YWC

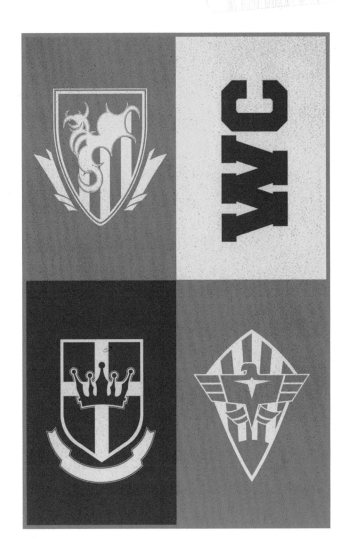

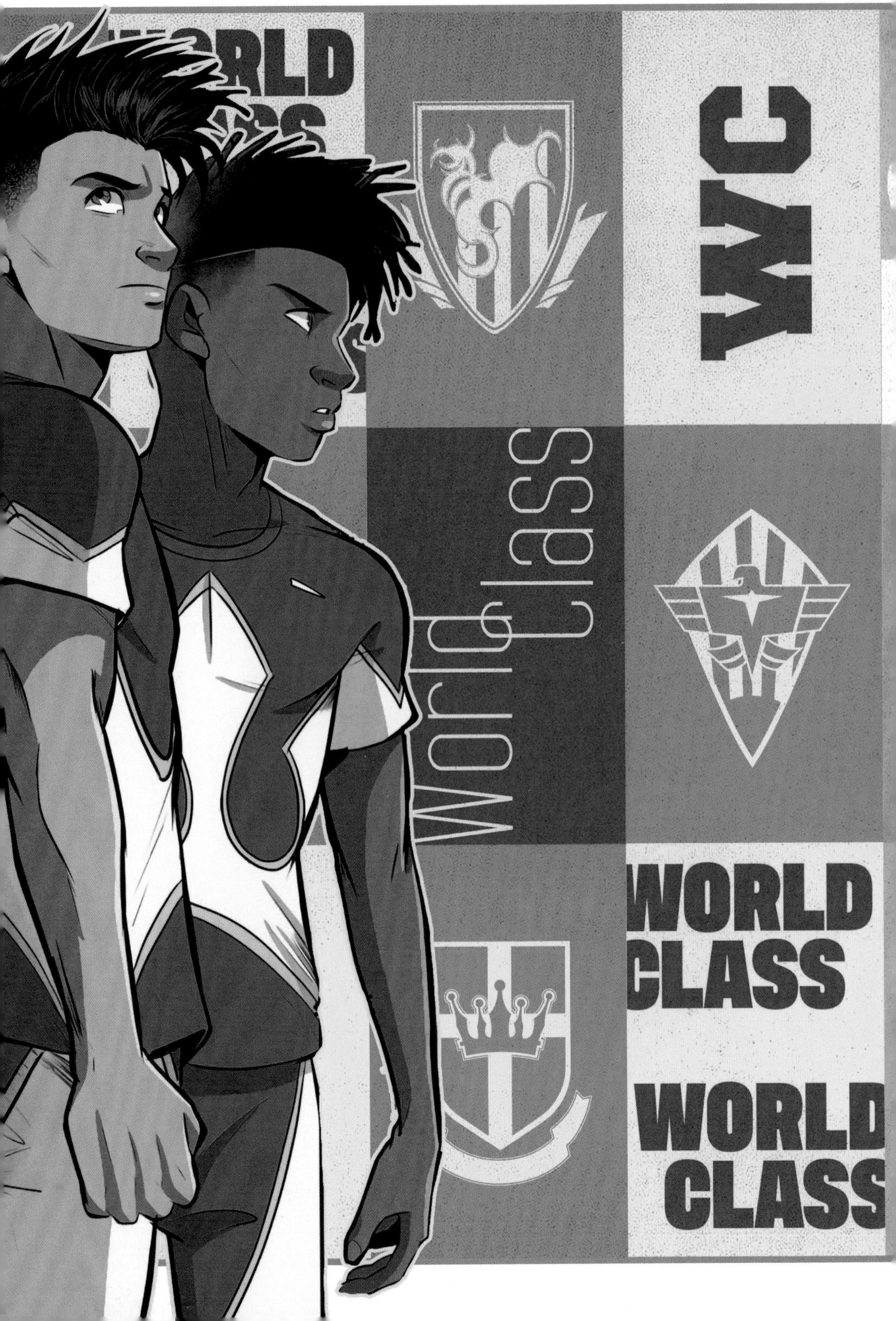
WYC
World Class
WORLD CLASS
WORLD CLASS

WORLD CLASS

A Graphic Novel

Words by
Jay Sandlin

Art by
Patrick Mulholland

Colors by
Rebecca Nalty

Letters by
Justin Birch

Logo and Book Design by
Miguel A. Zapata

Edits by
Chris Sanchez

MAVERICK

Laura Chacón - *Founder*

Mark London - *CEO and Chief Creative Officer*

Mark Irwin - *VP of Business Development*

Chris Fernandez - *Publisher*

Cecilia Medina - *Chief Financial Officer*

Allison Pond - *Marketing Director*

Manny Castellanos - *Sales and Retailer Relations*

Giovanna T. Orozco - *Production Manager*

Miguel A. Zapata - *Design Director*

Chris Sanchez - *Senior Editor*

Chas! Pangburn - *Senior Editor*

Maya Lopez - *Marketing Manager*

Brian Hawkins - *Assistant Editor*

Diana Bermúdez - *Graphic Designer*

David Reyes - *Graphic Designer*

Adriana T. Orozco - *Interactive Media Designer*

Nicolás Zea Arias - *Audiovisual Production*

Frank Silva - *Executive Assistant*

Stephanie Hidalgo - *Office Manager*

MAVERICK

FOR MAD CAVE COMICS, INC.

World Class™ Published by Mad Cave Studios, Inc. 8838 SW 129 St. Miami, FL 33176. © 2022 Mad Cave Studios, Inc. All rights reserved. **World Class™** *characters and the distinctive likeness(es) thereof are Trademarks and Copyrights © 2022 Mad Cave Studios, Inc.*

First Printing. Printed in Canada.
ISBN: 978-1-952303-27-2

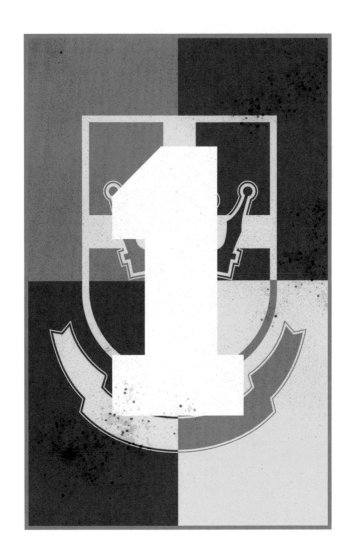

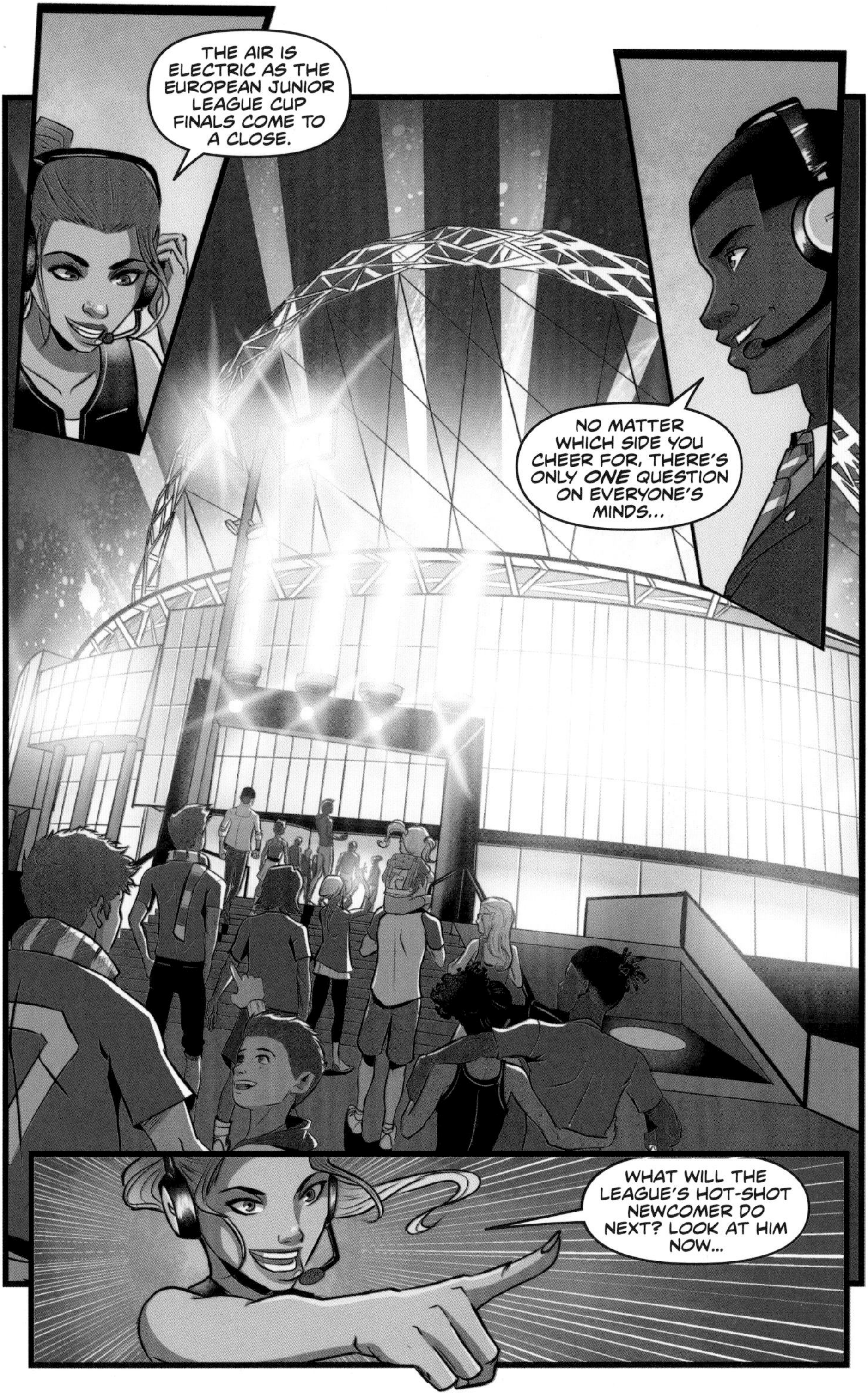
THE AIR IS ELECTRIC AS THE EUROPEAN JUNIOR LEAGUE CUP FINALS COME TO A CLOSE.
NO MATTER WHICH SIDE YOU CHEER FOR, THERE'S ONLY *ONE* QUESTION ON EVERYONE'S MINDS...
WHAT WILL THE LEAGUE'S HOT-SHOT NEWCOMER DO NEXT? LOOK AT HIM NOW...

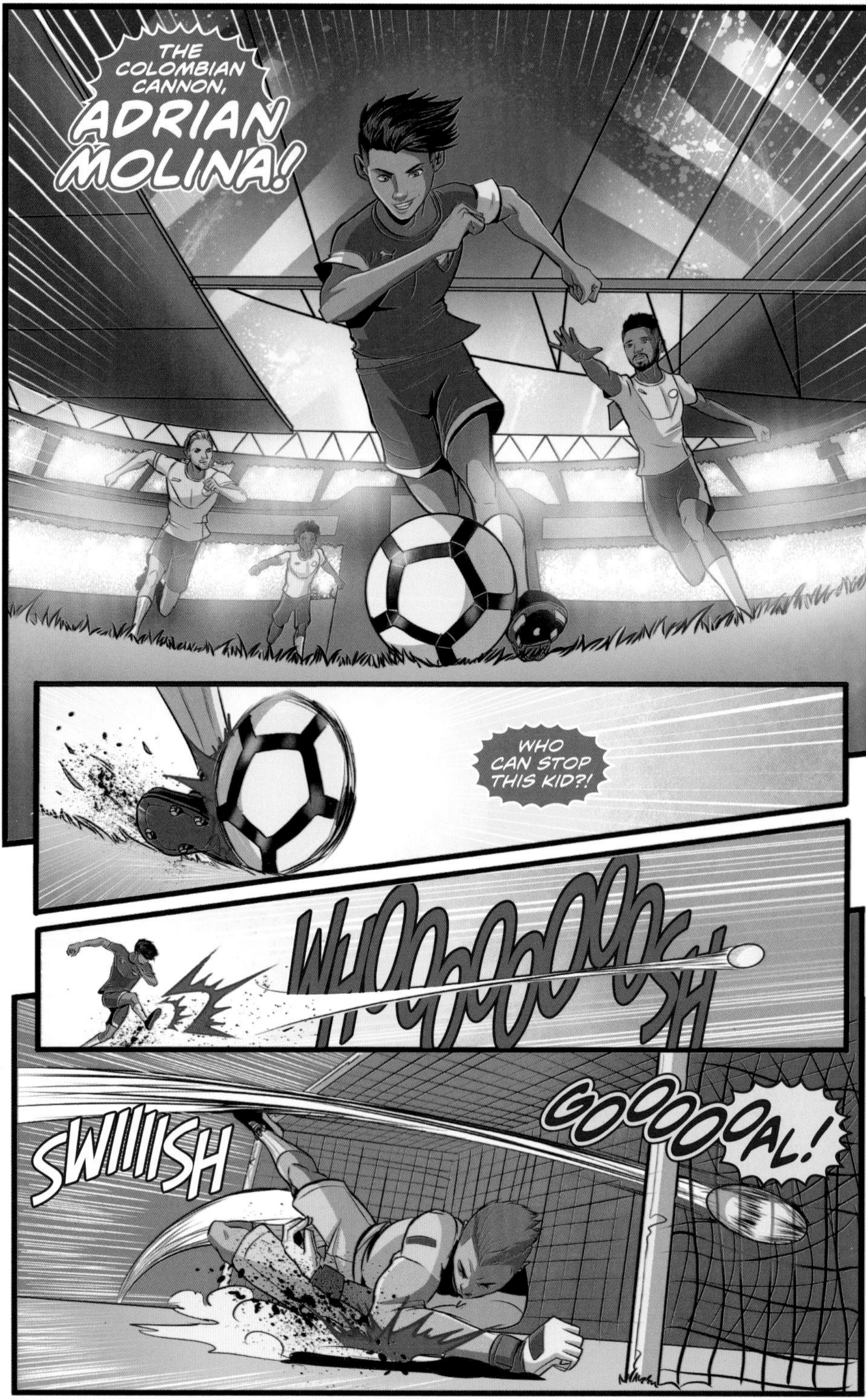
THE COLOMBIAN CANNON, ADRIAN MOLINA!
WHO CAN STOP THIS KID?!
WHOOOOOOOSH
SWIIIISH
GOOOOOOAL!

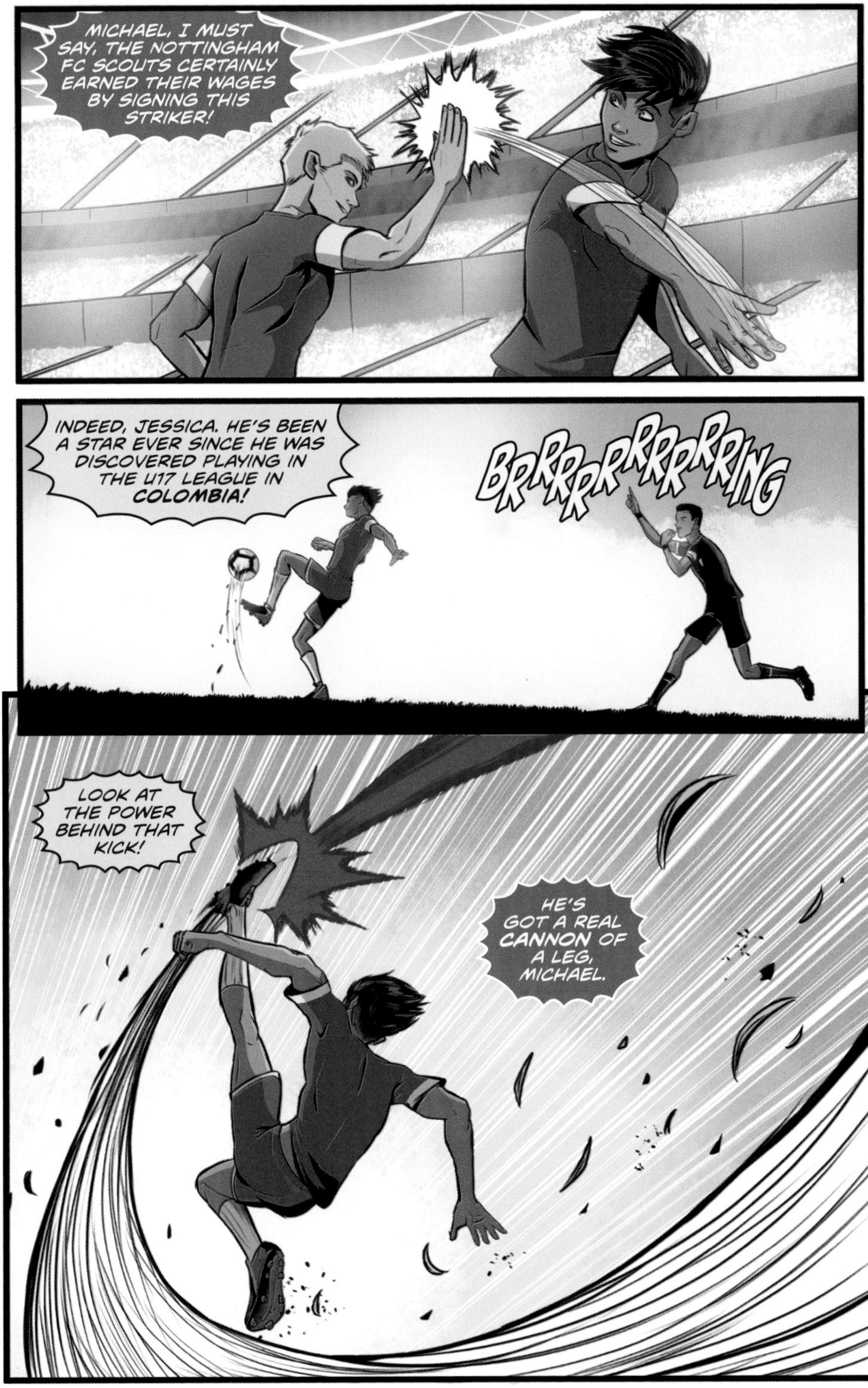
MICHAEL, I MUST SAY, THE NOTTINGHAM FC SCOUTS CERTAINLY EARNED THEIR WAGES BY SIGNING THIS STRIKER!
INDEED, JESSICA. HE'S BEEN A STAR EVER SINCE HE WAS DISCOVERED PLAYING IN THE U17 LEAGUE IN COLOMBIA!
BRRRRRRRRRRRING
LOOK AT THE POWER BEHIND THAT KICK!
HE'S GOT A REAL CANNON OF A LEG, MICHAEL.

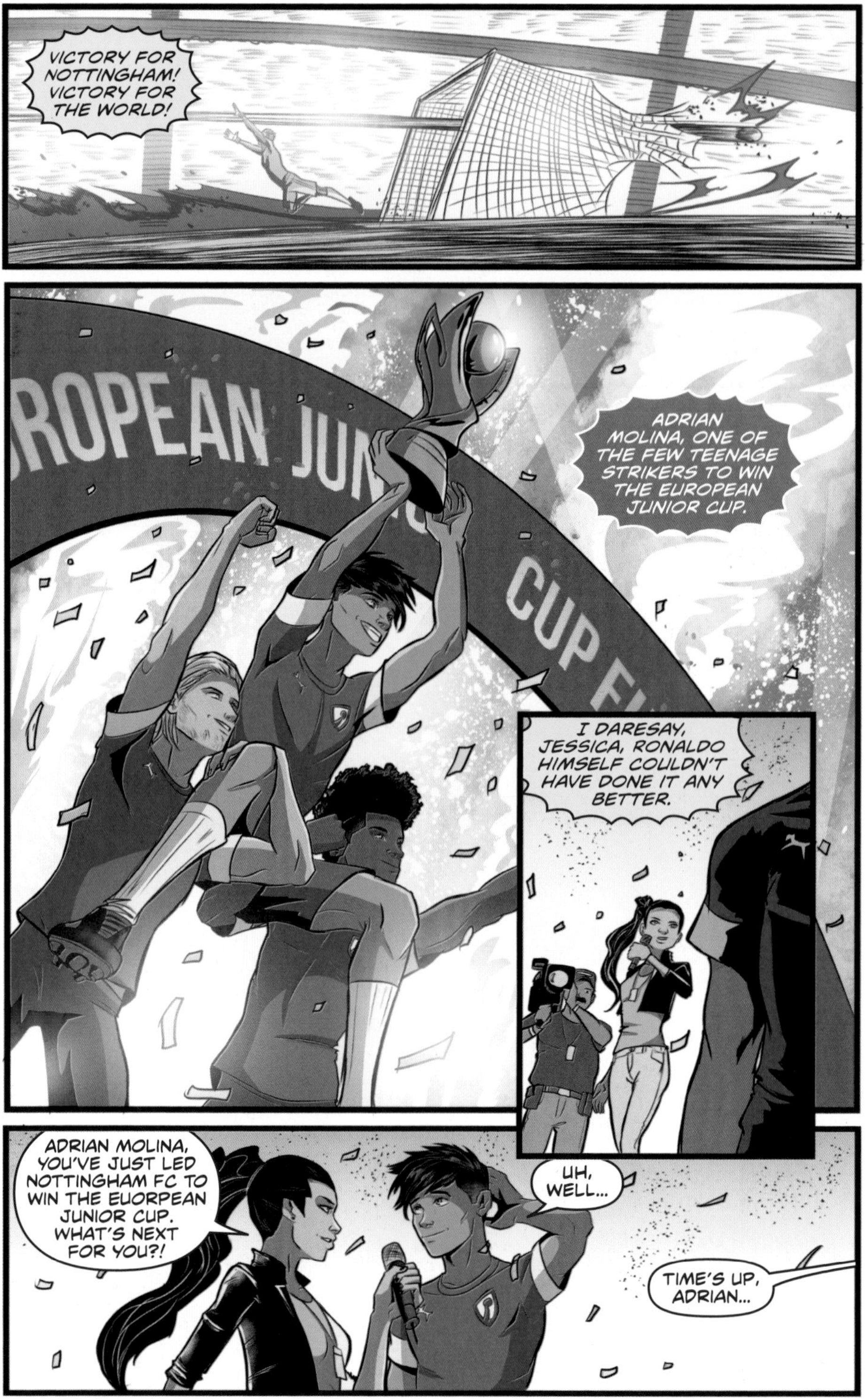
VICTORY FOR NOTTINGHAM! VICTORY FOR THE WORLD!
ROPEAN JUN
CUP FI
ADRIAN MOLINA, ONE OF THE FEW TEENAGE STRIKERS TO WIN THE EUROPEAN JUNIOR CUP.
I DARESAY, JESSICA, RONALDO HIMSELF COULDN'T HAVE DONE IT ANY BETTER.
ADRIAN MOLINA, YOU'VE JUST LED NOTTINGHAM FC TO WIN THE EUORPEAN JUNIOR CUP. WHAT'S NEXT FOR YOU?!
UH, WELL...
TIME'S UP, ADRIAN...

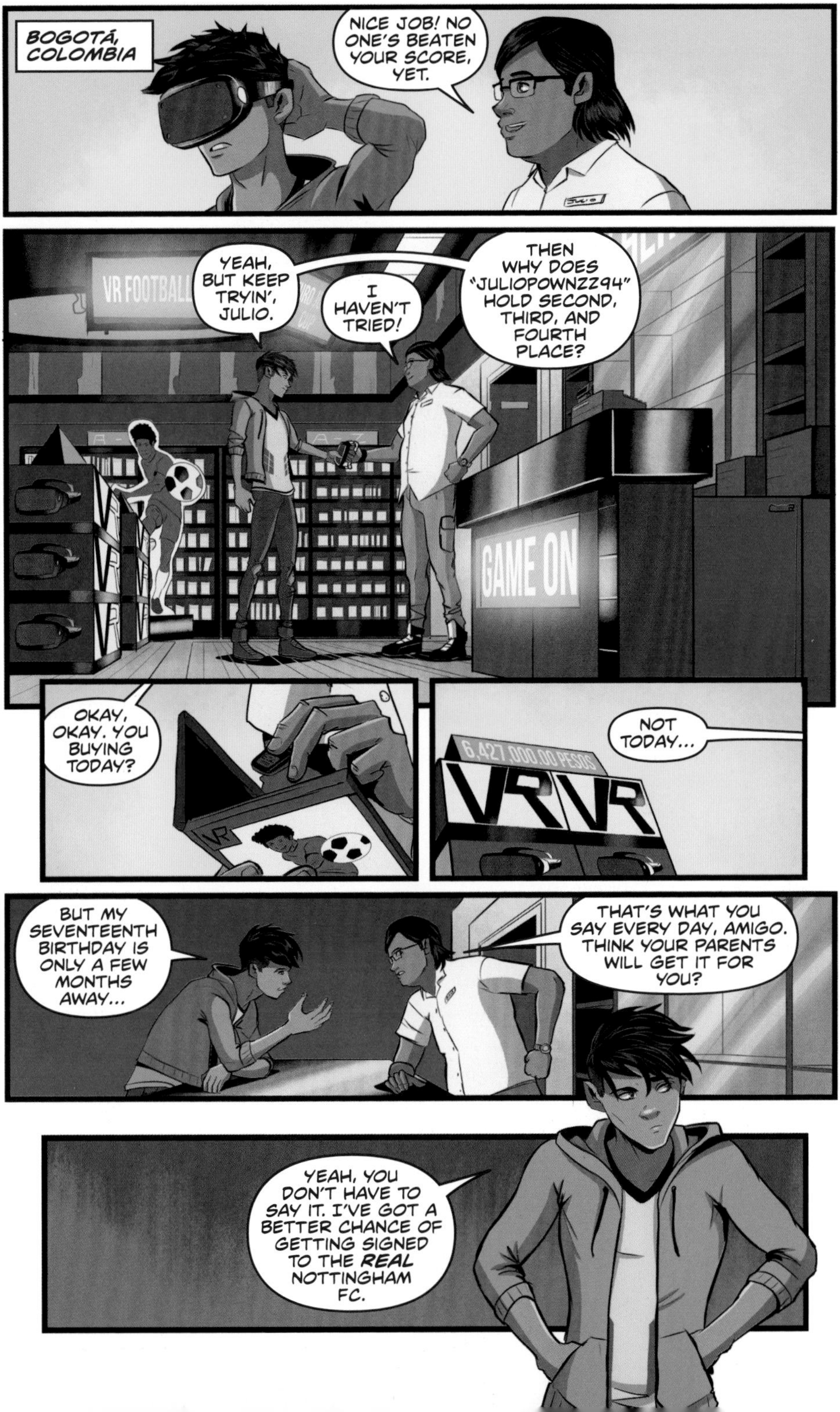
BOGOTÁ, COLOMBIA
NICE JOB! NO ONE'S BEATEN YOUR SCORE, YET.
YEAH, BUT KEEP TRYIN', JULIO.
I HAVEN'T TRIED!
THEN WHY DOES "JULIOPOWNZZ94" HOLD SECOND, THIRD, AND FOURTH PLACE?
VR FOOTBALL
GAME ON
OKAY, OKAY. YOU BUYING TODAY?
6,427,000.00 PESOS
VRVR
NOT TODAY...
BUT MY SEVENTEENTH BIRTHDAY IS ONLY A FEW MONTHS AWAY...
THAT'S WHAT YOU SAY EVERY DAY, AMIGO. THINK YOUR PARENTS WILL GET IT FOR YOU?
YEAH, YOU DON'T HAVE TO SAY IT. I'VE GOT A BETTER CHANCE OF GETTING SIGNED TO THE *REAL* NOTTINGHAM FC.

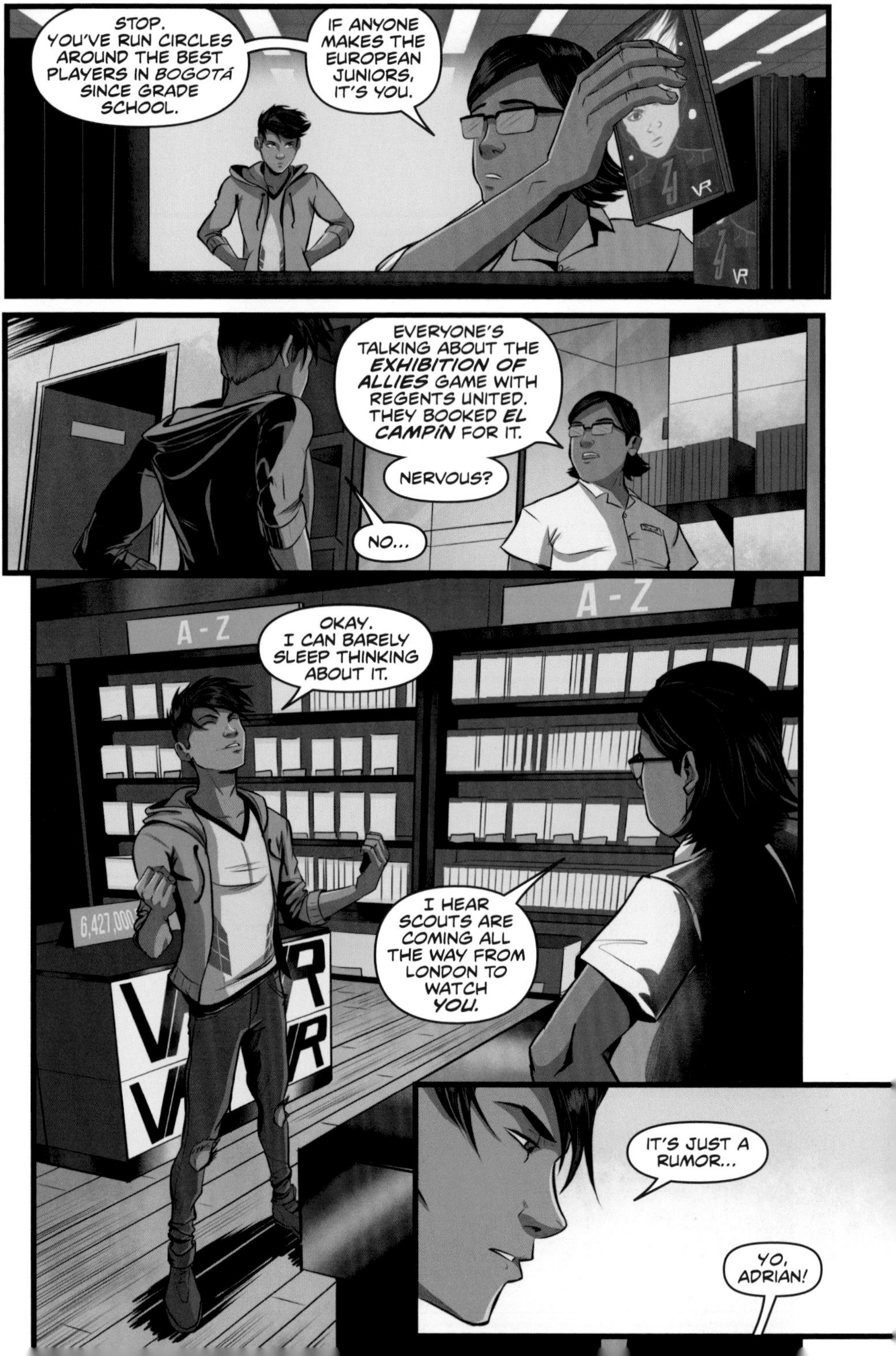
STOP. YOU'VE RUN CIRCLES AROUND THE BEST PLAYERS IN *BOGOTÁ* SINCE GRADE SCHOOL.
IF ANYONE MAKES THE EUROPEAN JUNIORS, IT'S YOU.
VR
VR
EVERYONE'S TALKING ABOUT THE ***EXHIBITION OF ALLIES*** GAME WITH REGENTS UNITED. THEY BOOKED ***EL CAMPÍN*** FOR IT.
NERVOUS?
NO...
A - Z
A - Z
OKAY. I CAN BARELY SLEEP THINKING ABOUT IT.
6,427,000
I HEAR SCOUTS ARE COMING ALL THE WAY FROM LONDON TO WATCH ***YOU***.
IT'S JUST A RUMOR...
YO, ADRIAN!

SEE YOU AT THE GAME, JULIO.

MAKE WAY!

EL CAÑÓN COLOMBIANO IS COMIN' THROUGH!

WHY DO YOU WASTE TIME PLAYING VR FOOTBALL? YOU THINK IT'LL IMPROVE YOUR AIM BEFORE THE EXHIBITION?!

GEE THANKS, MARIA. I HOPE YOU'RE THIS ENCOURAGING WHEN YOU CALL THE GAME.

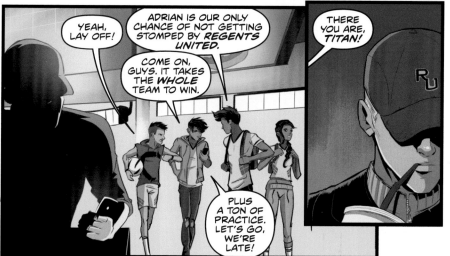

YEAH, LAY OFF!

ADRIAN IS OUR ONLY CHANCE OF NOT GETTING STOMPED BY REGENTS UNITED.

COME ON, GUYS. IT TAKES THE WHOLE TEAM TO WIN.

THERE YOU ARE, TITAN!

PLUS A TON OF PRACTICE. LET'S GO, WE'RE LATE!

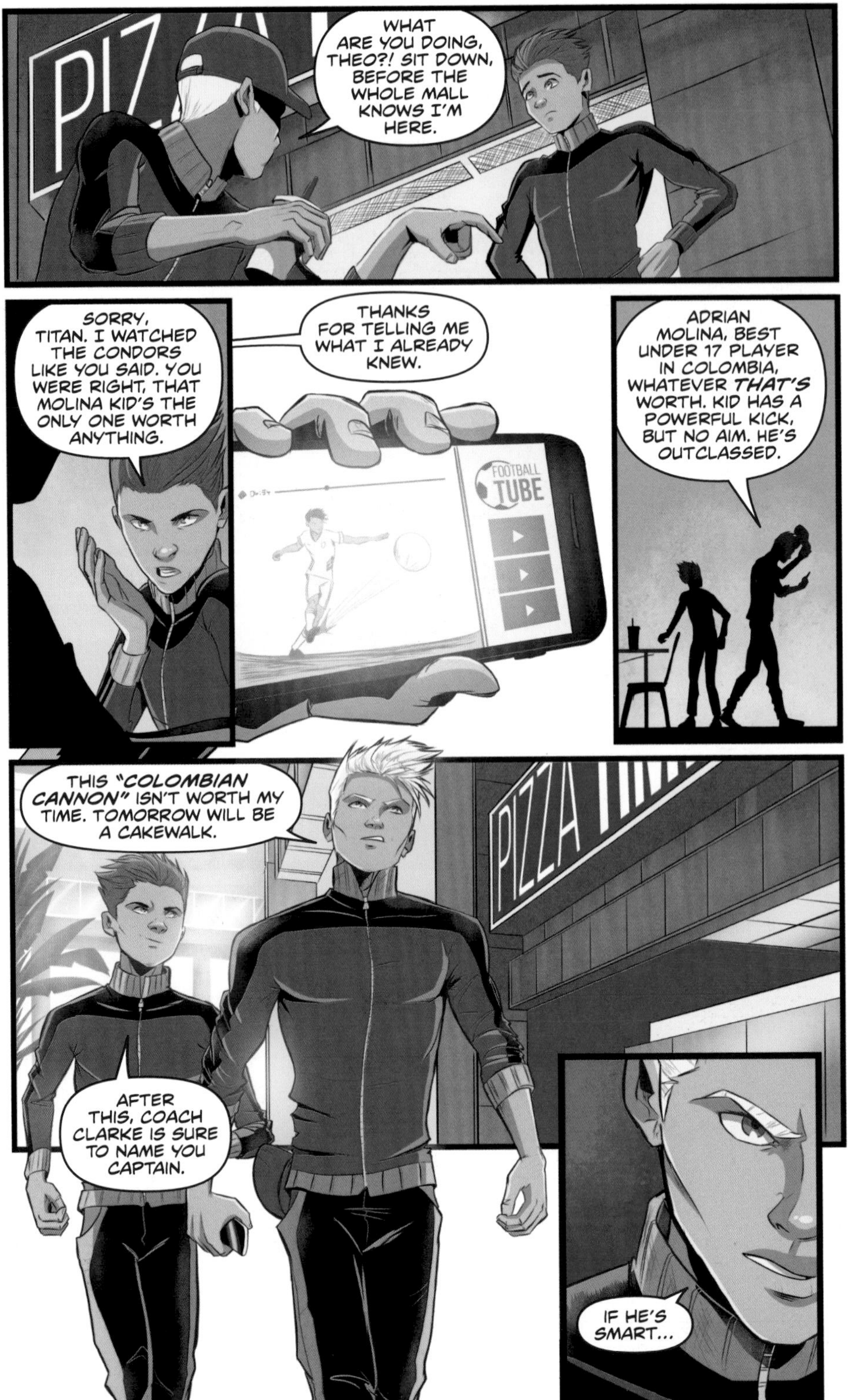
PIZZA
WHAT ARE YOU DOING, THEO?! SIT DOWN, BEFORE THE WHOLE MALL KNOWS I'M HERE.
SORRY, TITAN. I WATCHED THE CONDORS LIKE YOU SAID. YOU WERE RIGHT, THAT MOLINA KID'S THE ONLY ONE WORTH ANYTHING.
THANKS FOR TELLING ME WHAT I ALREADY KNEW.
FOOTBALL TUBE
ADRIAN MOLINA, BEST UNDER 17 PLAYER IN COLOMBIA, WHATEVER *THAT'S* WORTH. KID HAS A POWERFUL KICK, BUT NO AIM. HE'S OUTCLASSED.
THIS *"COLOMBIAN CANNON"* ISN'T WORTH MY TIME. TOMORROW WILL BE A CAKEWALK.
PIZZA TIME
AFTER THIS, COACH CLARKE IS SURE TO NAME YOU CAPTAIN.
IF HE'S SMART...

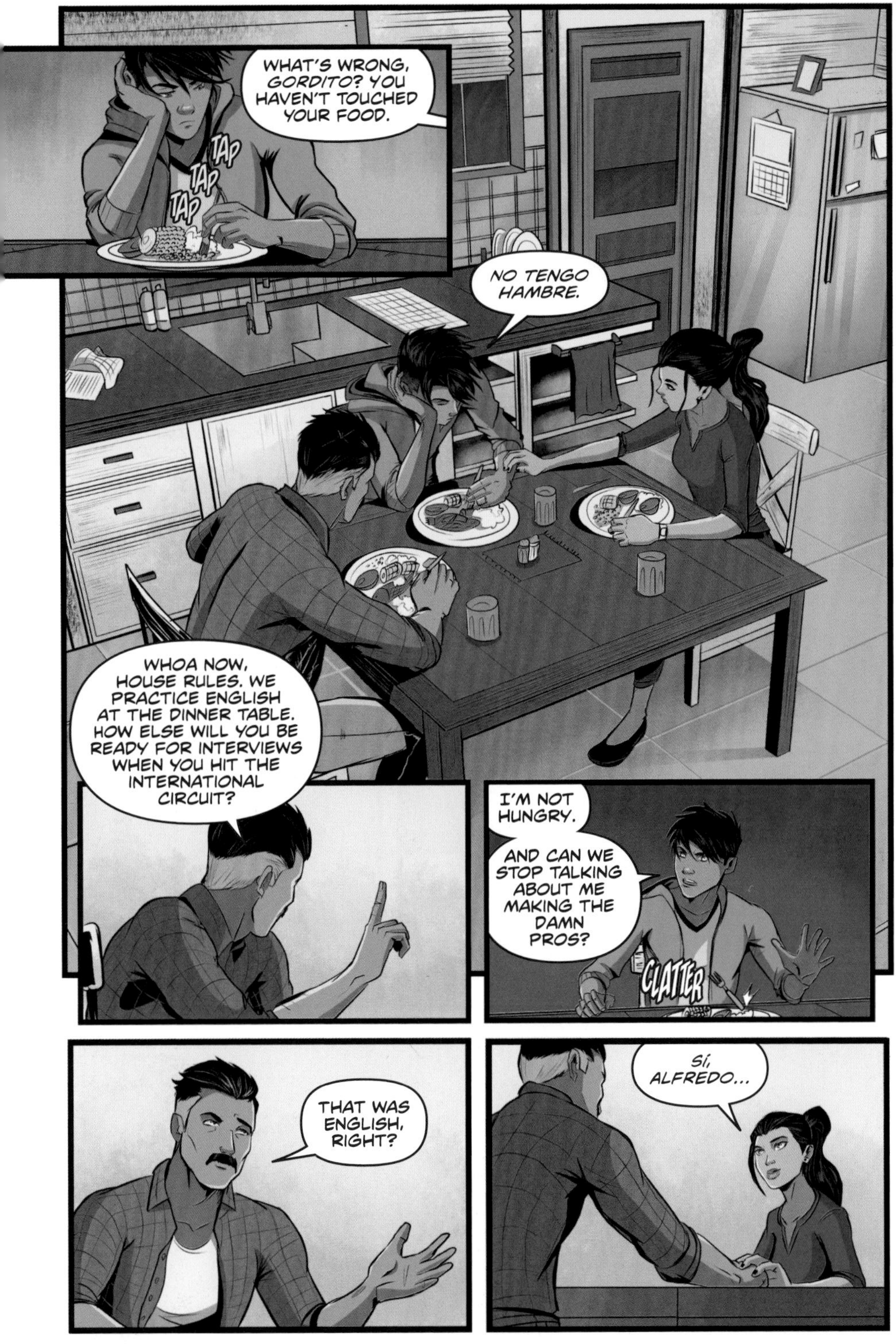
WHAT'S WRONG, GORDITO? YOU HAVEN'T TOUCHED YOUR FOOD.
TAP TAP TAP
NO TENGO HAMBRE.
WHOA NOW, HOUSE RULES. WE PRACTICE ENGLISH AT THE DINNER TABLE. HOW ELSE WILL YOU BE READY FOR INTERVIEWS WHEN YOU HIT THE INTERNATIONAL CIRCUIT?
I'M NOT HUNGRY.
AND CAN WE STOP TALKING ABOUT ME MAKING THE DAMN PROS?
CLATTER
THAT WAS ENGLISH, RIGHT?
SÍ, ALFREDO...

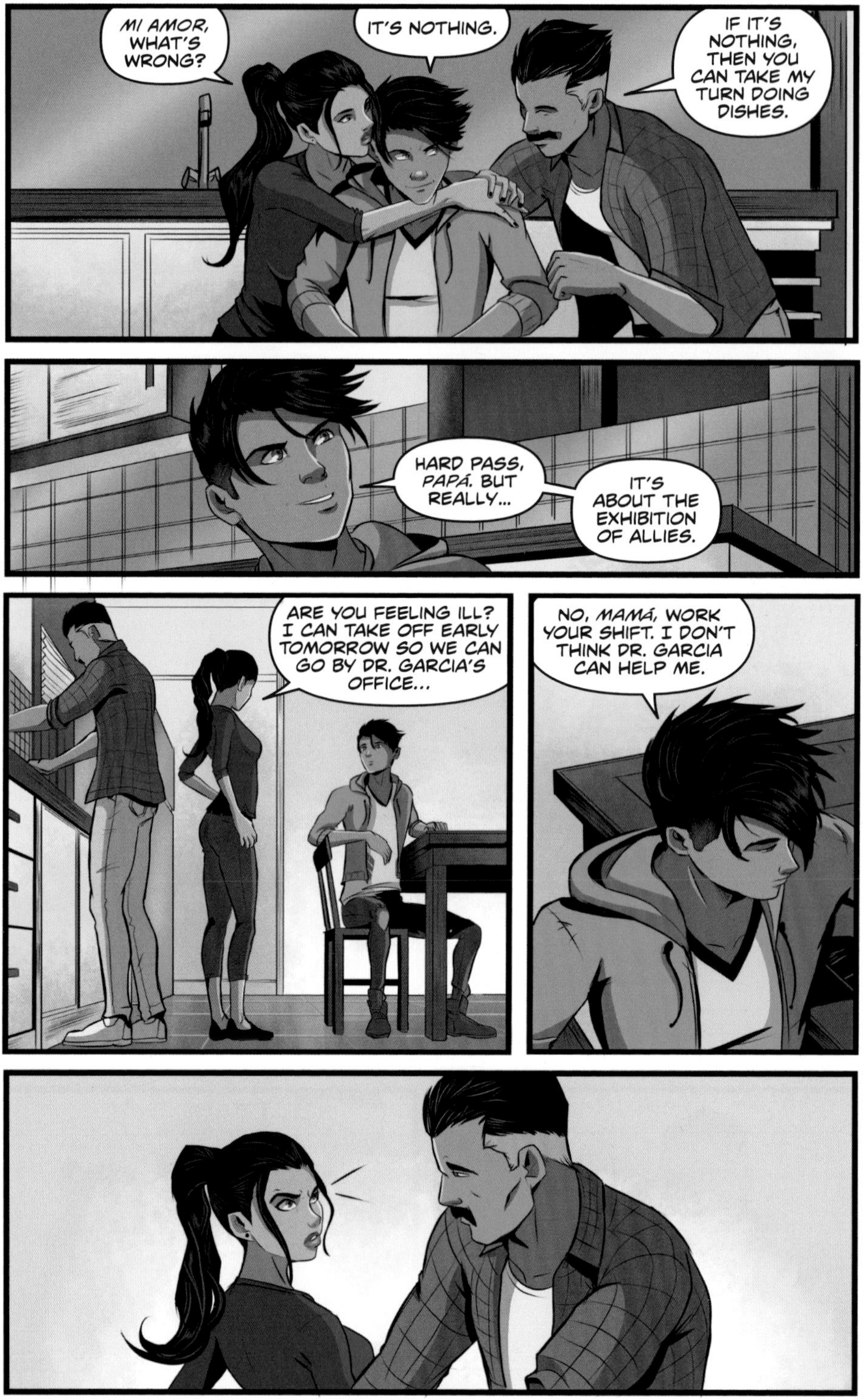
MI AMOR, WHAT'S WRONG?
IT'S NOTHING.
IF IT'S NOTHING, THEN YOU CAN TAKE MY TURN DOING DISHES.
HARD PASS, PAPÁ. BUT REALLY...
IT'S ABOUT THE EXHIBITION OF ALLIES.
ARE YOU FEELING ILL? I CAN TAKE OFF EARLY TOMORROW SO WE CAN GO BY DR. GARCIA'S OFFICE...
NO, MAMÁ, WORK YOUR SHIFT. I DON'T THINK DR. GARCIA CAN HELP ME.

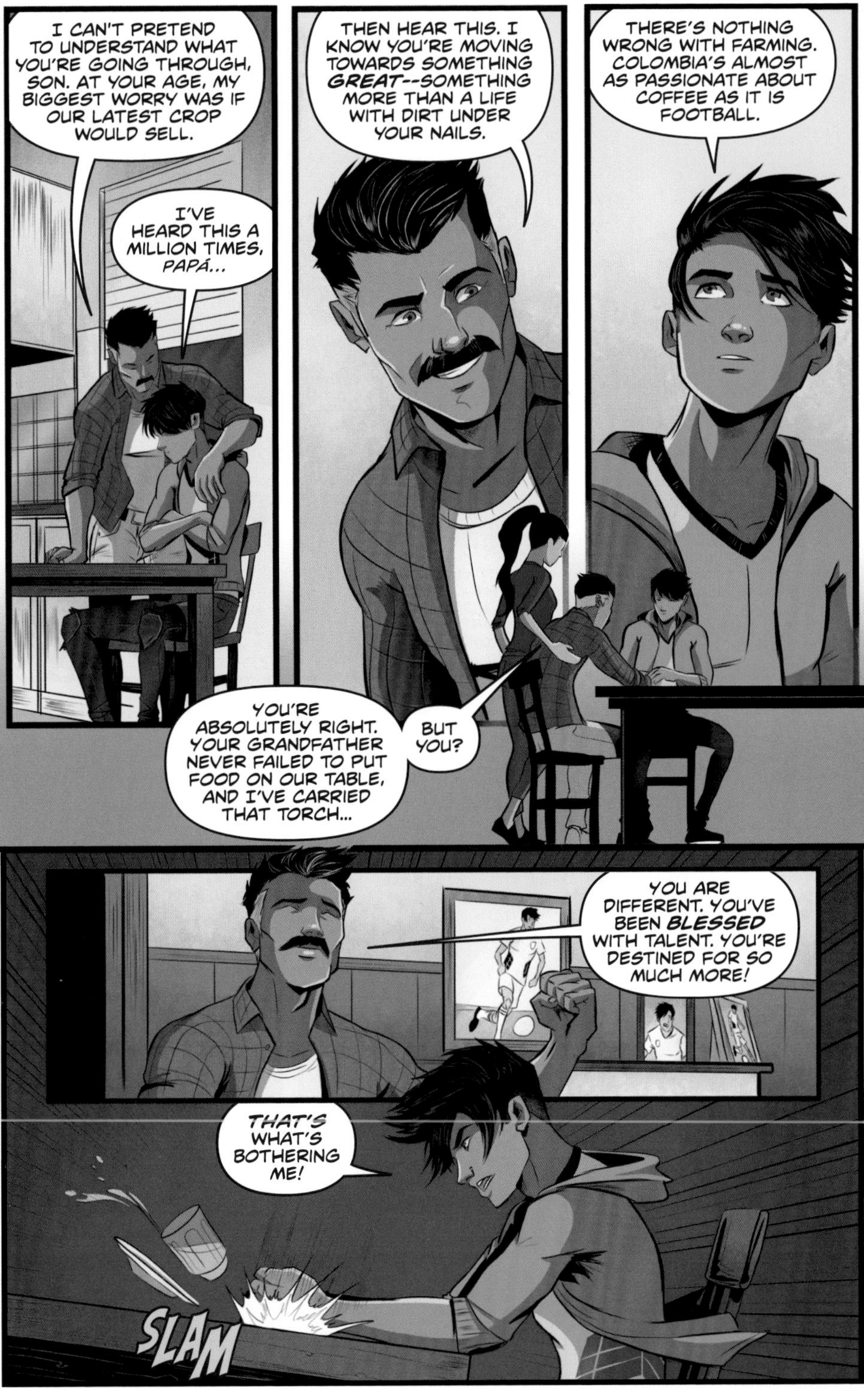
I CAN'T PRETEND TO UNDERSTAND WHAT YOU'RE GOING THROUGH, SON. AT YOUR AGE, MY BIGGEST WORRY WAS IF OUR LATEST CROP WOULD SELL.
I'VE HEARD THIS A MILLION TIMES, *PAPÁ*...
THEN HEAR THIS. I KNOW YOU'RE MOVING TOWARDS SOMETHING ***GREAT***--SOMETHING MORE THAN A LIFE WITH DIRT UNDER YOUR NAILS.
THERE'S NOTHING WRONG WITH FARMING. COLOMBIA'S ALMOST AS PASSIONATE ABOUT COFFEE AS IT IS FOOTBALL.
YOU'RE ABSOLUTELY RIGHT. YOUR GRANDFATHER NEVER FAILED TO PUT FOOD ON OUR TABLE, AND I'VE CARRIED THAT TORCH...
BUT YOU?
YOU ARE DIFFERENT. YOU'VE BEEN ***BLESSED*** WITH TALENT. YOU'RE DESTINED FOR SO MUCH MORE!
THAT'S WHAT'S BOTHERING ME!
SLAM

DESTINY. GREATNESS. I HEAR IT *EVERYWHERE.* MY TEACHERS, COACH, FRIENDS. *YOU!*

EVERYONE THINKS I'LL MAKE IT TO THE PROS JUST BECAUSE I'VE GOT A GREAT LEG.

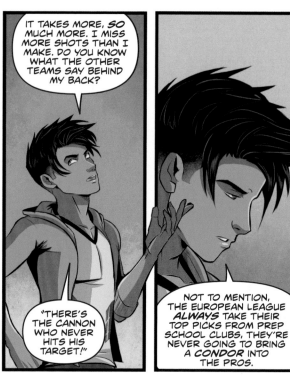

IT TAKES MORE, *SO MUCH MORE.* I MISS MORE SHOTS THAN I MAKE. DO YOU KNOW WHAT THE OTHER TEAMS SAY BEHIND MY BACK?

"THERE'S THE CANNON WHO NEVER HITS HIS TARGET!"

NOT TO MENTION, THE EUROPEAN LEAGUE *ALWAYS* TAKE THEIR TOP PICKS FROM PREP SCHOOL CLUBS, THEY'RE NEVER GOING TO BRING A *CONDOR* INTO THE PROS.

PREP SCHOOL CLUBS LIKE REGENTS UNITED...

EASY, *MI AMOR.* BREATHE.

SORRY, *MAMÁ.*

IT'S JUST...ALL THE PRESSURE GETS TO ME.

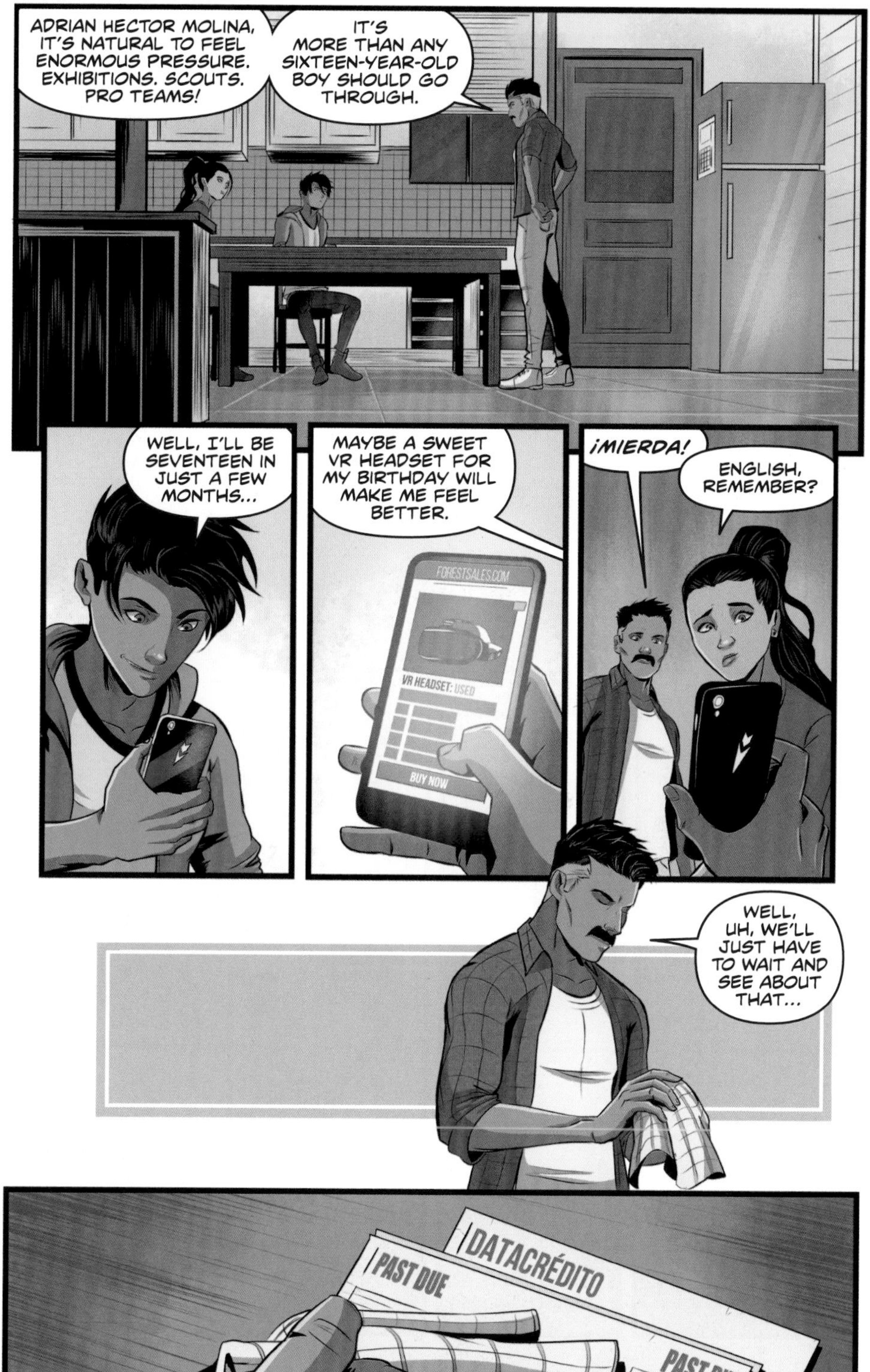
ADRIAN HECTOR MOLINA, IT'S NATURAL TO FEEL ENORMOUS PRESSURE. EXHIBITIONS. SCOUTS. PRO TEAMS!
IT'S MORE THAN ANY SIXTEEN-YEAR-OLD BOY SHOULD GO THROUGH.
WELL, I'LL BE SEVENTEEN IN JUST A FEW MONTHS...
MAYBE A SWEET VR HEADSET FOR MY BIRTHDAY WILL MAKE ME FEEL BETTER.
FORESTSALES.COM
VR HEADSET: USED
BUY NOW
¡MIERDA!
ENGLISH, REMEMBER?
WELL, UH, WE'LL JUST HAVE TO WAIT AND SEE ABOUT THAT...
DATACRÉDITO
PAST DUE
PAST DUE

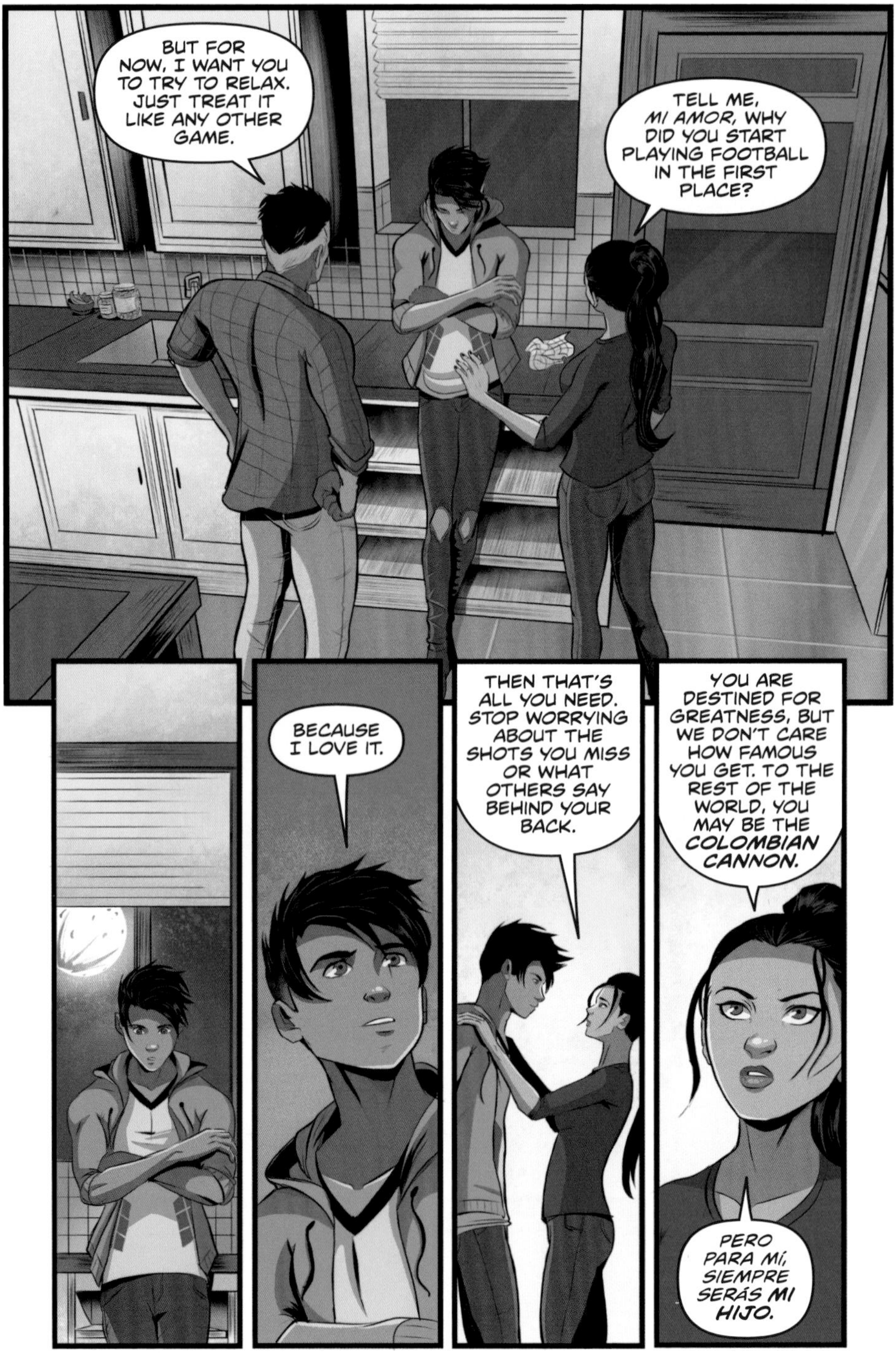
BUT FOR NOW, I WANT YOU TO TRY TO RELAX. JUST TREAT IT LIKE ANY OTHER GAME.
TELL ME, *MI AMOR*, WHY DID YOU START PLAYING FOOTBALL IN THE FIRST PLACE?
BECAUSE I LOVE IT.
THEN THAT'S ALL YOU NEED. STOP WORRYING ABOUT THE SHOTS YOU MISS OR WHAT OTHERS SAY BEHIND YOUR BACK.
YOU ARE DESTINED FOR GREATNESS, BUT WE DON'T CARE HOW FAMOUS YOU GET. TO THE REST OF THE WORLD, YOU MAY BE THE **COLOMBIAN CANNON.**
PERO PARA MÍ, SIEMPRE SERÁS ***MI HIJO.***

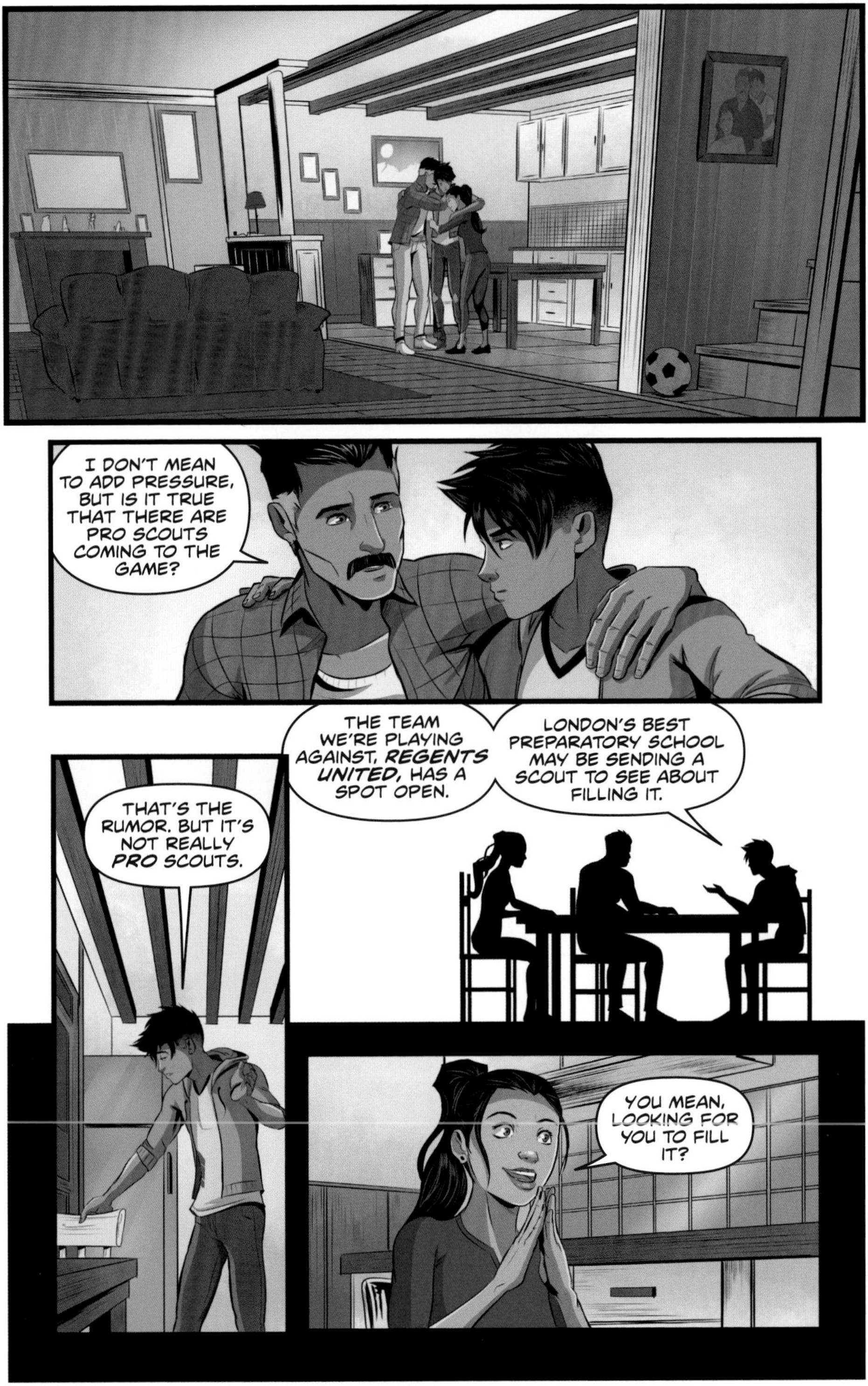
I DON'T MEAN TO ADD PRESSURE, BUT IS IT TRUE THAT THERE ARE PRO SCOUTS COMING TO THE GAME?
THAT'S THE RUMOR. BUT IT'S NOT REALLY *PRO* SCOUTS.
THE TEAM WE'RE PLAYING AGAINST, *REGENTS UNITED,* HAS A SPOT OPEN.
LONDON'S BEST PREPARATORY SCHOOL MAY BE SENDING A SCOUT TO SEE ABOUT FILLING IT.
YOU MEAN, LOOKING FOR YOU TO FILL IT?

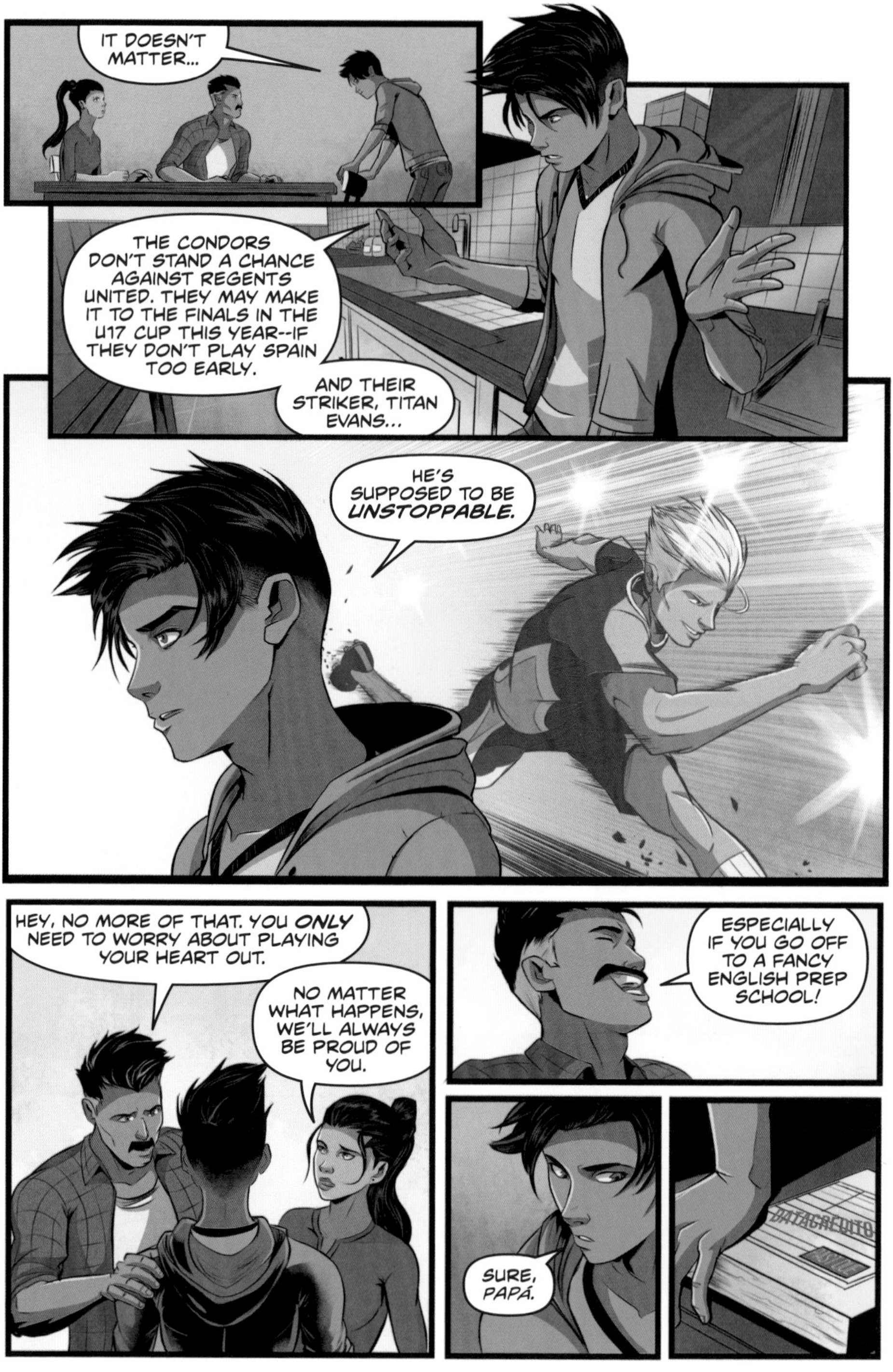
IT DOESN'T MATTER...
THE CONDORS DON'T STAND A CHANCE AGAINST REGENTS UNITED. THEY MAY MAKE IT TO THE FINALS IN THE U17 CUP THIS YEAR--IF THEY DON'T PLAY SPAIN TOO EARLY.
AND THEIR STRIKER, TITAN EVANS...
HE'S SUPPOSED TO BE *UNSTOPPABLE.*
HEY, NO MORE OF THAT. YOU *ONLY* NEED TO WORRY ABOUT PLAYING YOUR HEART OUT.
NO MATTER WHAT HAPPENS, WE'LL ALWAYS BE PROUD OF YOU.
ESPECIALLY IF YOU GO OFF TO A FANCY ENGLISH PREP SCHOOL!
SURE, *PAPÁ.*

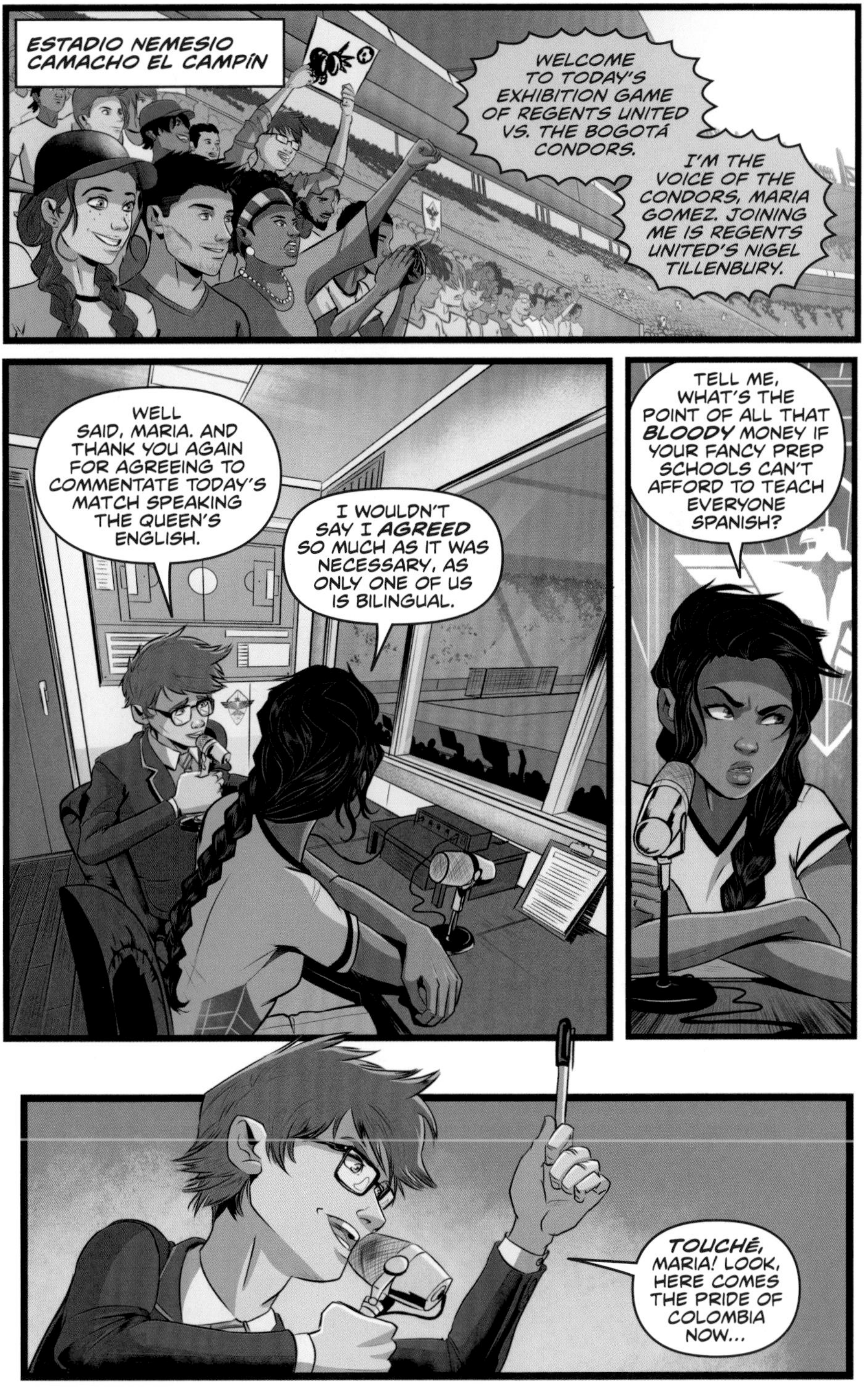
ESTADIO NEMESIO CAMACHO EL CAMPÍN
WELCOME TO TODAY'S EXHIBITION GAME OF REGENTS UNITED VS. THE BOGOTÁ CONDORS.
I'M THE VOICE OF THE CONDORS, MARIA GOMEZ. JOINING ME IS REGENTS UNITED'S NIGEL TILLENBURY.
WELL SAID, MARIA. AND THANK YOU AGAIN FOR AGREEING TO COMMENTATE TODAY'S MATCH SPEAKING THE QUEEN'S ENGLISH.
I WOULDN'T SAY I AGREED SO MUCH AS IT WAS NECESSARY, AS ONLY ONE OF US IS BILINGUAL.
TELL ME, WHAT'S THE POINT OF ALL THAT BLOODY MONEY IF YOUR FANCY PREP SCHOOLS CAN'T AFFORD TO TEACH EVERYONE SPANISH?
TOUCHÉ, MARIA! LOOK, HERE COMES THE PRIDE OF COLOMBIA NOW...

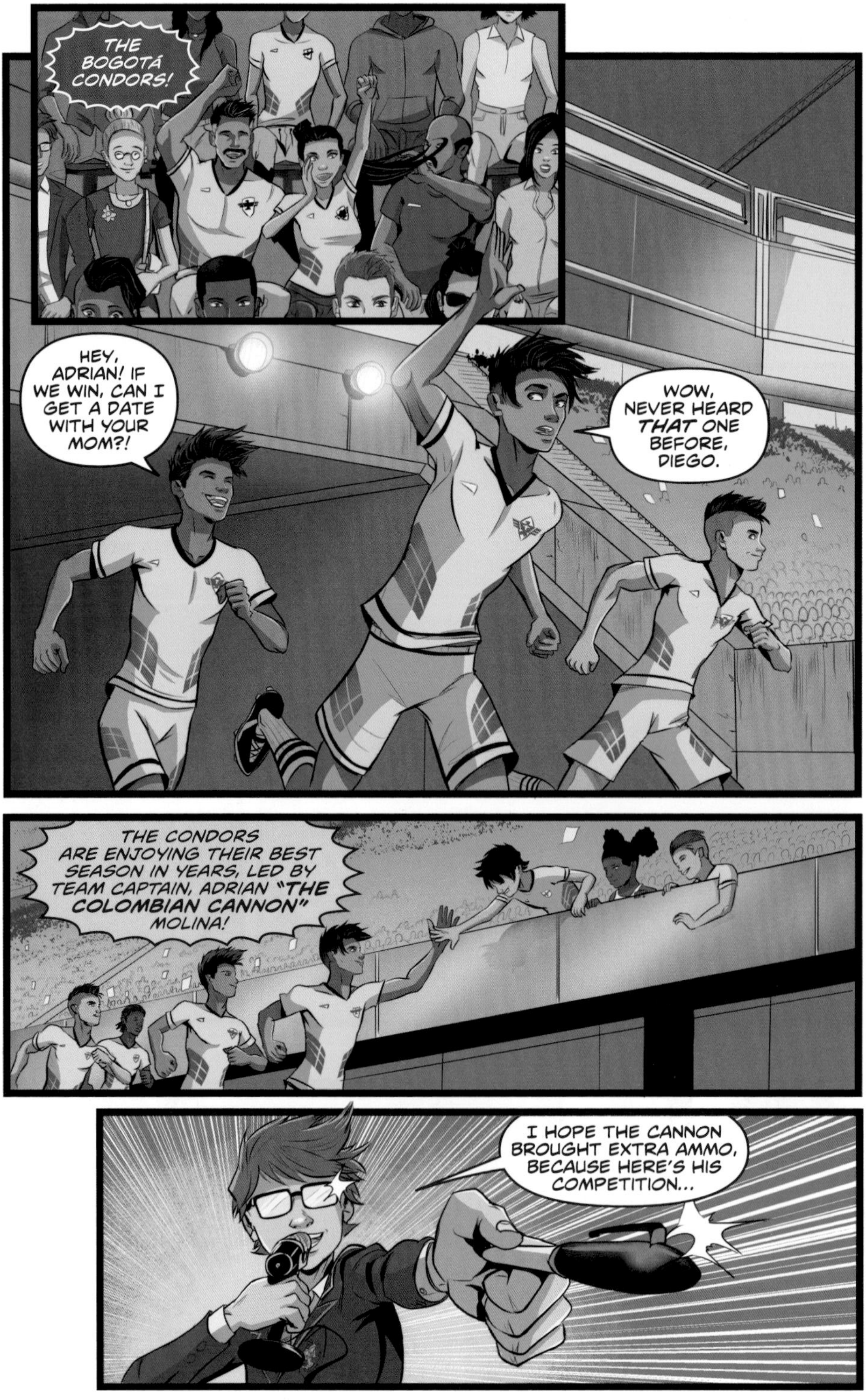
THE BOGOTÁ CONDORS!
HEY, ADRIAN! IF WE WIN, CAN I GET A DATE WITH YOUR MOM?!
WOW, NEVER HEARD THAT ONE BEFORE, DIEGO.
THE CONDORS ARE ENJOYING THEIR BEST SEASON IN YEARS, LED BY TEAM CAPTAIN, ADRIAN "THE COLOMBIAN CANNON" MOLINA!
I HOPE THE CANNON BROUGHT EXTRA AMMO, BECAUSE HERE'S HIS COMPETITION...

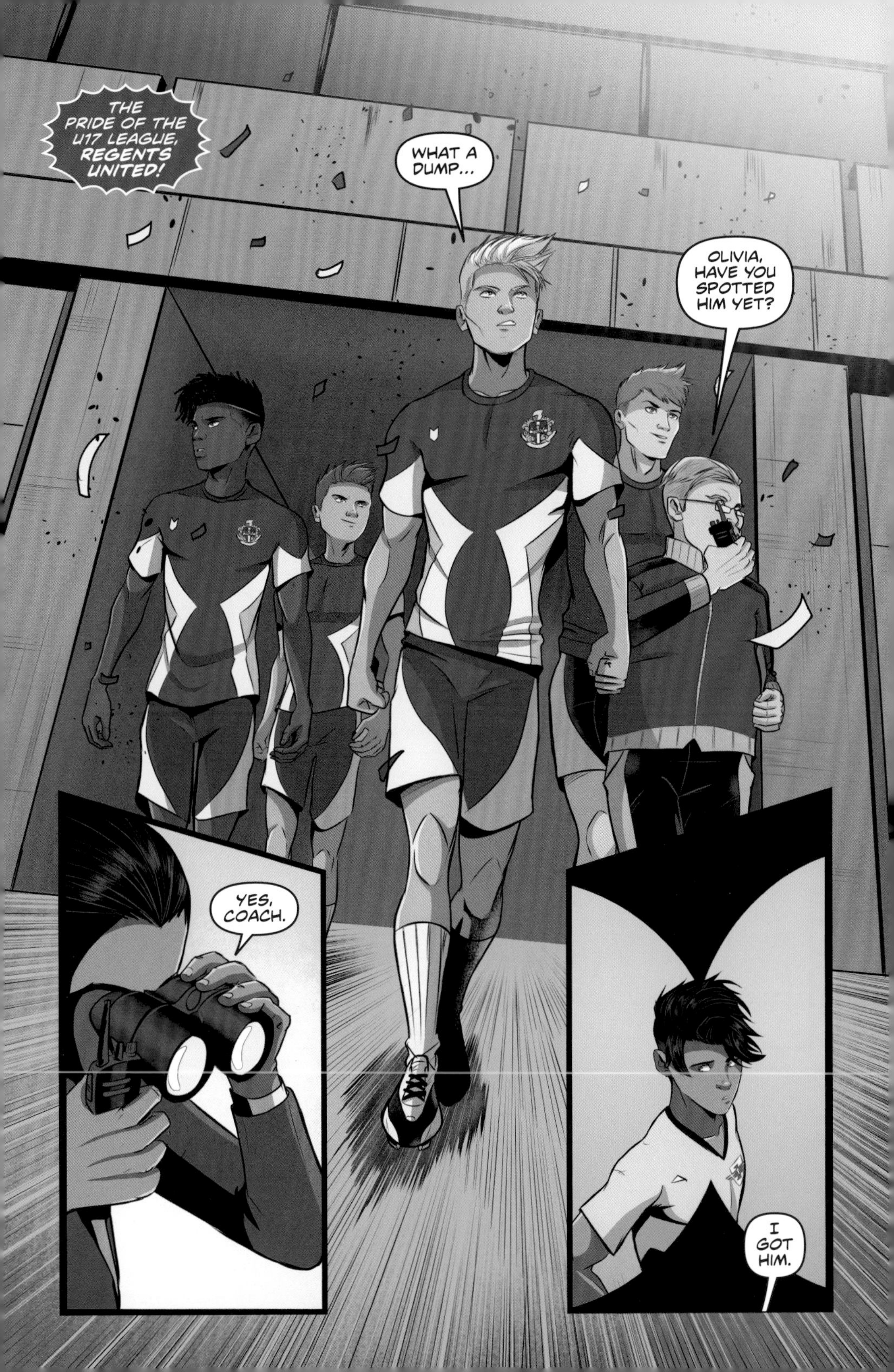
THE PRIDE OF THE U17 LEAGUE, REGENTS UNITED!
WHAT A DUMP...
OLIVIA, HAVE YOU SPOTTED HIM YET?
YES, COACH.
I GOT HIM.

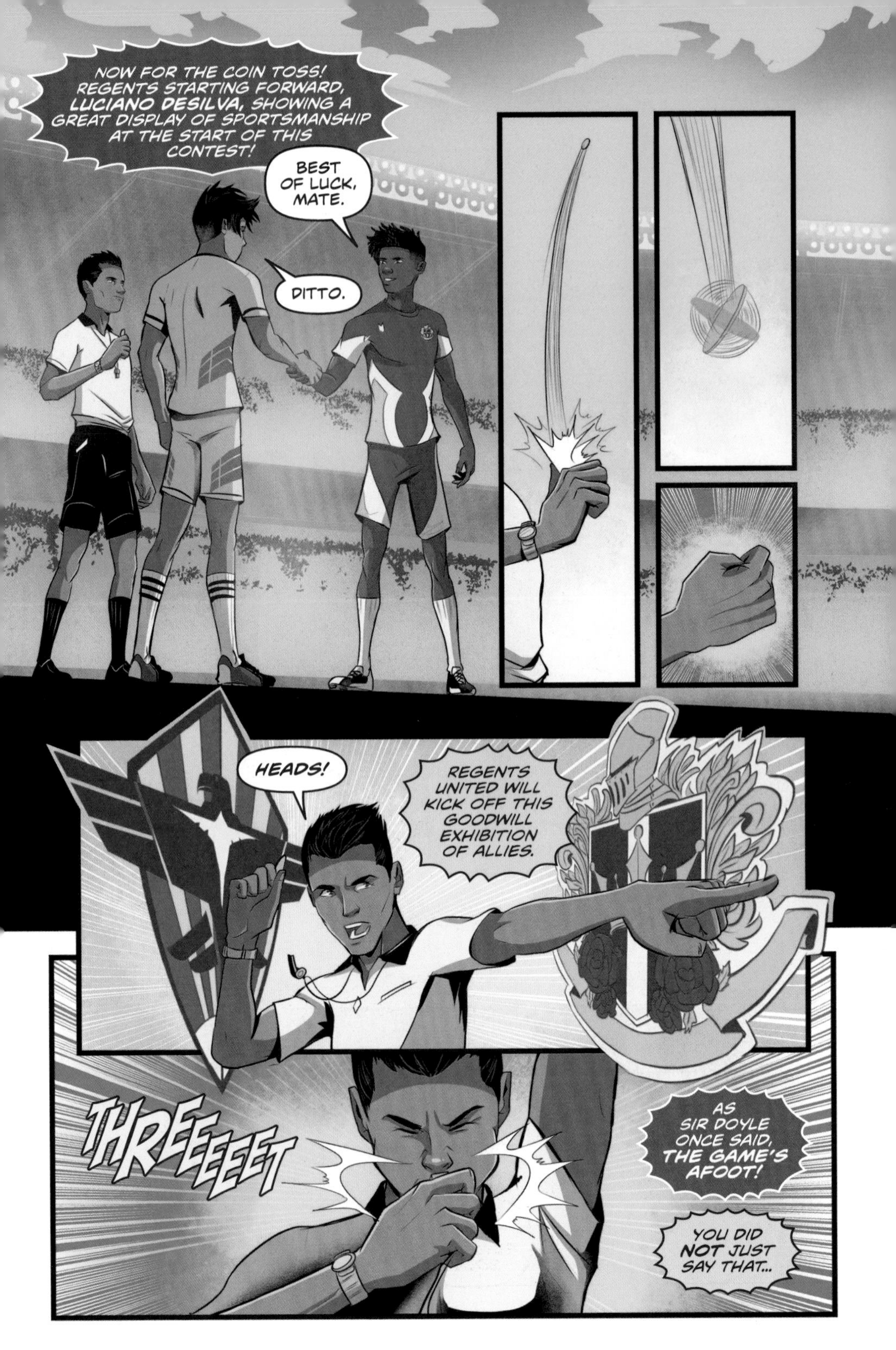
NOW FOR THE COIN TOSS! REGENTS STARTING FORWARD, **LUCIANO DESILVA,** SHOWING A GREAT DISPLAY OF SPORTSMANSHIP AT THE START OF THIS CONTEST!
BEST OF LUCK, MATE.
DITTO.
HEADS!
REGENTS UNITED WILL KICK OFF THIS GOODWILL EXHIBITION OF ALLIES.
THREEEEEET
AS SIR DOYLE ONCE SAID, **THE GAME'S AFOOT!**
YOU DID **NOT** JUST SAY THAT...

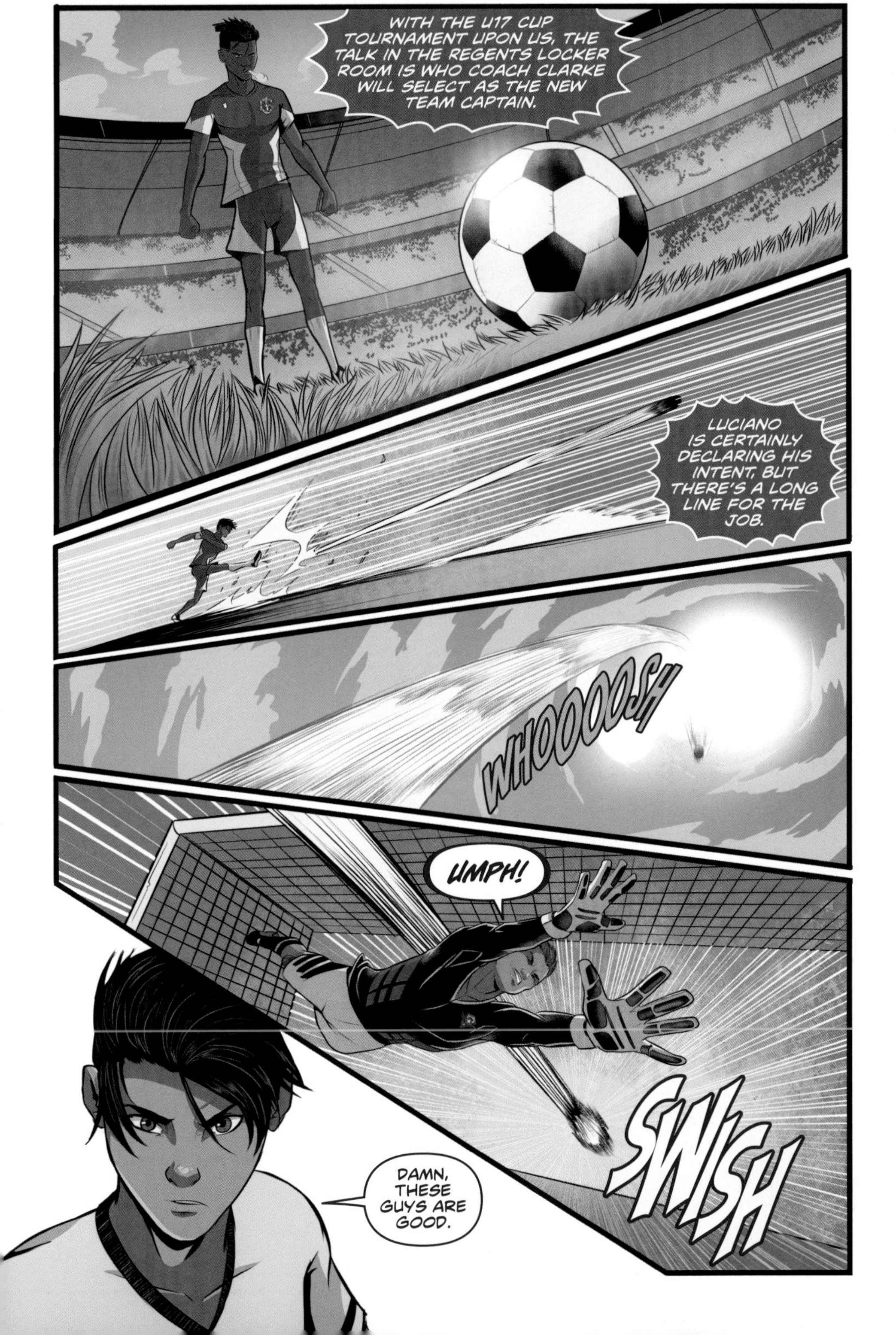
WITH THE U17 CUP TOURNAMENT UPON US, THE TALK IN THE REGENTS LOCKER ROOM IS WHO COACH CLARKE WILL SELECT AS THE NEW TEAM CAPTAIN.
LUCIANO IS CERTAINLY DECLARING HIS INTENT, BUT THERE'S A LONG LINE FOR THE JOB.
WHOOOOOSH
UMPH!
SWISH
DAMN, THESE GUYS ARE GOOD.

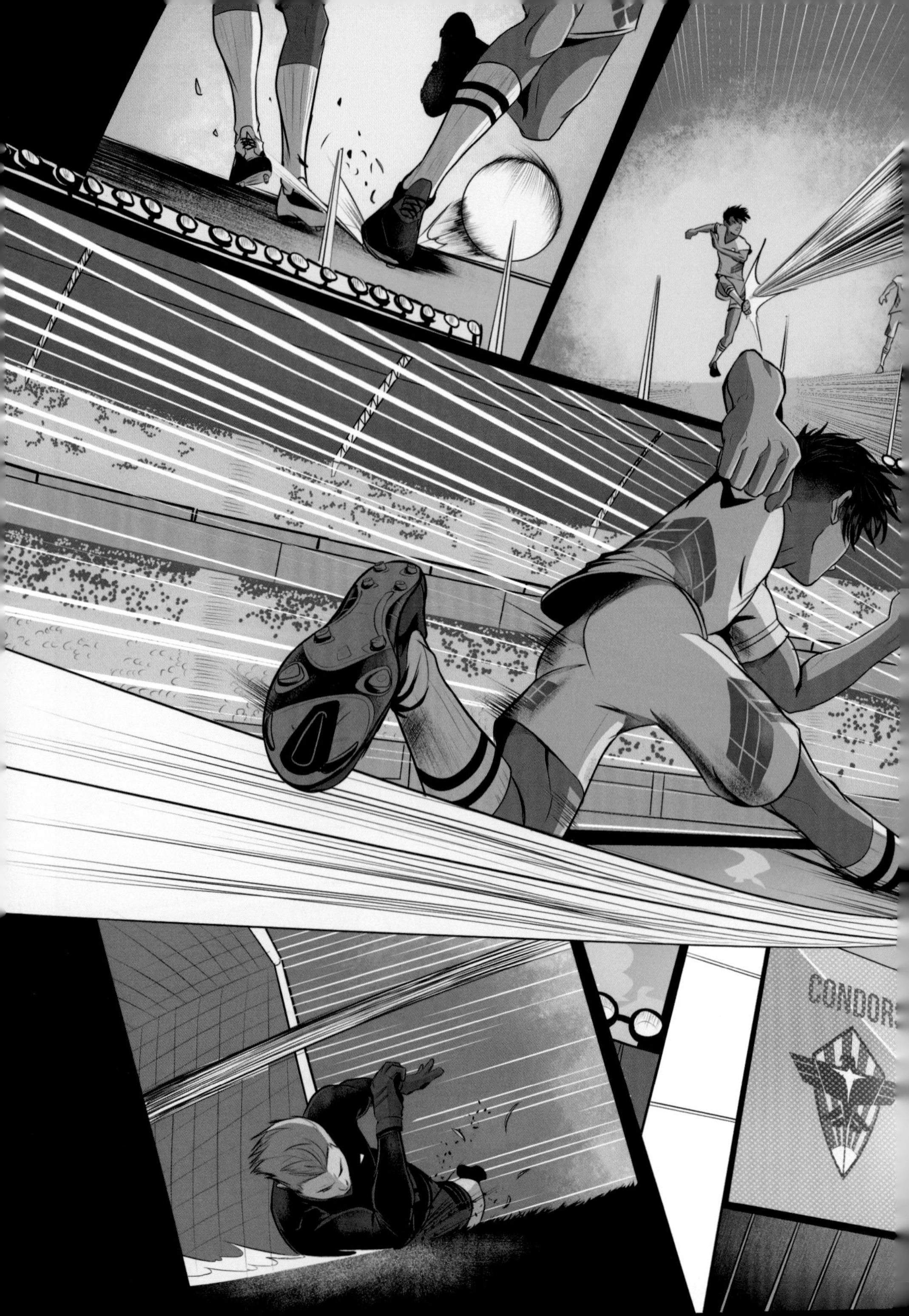
CONDOR

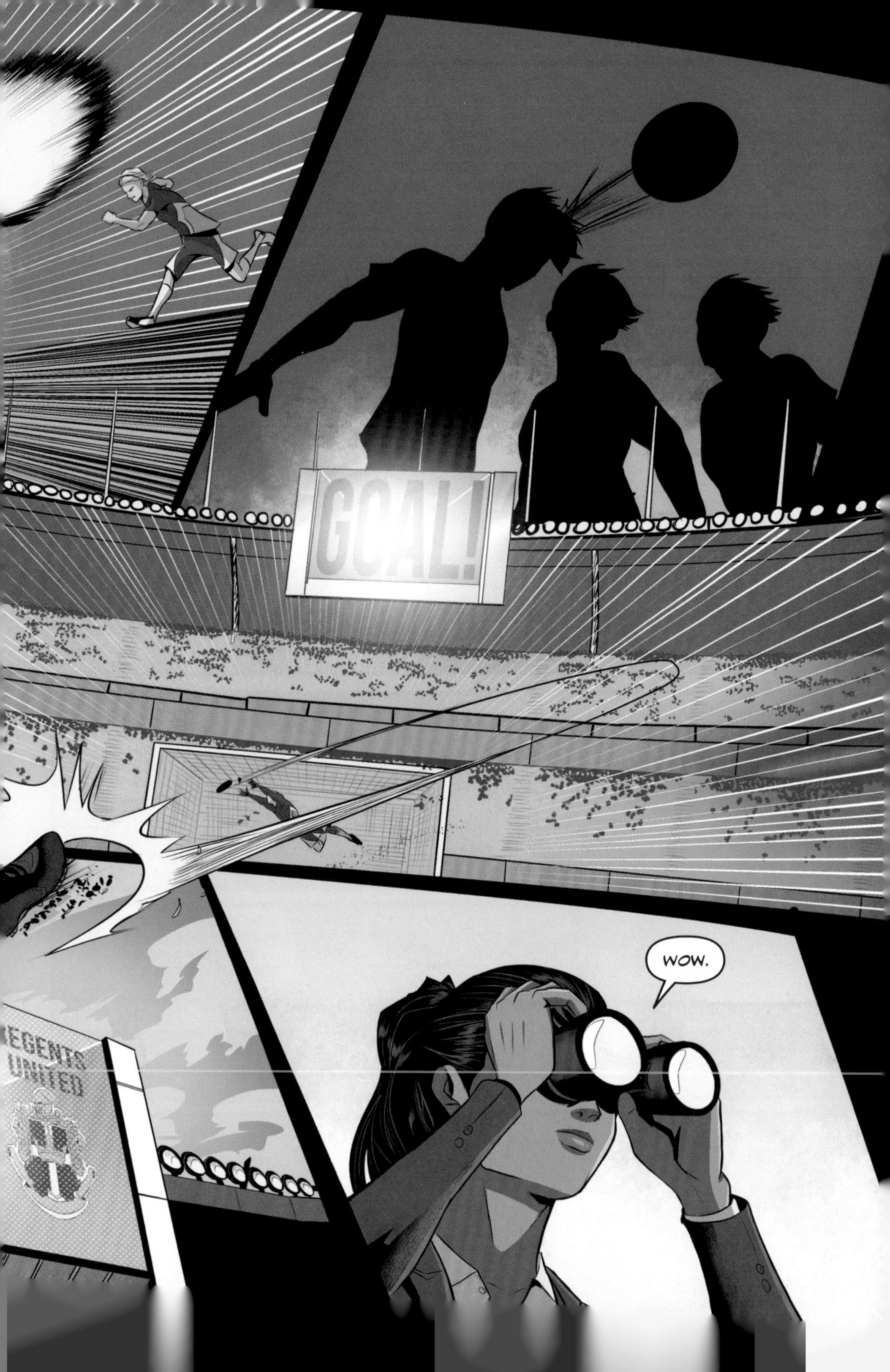
GOAL!
WOW.
REGENTS UNITED

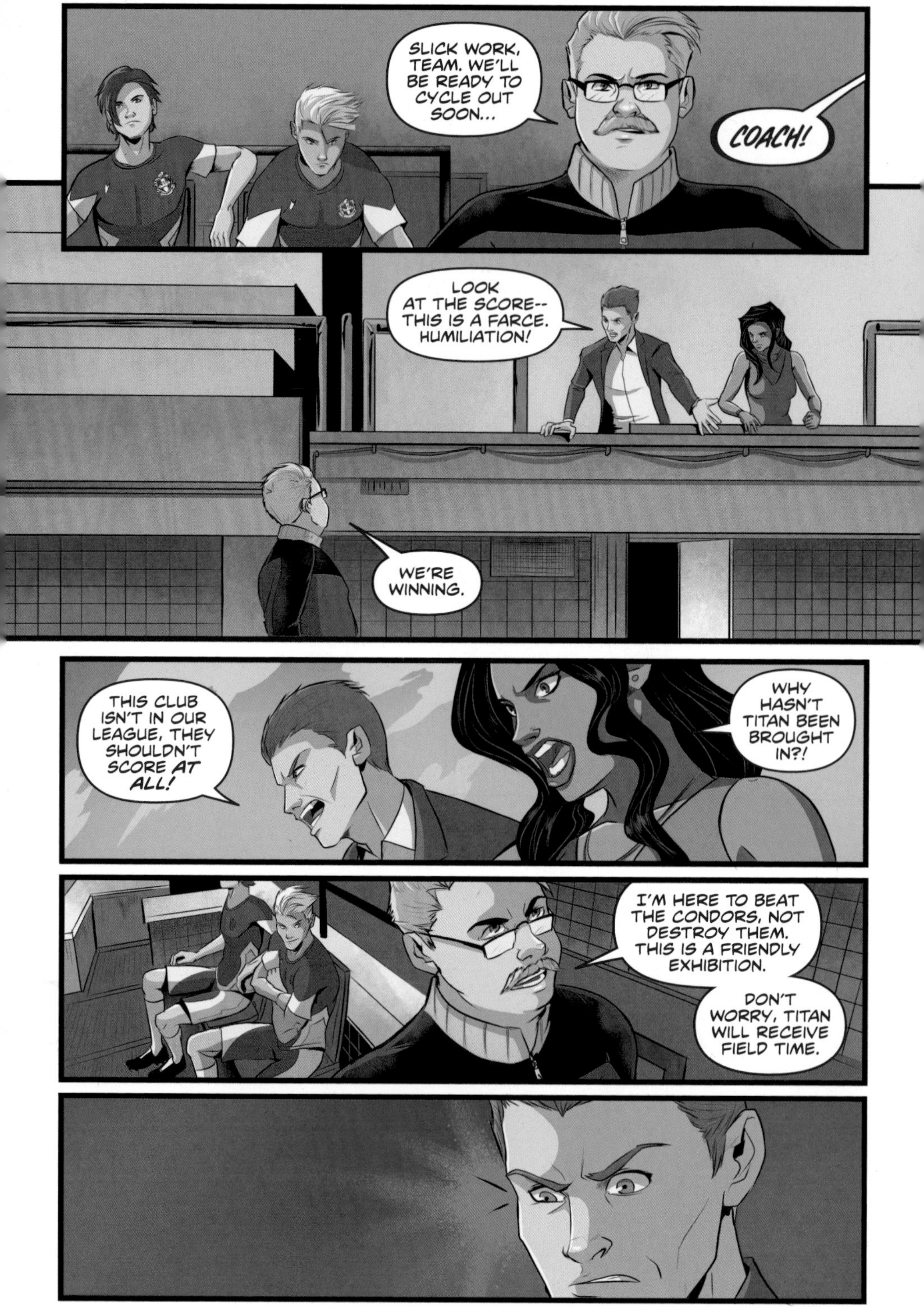
SLICK WORK, TEAM. WE'LL BE READY TO CYCLE OUT SOON...
COACH!
LOOK AT THE SCORE-- THIS IS A FARCE. HUMILIATION!
WE'RE WINNING.
THIS CLUB ISN'T IN OUR LEAGUE, THEY SHOULDN'T SCORE AT ALL!
WHY HASN'T TITAN BEEN BROUGHT IN?!
I'M HERE TO BEAT THE CONDORS, NOT DESTROY THEM. THIS IS A FRIENDLY EXHIBITION.
DON'T WORRY, TITAN WILL RECEIVE FIELD TIME.

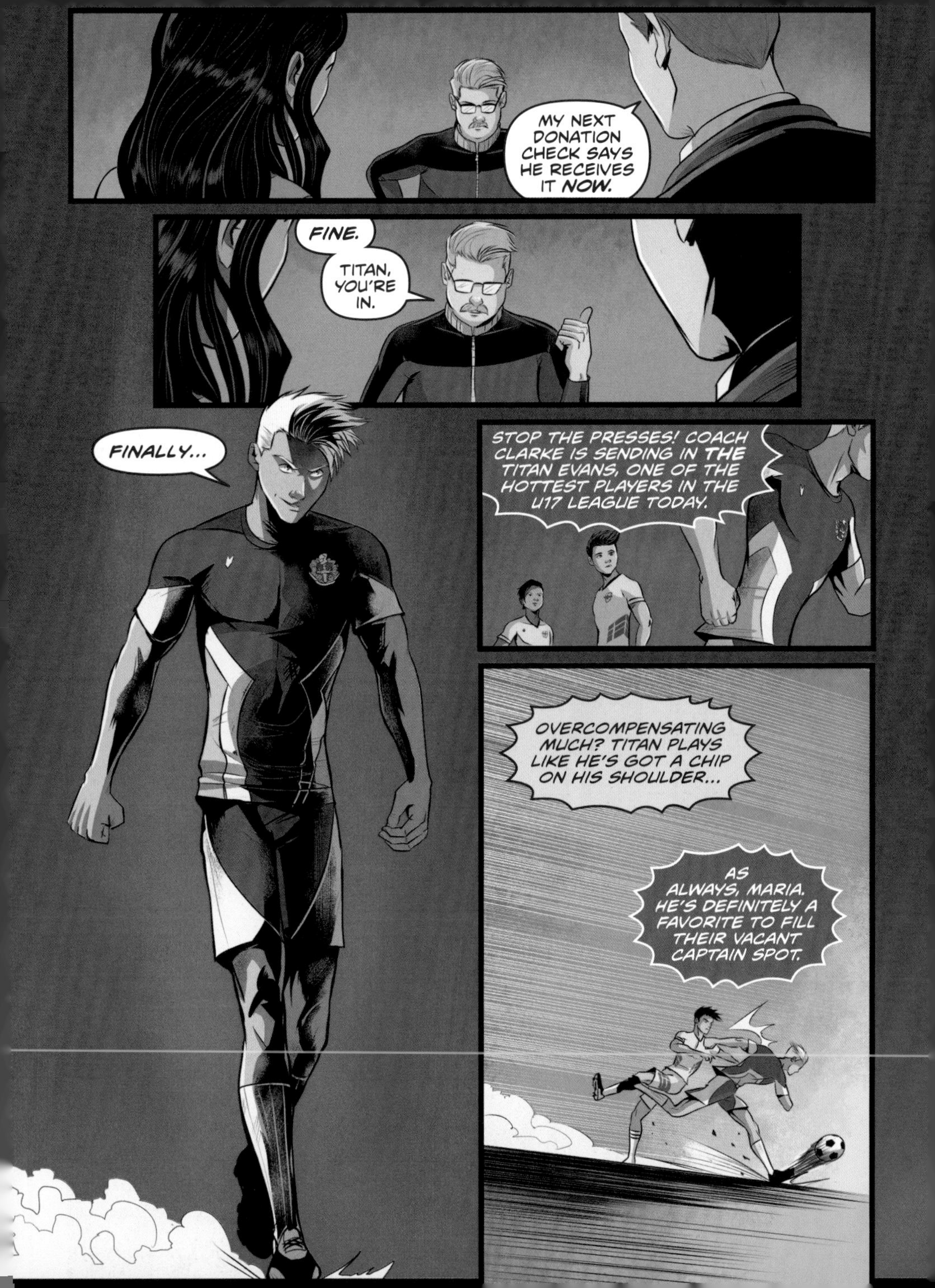
MY NEXT DONATION CHECK SAYS HE RECEIVES IT NOW.
FINE.
TITAN, YOU'RE IN.
FINALLY...
STOP THE PRESSES! COACH CLARKE IS SENDING IN THE TITAN EVANS, ONE OF THE HOTTEST PLAYERS IN THE U17 LEAGUE TODAY.
OVERCOMPENSATING MUCH? TITAN PLAYS LIKE HE'S GOT A CHIP ON HIS SHOULDER...
AS ALWAYS, MARIA. HE'S DEFINITELY A FAVORITE TO FILL THEIR VACANT CAPTAIN SPOT.

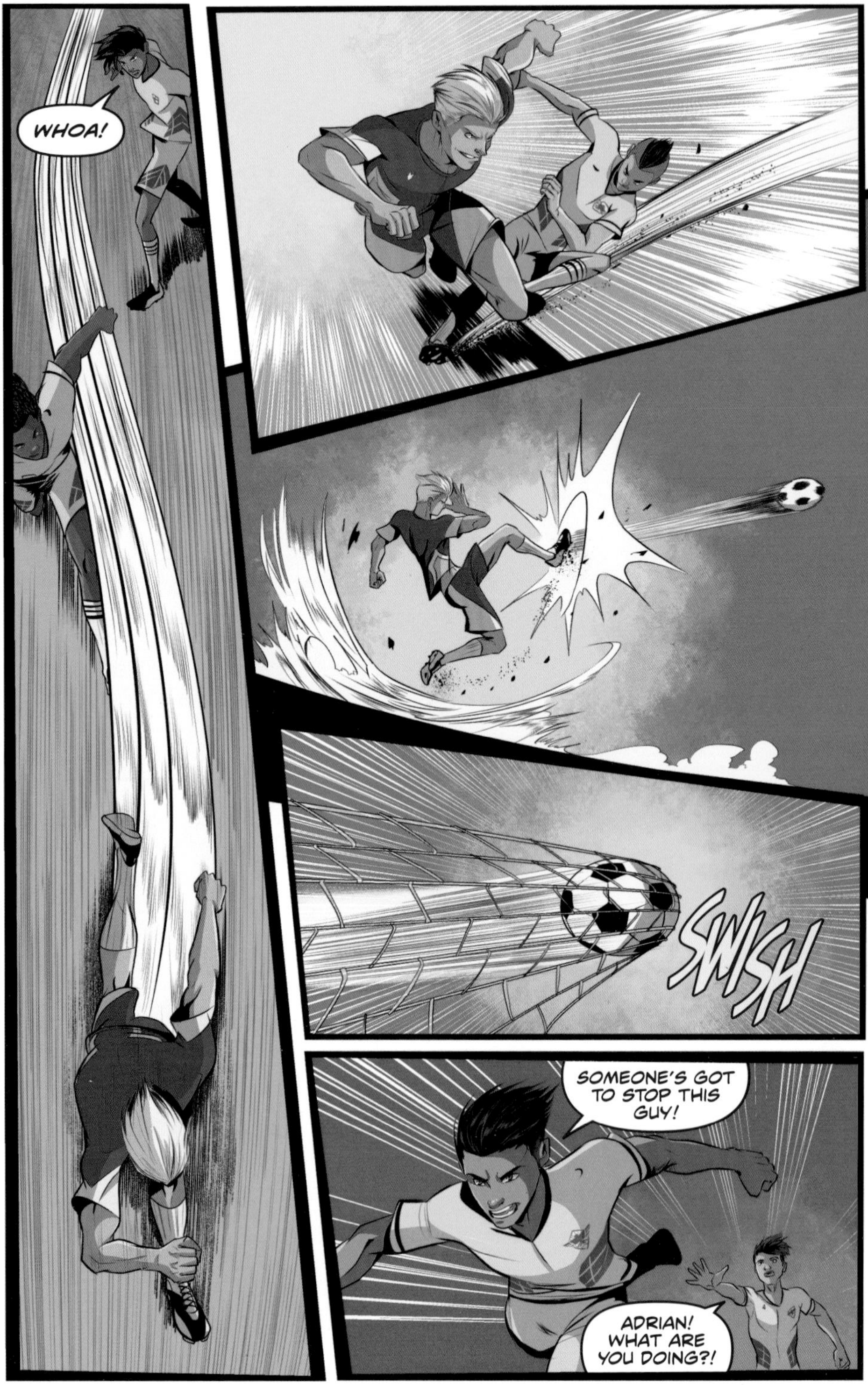
WHOA!
SWISH
SOMEONE'S GOT TO STOP THIS GUY!
ADRIAN! WHAT ARE YOU DOING?!

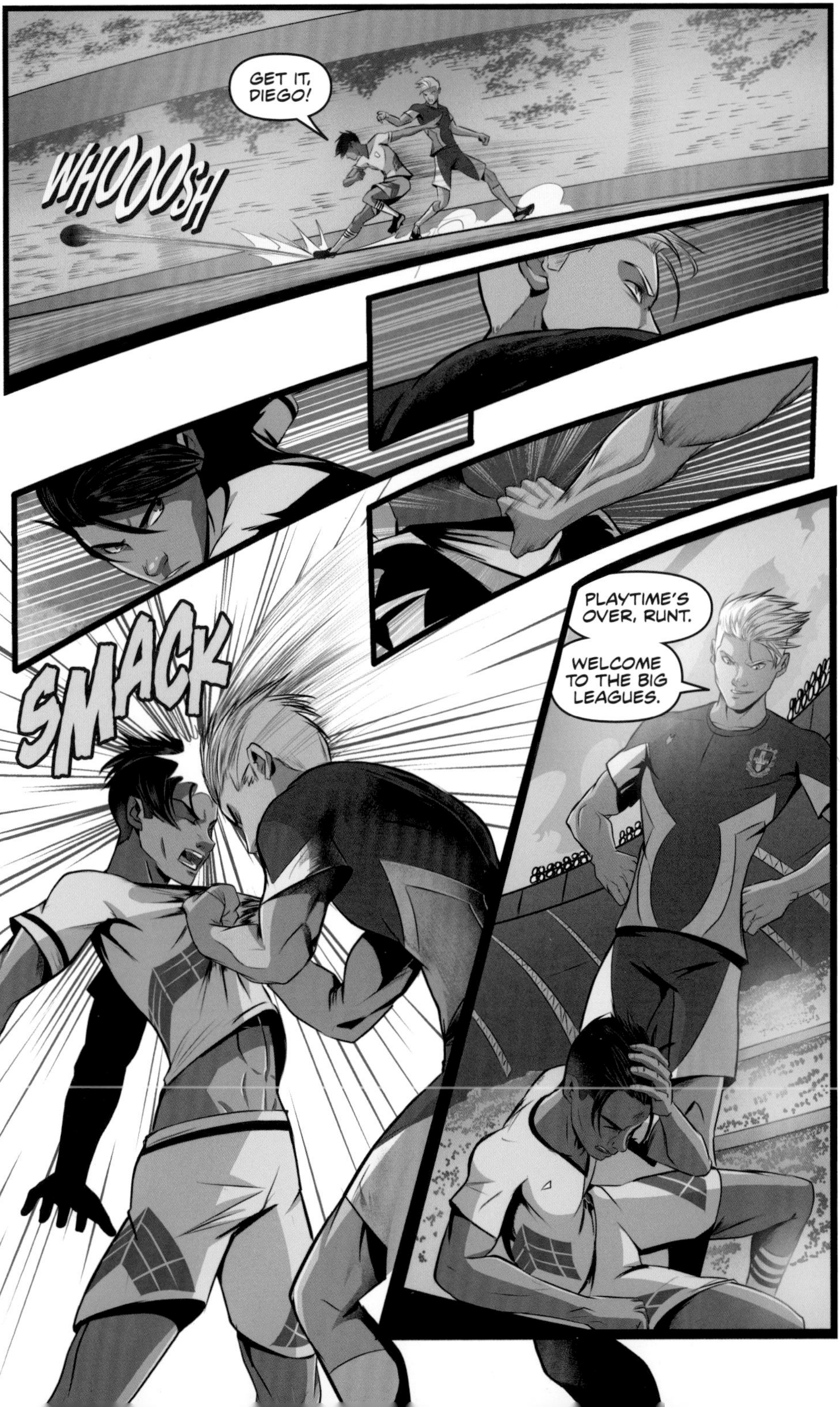
GET IT, DIEGO!
WHOOOSH
SMACK
PLAYTIME'S OVER, RUNT.
WELCOME TO THE BIG LEAGUES.

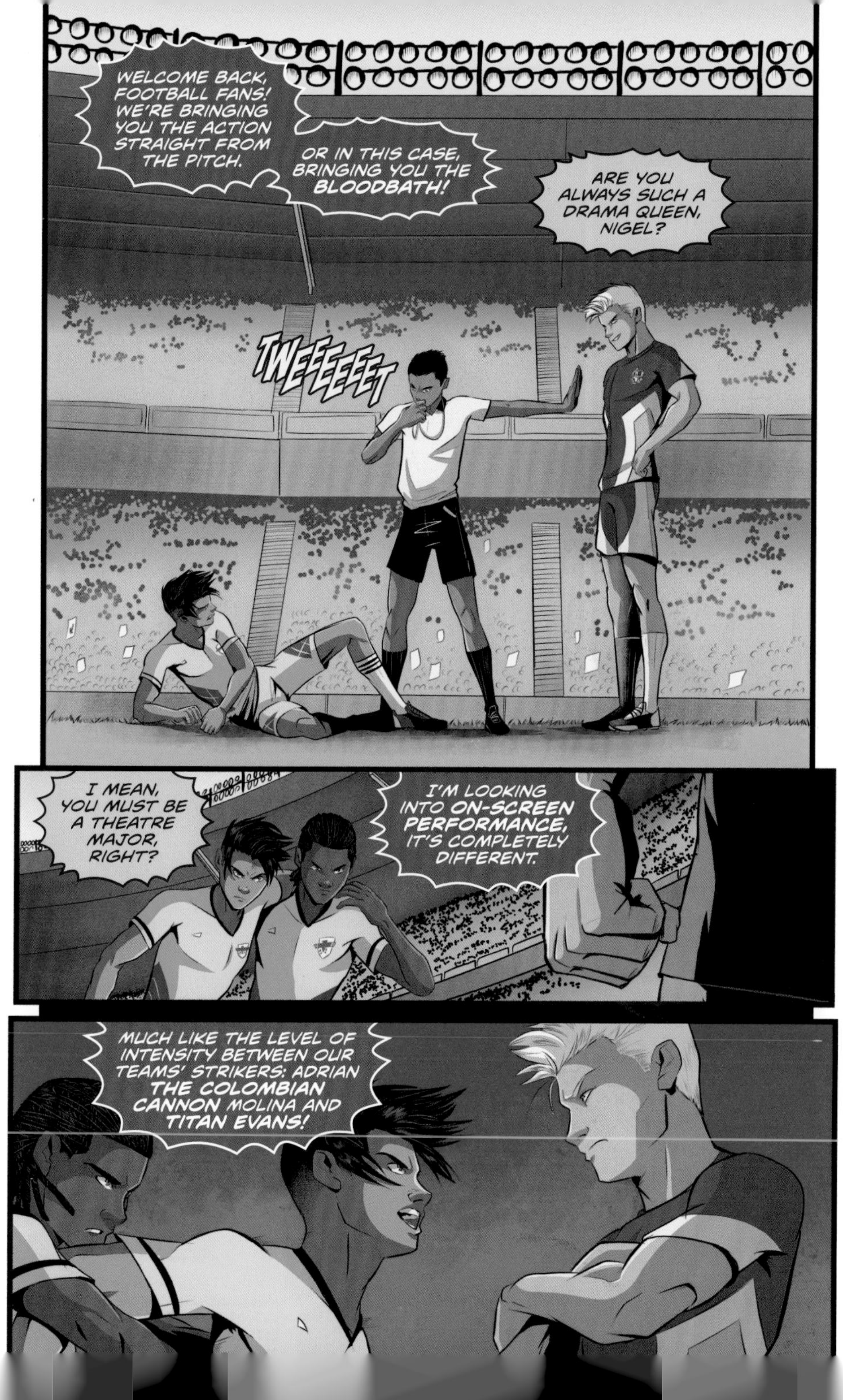
WELCOME BACK, FOOTBALL FANS! WE'RE BRINGING YOU THE ACTION STRAIGHT FROM THE PITCH.
OR IN THIS CASE, BRINGING YOU THE BLOODBATH!
ARE YOU ALWAYS SUCH A DRAMA QUEEN, NIGEL?
TWEEEEEET
I MEAN, YOU MUST BE A THEATRE MAJOR, RIGHT?
I'M LOOKING INTO ON-SCREEN PERFORMANCE, IT'S COMPLETELY DIFFERENT.
MUCH LIKE THE LEVEL OF INTENSITY BETWEEN OUR TEAMS' STRIKERS: ADRIAN THE COLOMBIAN CANNON MOLINA AND TITAN EVANS!

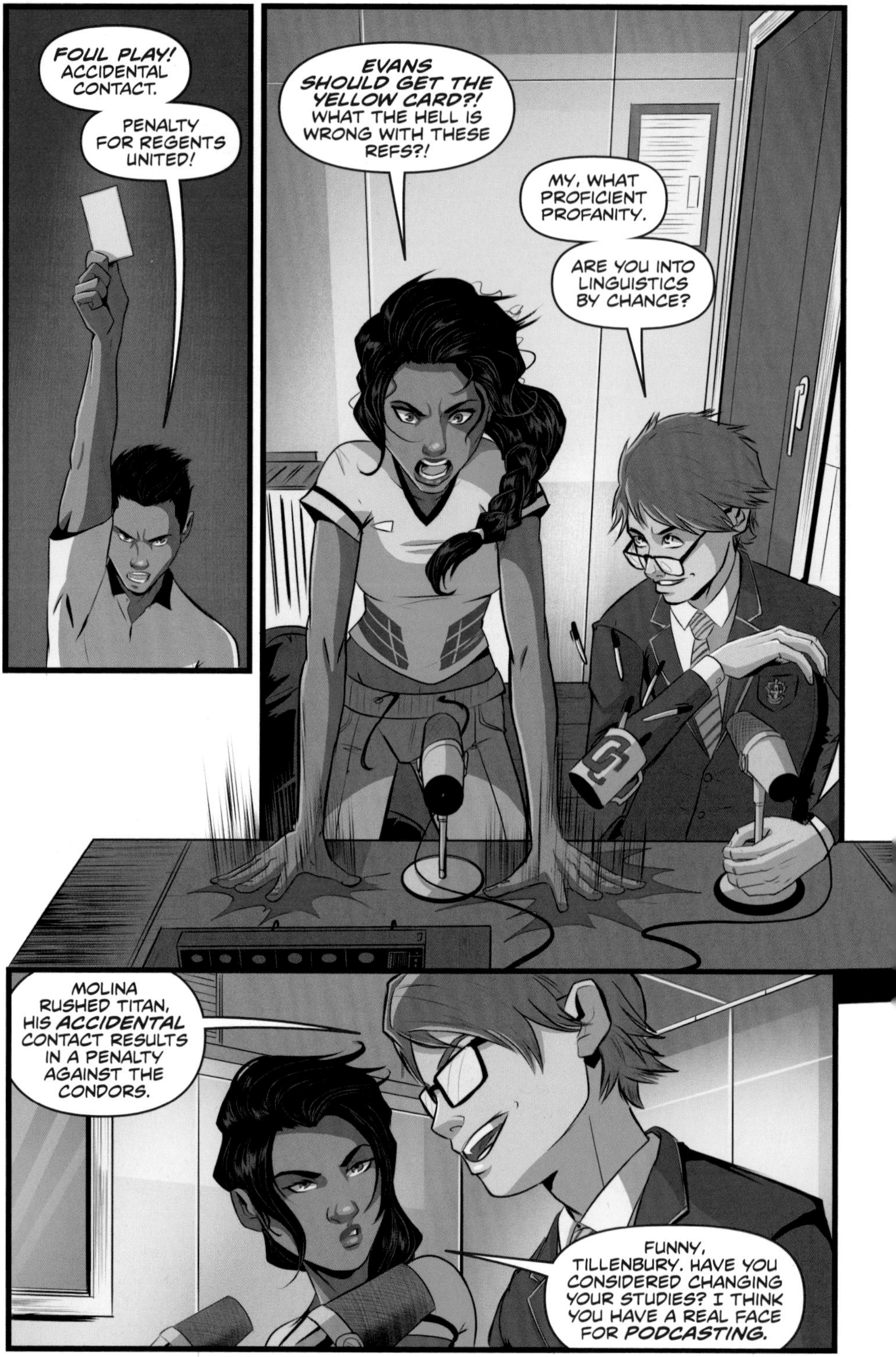
FOUL PLAY! ACCIDENTAL CONTACT.
PENALTY FOR REGENTS UNITED!
EVANS SHOULD GET THE YELLOW CARD?! WHAT THE HELL IS WRONG WITH THESE REFS?!
MY, WHAT PROFICIENT PROFANITY.
ARE YOU INTO LINGUISTICS BY CHANCE?
MOLINA RUSHED TITAN, HIS ACCIDENTAL CONTACT RESULTS IN A PENALTY AGAINST THE CONDORS.
FUNNY, TILLENBURY. HAVE YOU CONSIDERED CHANGING YOUR STUDIES? I THINK YOU HAVE A REAL FACE FOR PODCASTING.

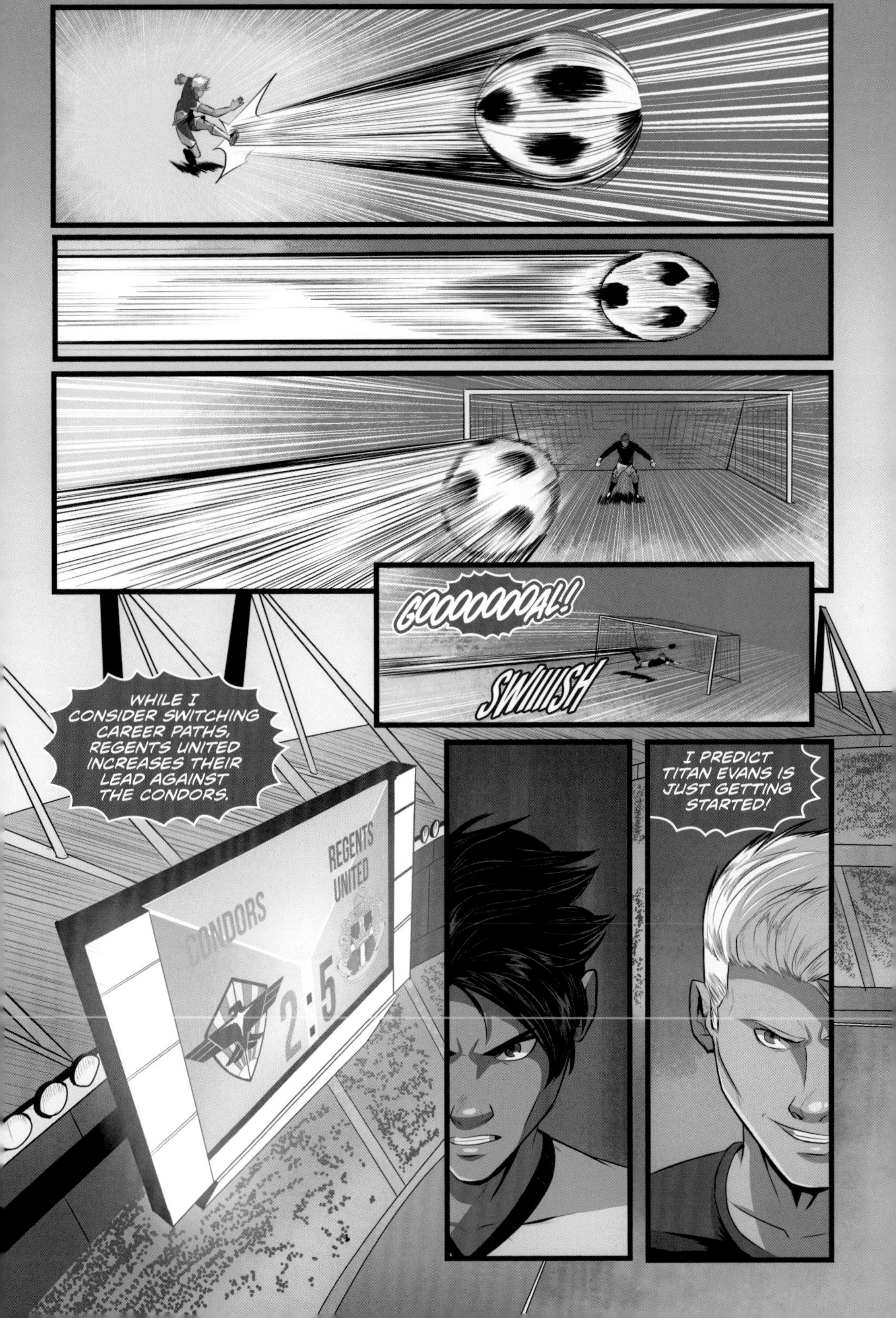
GOOOOOOOAL!
SWIIISH
WHILE I CONSIDER SWITCHING CAREER PATHS, REGENTS UNITED INCREASES THEIR LEAD AGAINST THE CONDORS.
CONDORS
REGENTS UNITED
2 : 5
I PREDICT TITAN EVANS IS JUST GETTING STARTED!

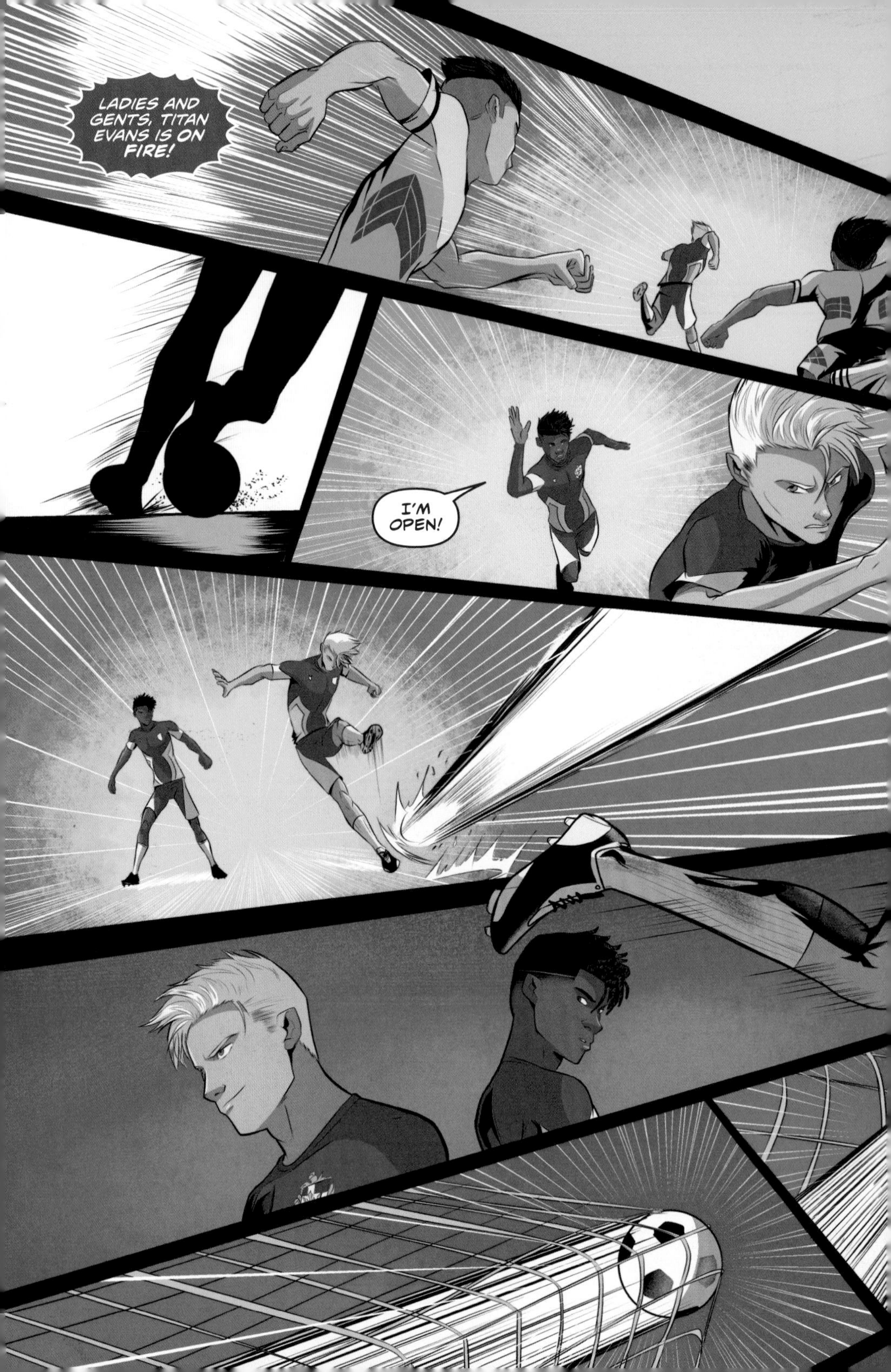
LADIES AND GENTS, TITAN EVANS IS ON FIRE!
I'M OPEN!

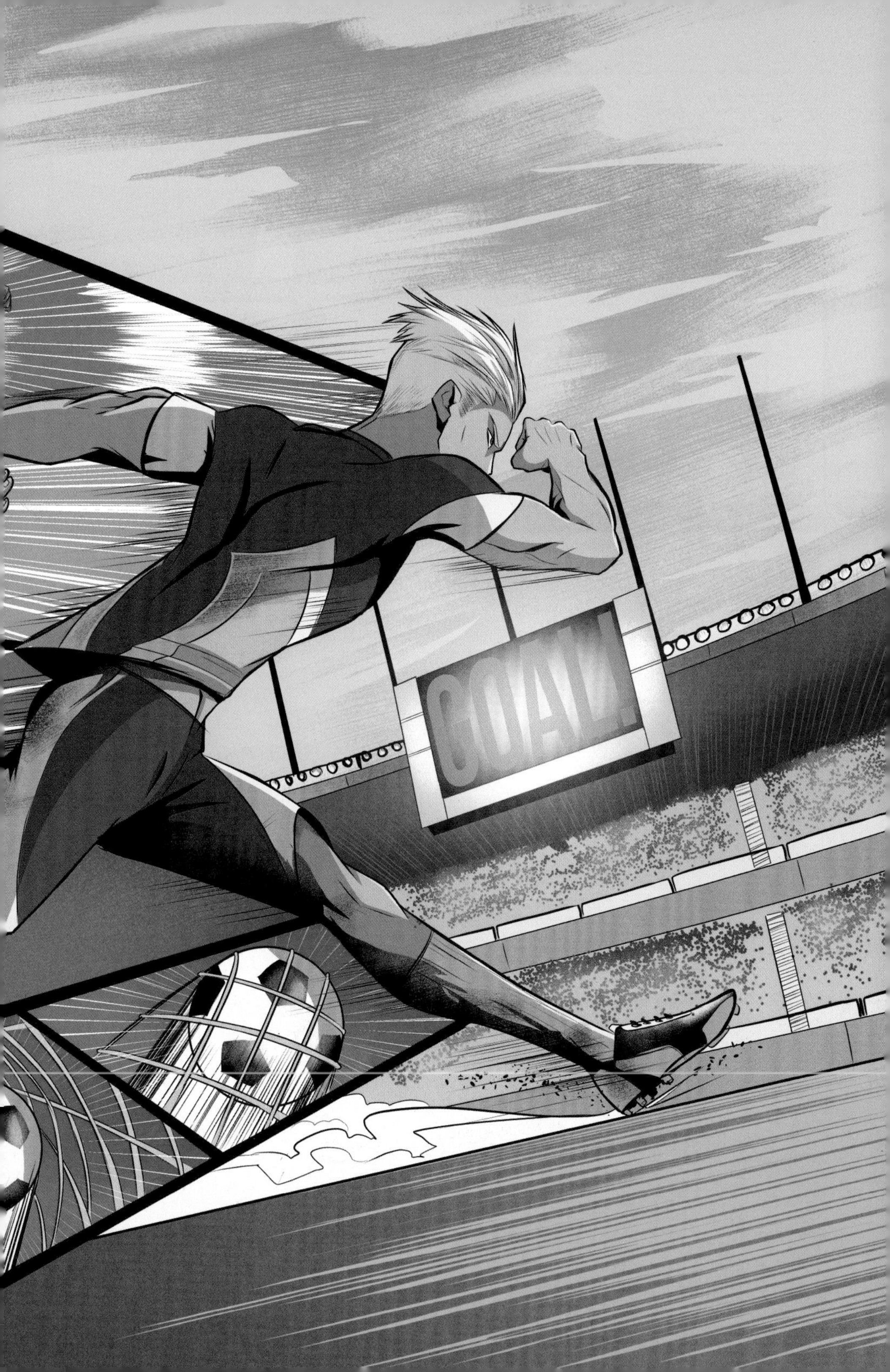
GOAL!

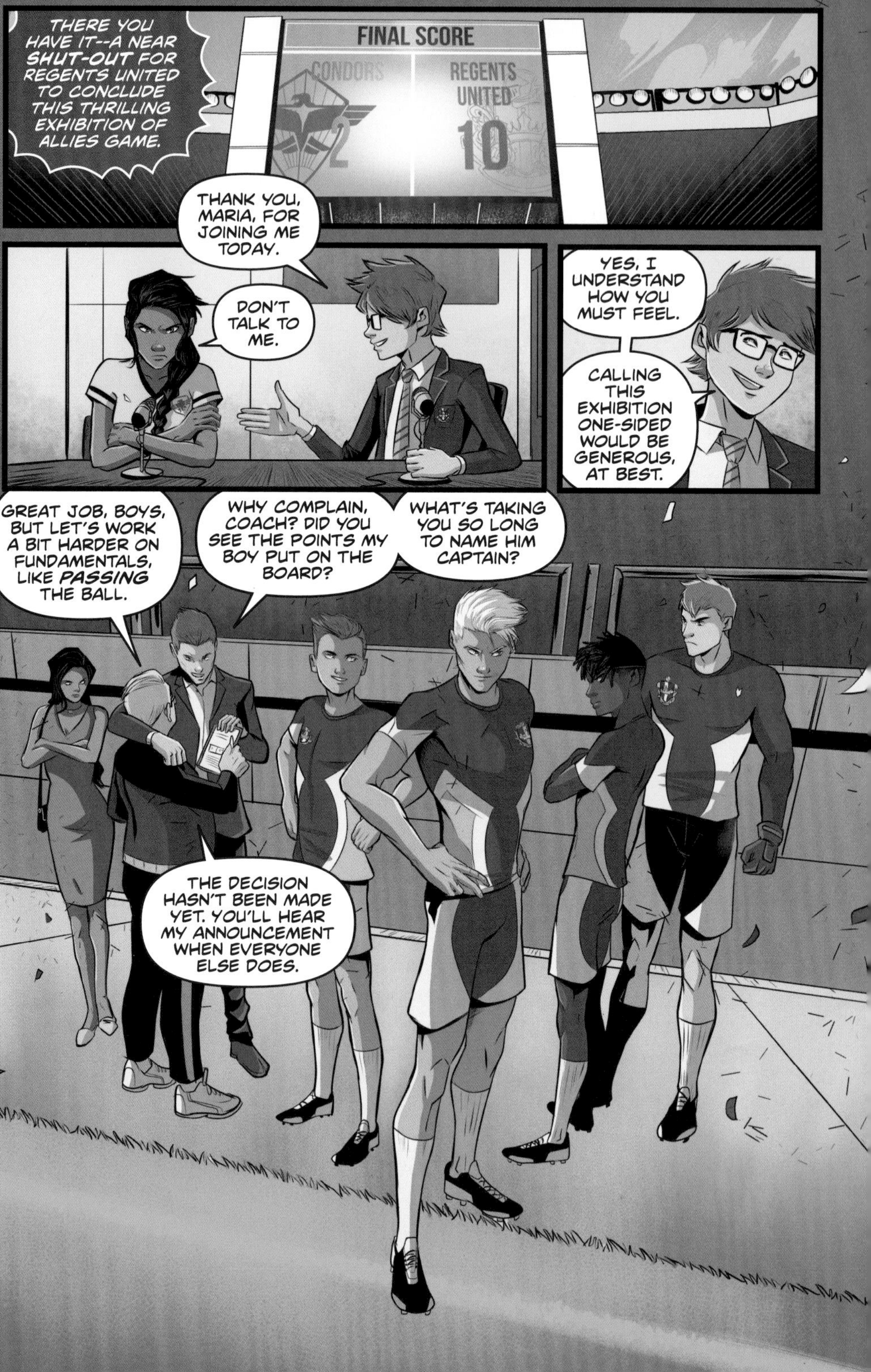
THERE YOU HAVE IT--A NEAR *SHUT-OUT* FOR REGENTS UNITED TO CONCLUDE THIS THRILLING EXHIBITION OF ALLIES GAME.
FINAL SCORE
CONDORS
REGENTS UNITED
2
10
THANK YOU, MARIA, FOR JOINING ME TODAY.
DON'T TALK TO ME.
YES, I UNDERSTAND HOW YOU MUST FEEL.
CALLING THIS EXHIBITION ONE-SIDED WOULD BE GENEROUS, AT BEST.
GREAT JOB, BOYS, BUT LET'S WORK A BIT HARDER ON FUNDAMENTALS, LIKE *PASSING* THE BALL.
WHY COMPLAIN, COACH? DID YOU SEE THE POINTS MY BOY PUT ON THE BOARD?
WHAT'S TAKING YOU SO LONG TO NAME HIM CAPTAIN?
THE DECISION HASN'T BEEN MADE YET. YOU'LL HEAR MY ANNOUNCEMENT WHEN EVERYONE ELSE DOES.

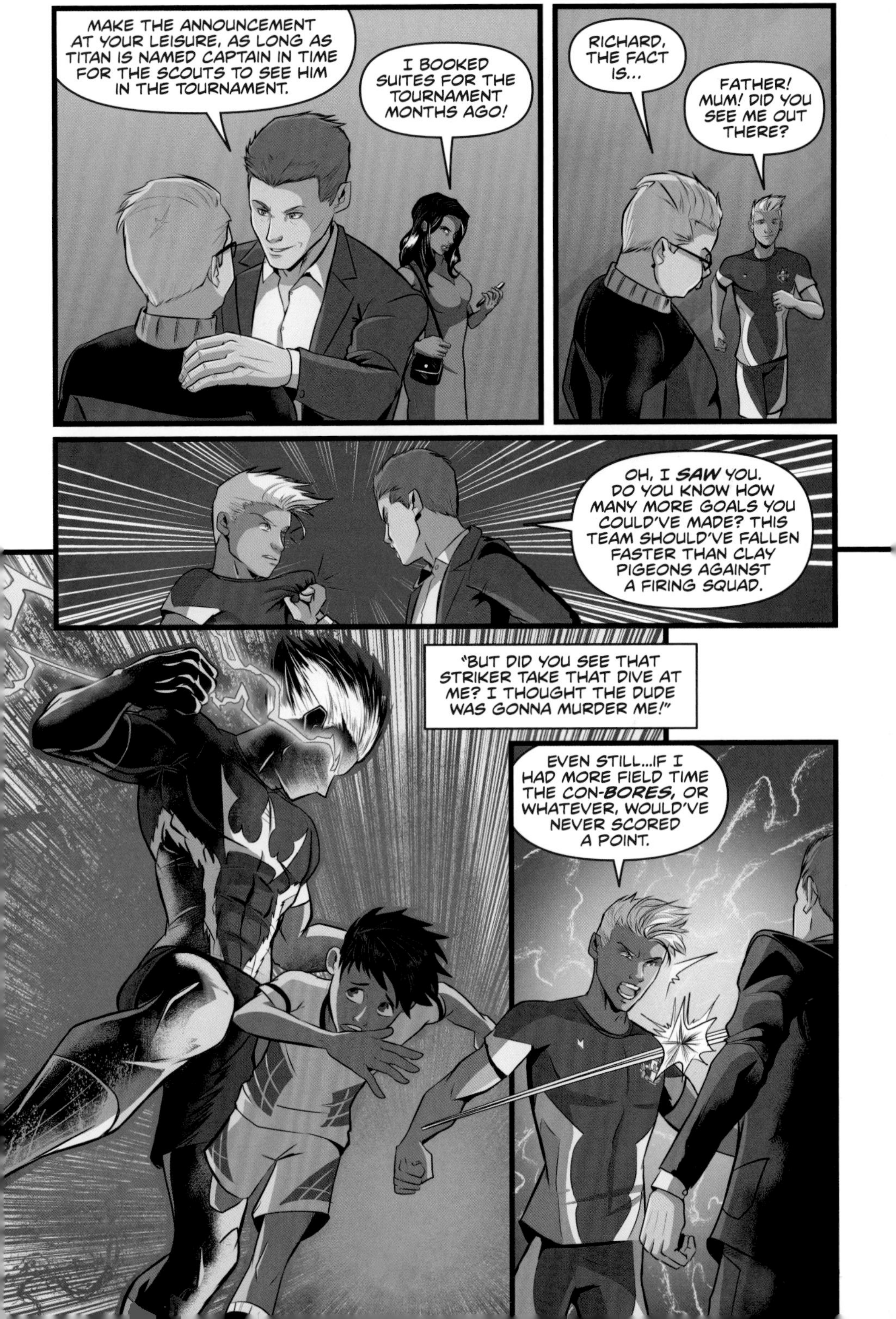
MAKE THE ANNOUNCEMENT AT YOUR LEISURE, AS LONG AS TITAN IS NAMED CAPTAIN IN TIME FOR THE SCOUTS TO SEE HIM IN THE TOURNAMENT.
I BOOKED SUITES FOR THE TOURNAMENT MONTHS AGO!
RICHARD, THE FACT IS...
FATHER! MUM! DID YOU SEE ME OUT THERE?
OH, I SAW YOU. DO YOU KNOW HOW MANY MORE GOALS YOU COULD'VE MADE? THIS TEAM SHOULD'VE FALLEN FASTER THAN CLAY PIGEONS AGAINST A FIRING SQUAD.
"BUT DID YOU SEE THAT STRIKER TAKE THAT DIVE AT ME? I THOUGHT THE DUDE WAS GONNA MURDER ME!"
EVEN STILL...IF I HAD MORE FIELD TIME THE CON-BORES, OR WHATEVER, WOULD'VE NEVER SCORED A POINT.

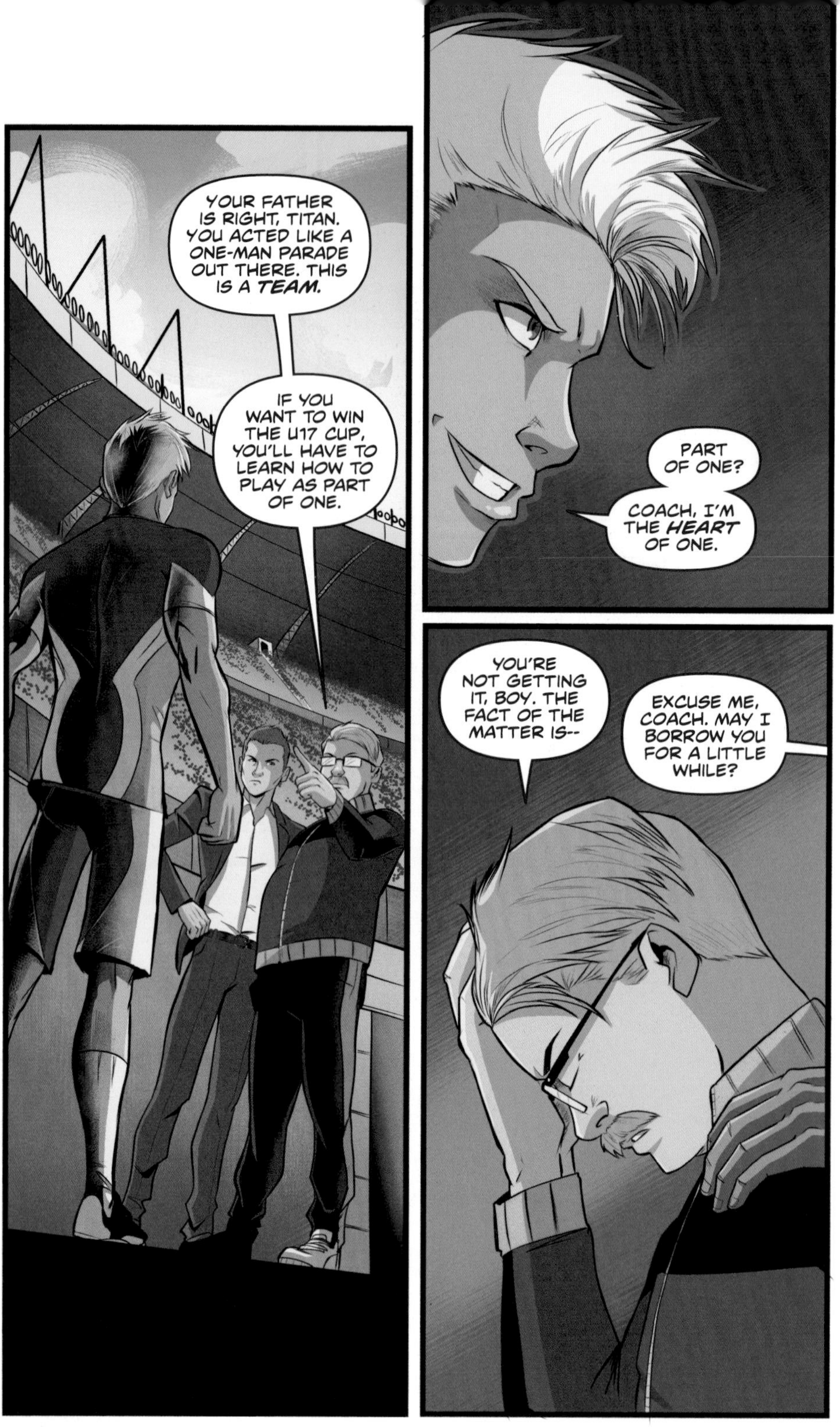
YOUR FATHER IS RIGHT, TITAN. YOU ACTED LIKE A ONE-MAN PARADE OUT THERE. THIS IS A *TEAM.*
IF YOU WANT TO WIN THE U17 CUP, YOU'LL HAVE TO LEARN HOW TO PLAY AS PART OF ONE.
PART OF ONE?
COACH, I'M THE ***HEART*** OF ONE.
YOU'RE NOT GETTING IT, BOY. THE FACT OF THE MATTER IS--
EXCUSE ME, COACH. MAY I BORROW YOU FOR A LITTLE WHILE?

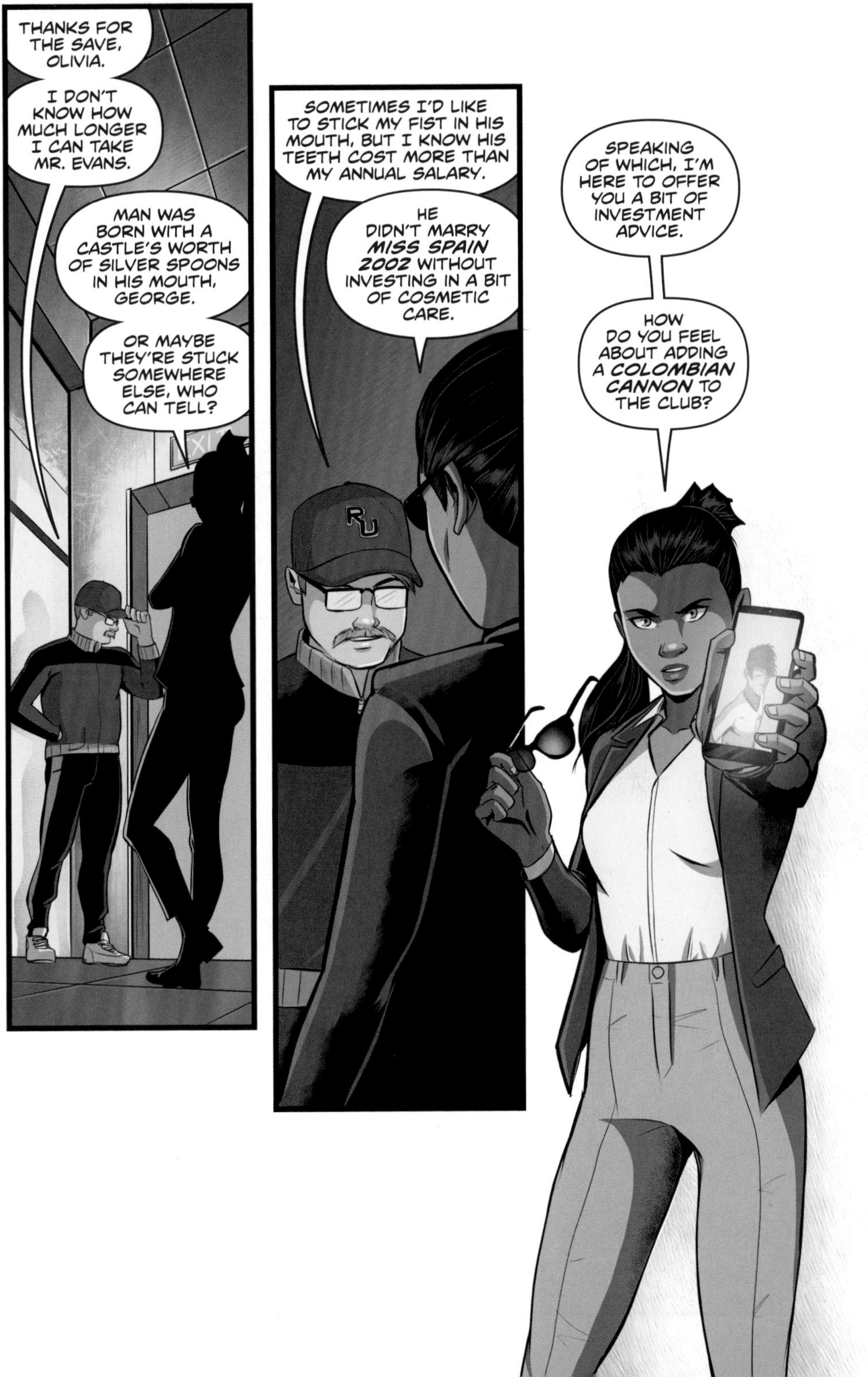
THANKS FOR THE SAVE, OLIVIA.
I DON'T KNOW HOW MUCH LONGER I CAN TAKE MR. EVANS.
MAN WAS BORN WITH A CASTLE'S WORTH OF SILVER SPOONS IN HIS MOUTH, GEORGE.
OR MAYBE THEY'RE STUCK SOMEWHERE ELSE, WHO CAN TELL?
EXIT
SOMETIMES I'D LIKE TO STICK MY FIST IN HIS MOUTH, BUT I KNOW HIS TEETH COST MORE THAN MY ANNUAL SALARY.
HE DIDN'T MARRY ***MISS SPAIN 2002*** WITHOUT INVESTING IN A BIT OF COSMETIC CARE.
RU
SPEAKING OF WHICH, I'M HERE TO OFFER YOU A BIT OF INVESTMENT ADVICE.
HOW DO YOU FEEL ABOUT ADDING A ***COLOMBIAN CANNON*** TO THE CLUB?

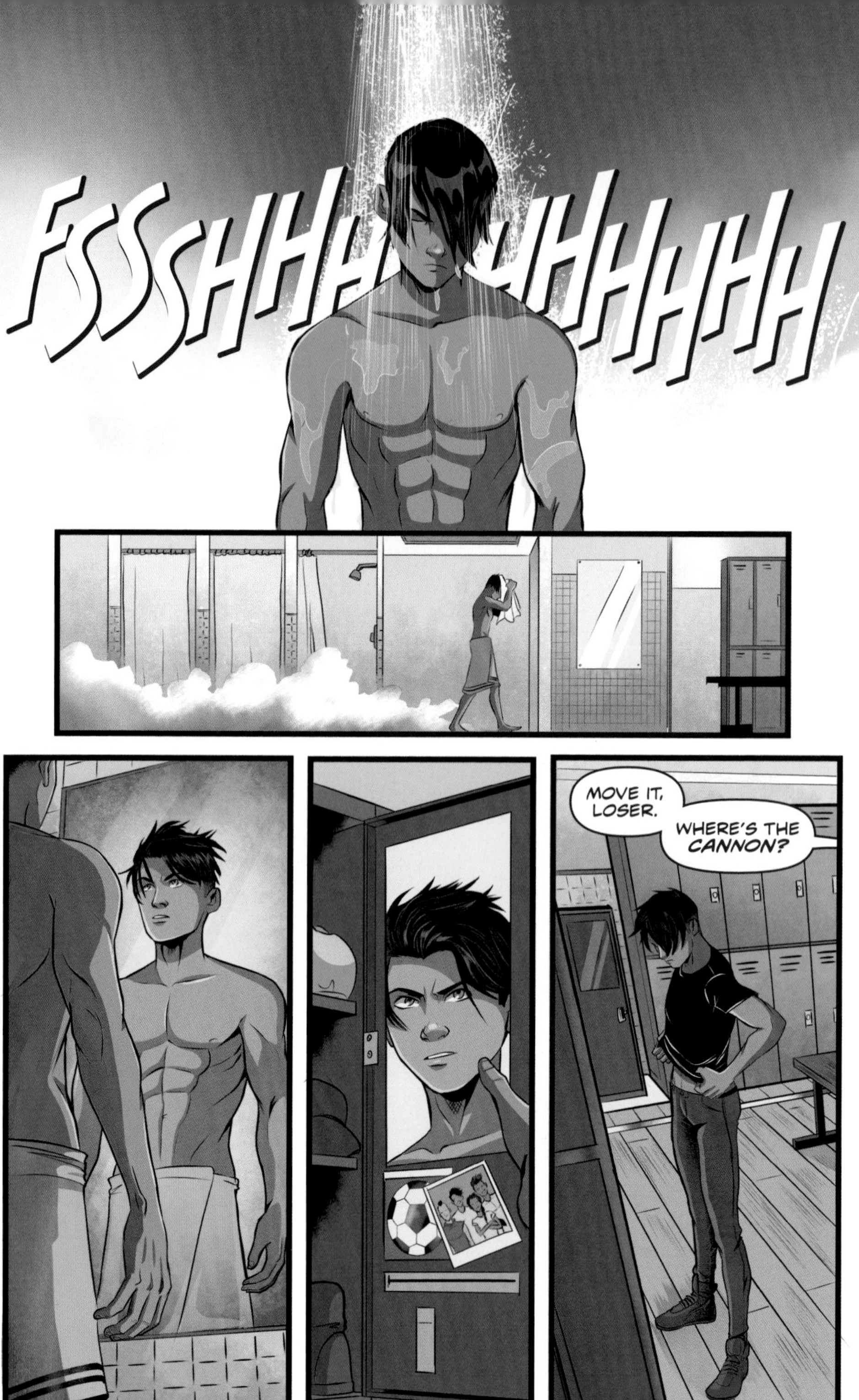
FSSSHHHHHHHHHHH
MOVE IT, LOSER.
WHERE'S THE *CANNON*?

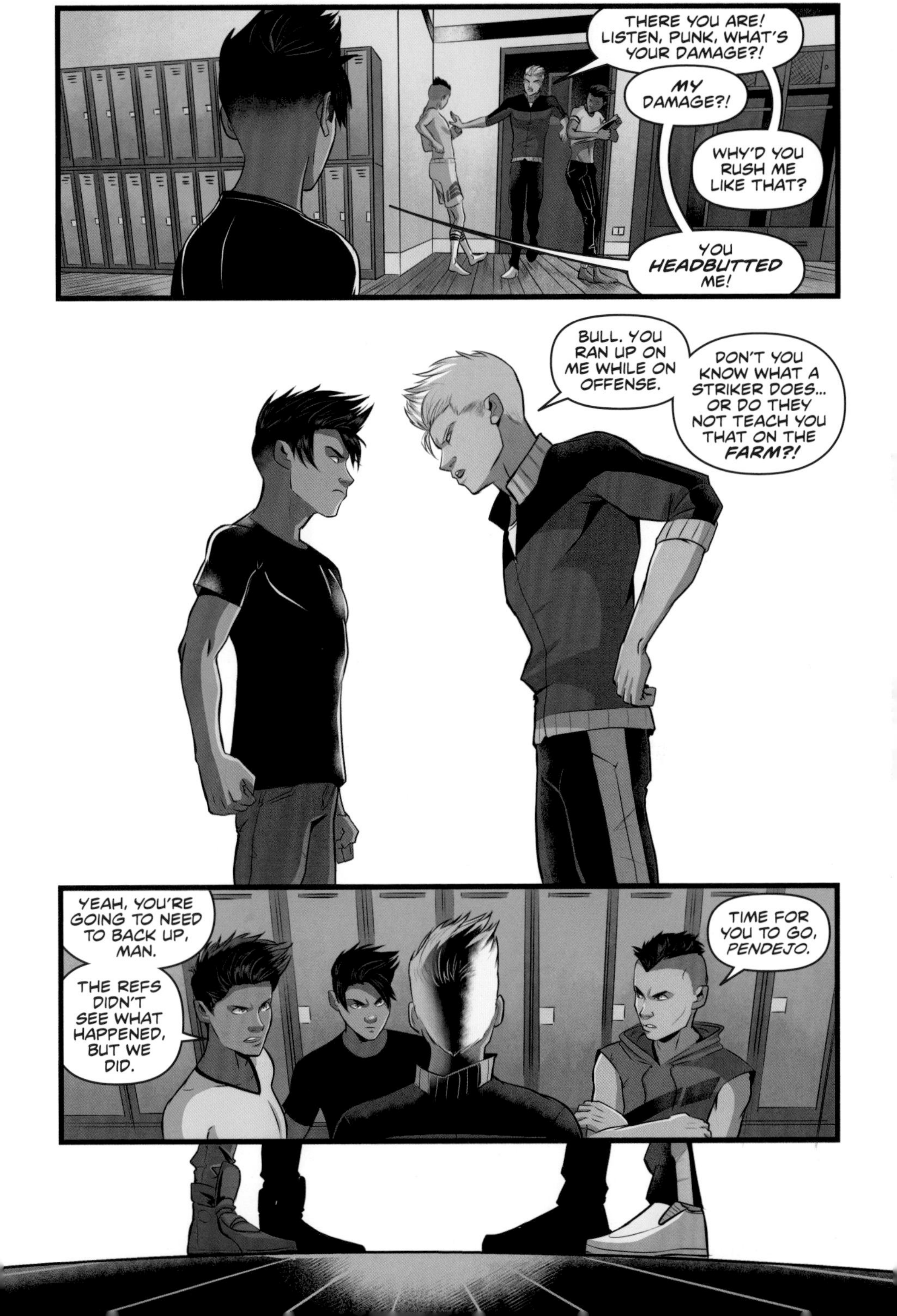
THERE YOU ARE! LISTEN, PUNK, WHAT'S YOUR DAMAGE?!
MY DAMAGE?!
WHY'D YOU RUSH ME LIKE THAT?
YOU HEADBUTTED ME!
BULL. YOU RAN UP ON ME WHILE ON OFFENSE.
DON'T YOU KNOW WHAT A STRIKER DOES... OR DO THEY NOT TEACH YOU THAT ON THE FARM?!
YEAH, YOU'RE GOING TO NEED TO BACK UP, MAN.
THE REFS DIDN'T SEE WHAT HAPPENED, BUT WE DID.
TIME FOR YOU TO GO, PENDEJO.

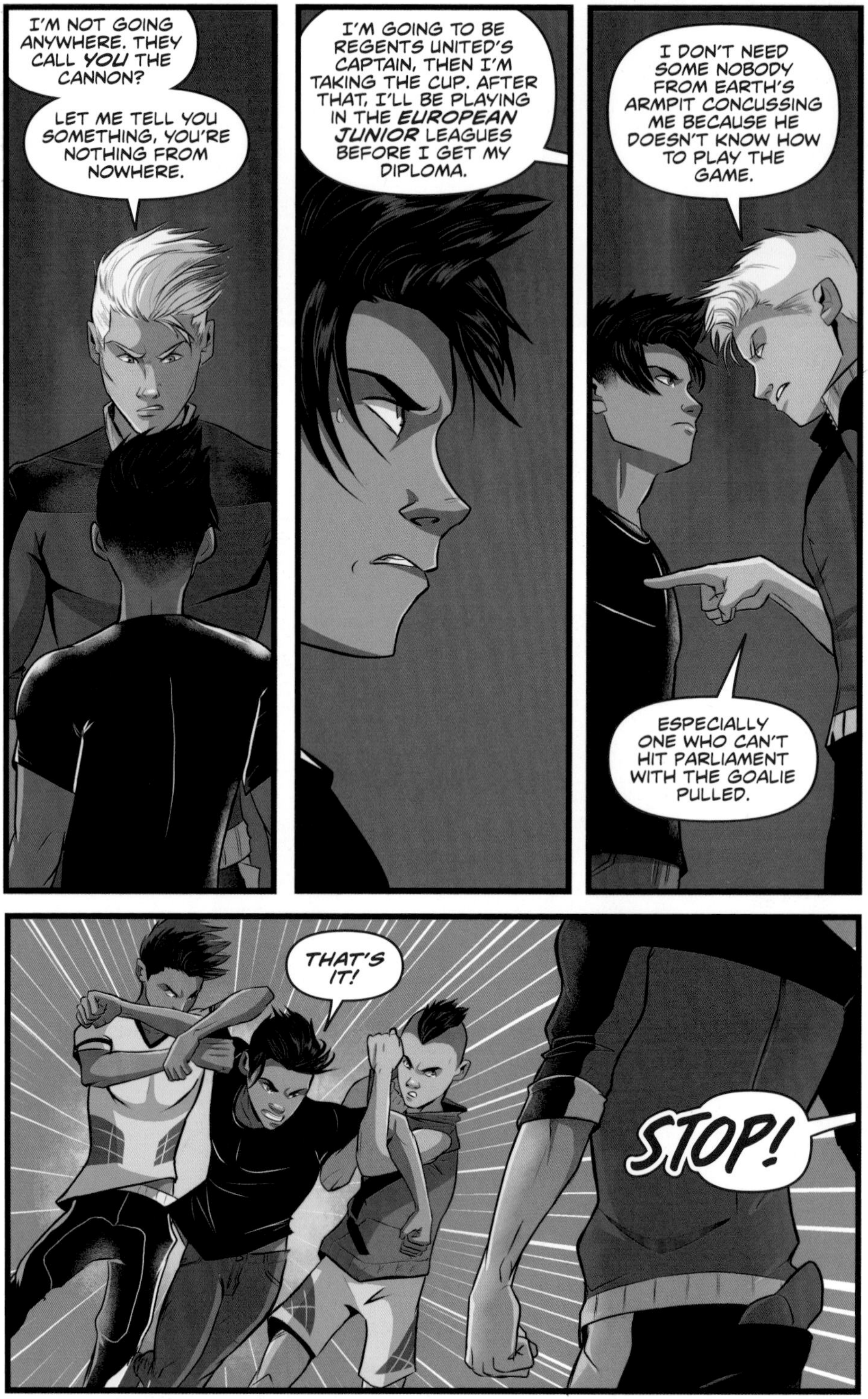
I'M NOT GOING ANYWHERE. THEY CALL *YOU* THE CANNON?
LET ME TELL YOU SOMETHING, YOU'RE NOTHING FROM NOWHERE.
I'M GOING TO BE REGENTS UNITED'S CAPTAIN, THEN I'M TAKING THE CUP. AFTER THAT, I'LL BE PLAYING IN THE *EUROPEAN JUNIOR* LEAGUES BEFORE I GET MY DIPLOMA.
I DON'T NEED SOME NOBODY FROM EARTH'S ARMPIT CONCUSSING ME BECAUSE HE DOESN'T KNOW HOW TO PLAY THE GAME.
ESPECIALLY ONE WHO CAN'T HIT PARLIAMENT WITH THE GOALIE PULLED.
THAT'S IT!
STOP!

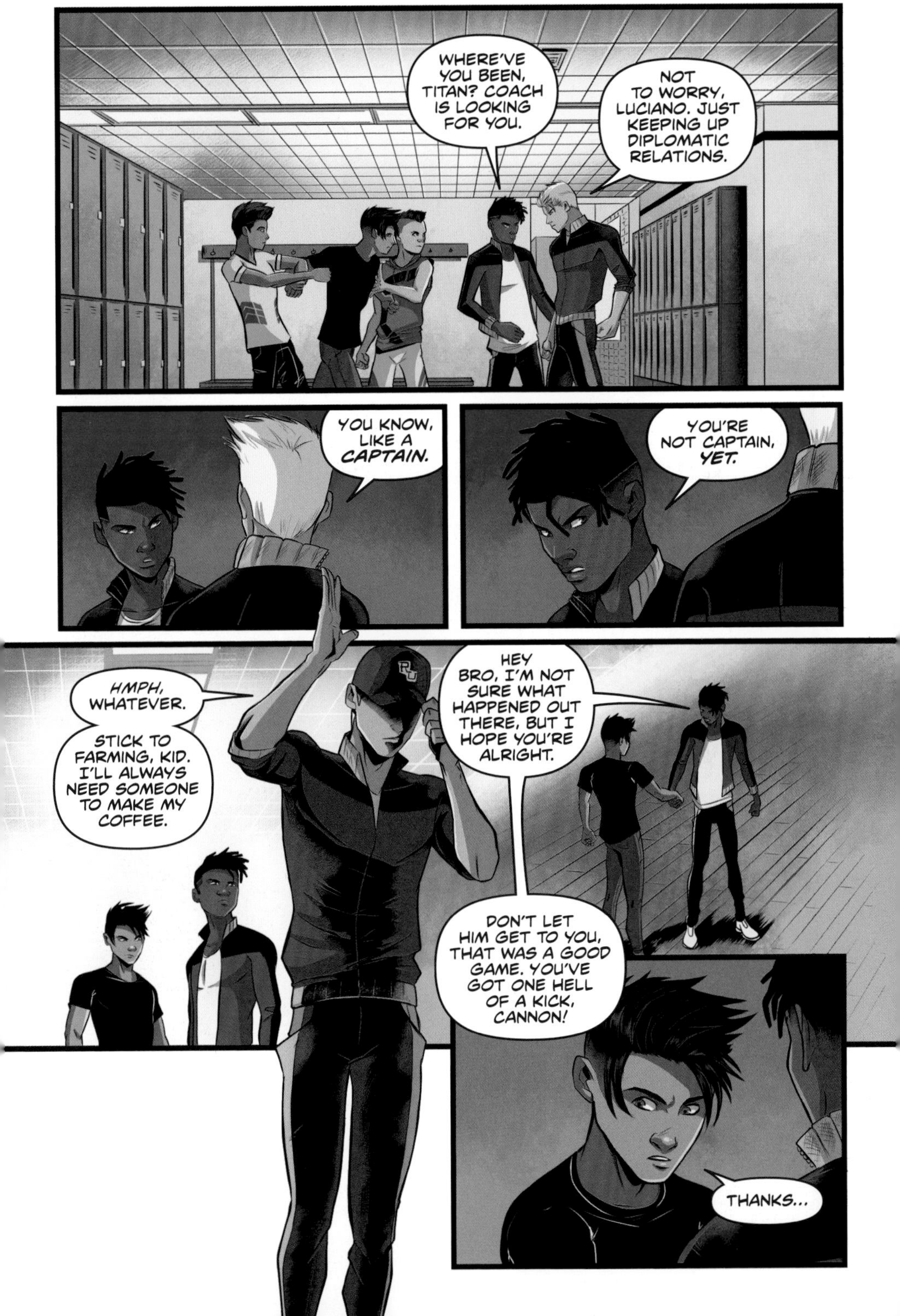
WHERE'VE YOU BEEN, TITAN? COACH IS LOOKING FOR YOU.
NOT TO WORRY, LUCIANO. JUST KEEPING UP DIPLOMATIC RELATIONS.
YOU KNOW, LIKE A *CAPTAIN.*
YOU'RE NOT CAPTAIN, ***YET.***
HMPH, WHATEVER.
STICK TO FARMING, KID. I'LL ALWAYS NEED SOMEONE TO MAKE MY COFFEE.
HEY BRO, I'M NOT SURE WHAT HAPPENED OUT THERE, BUT I HOPE YOU'RE ALRIGHT.
DON'T LET HIM GET TO YOU, THAT WAS A GOOD GAME. YOU'VE GOT ONE HELL OF A KICK, CANNON!
THANKS...

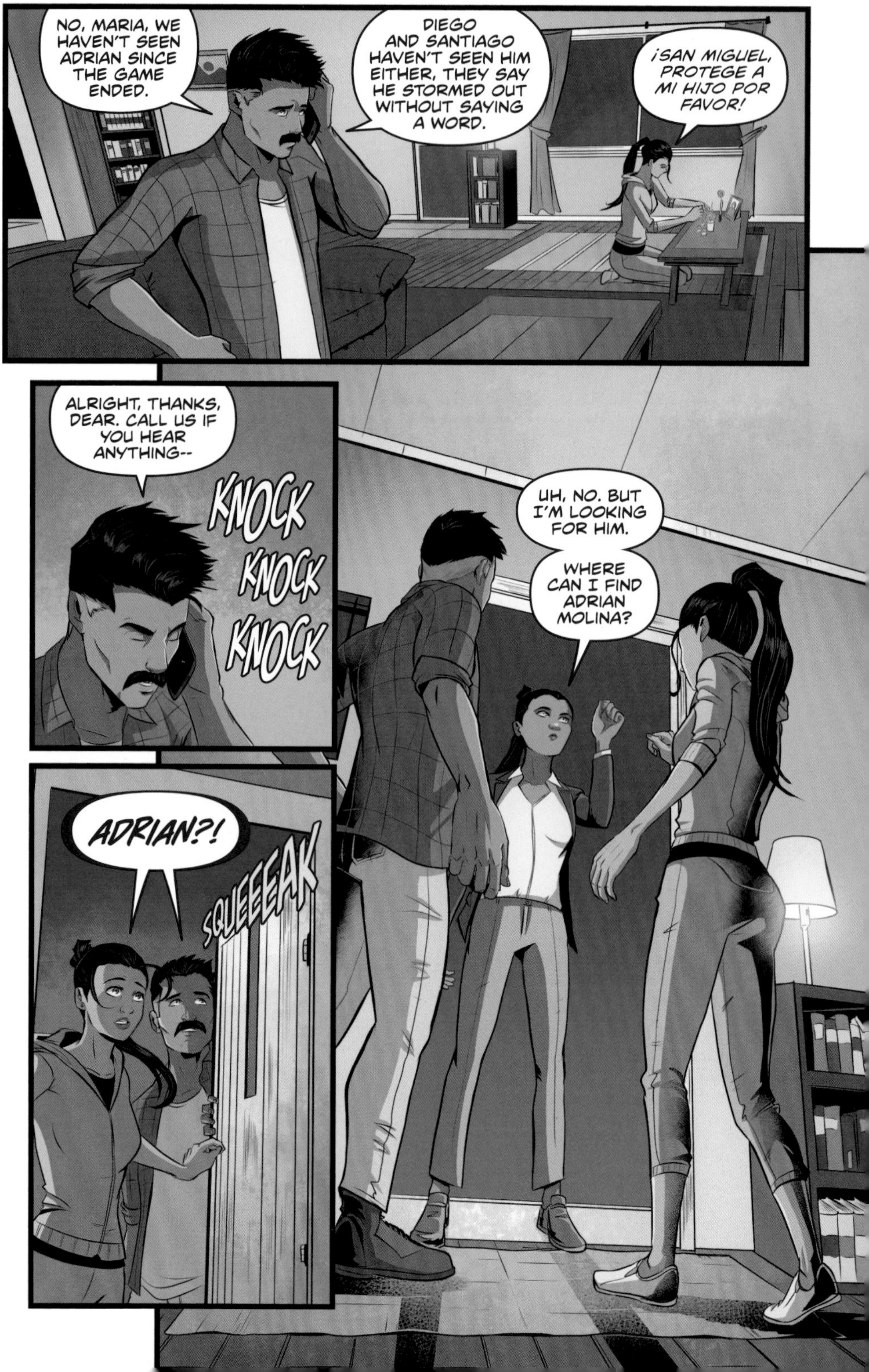
NO, MARIA, WE HAVEN'T SEEN ADRIAN SINCE THE GAME ENDED.
DIEGO AND SANTIAGO HAVEN'T SEEN HIM EITHER, THEY SAY HE STORMED OUT WITHOUT SAYING A WORD.
¡SAN MIGUEL, PROTEGE A MI HIJO POR FAVOR!
ALRIGHT, THANKS, DEAR. CALL US IF YOU HEAR ANYTHING--
KNOCK
KNOCK
KNOCK
ADRIAN?!
SQUEEEAK
UH, NO. BUT I'M LOOKING FOR HIM.
WHERE CAN I FIND ADRIAN MOLINA?

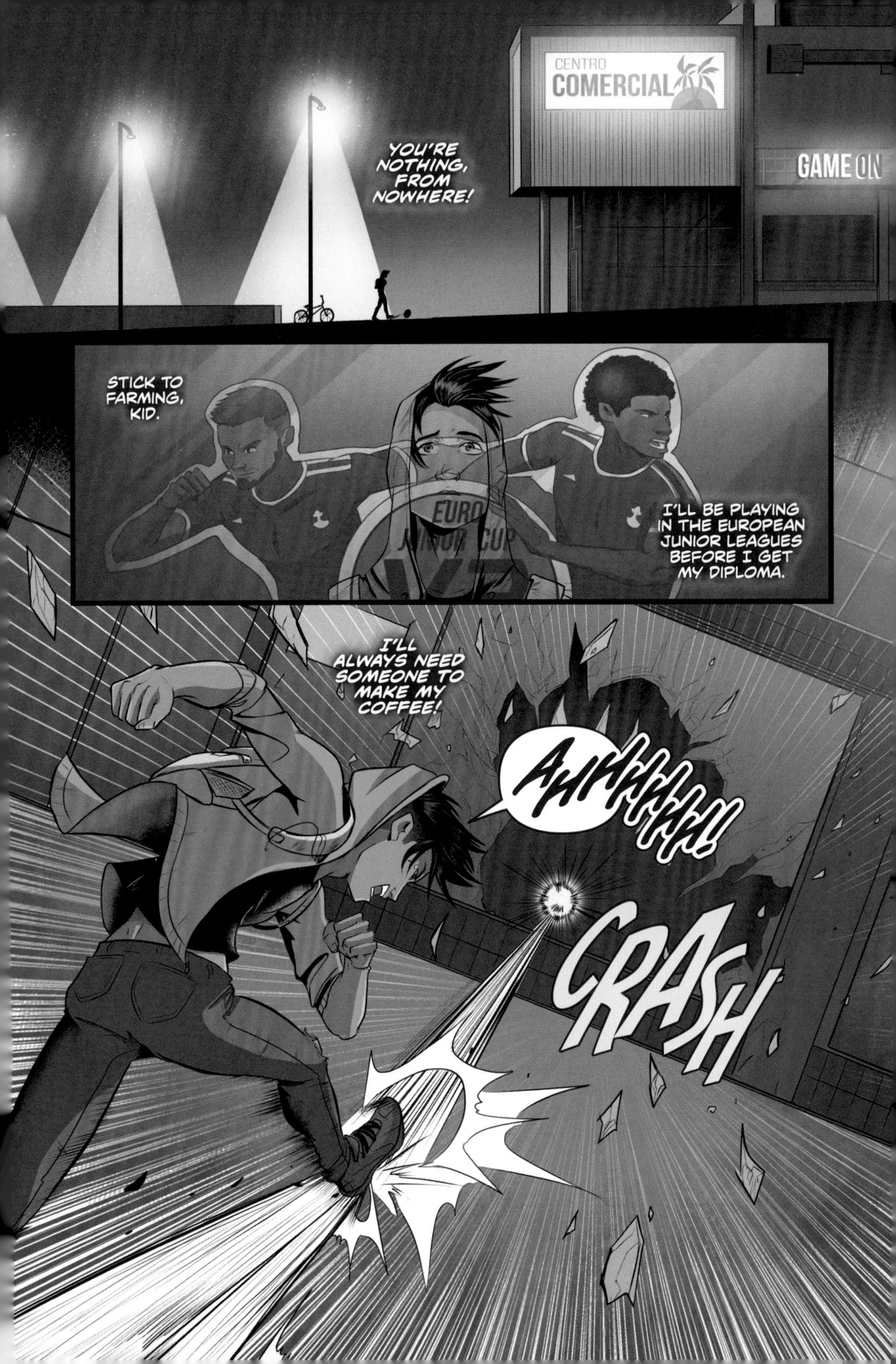
CENTRO
COMERCIAL
GAME ON
YOU'RE NOTHING, FROM NOWHERE!
STICK TO FARMING, KID.
I'LL BE PLAYING IN THE EUROPEAN JUNIOR LEAGUES BEFORE I GET MY DIPLOMA.
I'LL ALWAYS NEED SOMEONE TO MAKE MY COFFEE!
AHHHHHHH!
CRASH

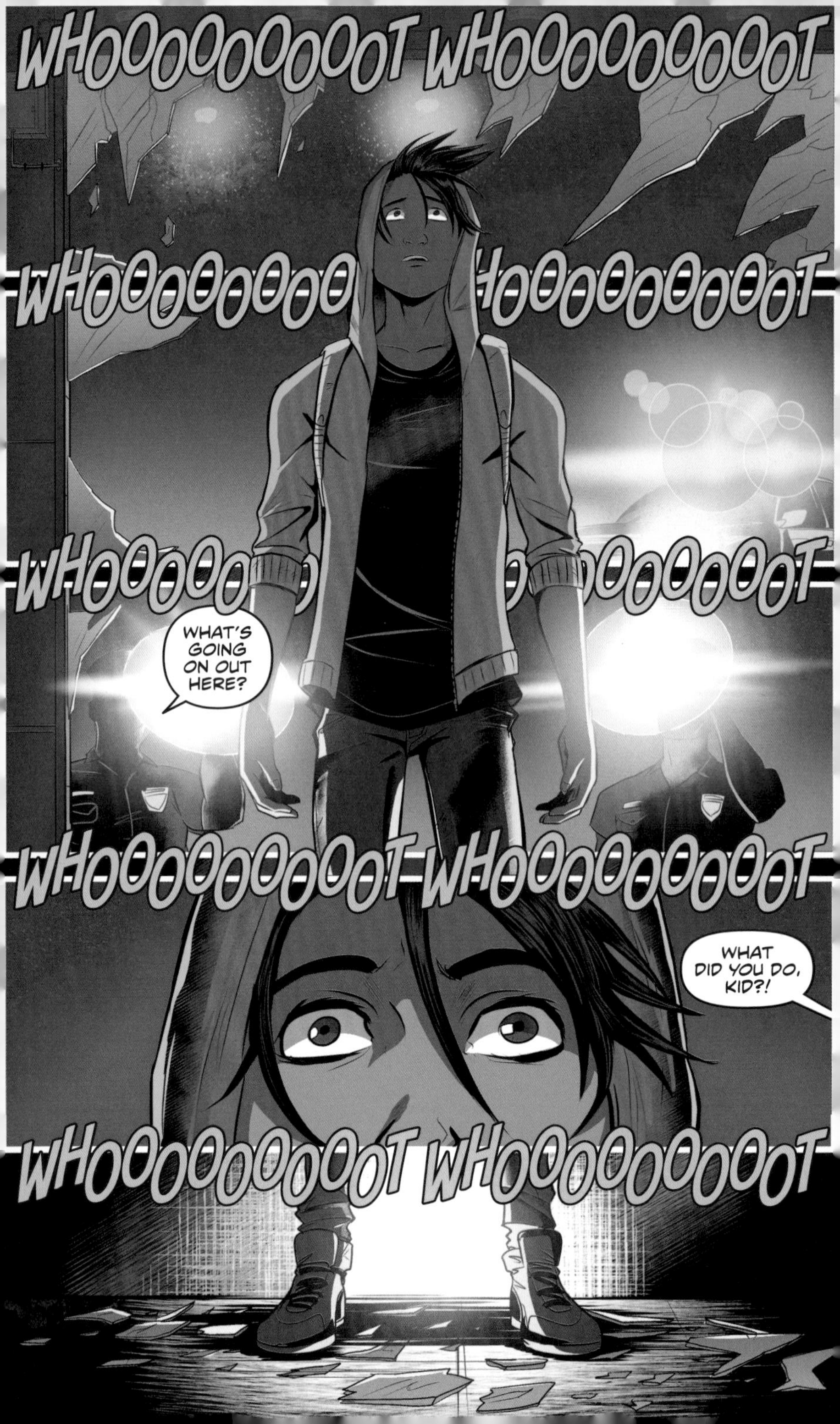
WHOOOOOOOOOOT WHOOOOOOOOOOT
WHAT'S GOING ON OUT HERE?
WHOOOOOOOOOOT WHOOOOOOOOOOT
WHAT DID YOU DO, KID?!
WHOOOOOOOOOOT WHOOOOOOOOOOT

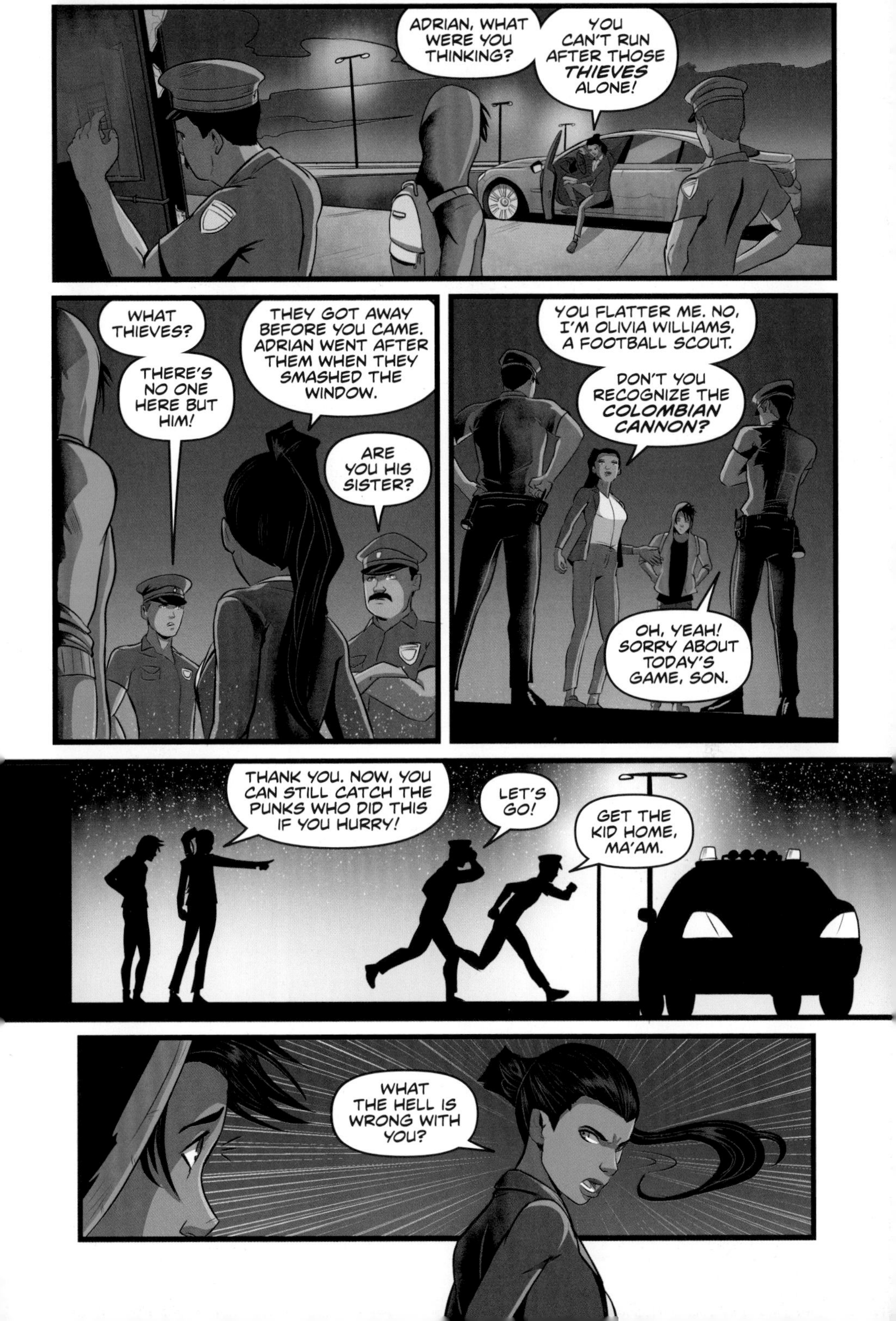
ADRIAN, WHAT WERE YOU THINKING?
YOU CAN'T RUN AFTER THOSE THIEVES ALONE!
WHAT THIEVES?
THERE'S NO ONE HERE BUT HIM!
THEY GOT AWAY BEFORE YOU CAME. ADRIAN WENT AFTER THEM WHEN THEY SMASHED THE WINDOW.
ARE YOU HIS SISTER?
YOU FLATTER ME. NO, I'M OLIVIA WILLIAMS, A FOOTBALL SCOUT.
DON'T YOU RECOGNIZE THE COLOMBIAN CANNON?
OH, YEAH! SORRY ABOUT TODAY'S GAME, SON.
THANK YOU. NOW, YOU CAN STILL CATCH THE PUNKS WHO DID THIS IF YOU HURRY!
LET'S GO!
GET THE KID HOME, MA'AM.
WHAT THE HELL IS WRONG WITH YOU?

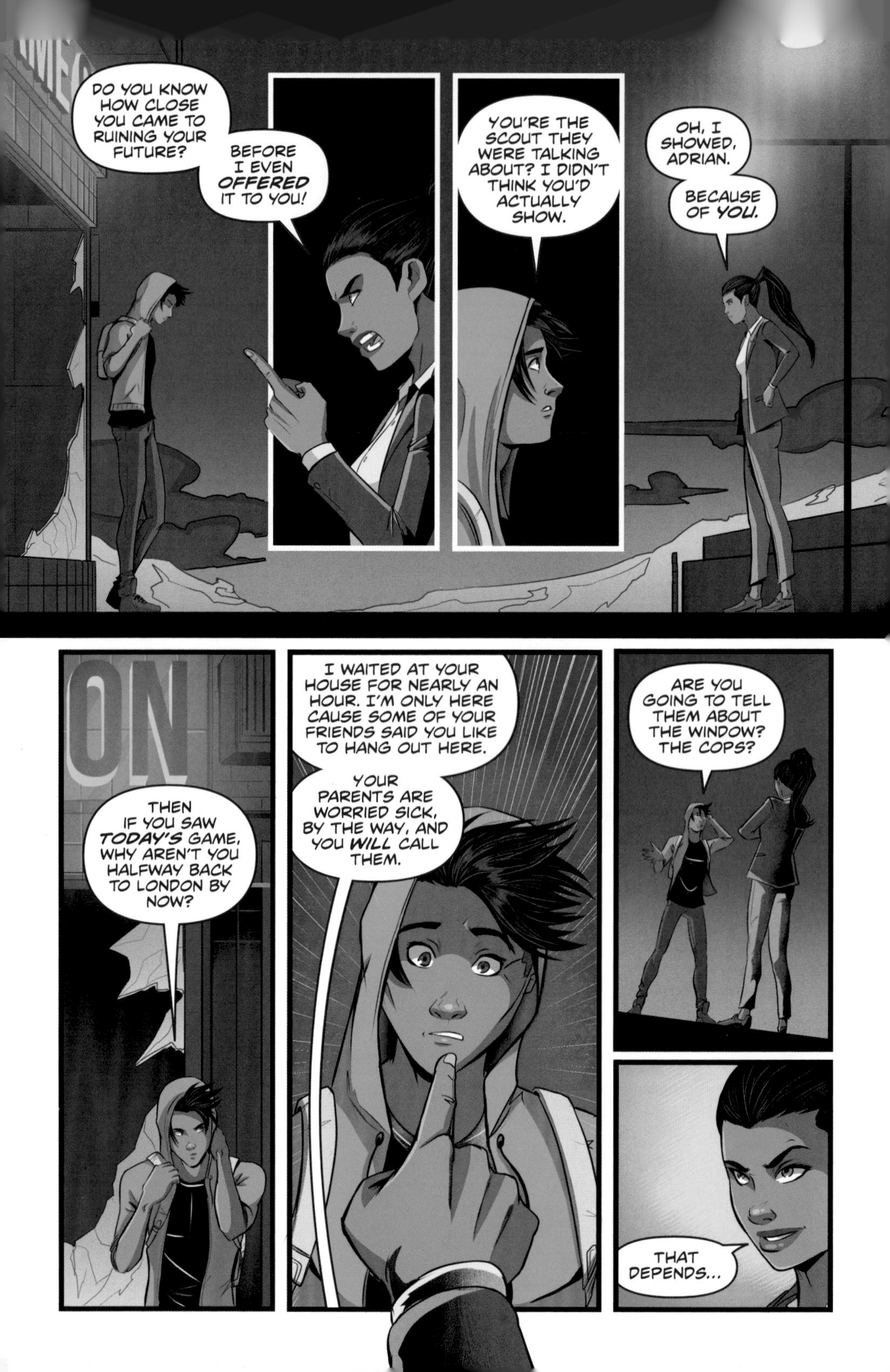

DO YOU KNOW HOW CLOSE YOU CAME TO RUINING YOUR FUTURE?
BEFORE I EVEN OFFERED IT TO YOU!
YOU'RE THE SCOUT THEY WERE TALKING ABOUT? I DIDN'T THINK YOU'D ACTUALLY SHOW.
OH, I SHOWED, ADRIAN.
BECAUSE OF YOU.
THEN IF YOU SAW TODAY'S GAME, WHY AREN'T YOU HALFWAY BACK TO LONDON BY NOW?
I WAITED AT YOUR HOUSE FOR NEARLY AN HOUR. I'M ONLY HERE CAUSE SOME OF YOUR FRIENDS SAID YOU LIKE TO HANG OUT HERE.
YOUR PARENTS ARE WORRIED SICK, BY THE WAY, AND YOU WILL CALL THEM.
ARE YOU GOING TO TELL THEM ABOUT THE WINDOW? THE COPS?
THAT DEPENDS...

PEOPLE *ALWAYS* NEED COFFEE...

IS THAT WHAT *YOU* WANT TO DO?

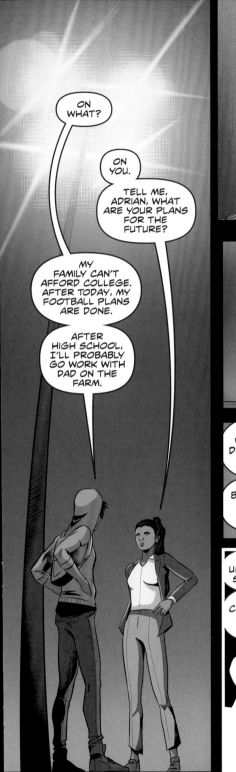

ON WHAT?

ON YOU.

TELL ME, ADRIAN, WHAT ARE YOUR PLANS FOR THE FUTURE?

MY FAMILY CAN'T AFFORD COLLEGE. AFTER TODAY, MY FOOTBALL PLANS ARE DONE.

AFTER HIGH SCHOOL, I'LL PROBABLY GO WORK WITH DAD ON THE FARM.

MY DAD'S THE BEST MAN I KNOW. I WOULD BE LUCKY TO TURN OUT LIKE HIM.

YOU'RE RIGHT. I MET YOUR FOLKS TONIGHT. YOU HIT THE LOTTERY, KID.

AND THEY WANT ALL YOUR DREAMS TO COME TRUE. I WANT THE SAME.

IT'S WHY I BECAME A SCOUT. TO TURN THEIR DREAMS INTO REALITY.

REGENTS UNITED HAS A SPOT OPEN.

I SPOKE TO COACH CLARKE, IT'S YOURS IF YOU WANT IT.

WHAT DO YOU SAY, COLOMBIAN CANNON, WANT TO FIRE FOR LONDON?

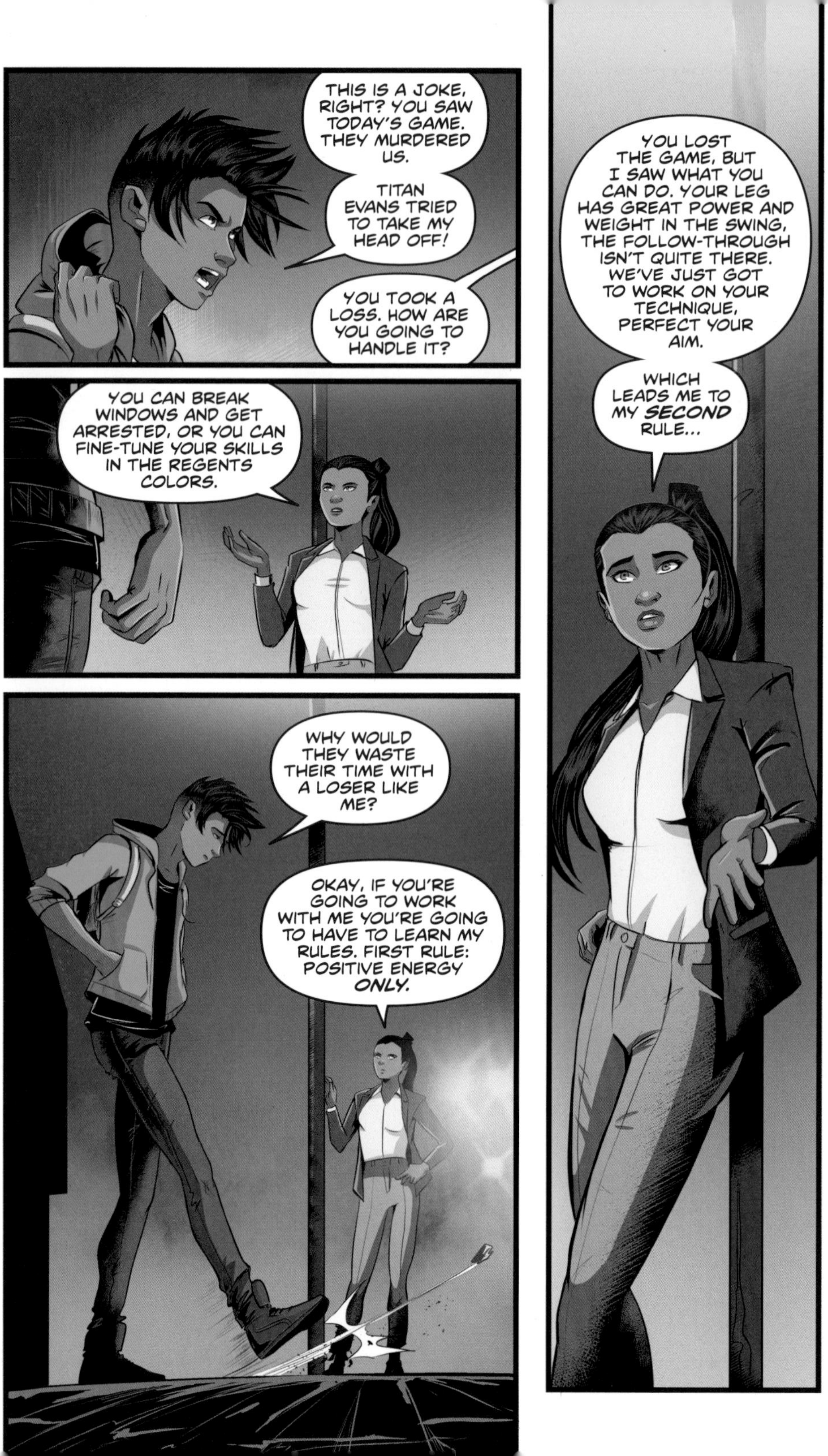
THIS IS A JOKE, RIGHT? YOU SAW TODAY'S GAME. THEY MURDERED US.
TITAN EVANS TRIED TO TAKE MY HEAD OFF!
YOU TOOK A LOSS. HOW ARE YOU GOING TO HANDLE IT?
YOU CAN BREAK WINDOWS AND GET ARRESTED, OR YOU CAN FINE-TUNE YOUR SKILLS IN THE REGENTS COLORS.
WHY WOULD THEY WASTE THEIR TIME WITH A LOSER LIKE ME?
OKAY, IF YOU'RE GOING TO WORK WITH ME YOU'RE GOING TO HAVE TO LEARN MY RULES. FIRST RULE: POSITIVE ENERGY ONLY.
YOU LOST THE GAME, BUT I SAW WHAT YOU CAN DO. YOUR LEG HAS GREAT POWER AND WEIGHT IN THE SWING, THE FOLLOW-THROUGH ISN'T QUITE THERE. WE'VE JUST GOT TO WORK ON YOUR TECHNIQUE, PERFECT YOUR AIM.
WHICH LEADS ME TO MY SECOND RULE...

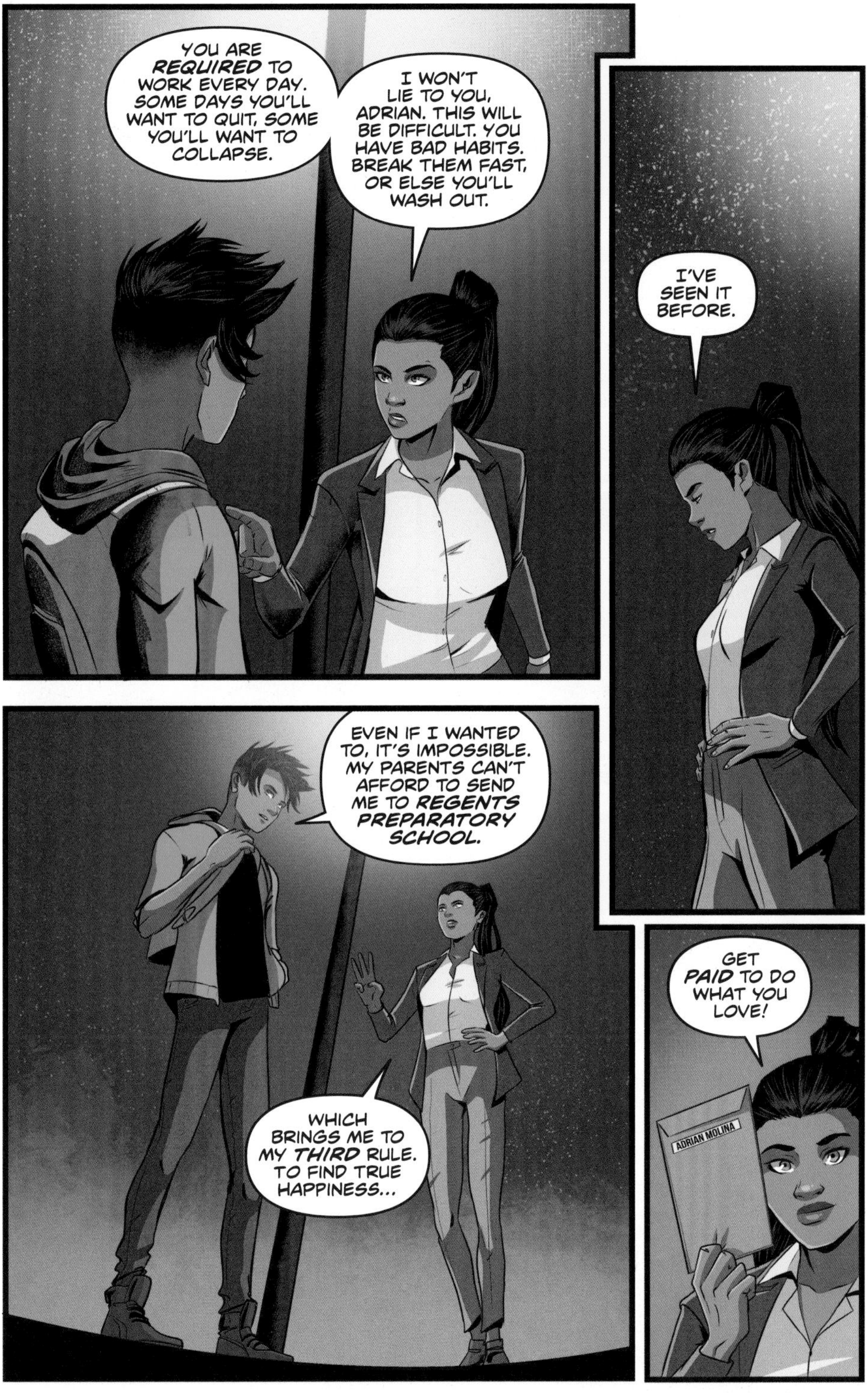
YOU ARE *REQUIRED* TO WORK EVERY DAY. SOME DAYS YOU'LL WANT TO QUIT, SOME YOU'LL WANT TO COLLAPSE.
I WON'T LIE TO YOU, ADRIAN. THIS WILL BE DIFFICULT. YOU HAVE BAD HABITS. BREAK THEM FAST, OR ELSE YOU'LL WASH OUT.
I'VE SEEN IT BEFORE.
EVEN IF I WANTED TO, IT'S IMPOSSIBLE. MY PARENTS CAN'T AFFORD TO SEND ME TO *REGENTS PREPARATORY SCHOOL.*
WHICH BRINGS ME TO MY *THIRD* RULE. TO FIND TRUE HAPPINESS...
GET *PAID* TO DO WHAT YOU LOVE!
ADRIAN MOLINA

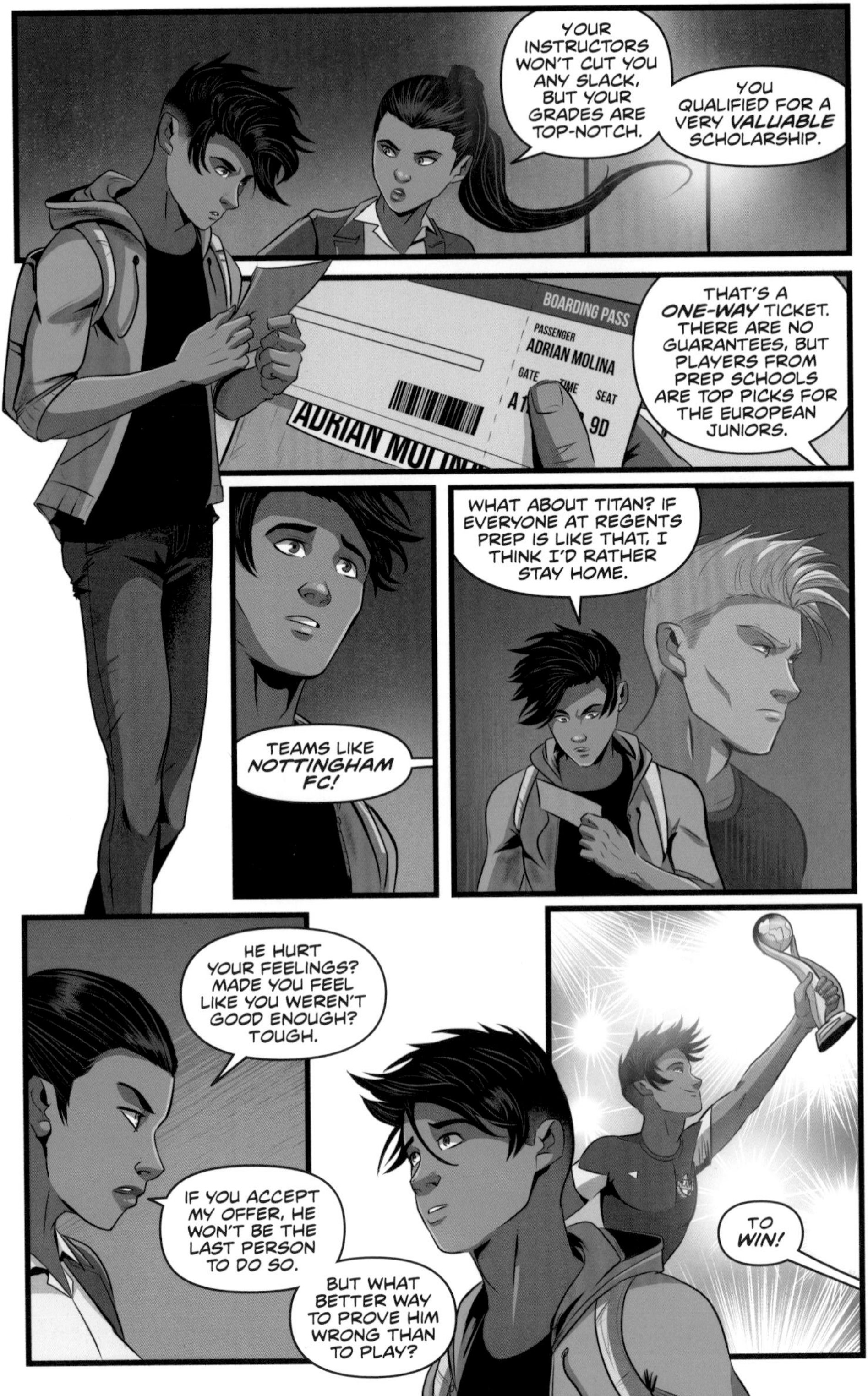
YOUR INSTRUCTORS WON'T CUT YOU ANY SLACK, BUT YOUR GRADES ARE TOP-NOTCH.
YOU QUALIFIED FOR A VERY VALUABLE SCHOLARSHIP.
BOARDING PASS
PASSENGER
ADRIAN MOLINA
GATE
TIME
SEAT
9D
THAT'S A ONE-WAY TICKET. THERE ARE NO GUARANTEES, BUT PLAYERS FROM PREP SCHOOLS ARE TOP PICKS FOR THE EUROPEAN JUNIORS.
TEAMS LIKE NOTTINGHAM FC!
WHAT ABOUT TITAN? IF EVERYONE AT REGENTS PREP IS LIKE THAT, I THINK I'D RATHER STAY HOME.
HE HURT YOUR FEELINGS? MADE YOU FEEL LIKE YOU WEREN'T GOOD ENOUGH? TOUGH.
IF YOU ACCEPT MY OFFER, HE WON'T BE THE LAST PERSON TO DO SO.
BUT WHAT BETTER WAY TO PROVE HIM WRONG THAN TO PLAY?
TO WIN!

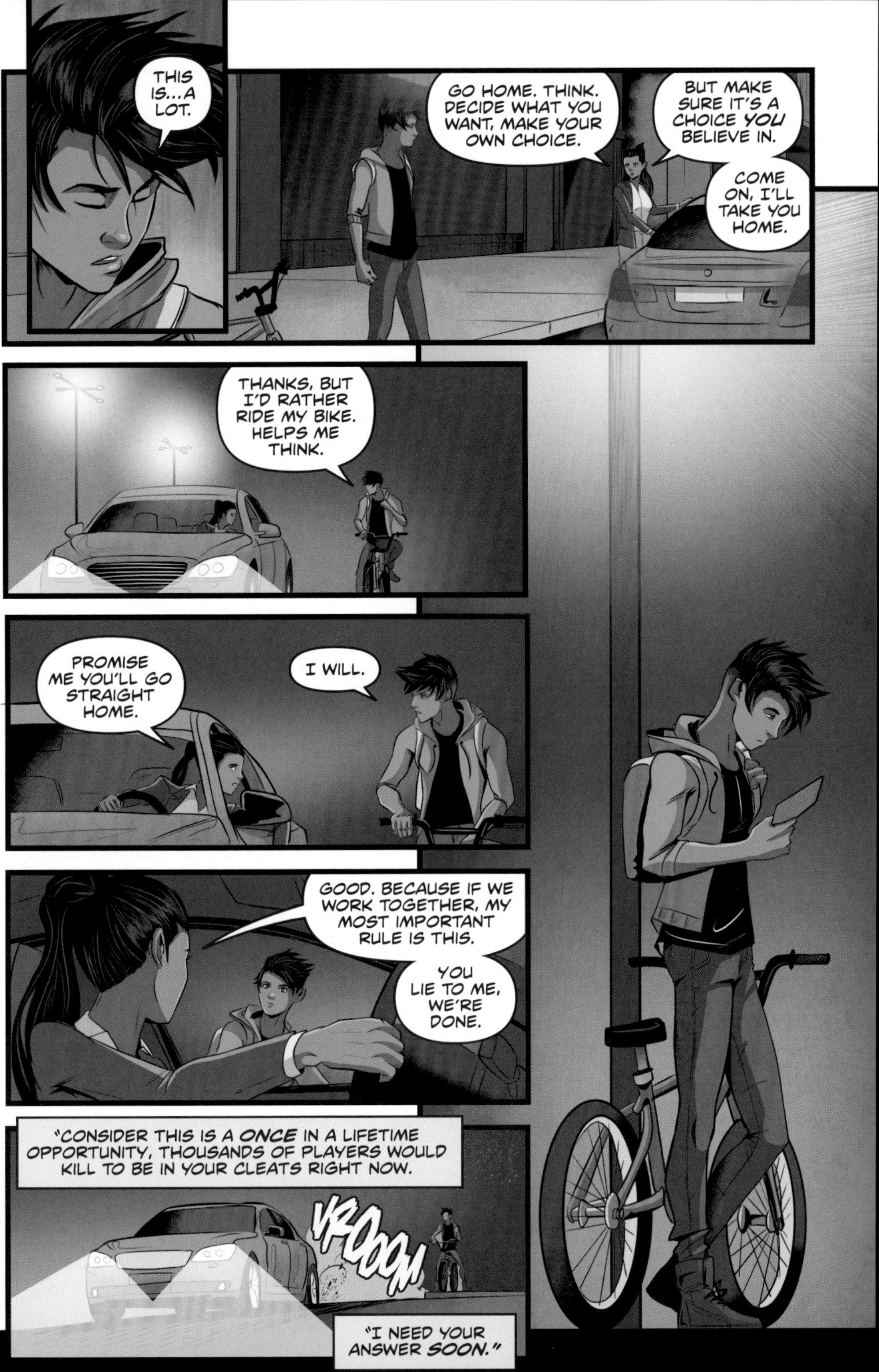

THIS IS...A LOT.
GO HOME. THINK. DECIDE WHAT YOU WANT, MAKE YOUR OWN CHOICE.
BUT MAKE SURE IT'S A CHOICE *YOU* BELIEVE IN.
COME ON, I'LL TAKE YOU HOME.
THANKS, BUT I'D RATHER RIDE MY BIKE. HELPS ME THINK.
PROMISE ME YOU'LL GO STRAIGHT HOME.
I WILL.
GOOD. BECAUSE IF WE WORK TOGETHER, MY MOST IMPORTANT RULE IS THIS.
YOU LIE TO ME, WE'RE DONE.
"CONSIDER THIS IS A *ONCE* IN A LIFETIME OPPORTUNITY, THOUSANDS OF PLAYERS WOULD KILL TO BE IN YOUR CLEATS RIGHT NOW.
VROOOM
"I NEED YOUR ANSWER *SOON.*"

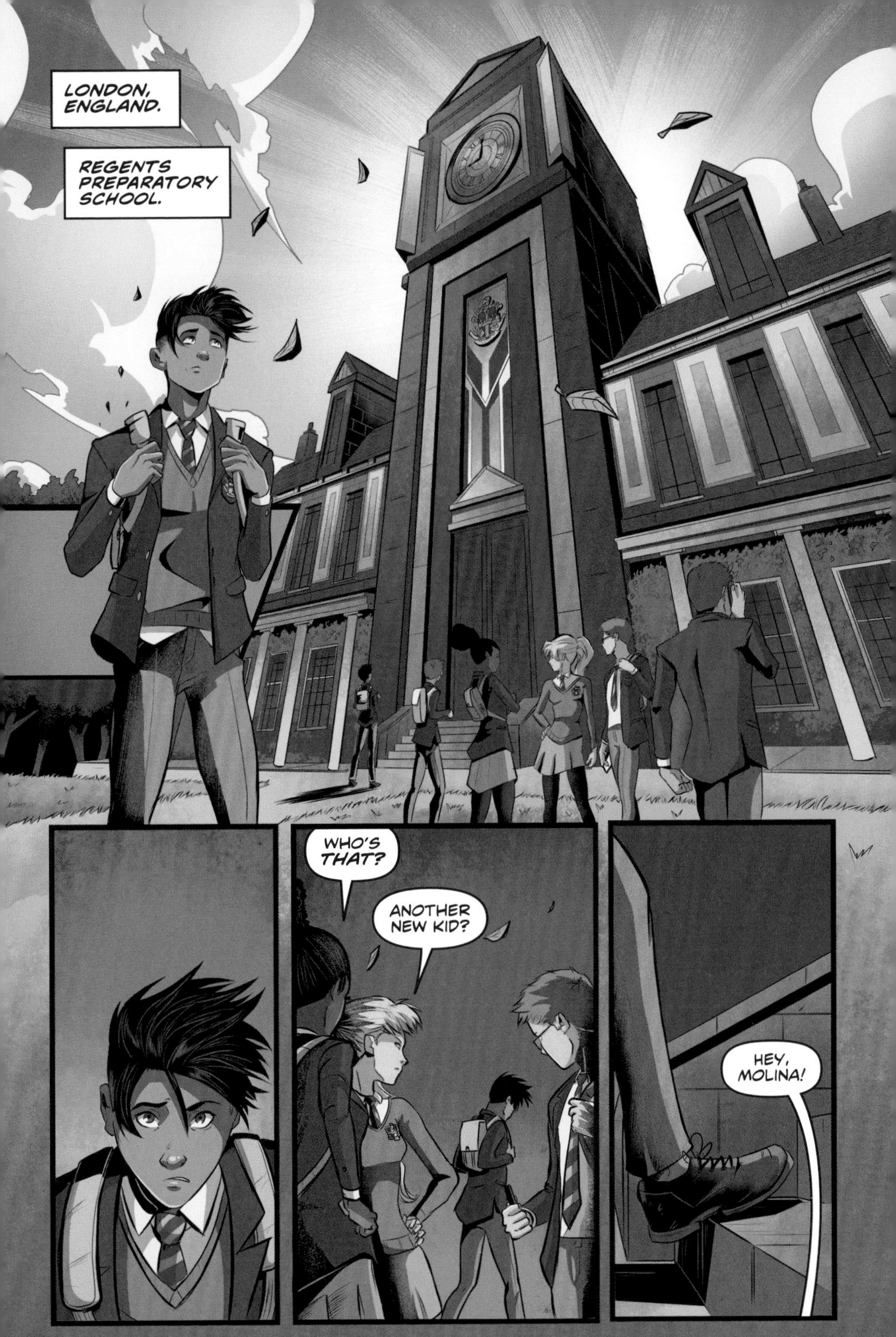
LONDON, ENGLAND.
REGENTS PREPARATORY SCHOOL.
WHO'S *THAT?*
ANOTHER NEW KID?
HEY, MOLINA!

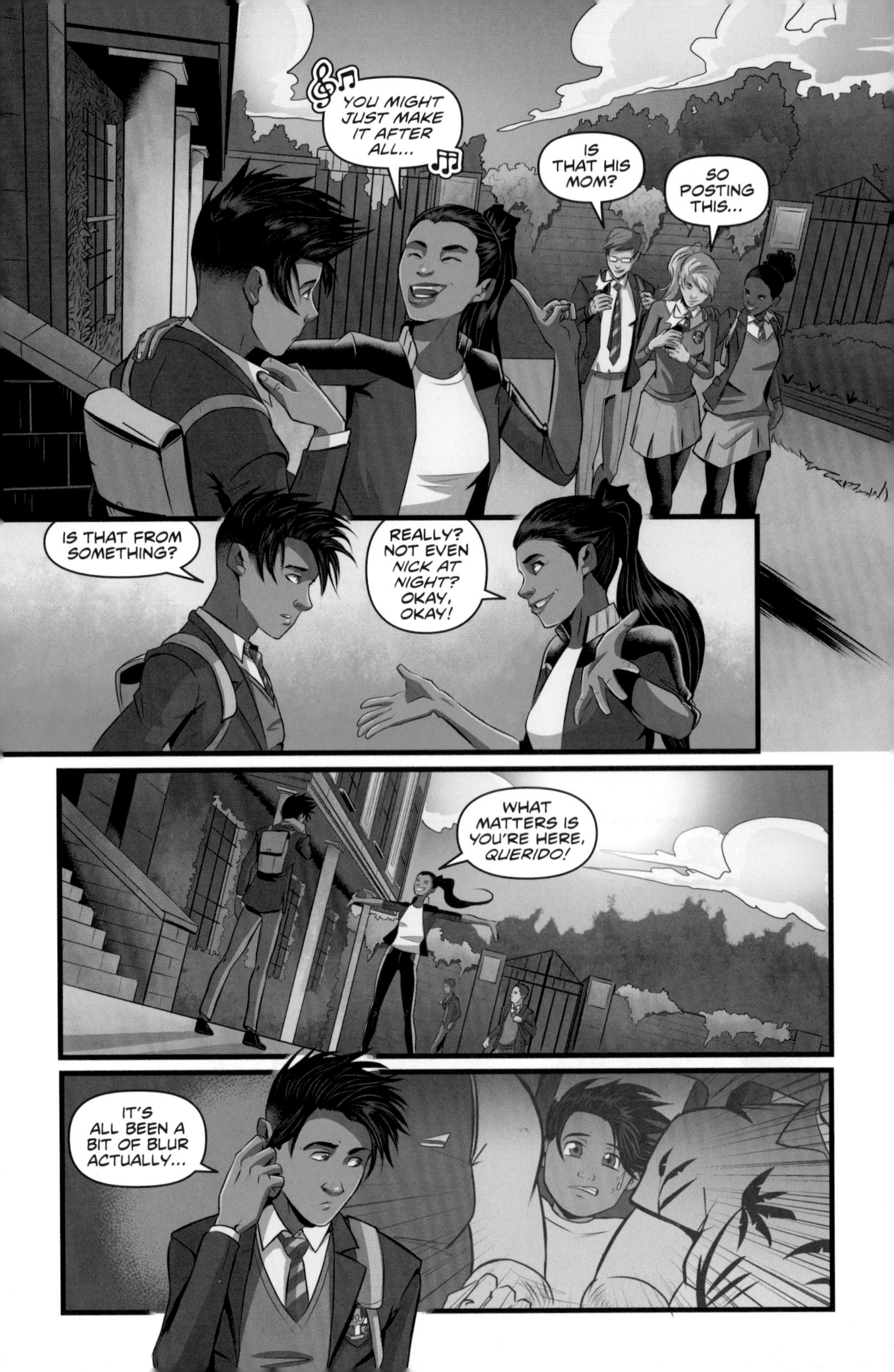
YOU MIGHT JUST MAKE IT AFTER ALL...
IS THAT HIS MOM?
SO POSTING THIS...
IS THAT FROM SOMETHING?
REALLY? NOT EVEN NICK AT NIGHT? OKAY, OKAY!
WHAT MATTERS IS YOU'RE HERE, QUERIDO!
IT'S ALL BEEN A BIT OF BLUR ACTUALLY...

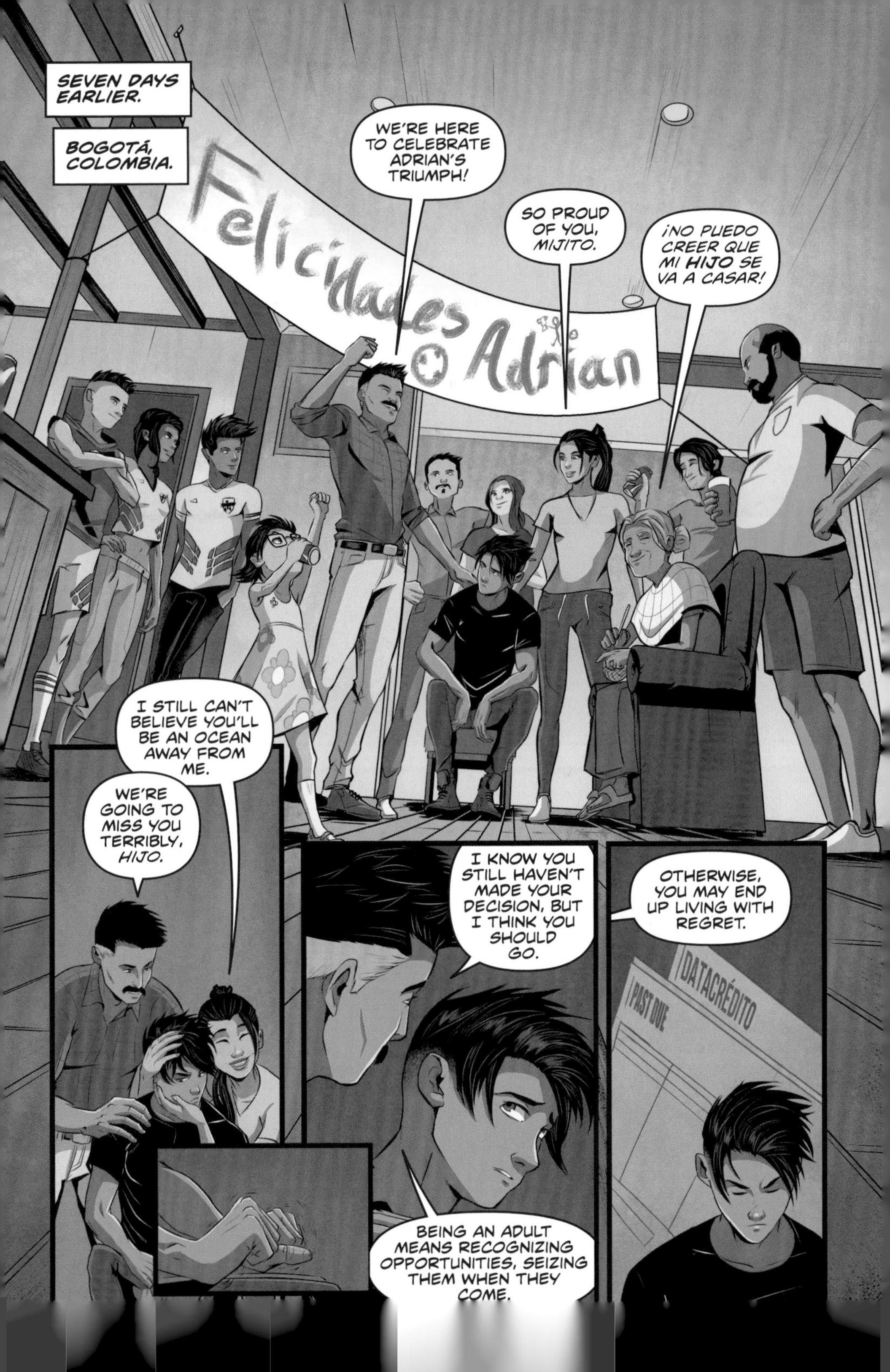
SEVEN DAYS EARLIER.
BOGOTÁ, COLOMBIA.
Felicidades Adrian
WE'RE HERE TO CELEBRATE ADRIAN'S TRIUMPH!
SO PROUD OF YOU, MIJITO.
¡NO PUEDO CREER QUE MI HIJO SE VA A CASAR!
I STILL CAN'T BELIEVE YOU'LL BE AN OCEAN AWAY FROM ME.
WE'RE GOING TO MISS YOU TERRIBLY, HIJO.
I KNOW YOU STILL HAVEN'T MADE YOUR DECISION, BUT I THINK YOU SHOULD GO.
BEING AN ADULT MEANS RECOGNIZING OPPORTUNITIES, SEIZING THEM WHEN THEY COME.
OTHERWISE, YOU MAY END UP LIVING WITH REGRET.
DATACRÉDITO
PAST DUE

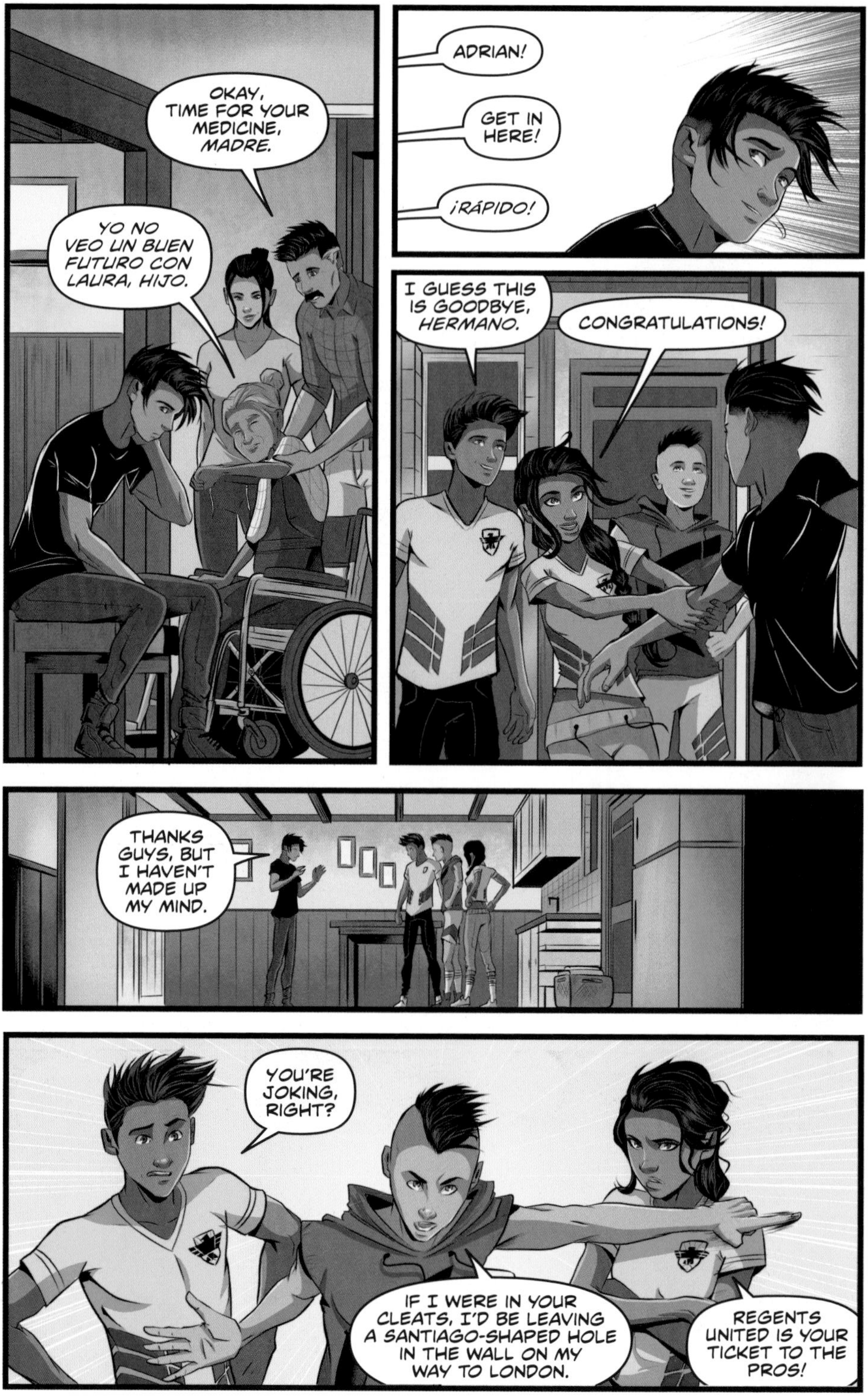
OKAY, TIME FOR YOUR MEDICINE, MADRE.
YO NO VEO UN BUEN FUTURO CON LAURA, HIJO.
ADRIAN!
GET IN HERE!
¡RÁPIDO!
I GUESS THIS IS GOODBYE, HERMANO.
CONGRATULATIONS!
THANKS GUYS, BUT I HAVEN'T MADE UP MY MIND.
YOU'RE JOKING, RIGHT?
IF I WERE IN YOUR CLEATS, I'D BE LEAVING A SANTIAGO-SHAPED HOLE IN THE WALL ON MY WAY TO LONDON.
REGENTS UNITED IS YOUR TICKET TO THE PROS!

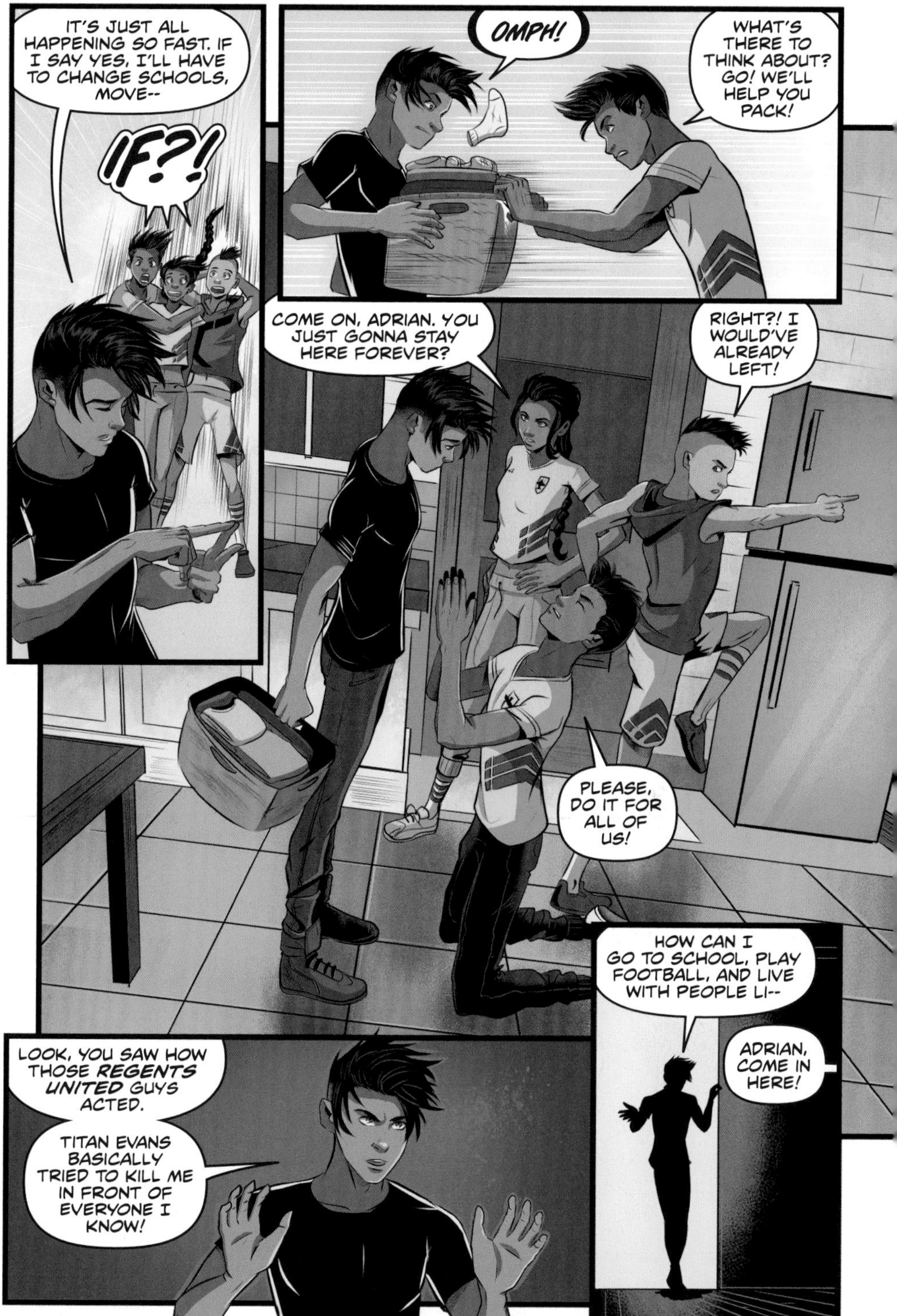
IT'S JUST ALL HAPPENING SO FAST. IF I SAY YES, I'LL HAVE TO CHANGE SCHOOLS, MOVE--
IF?!
OMPH!
WHAT'S THERE TO THINK ABOUT? GO! WE'LL HELP YOU PACK!
COME ON, ADRIAN. YOU JUST GONNA STAY HERE FOREVER?
RIGHT?! I WOULD'VE ALREADY LEFT!
PLEASE, DO IT FOR ALL OF US!
LOOK, YOU SAW HOW THOSE REGENTS UNITED GUYS ACTED.
TITAN EVANS BASICALLY TRIED TO KILL ME IN FRONT OF EVERYONE I KNOW!
HOW CAN I GO TO SCHOOL, PLAY FOOTBALL, AND LIVE WITH PEOPLE LI--
ADRIAN, COME IN HERE!

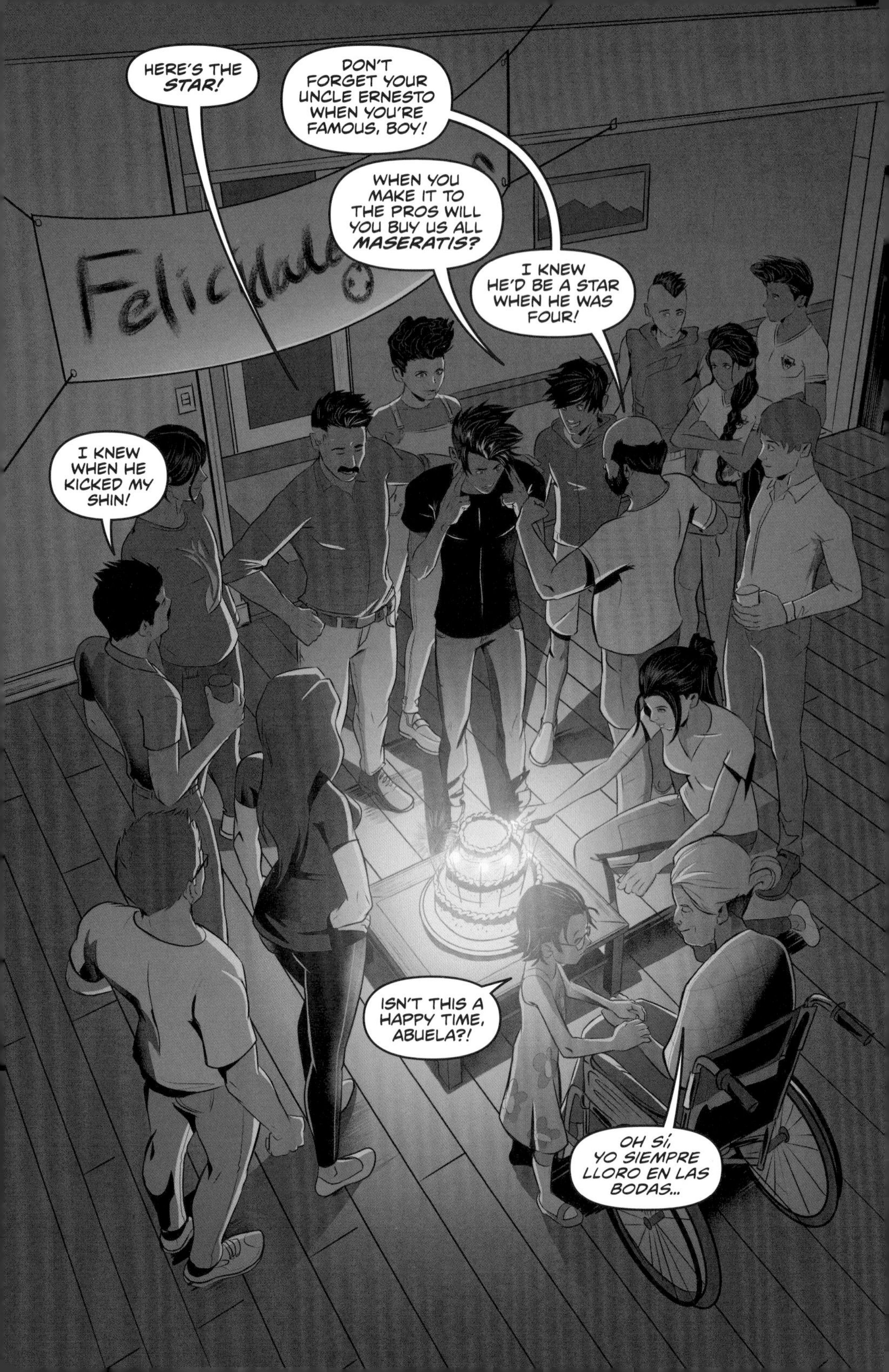
Felicidade
HERE'S THE STAR!
DON'T FORGET YOUR UNCLE ERNESTO WHEN YOU'RE FAMOUS, BOY!
WHEN YOU MAKE IT TO THE PROS WILL YOU BUY US ALL MASERATIS?
I KNEW HE'D BE A STAR WHEN HE WAS FOUR!
I KNEW WHEN HE KICKED MY SHIN!
ISN'T THIS A HAPPY TIME, ABUELA?!
OH SÍ, YO SIEMPRE LLORO EN LAS BODAS...

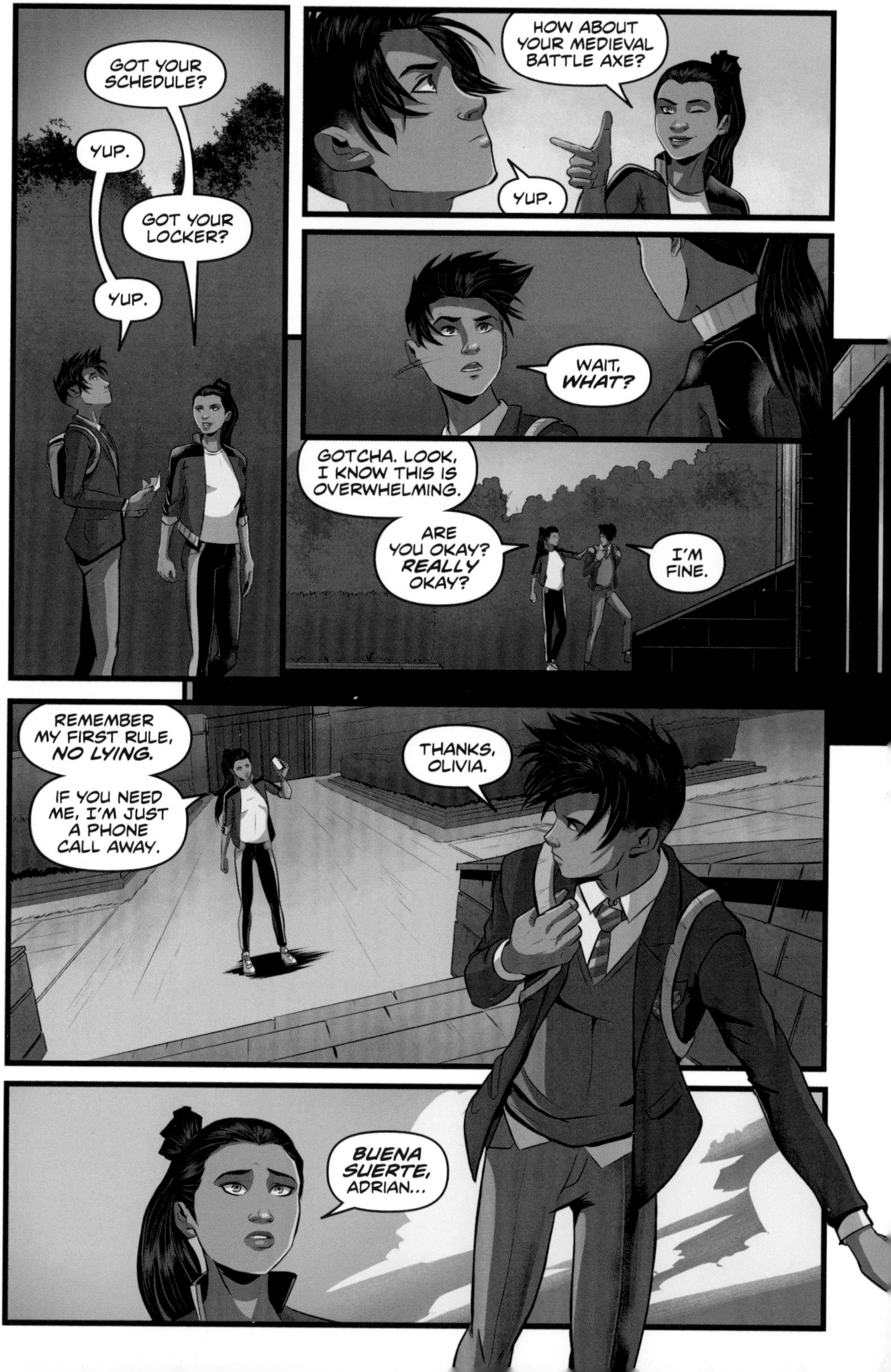
GOT YOUR SCHEDULE?
YUP.
GOT YOUR LOCKER?
YUP.
HOW ABOUT YOUR MEDIEVAL BATTLE AXE?
YUP.
WAIT, WHAT?
GOTCHA. LOOK, I KNOW THIS IS OVERWHELMING.
ARE YOU OKAY? REALLY OKAY?
I'M FINE.
REMEMBER MY FIRST RULE, NO LYING.
IF YOU NEED ME, I'M JUST A PHONE CALL AWAY.
THANKS, OLIVIA.
BUENA SUERTE, ADRIAN...

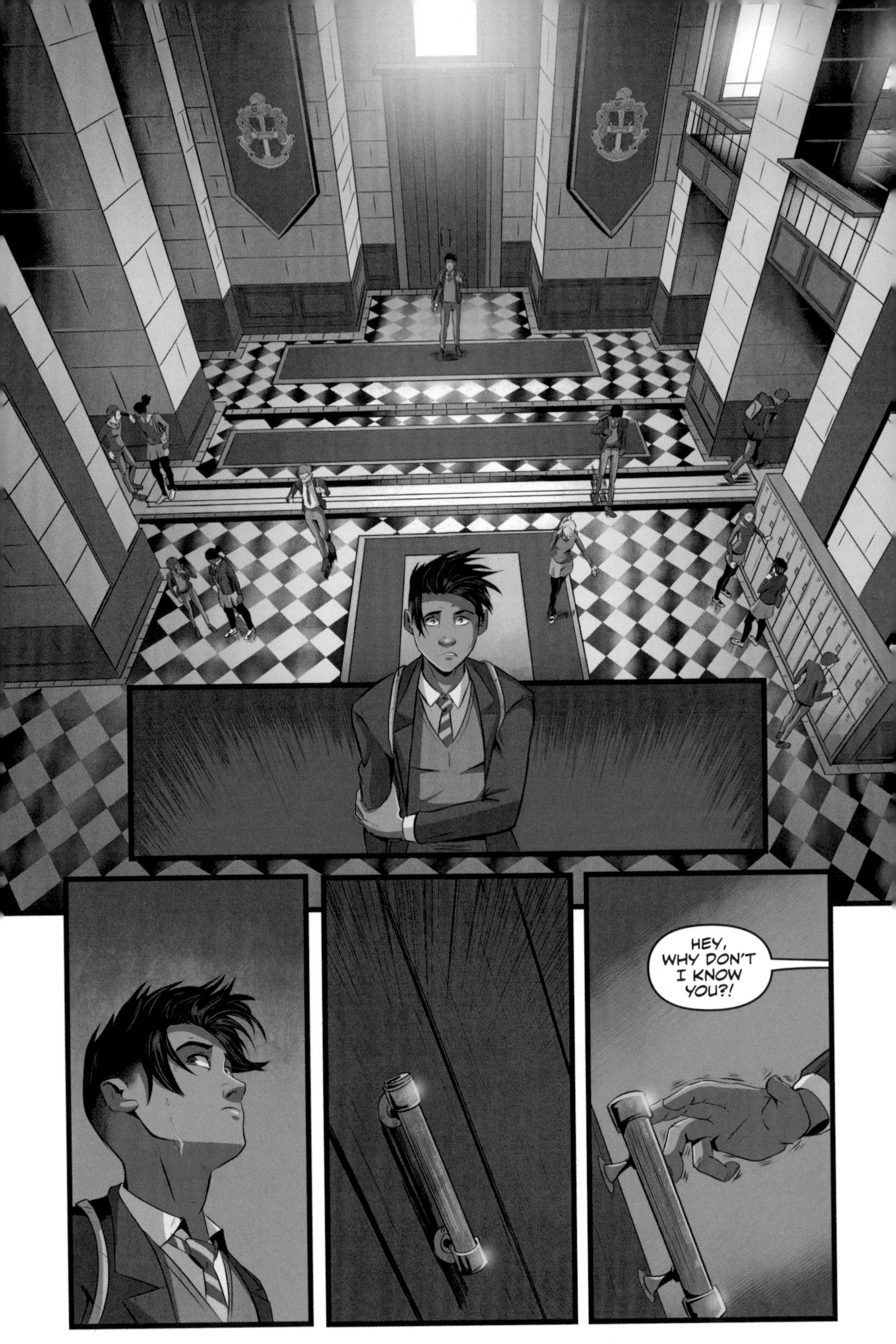
HEY, WHY DON'T I KNOW YOU?!

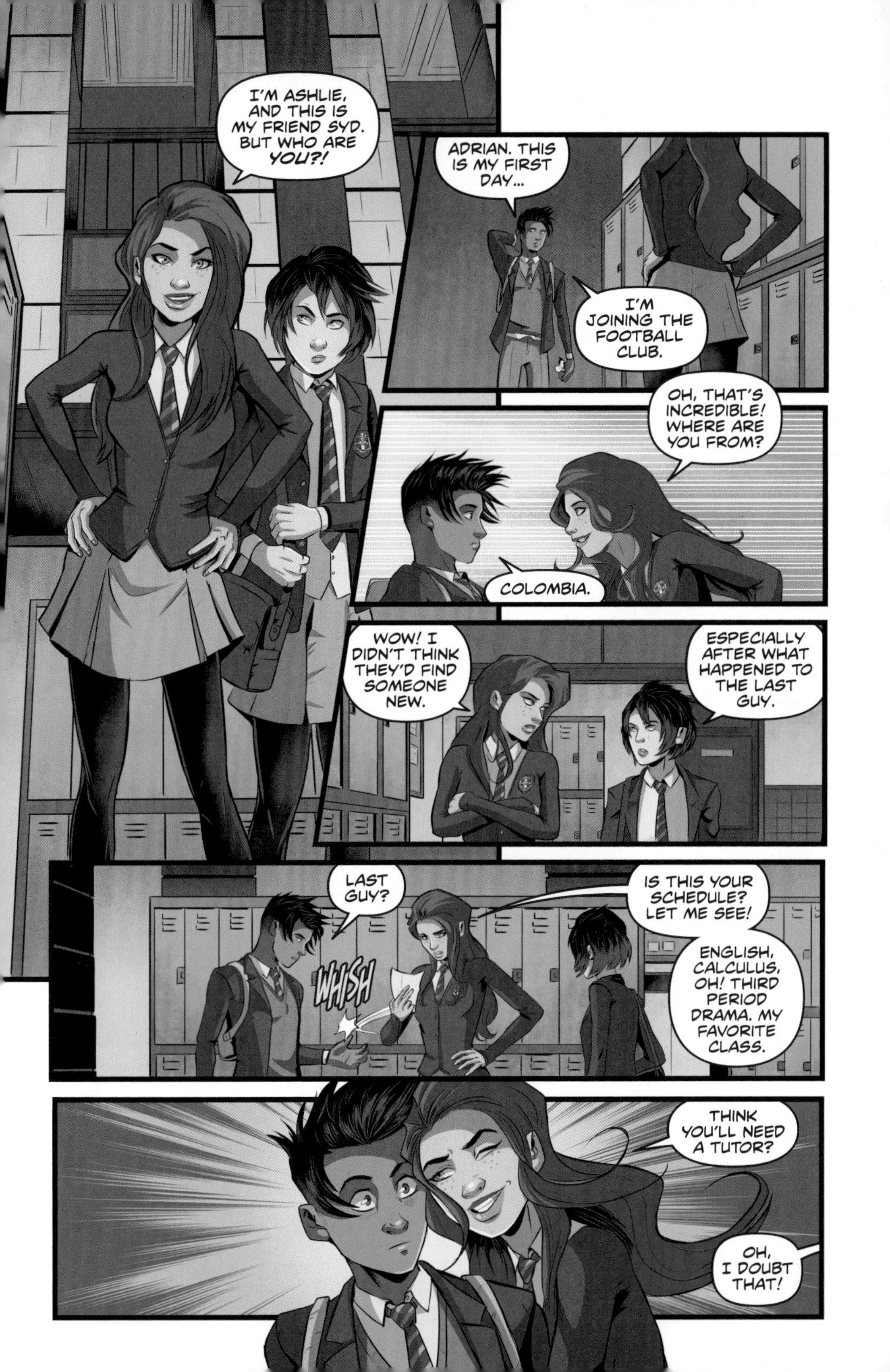
I'M ASHLIE, AND THIS IS MY FRIEND SYD. BUT WHO ARE *YOU?!*
ADRIAN. THIS IS MY FIRST DAY...
I'M JOINING THE FOOTBALL CLUB.
OH, THAT'S INCREDIBLE! WHERE ARE YOU FROM?
COLOMBIA.
WOW! I DIDN'T THINK THEY'D FIND SOMEONE NEW.
ESPECIALLY AFTER WHAT HAPPENED TO THE LAST GUY.
LAST GUY?
WHISH
IS THIS YOUR SCHEDULE? LET ME SEE!
ENGLISH, CALCULUS, OH! THIRD PERIOD DRAMA. MY FAVORITE CLASS.
THINK YOU'LL NEED A TUTOR?
OH, I DOUBT THAT!

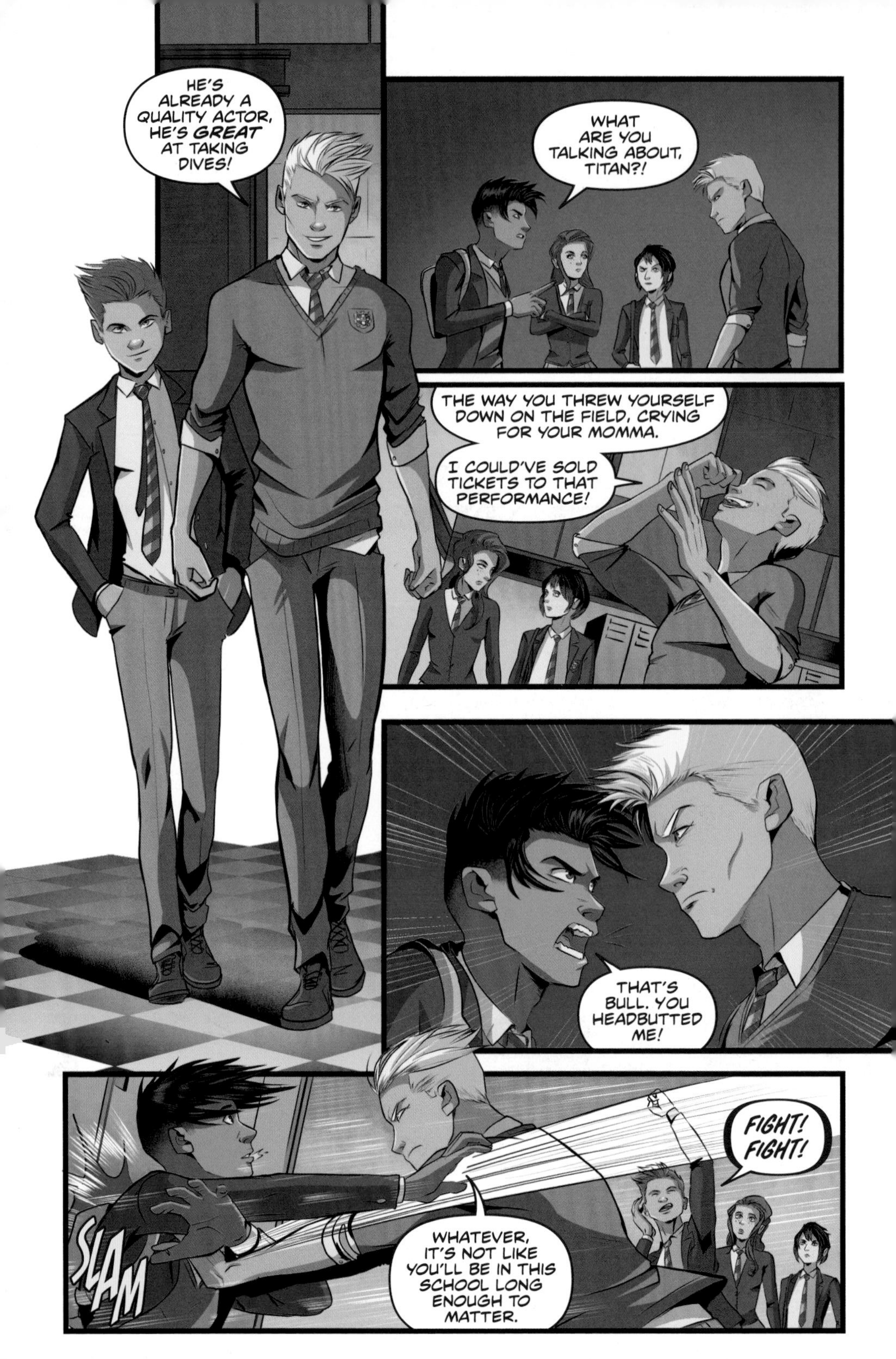
HE'S ALREADY A QUALITY ACTOR, HE'S GREAT AT TAKING DIVES!
WHAT ARE YOU TALKING ABOUT, TITAN?!
THE WAY YOU THREW YOURSELF DOWN ON THE FIELD, CRYING FOR YOUR MOMMA.
I COULD'VE SOLD TICKETS TO THAT PERFORMANCE!
THAT'S BULL. YOU HEADBUTTED ME!
SLAM
WHATEVER, IT'S NOT LIKE YOU'LL BE IN THIS SCHOOL LONG ENOUGH TO MATTER.
FIGHT! FIGHT!

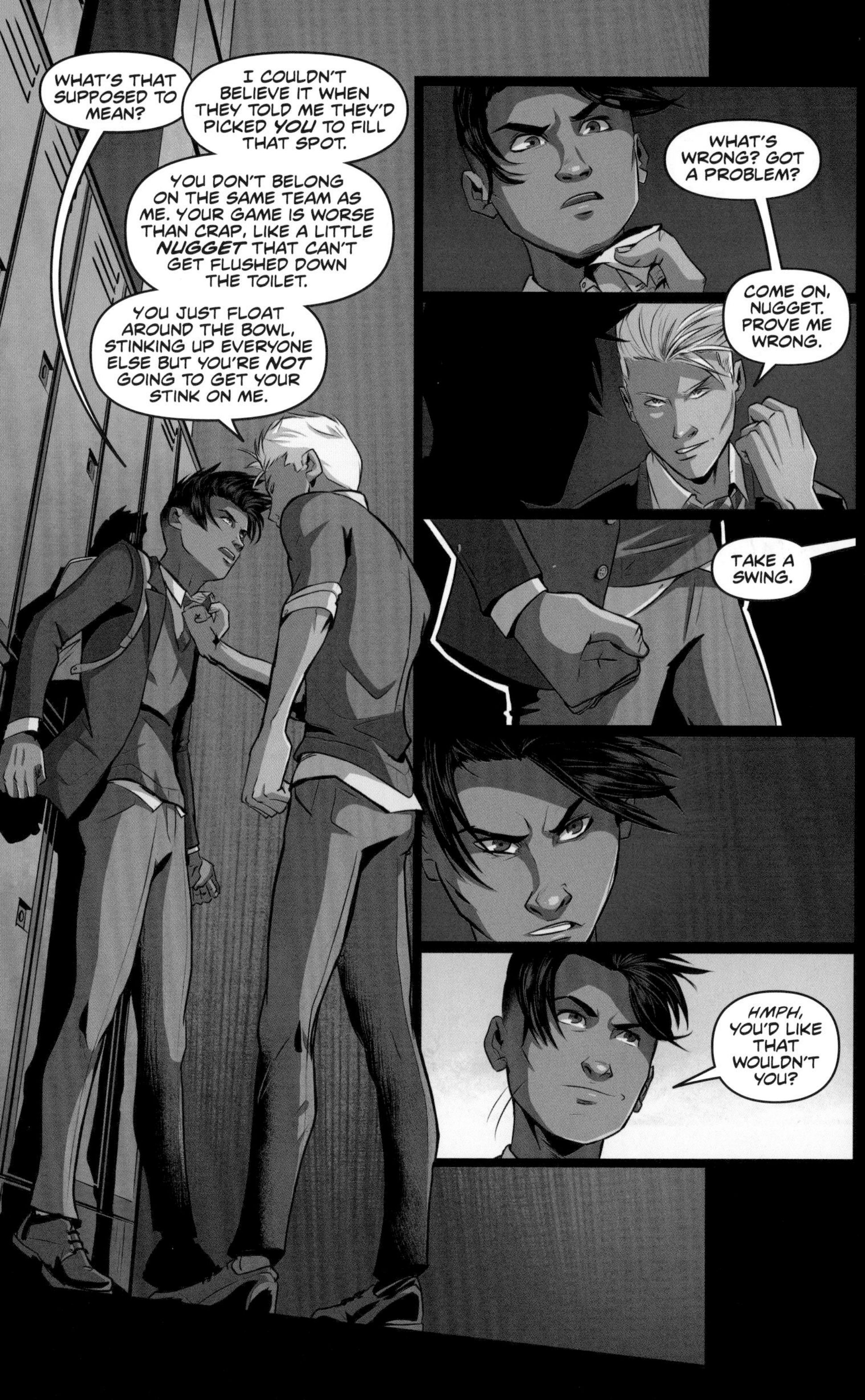

WHAT'S THAT SUPPOSED TO MEAN?
I COULDN'T BELIEVE IT WHEN THEY TOLD ME THEY'D PICKED *YOU* TO FILL THAT SPOT.
YOU DON'T BELONG ON THE SAME TEAM AS ME. YOUR GAME IS WORSE THAN CRAP, LIKE A LITTLE ***NUGGET*** THAT CAN'T GET FLUSHED DOWN THE TOILET.
YOU JUST FLOAT AROUND THE BOWL, STINKING UP EVERYONE ELSE BUT YOU'RE ***NOT*** GOING TO GET YOUR STINK ON ME.
WHAT'S WRONG? GOT A PROBLEM?
COME ON, NUGGET. PROVE ME WRONG.
TAKE A SWING.
HMPH, YOU'D LIKE THAT WOULDN'T YOU?

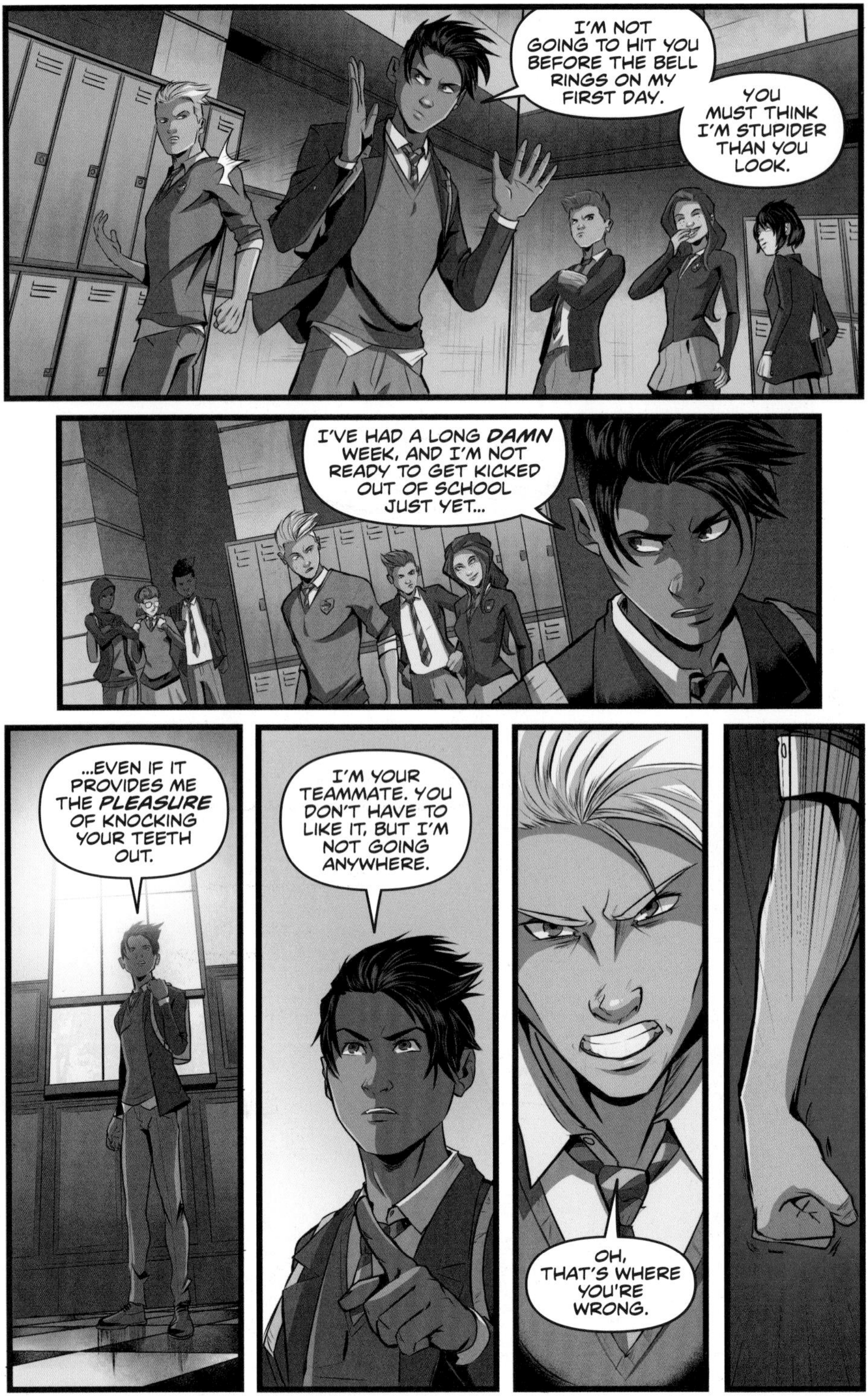
I'M NOT GOING TO HIT YOU BEFORE THE BELL RINGS ON MY FIRST DAY.
YOU MUST THINK I'M STUPIDER THAN YOU LOOK.
I'VE HAD A LONG *DAMN* WEEK, AND I'M NOT READY TO GET KICKED OUT OF SCHOOL JUST YET...
...EVEN IF IT PROVIDES ME THE *PLEASURE* OF KNOCKING YOUR TEETH OUT.
I'M YOUR TEAMMATE. YOU DON'T HAVE TO LIKE IT, BUT I'M NOT GOING ANYWHERE.
OH, THAT'S WHERE YOU'RE WRONG.

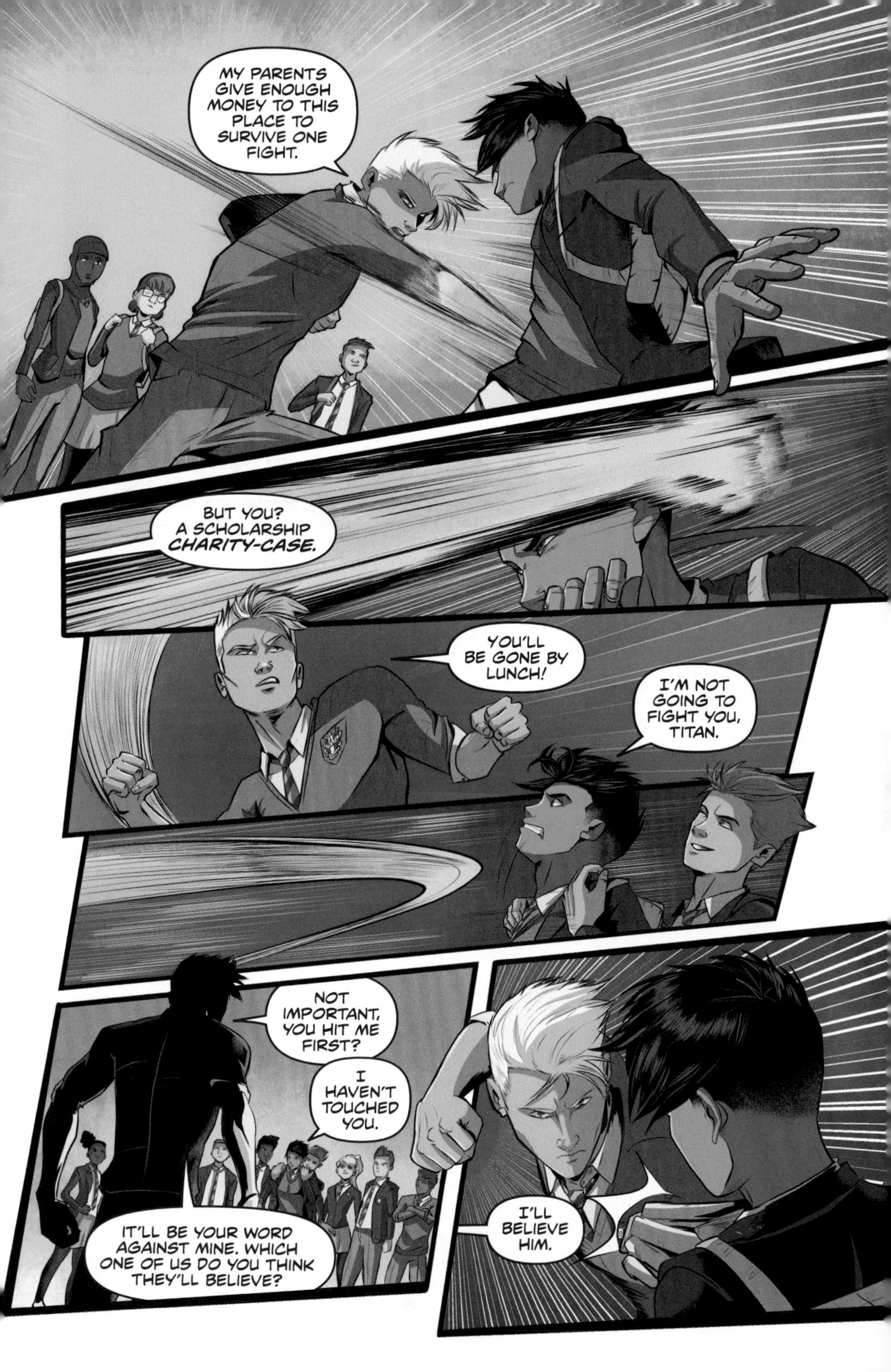
MY PARENTS GIVE ENOUGH MONEY TO THIS PLACE TO SURVIVE ONE FIGHT.
BUT YOU? A SCHOLARSHIP CHARITY-CASE.
YOU'LL BE GONE BY LUNCH!
I'M NOT GOING TO FIGHT YOU, TITAN.
NOT IMPORTANT, YOU HIT ME FIRST?
I HAVEN'T TOUCHED YOU.
IT'LL BE YOUR WORD AGAINST MINE. WHICH ONE OF US DO YOU THINK THEY'LL BELIEVE?
I'LL BELIEVE HIM.

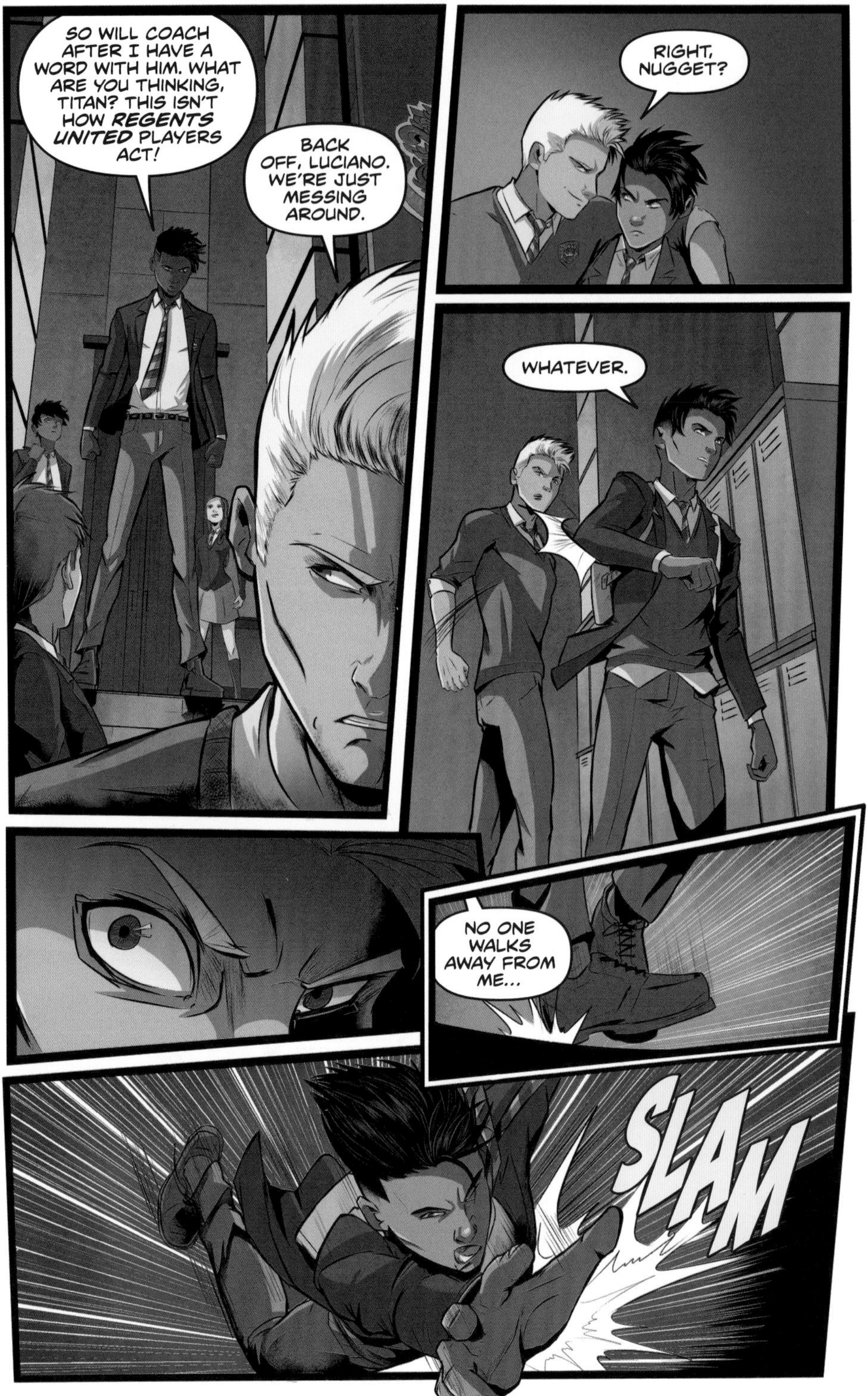
SO WILL COACH AFTER I HAVE A WORD WITH HIM. WHAT ARE YOU THINKING, TITAN? THIS ISN'T HOW *REGENTS UNITED* PLAYERS ACT!
BACK OFF, LUCIANO. WE'RE JUST MESSING AROUND.
RIGHT, NUGGET?
WHATEVER.
NO ONE WALKS AWAY FROM ME...
SLAM

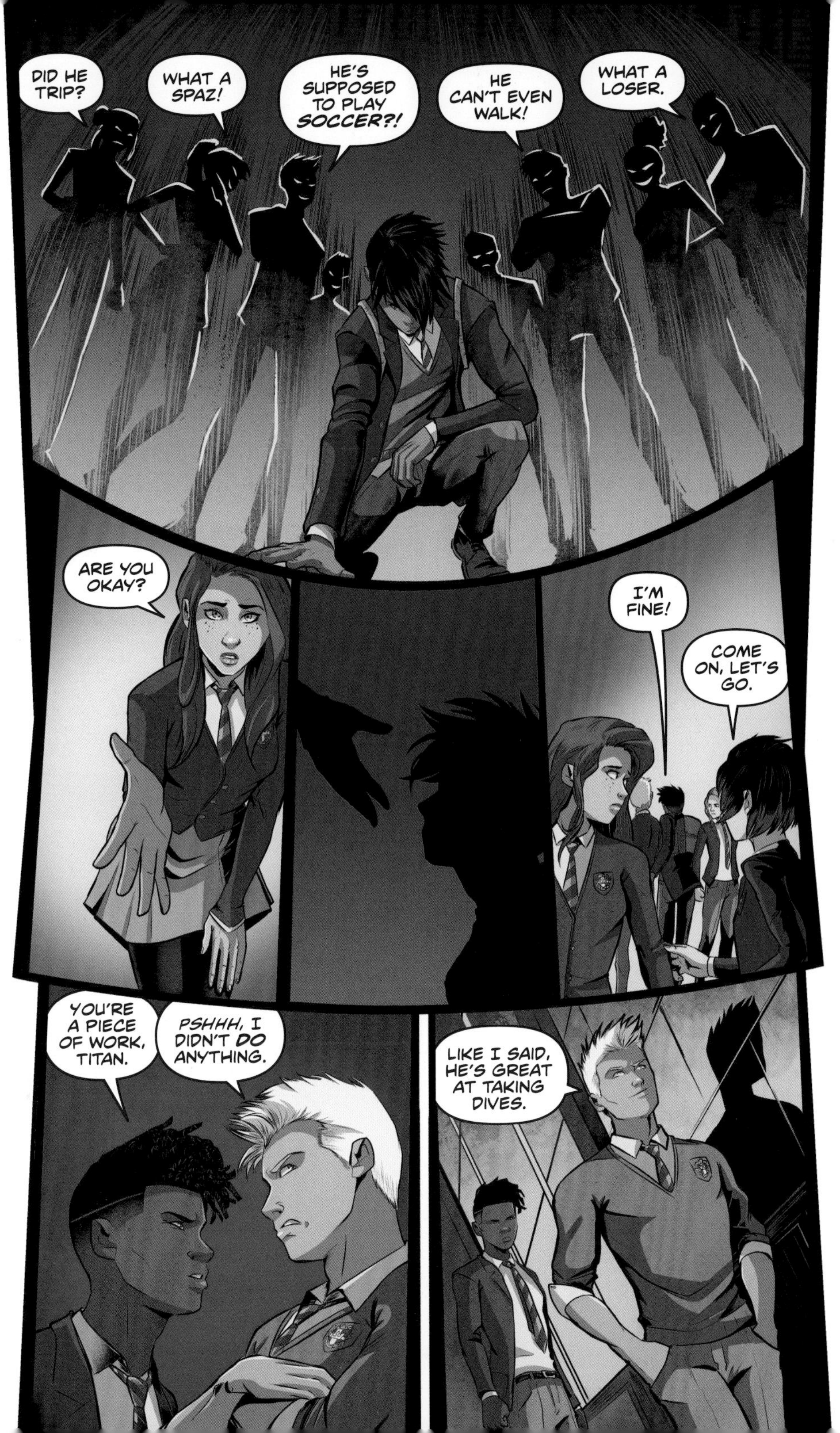
DID HE TRIP?
WHAT A SPAZ!
HE'S SUPPOSED TO PLAY SOCCER?!
HE CAN'T EVEN WALK!
WHAT A LOSER.
ARE YOU OKAY?
I'M FINE!
COME ON, LET'S GO.
YOU'RE A PIECE OF WORK, TITAN.
PSHHH, I DIDN'T DO ANYTHING.
LIKE I SAID, HE'S GREAT AT TAKING DIVES.

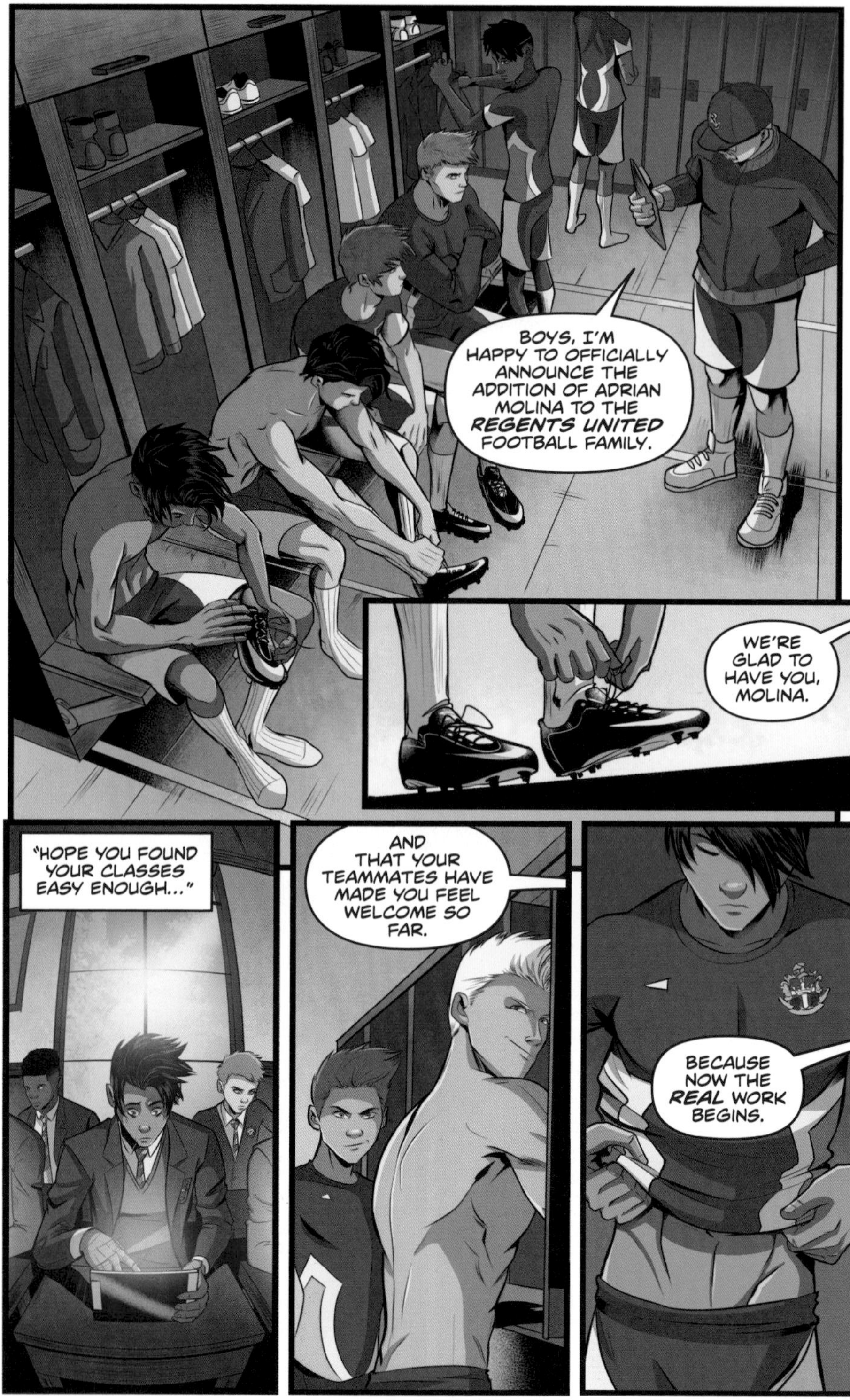
BOYS, I'M HAPPY TO OFFICIALLY ANNOUNCE THE ADDITION OF ADRIAN MOLINA TO THE *REGENTS UNITED* FOOTBALL FAMILY.
WE'RE GLAD TO HAVE YOU, MOLINA.
"HOPE YOU FOUND YOUR CLASSES EASY ENOUGH..."
AND THAT YOUR TEAMMATES HAVE MADE YOU FEEL WELCOME SO FAR.
BECAUSE NOW THE *REAL* WORK BEGINS.

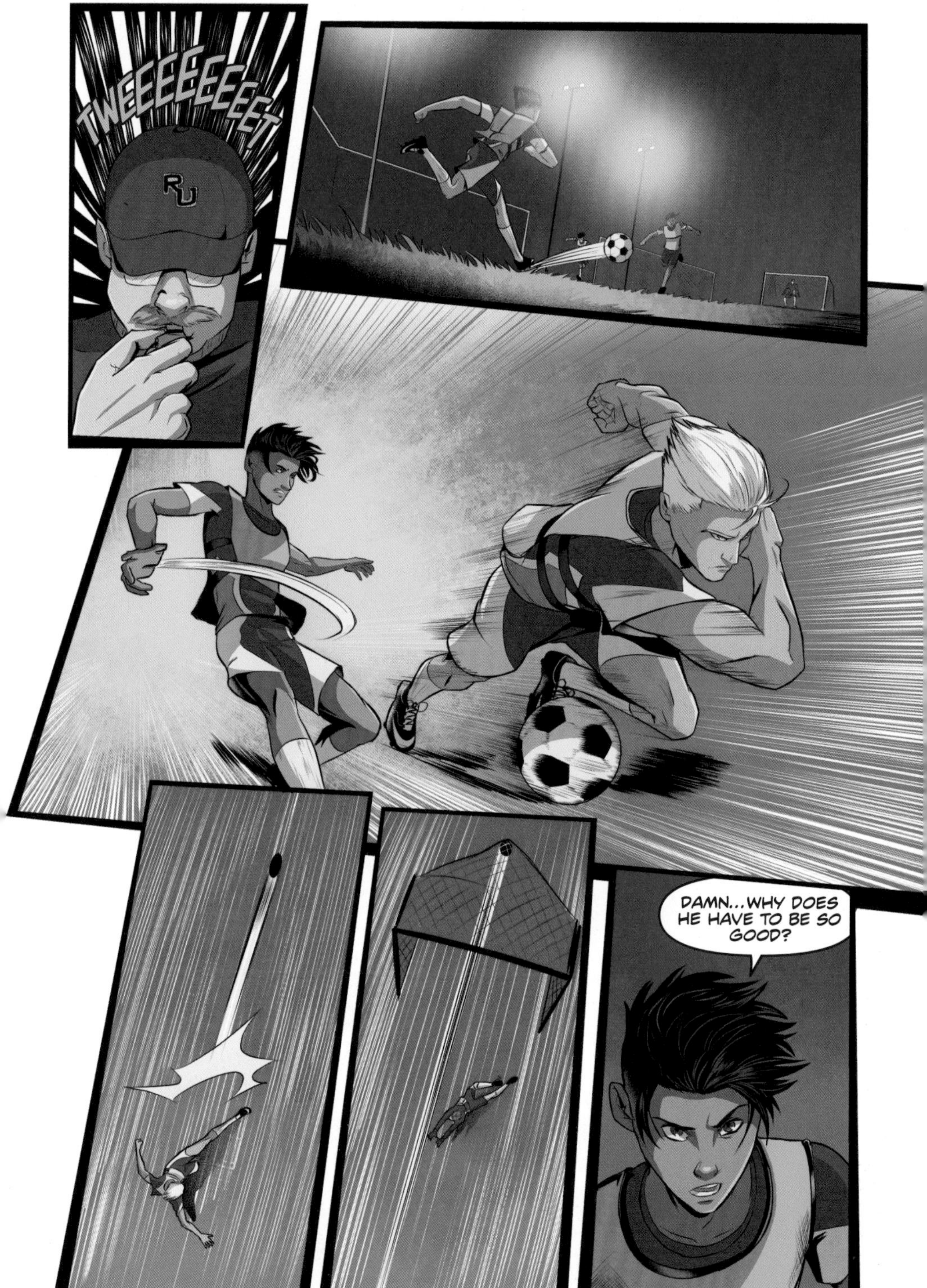
TWEEEEEEEEET
RU
DAMN...WHY DOES HE HAVE TO BE SO GOOD?

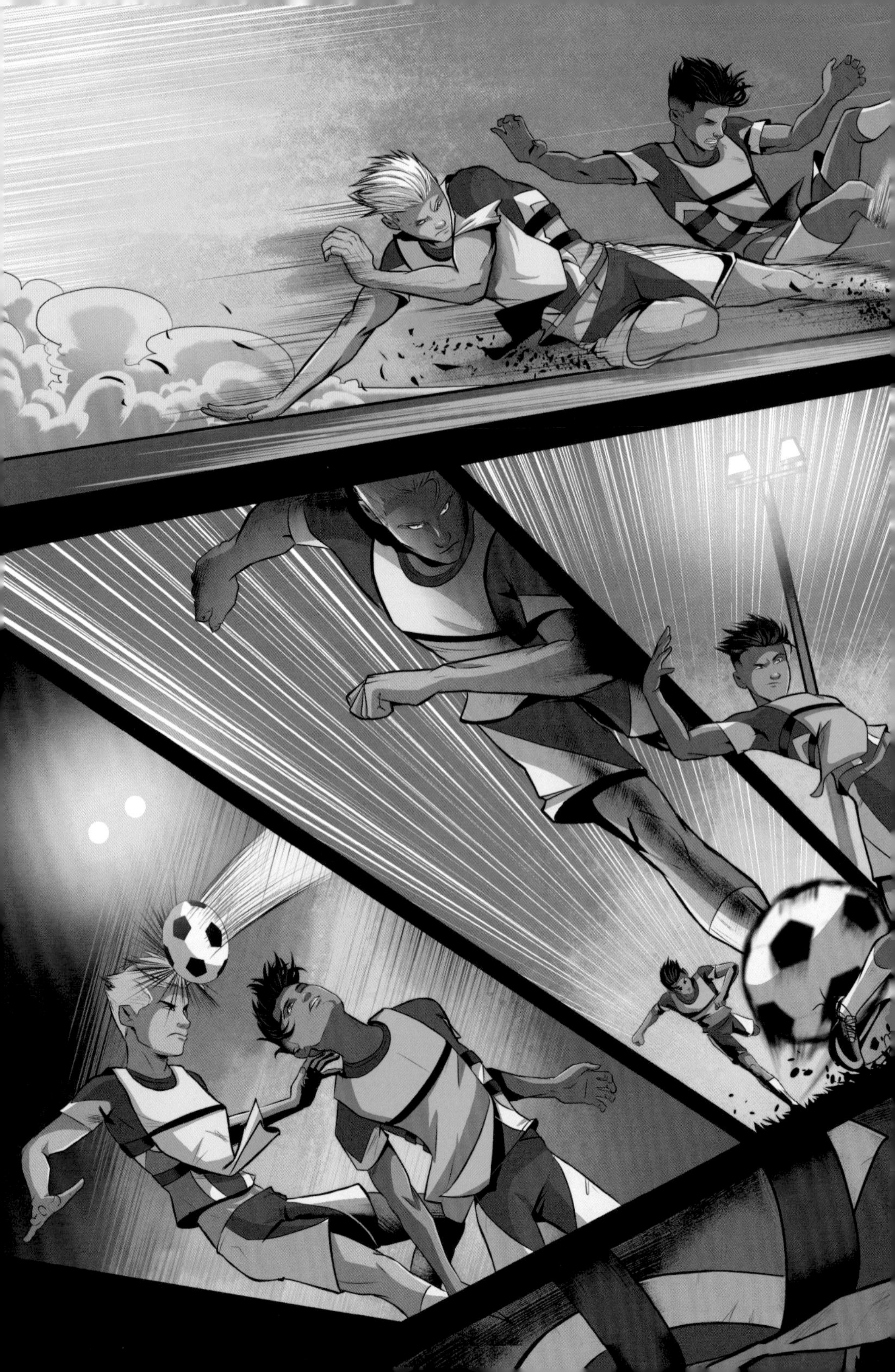

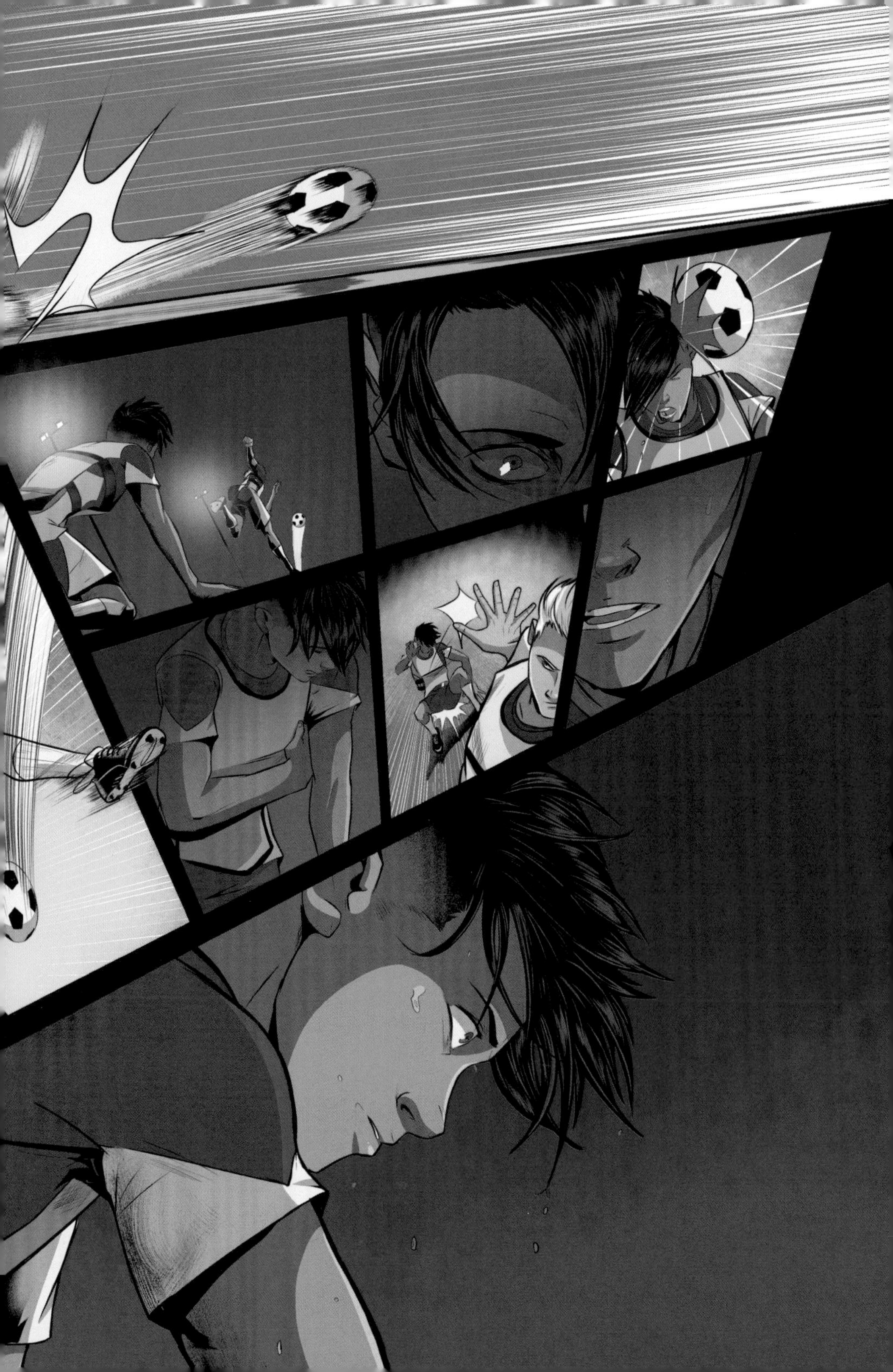

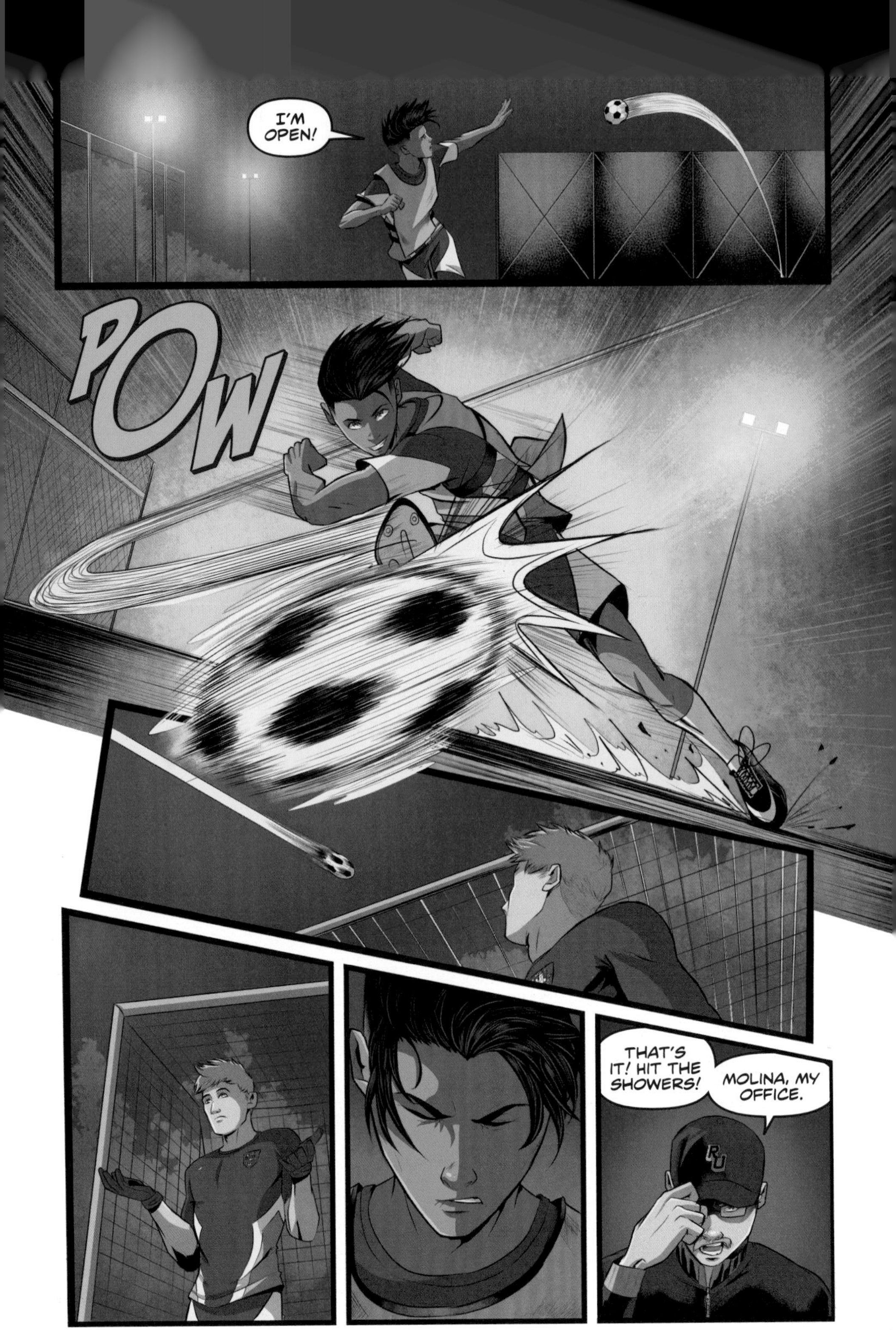
I'M OPEN!
POW
THAT'S IT! HIT THE SHOWERS!
MOLINA, MY OFFICE.

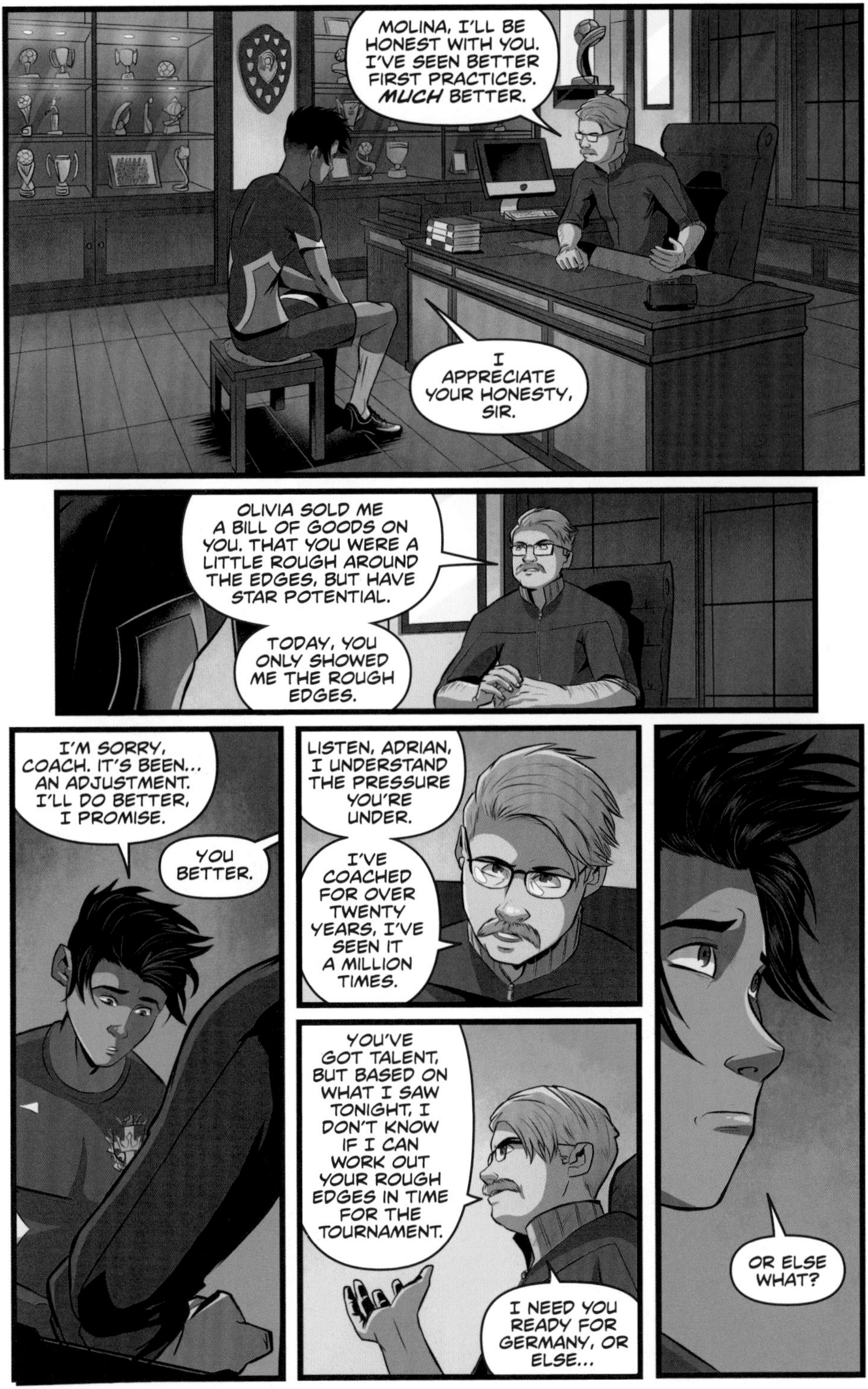
MOLINA, I'LL BE HONEST WITH YOU. I'VE SEEN BETTER FIRST PRACTICES. *MUCH* BETTER.
I APPRECIATE YOUR HONESTY, SIR.
OLIVIA SOLD ME A BILL OF GOODS ON YOU. THAT YOU WERE A LITTLE ROUGH AROUND THE EDGES, BUT HAVE STAR POTENTIAL.
TODAY, YOU ONLY SHOWED ME THE ROUGH EDGES.
I'M SORRY, COACH. IT'S BEEN... AN ADJUSTMENT. I'LL DO BETTER, I PROMISE.
YOU BETTER.
LISTEN, ADRIAN, I UNDERSTAND THE PRESSURE YOU'RE UNDER.
I'VE COACHED FOR OVER TWENTY YEARS, I'VE SEEN IT A MILLION TIMES.
YOU'VE GOT TALENT, BUT BASED ON WHAT I SAW TONIGHT, I DON'T KNOW IF I CAN WORK OUT YOUR ROUGH EDGES IN TIME FOR THE TOURNAMENT.
I NEED YOU READY FOR GERMANY, OR ELSE...
OR ELSE WHAT?

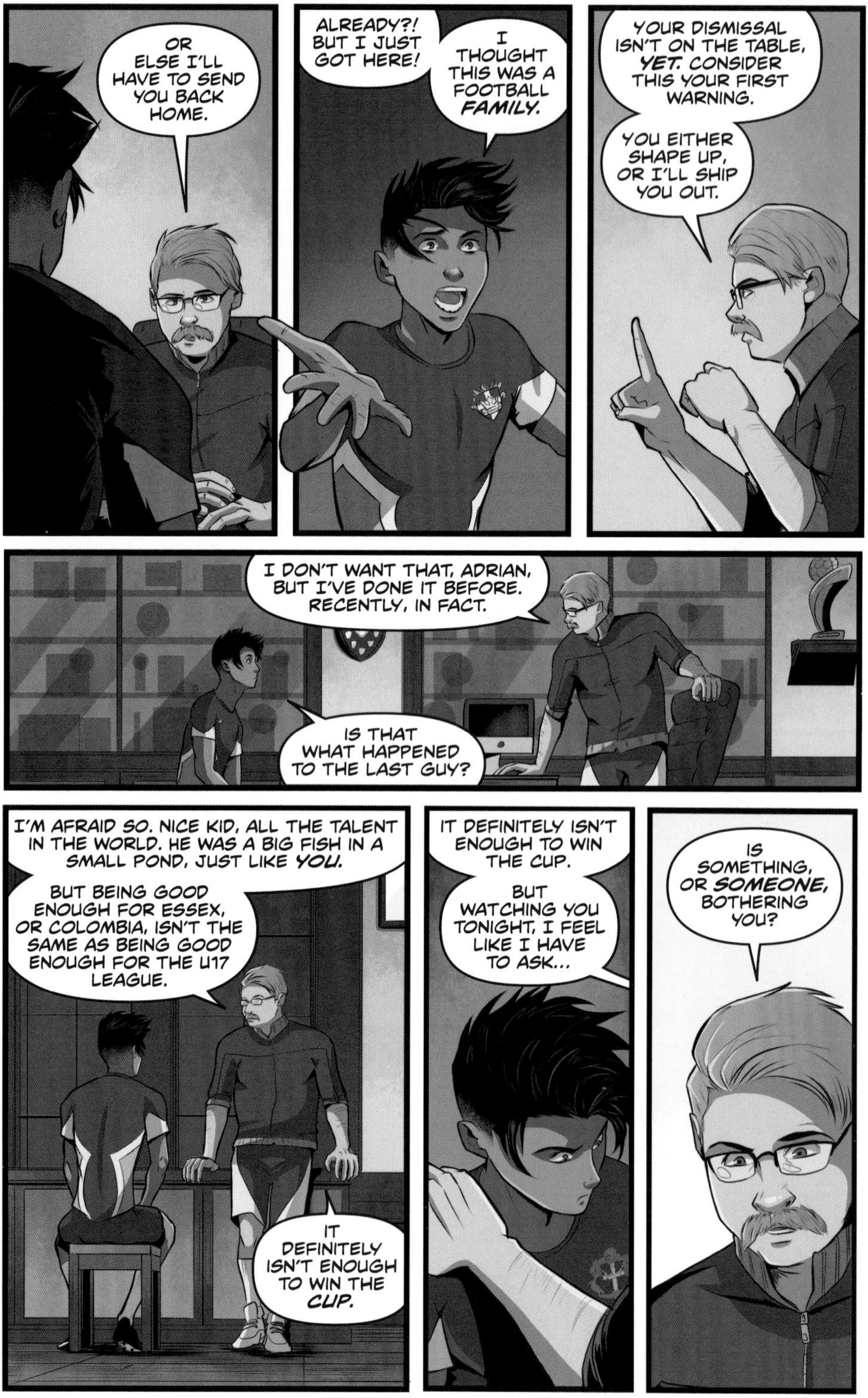
OR ELSE I'LL HAVE TO SEND YOU BACK HOME.
ALREADY?! BUT I JUST GOT HERE!
I THOUGHT THIS WAS A FOOTBALL FAMILY.
YOUR DISMISSAL ISN'T ON THE TABLE, YET. CONSIDER THIS YOUR FIRST WARNING.
YOU EITHER SHAPE UP, OR I'LL SHIP YOU OUT.
I DON'T WANT THAT, ADRIAN, BUT I'VE DONE IT BEFORE. RECENTLY, IN FACT.
IS THAT WHAT HAPPENED TO THE LAST GUY?
I'M AFRAID SO. NICE KID, ALL THE TALENT IN THE WORLD. HE WAS A BIG FISH IN A SMALL POND, JUST LIKE YOU.
BUT BEING GOOD ENOUGH FOR ESSEX, OR COLOMBIA, ISN'T THE SAME AS BEING GOOD ENOUGH FOR THE U17 LEAGUE.
IT DEFINITELY ISN'T ENOUGH TO WIN THE CUP.
IT DEFINITELY ISN'T ENOUGH TO WIN THE CUP.
BUT WATCHING YOU TONIGHT, I FEEL LIKE I HAVE TO ASK...
IS SOMETHING, OR SOMEONE, BOTHERING YOU?

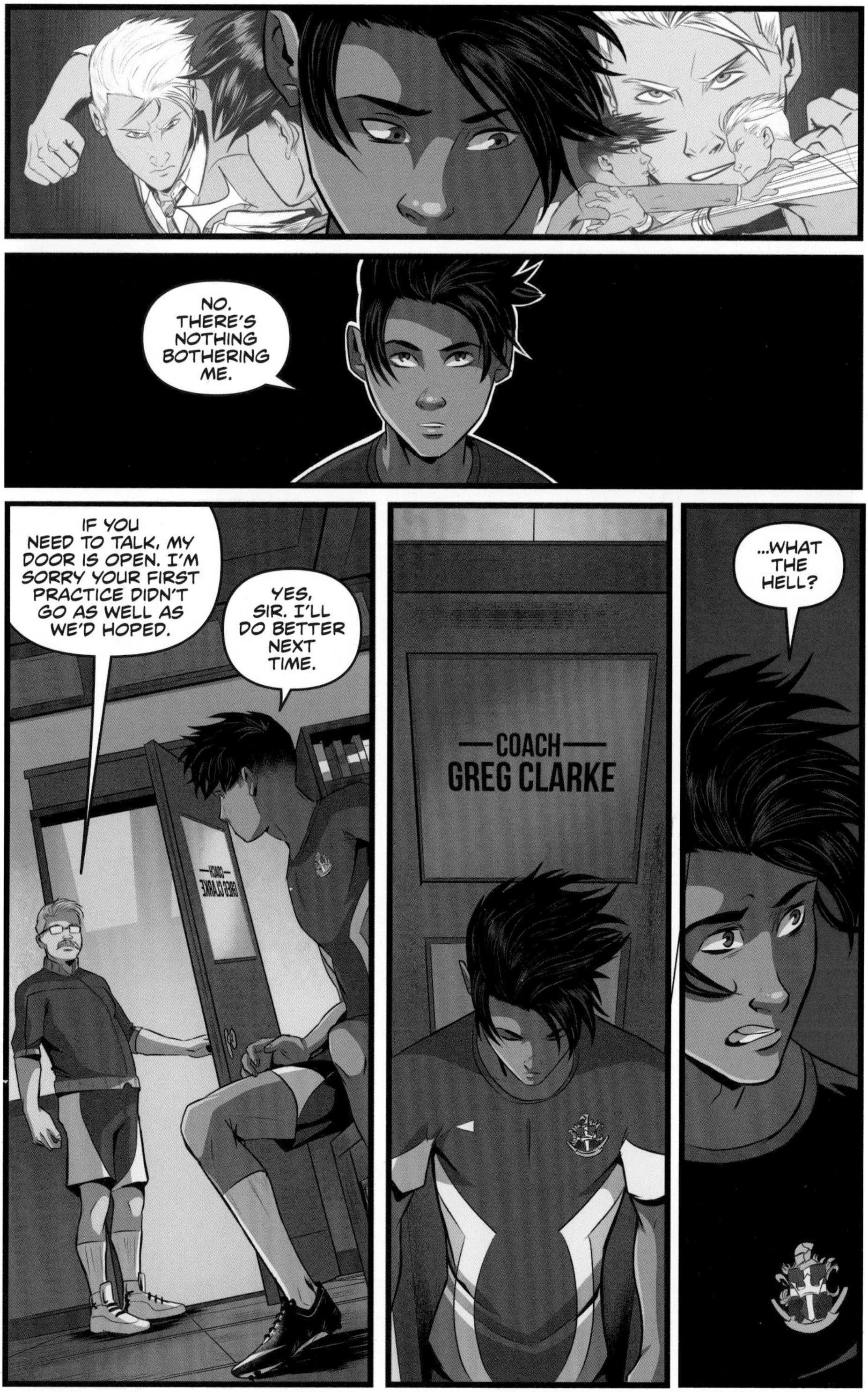
NO. THERE'S NOTHING BOTHERING ME.
IF YOU NEED TO TALK, MY DOOR IS OPEN. I'M SORRY YOUR FIRST PRACTICE DIDN'T GO AS WELL AS WE'D HOPED.
YES, SIR. I'LL DO BETTER NEXT TIME.
COACH
GREG CLARKE
COACH GREG CLARKE
...WHAT THE HELL?

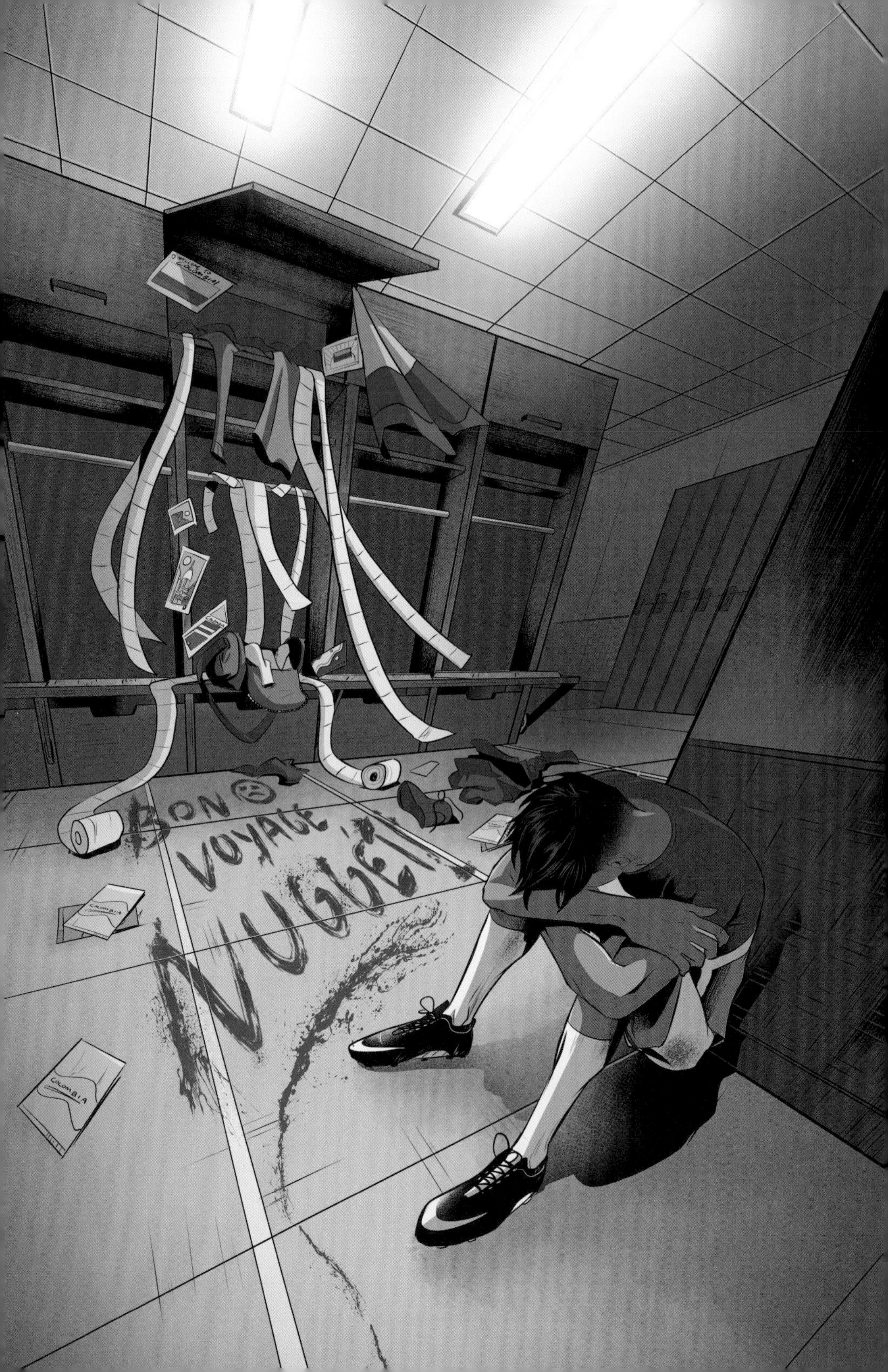
WELCOME TO COLOMBIA!
BON VOYAGE NUGGET!
COLOMBIA
COLOMBIA

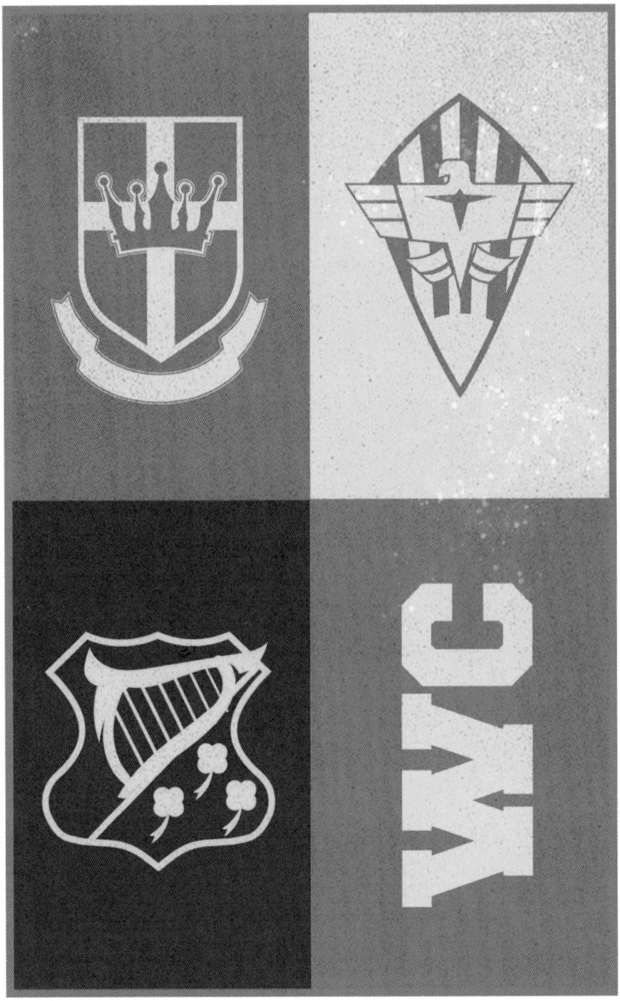
WC

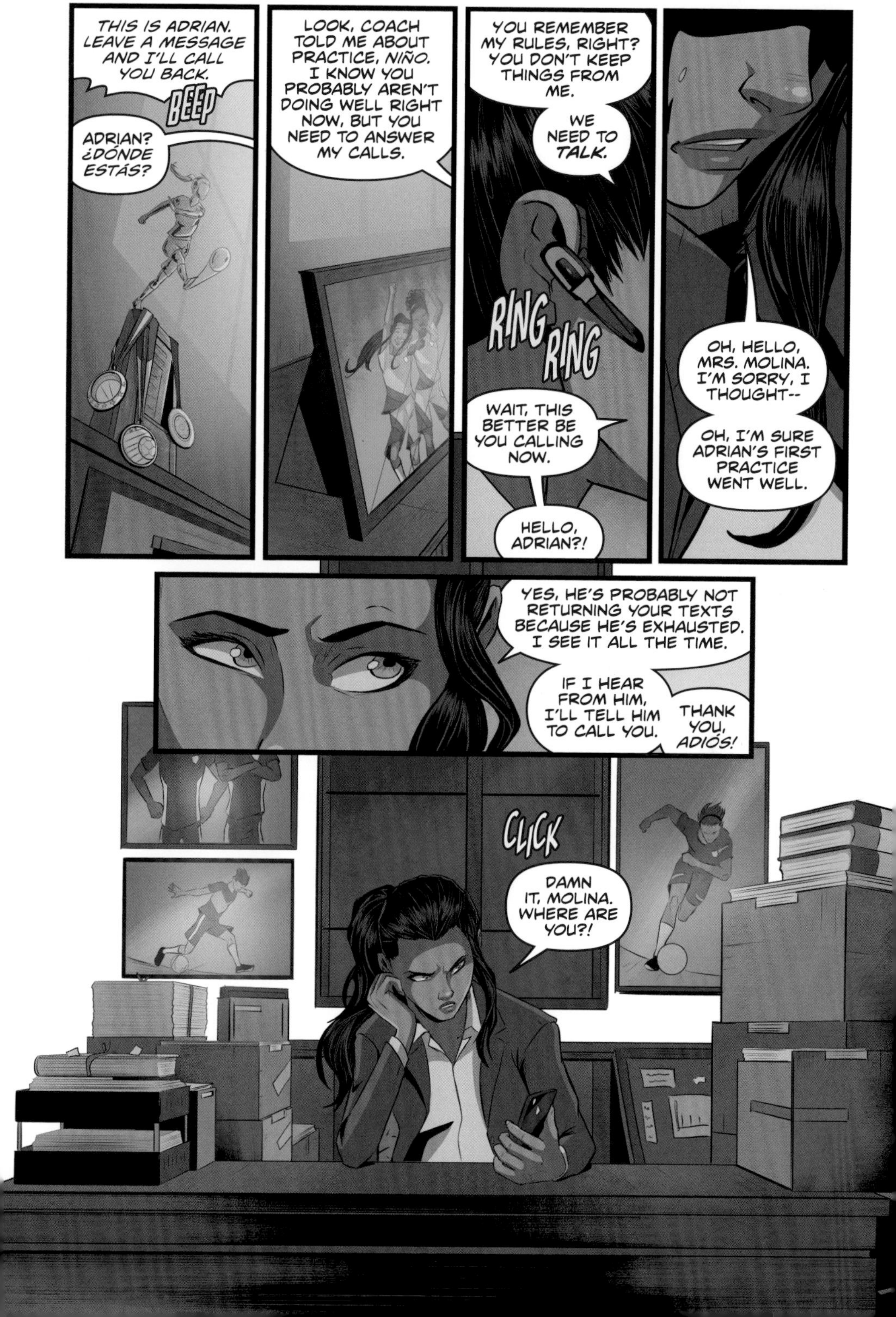
THIS IS ADRIAN. LEAVE A MESSAGE AND I'LL CALL YOU BACK.
BEEP
ADRIAN? ¿DÓNDE ESTÁS?
LOOK, COACH TOLD ME ABOUT PRACTICE, NIÑO. I KNOW YOU PROBABLY AREN'T DOING WELL RIGHT NOW, BUT YOU NEED TO ANSWER MY CALLS.
YOU REMEMBER MY RULES, RIGHT? YOU DON'T KEEP THINGS FROM ME.
WE NEED TO *TALK.*
RING RING
WAIT, THIS BETTER BE YOU CALLING NOW.
HELLO, ADRIAN?!
OH, HELLO, MRS. MOLINA. I'M SORRY, I THOUGHT--
OH, I'M SURE ADRIAN'S FIRST PRACTICE WENT WELL.
YES, HE'S PROBABLY NOT RETURNING YOUR TEXTS BECAUSE HE'S EXHAUSTED. I SEE IT ALL THE TIME.
IF I HEAR FROM HIM, I'LL TELL HIM TO CALL YOU.
THANK YOU, *ADIÓS!*
CLICK
DAMN IT, MOLINA. WHERE ARE YOU?!

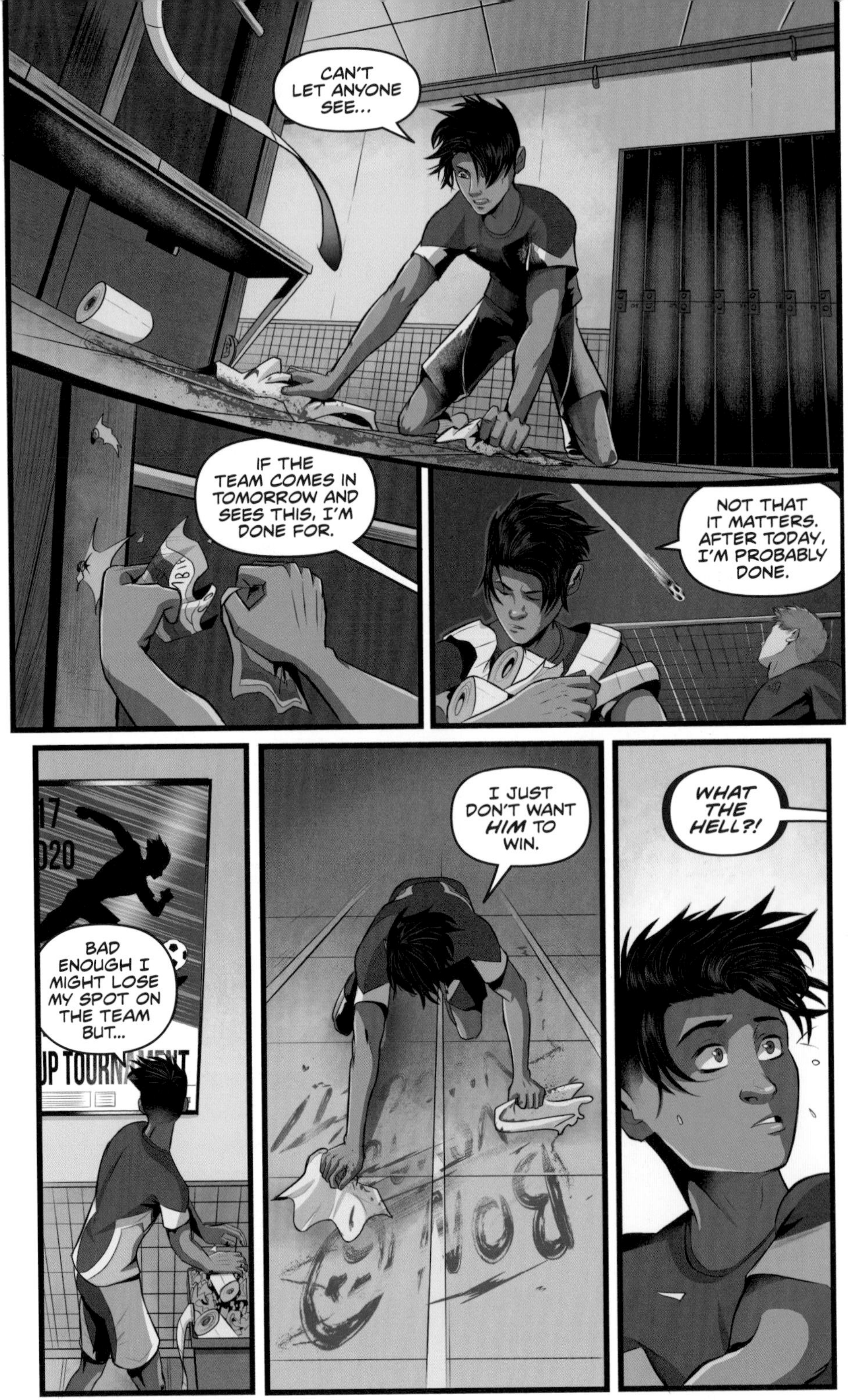
CAN'T LET ANYONE SEE...
IF THE TEAM COMES IN TOMORROW AND SEES THIS, I'M DONE FOR.
NOT THAT IT MATTERS. AFTER TODAY, I'M PROBABLY DONE.
BAD ENOUGH I MIGHT LOSE MY SPOT ON THE TEAM BUT...
UP TOURNAMENT
I JUST DON'T WANT *HIM* TO WIN.
WHAT THE HELL?!

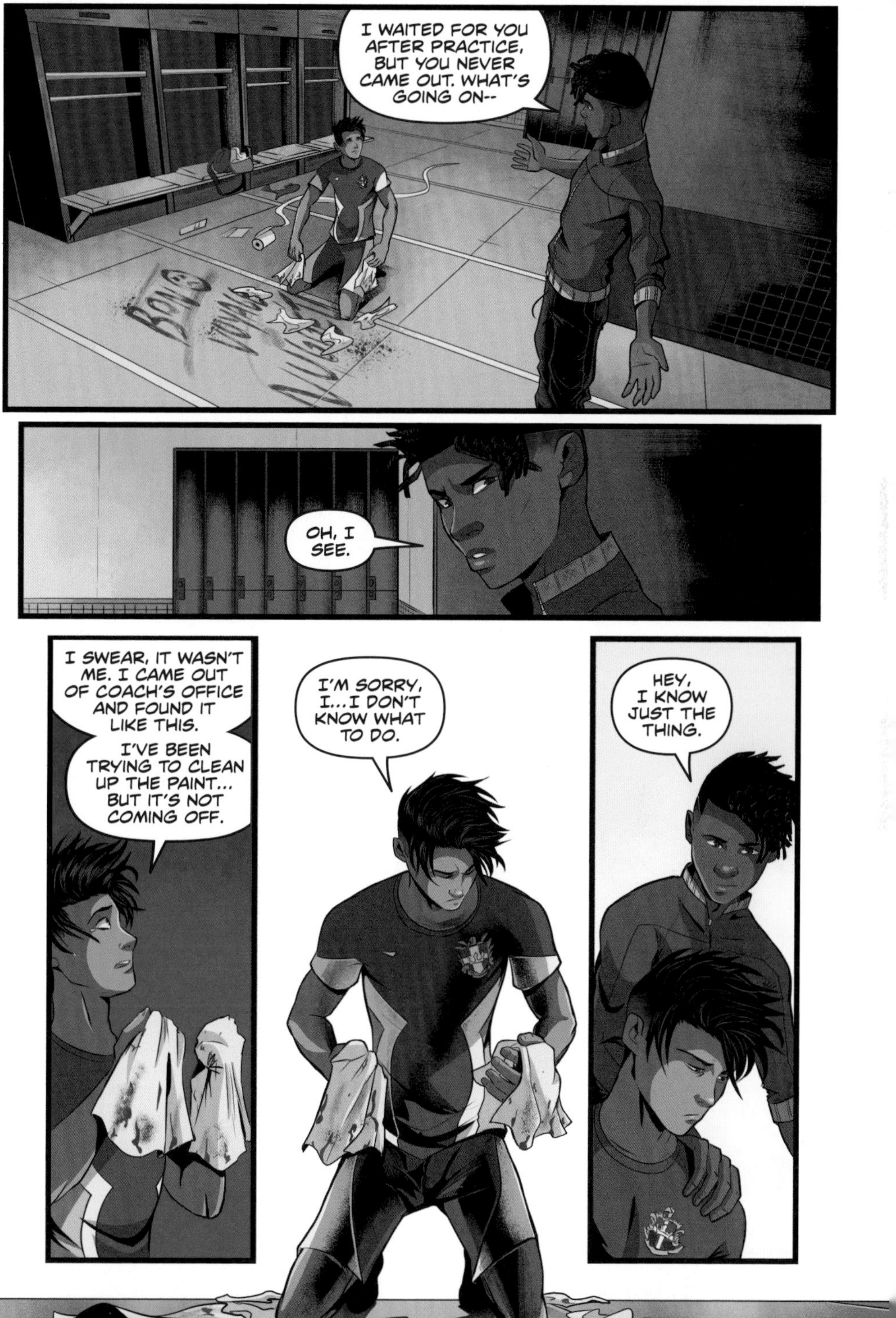
I WAITED FOR YOU AFTER PRACTICE, BUT YOU NEVER CAME OUT. WHAT'S GOING ON--
OH, I SEE.
I SWEAR, IT WASN'T ME. I CAME OUT OF COACH'S OFFICE AND FOUND IT LIKE THIS.
I'VE BEEN TRYING TO CLEAN UP THE PAINT... BUT IT'S NOT COMING OFF.
I'M SORRY, I...I DON'T KNOW WHAT TO DO.
HEY, I KNOW JUST THE THING.

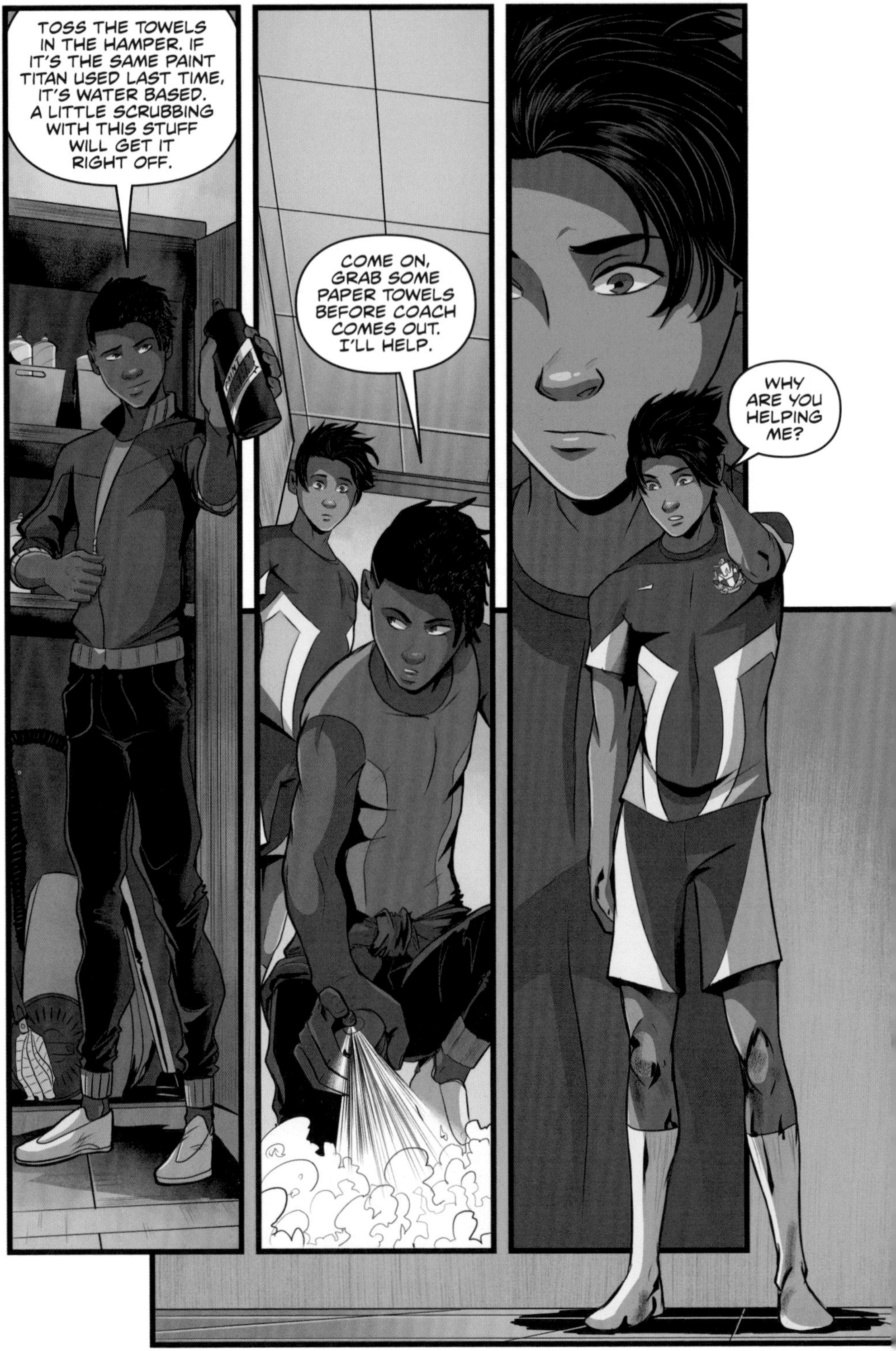
TOSS THE TOWELS IN THE HAMPER. IF IT'S THE SAME PAINT TITAN USED LAST TIME, IT'S WATER BASED. A LITTLE SCRUBBING WITH THIS STUFF WILL GET IT RIGHT OFF.
COME ON, GRAB SOME PAPER TOWELS BEFORE COACH COMES OUT. I'LL HELP.
WHY ARE YOU HELPING ME?

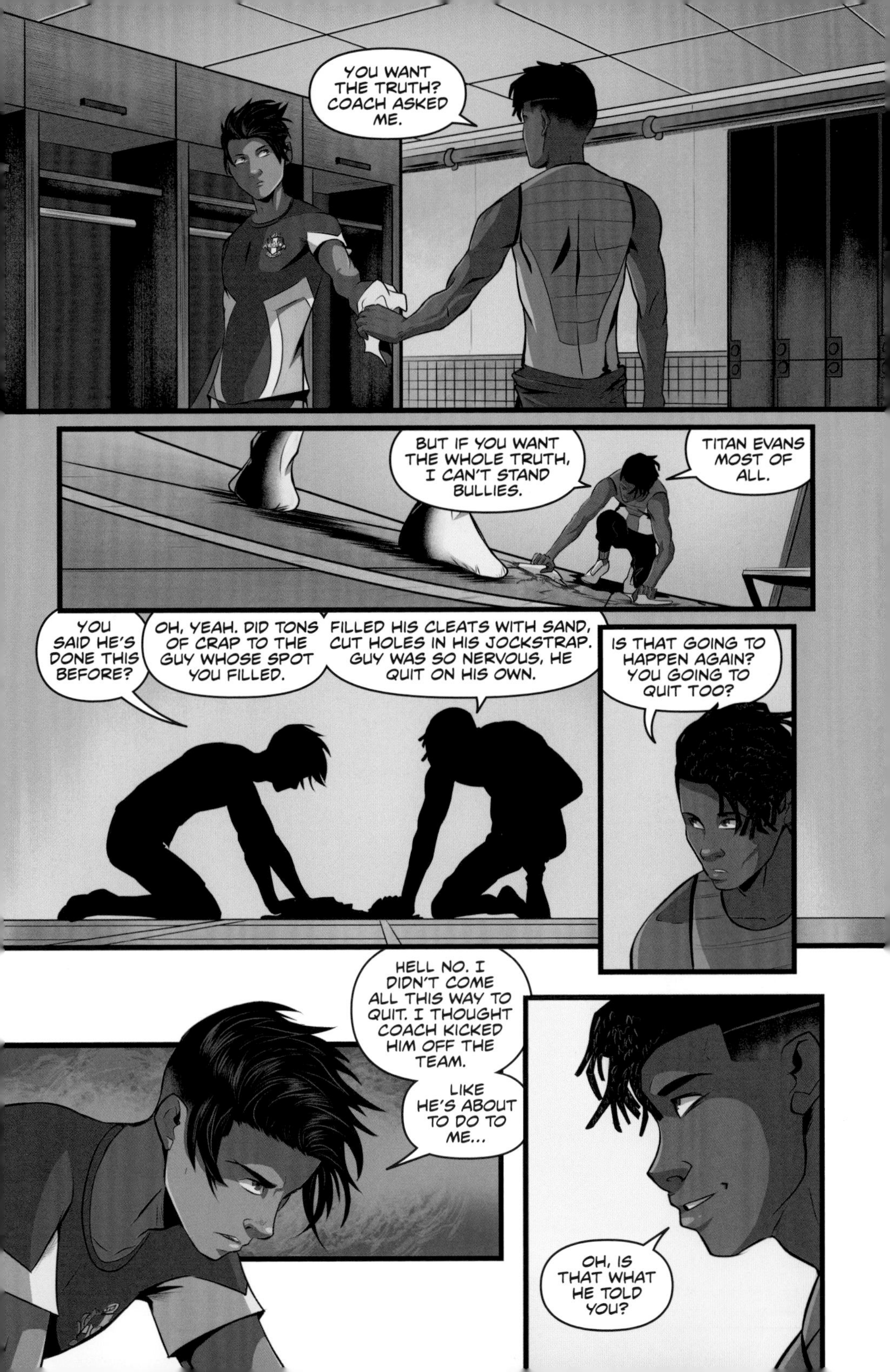
YOU WANT THE TRUTH? COACH ASKED ME.
BUT IF YOU WANT THE WHOLE TRUTH, I CAN'T STAND BULLIES.
TITAN EVANS MOST OF ALL.
YOU SAID HE'S DONE THIS BEFORE?
OH, YEAH. DID TONS OF CRAP TO THE GUY WHOSE SPOT YOU FILLED.
FILLED HIS CLEATS WITH SAND, CUT HOLES IN HIS JOCKSTRAP. GUY WAS SO NERVOUS, HE QUIT ON HIS OWN.
IS THAT GOING TO HAPPEN AGAIN? YOU GOING TO QUIT TOO?
HELL NO. I DIDN'T COME ALL THIS WAY TO QUIT. I THOUGHT COACH KICKED HIM OFF THE TEAM.
LIKE HE'S ABOUT TO DO TO ME...
OH, IS THAT WHAT HE TOLD YOU?

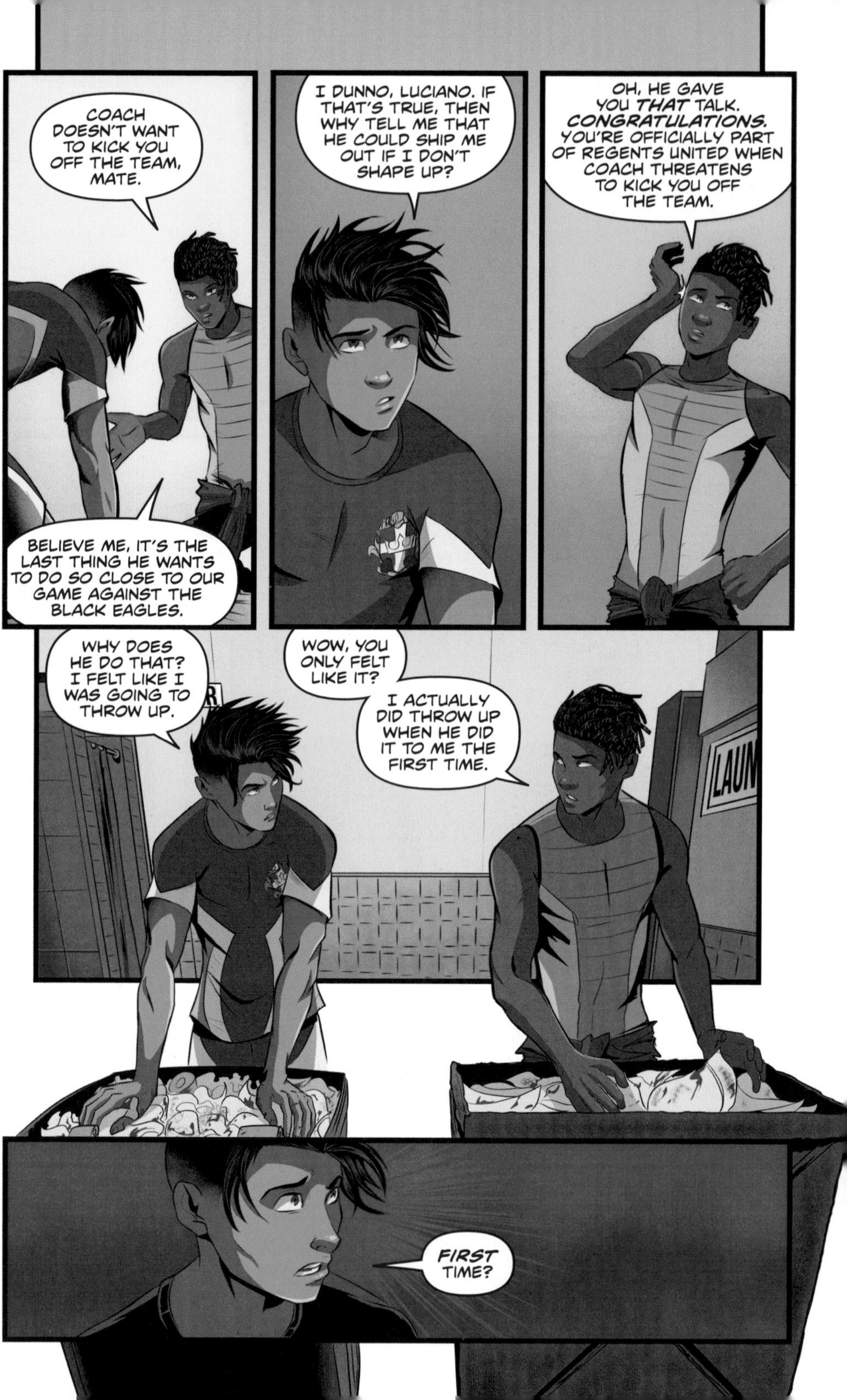
COACH DOESN'T WANT TO KICK YOU OFF THE TEAM, MATE.
BELIEVE ME, IT'S THE LAST THING HE WANTS TO DO SO CLOSE TO OUR GAME AGAINST THE BLACK EAGLES.
I DUNNO, LUCIANO. IF THAT'S TRUE, THEN WHY TELL ME THAT HE COULD SHIP ME OUT IF I DON'T SHAPE UP?
OH, HE GAVE YOU *THAT* TALK. ***CONGRATULATIONS.*** YOU'RE OFFICIALLY PART OF REGENTS UNITED WHEN COACH THREATENS TO KICK YOU OFF THE TEAM.
WHY DOES HE DO THAT? I FELT LIKE I WAS GOING TO THROW UP.
WOW, YOU ONLY FELT LIKE IT?
I ACTUALLY DID THROW UP WHEN HE DID IT TO ME THE FIRST TIME.
LAUN
FIRST TIME?

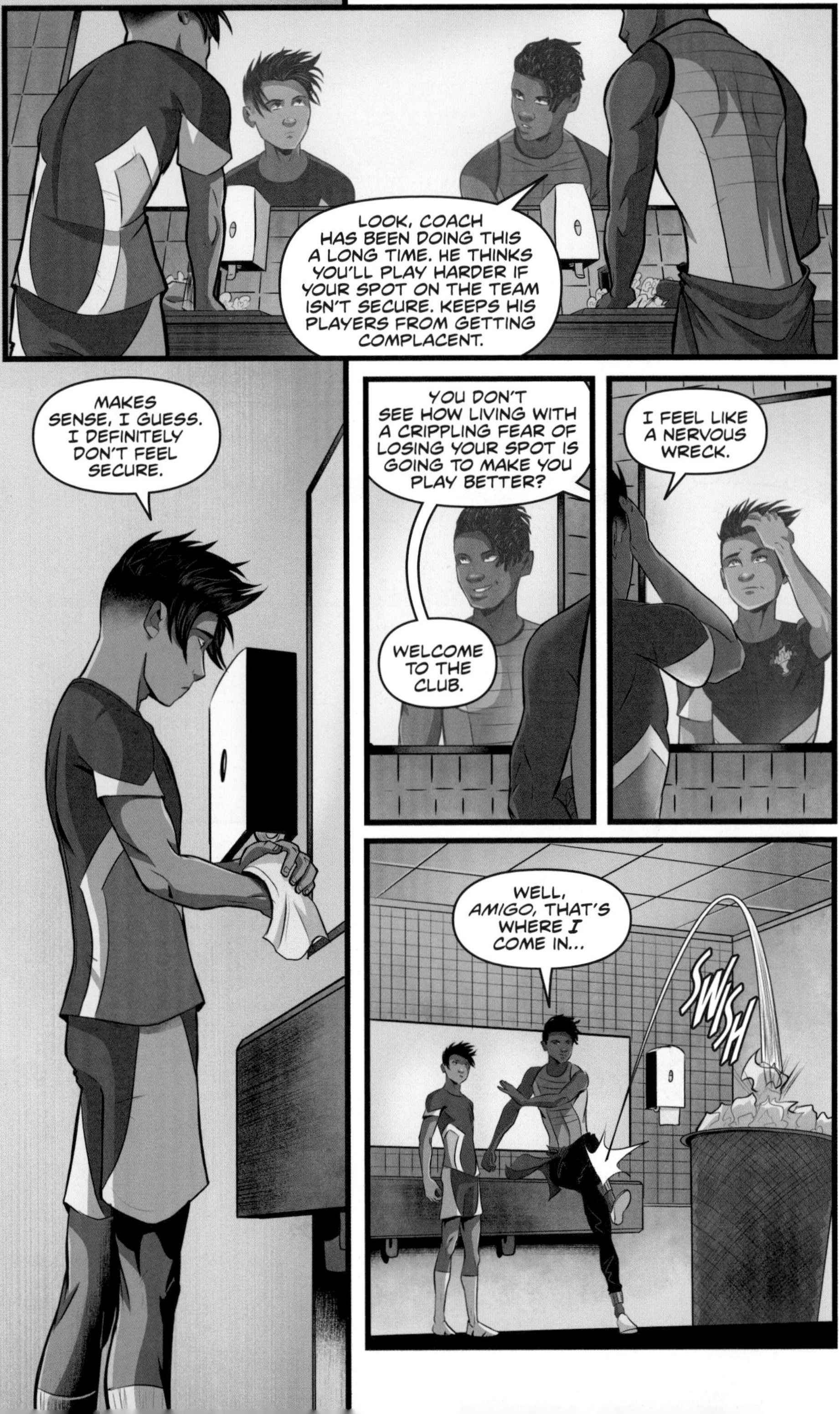
LOOK, COACH HAS BEEN DOING THIS A LONG TIME. HE THINKS YOU'LL PLAY HARDER IF YOUR SPOT ON THE TEAM ISN'T SECURE. KEEPS HIS PLAYERS FROM GETTING COMPLACENT.
MAKES SENSE, I GUESS. I DEFINITELY DON'T FEEL SECURE.
YOU DON'T SEE HOW LIVING WITH A CRIPPLING FEAR OF LOSING YOUR SPOT IS GOING TO MAKE YOU PLAY BETTER?
WELCOME TO THE CLUB.
I FEEL LIKE A NERVOUS WRECK.
WELL, AMIGO, THAT'S WHERE *I* COME IN...
SWISH

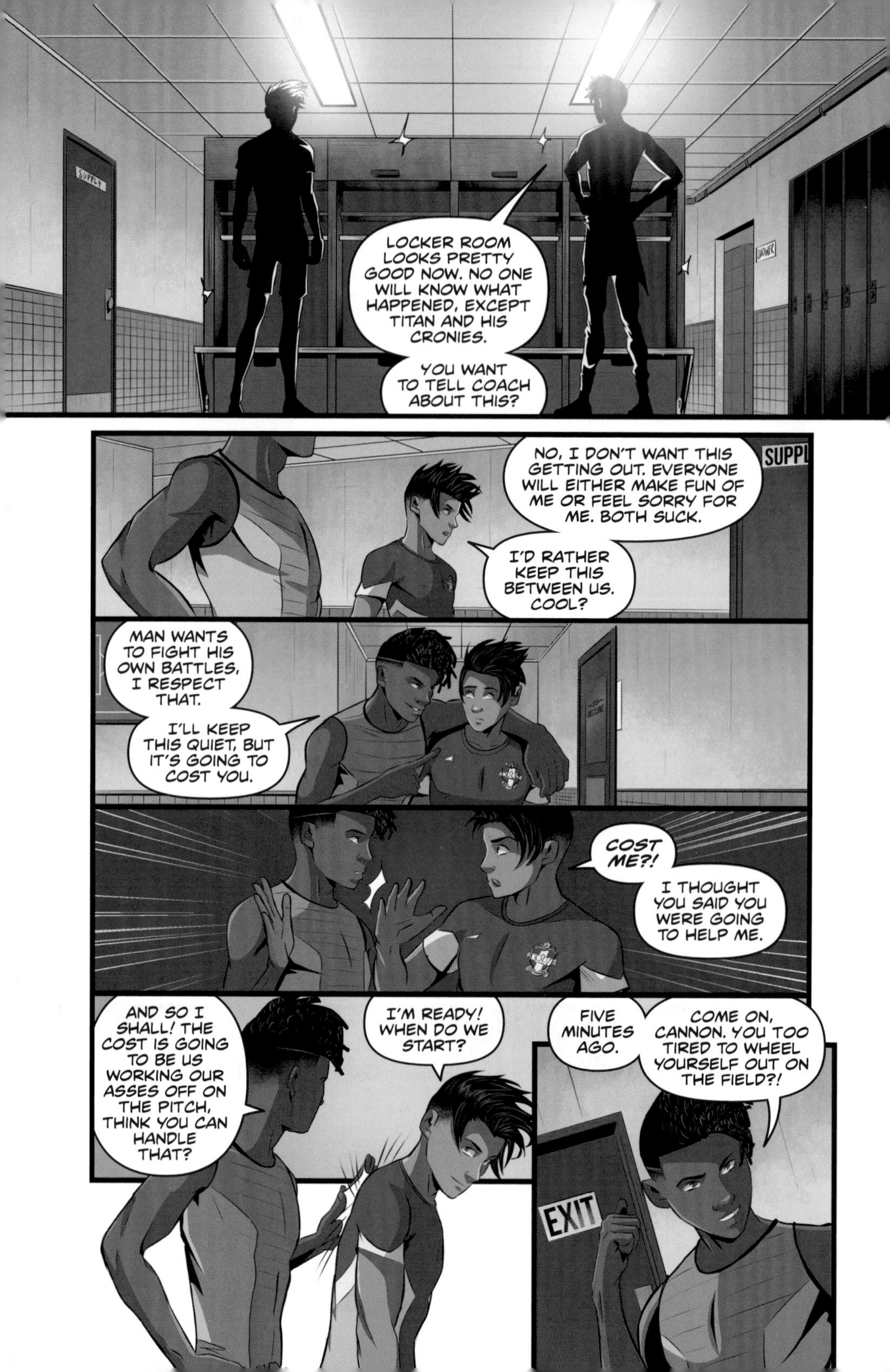
SUPPLY
SHOWER
LOCKER ROOM LOOKS PRETTY GOOD NOW. NO ONE WILL KNOW WHAT HAPPENED, EXCEPT TITAN AND HIS CRONIES.
YOU WANT TO TELL COACH ABOUT THIS?
SUPPL
NO, I DON'T WANT THIS GETTING OUT. EVERYONE WILL EITHER MAKE FUN OF ME OR FEEL SORRY FOR ME. BOTH SUCK.
I'D RATHER KEEP THIS BETWEEN US. COOL?
MAN WANTS TO FIGHT HIS OWN BATTLES, I RESPECT THAT.
I'LL KEEP THIS QUIET, BUT IT'S GOING TO COST YOU.
COST ME?!
I THOUGHT YOU SAID YOU WERE GOING TO HELP ME.
AND SO I SHALL! THE COST IS GOING TO BE US WORKING OUR ASSES OFF ON THE PITCH, THINK YOU CAN HANDLE THAT?
I'M READY! WHEN DO WE START?
FIVE MINUTES AGO.
COME ON, CANNON. YOU TOO TIRED TO WHEEL YOURSELF OUT ON THE FIELD?!
EXIT

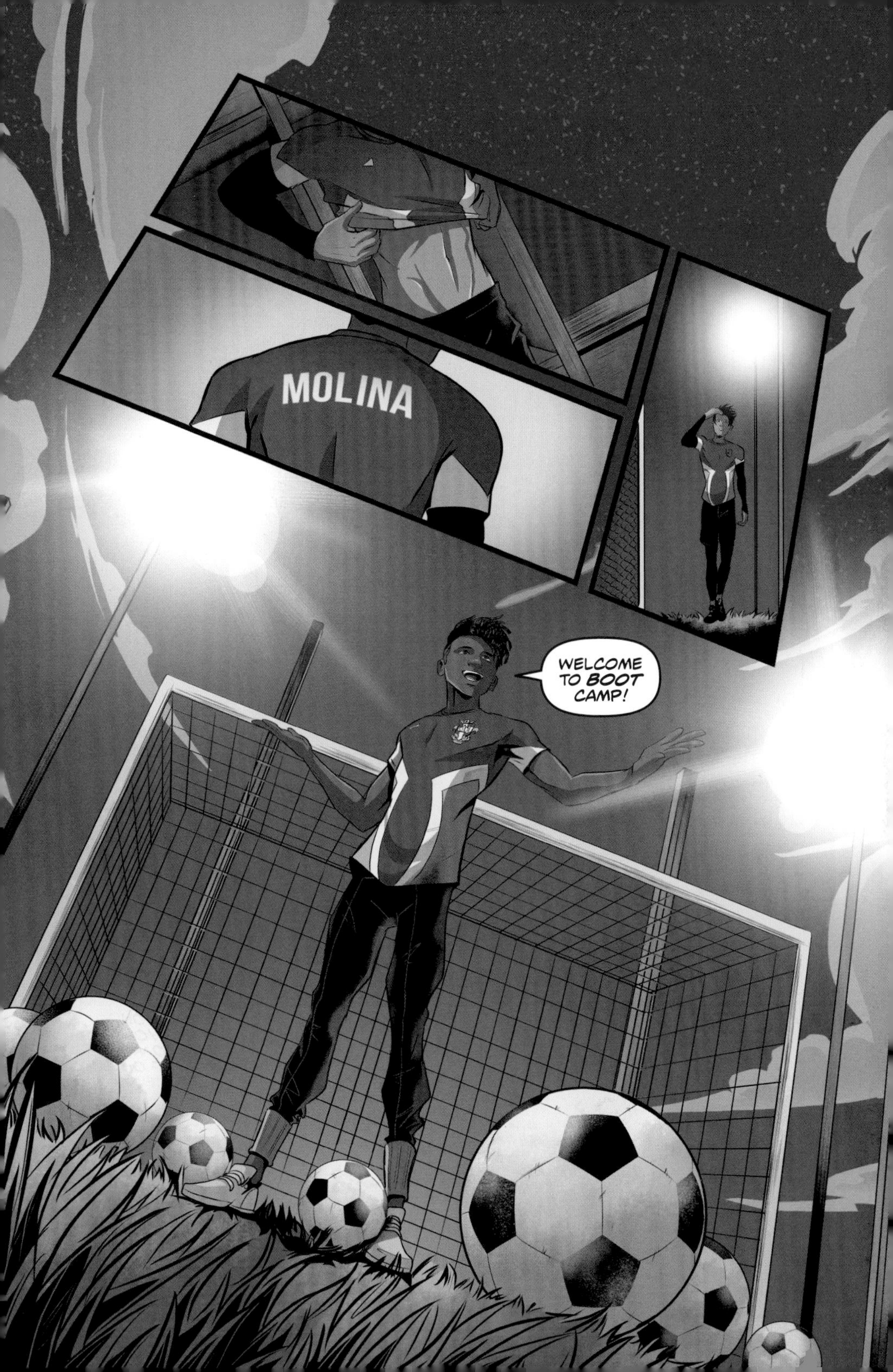
MOLINA
WELCOME TO BOOT CAMP!

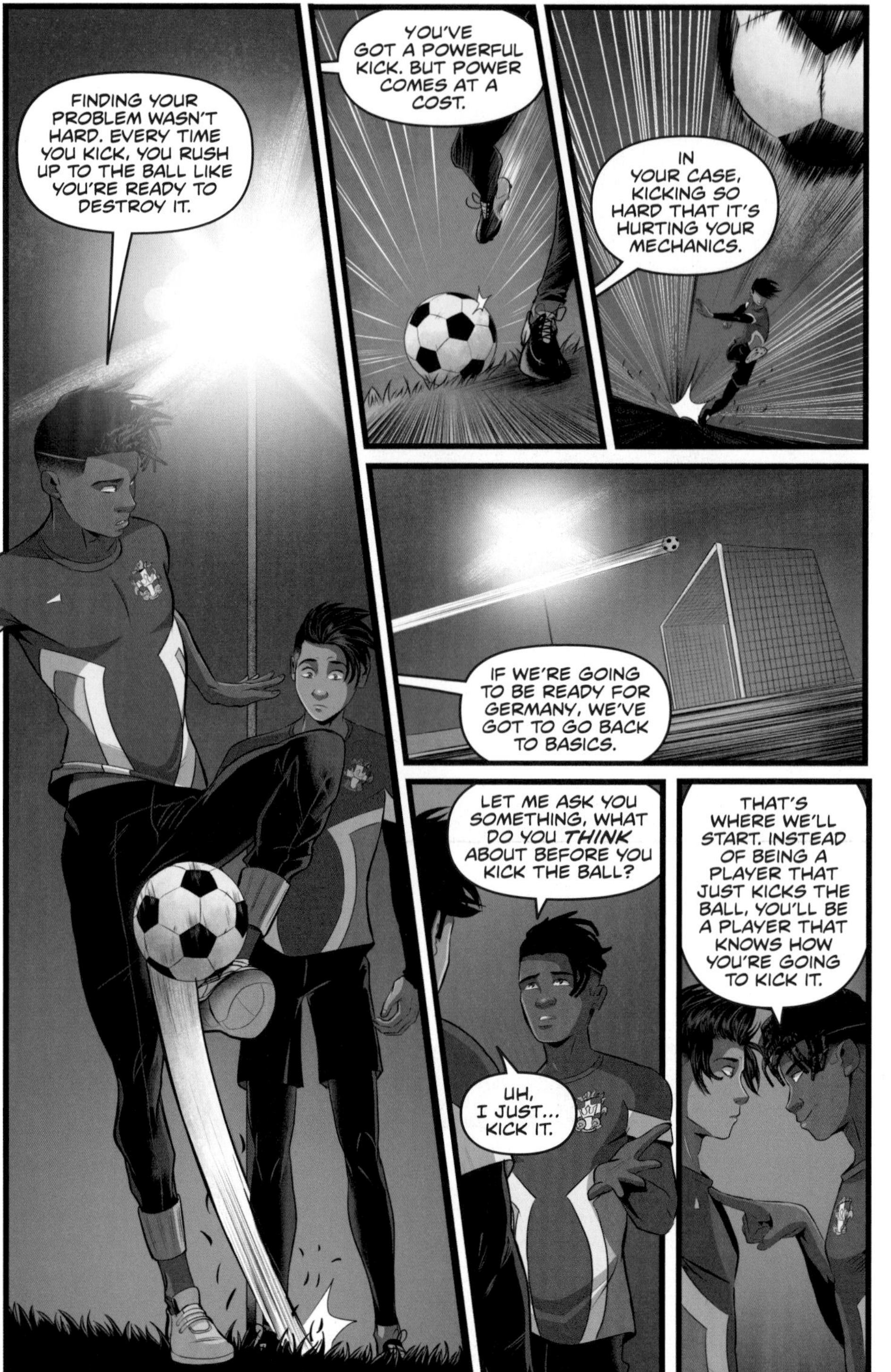

FINDING YOUR PROBLEM WASN'T HARD. EVERY TIME YOU KICK, YOU RUSH UP TO THE BALL LIKE YOU'RE READY TO DESTROY IT.
YOU'VE GOT A POWERFUL KICK. BUT POWER COMES AT A COST.
IN YOUR CASE, KICKING SO HARD THAT IT'S HURTING YOUR MECHANICS.
IF WE'RE GOING TO BE READY FOR GERMANY, WE'VE GOT TO GO BACK TO BASICS.
LET ME ASK YOU SOMETHING, WHAT DO YOU *THINK* ABOUT BEFORE YOU KICK THE BALL?
UH, I JUST... KICK IT.
THAT'S WHERE WE'LL START. INSTEAD OF BEING A PLAYER THAT JUST KICKS THE BALL, YOU'LL BE A PLAYER THAT KNOWS HOW YOU'RE GOING TO KICK IT.

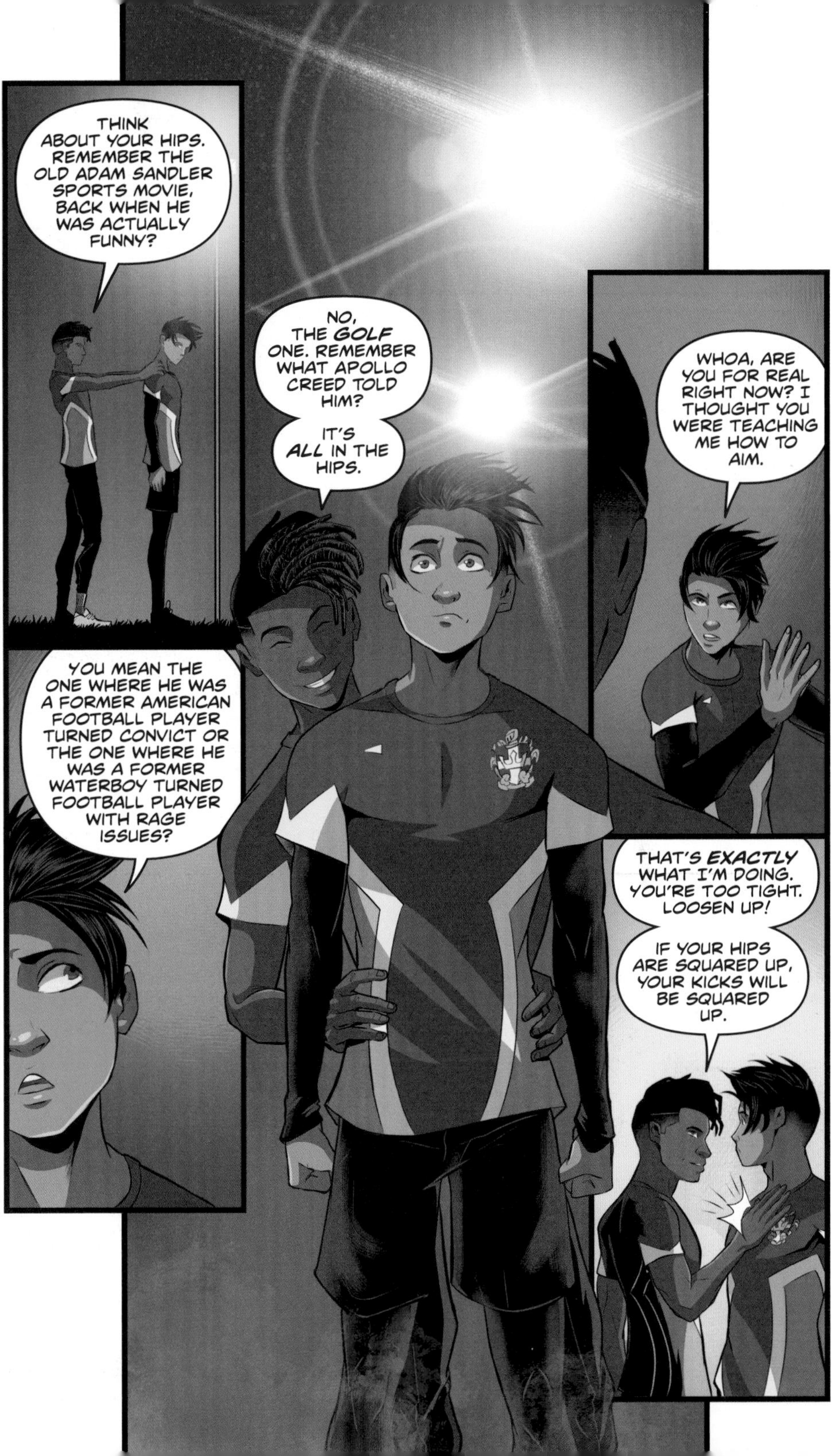
THINK ABOUT YOUR HIPS. REMEMBER THE OLD ADAM SANDLER SPORTS MOVIE, BACK WHEN HE WAS ACTUALLY FUNNY?
YOU MEAN THE ONE WHERE HE WAS A FORMER AMERICAN FOOTBALL PLAYER TURNED CONVICT OR THE ONE WHERE HE WAS A FORMER WATERBOY TURNED FOOTBALL PLAYER WITH RAGE ISSUES?
NO, THE GOLF ONE. REMEMBER WHAT APOLLO CREED TOLD HIM?
IT'S ALL IN THE HIPS.
WHOA, ARE YOU FOR REAL RIGHT NOW? I THOUGHT YOU WERE TEACHING ME HOW TO AIM.
THAT'S EXACTLY WHAT I'M DOING. YOU'RE TOO TIGHT. LOOSEN UP!
IF YOUR HIPS ARE SQUARED UP, YOUR KICKS WILL BE SQUARED UP.

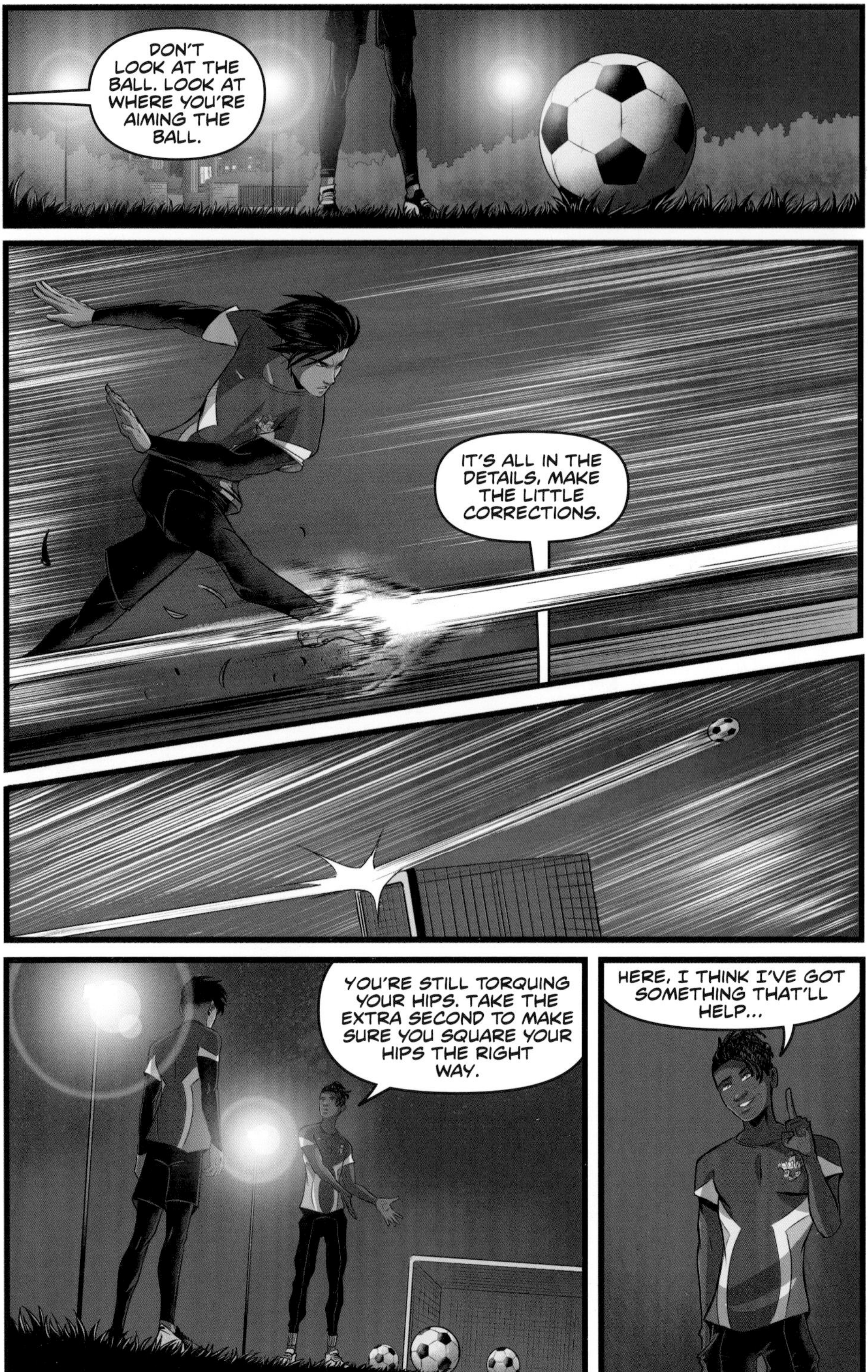
DON'T LOOK AT THE BALL. LOOK AT WHERE YOU'RE AIMING THE BALL.
IT'S ALL IN THE DETAILS, MAKE THE LITTLE CORRECTIONS.
YOU'RE STILL TORQUING YOUR HIPS. TAKE THE EXTRA SECOND TO MAKE SURE YOU SQUARE YOUR HIPS THE RIGHT WAY.
HERE, I THINK I'VE GOT SOMETHING THAT'LL HELP...

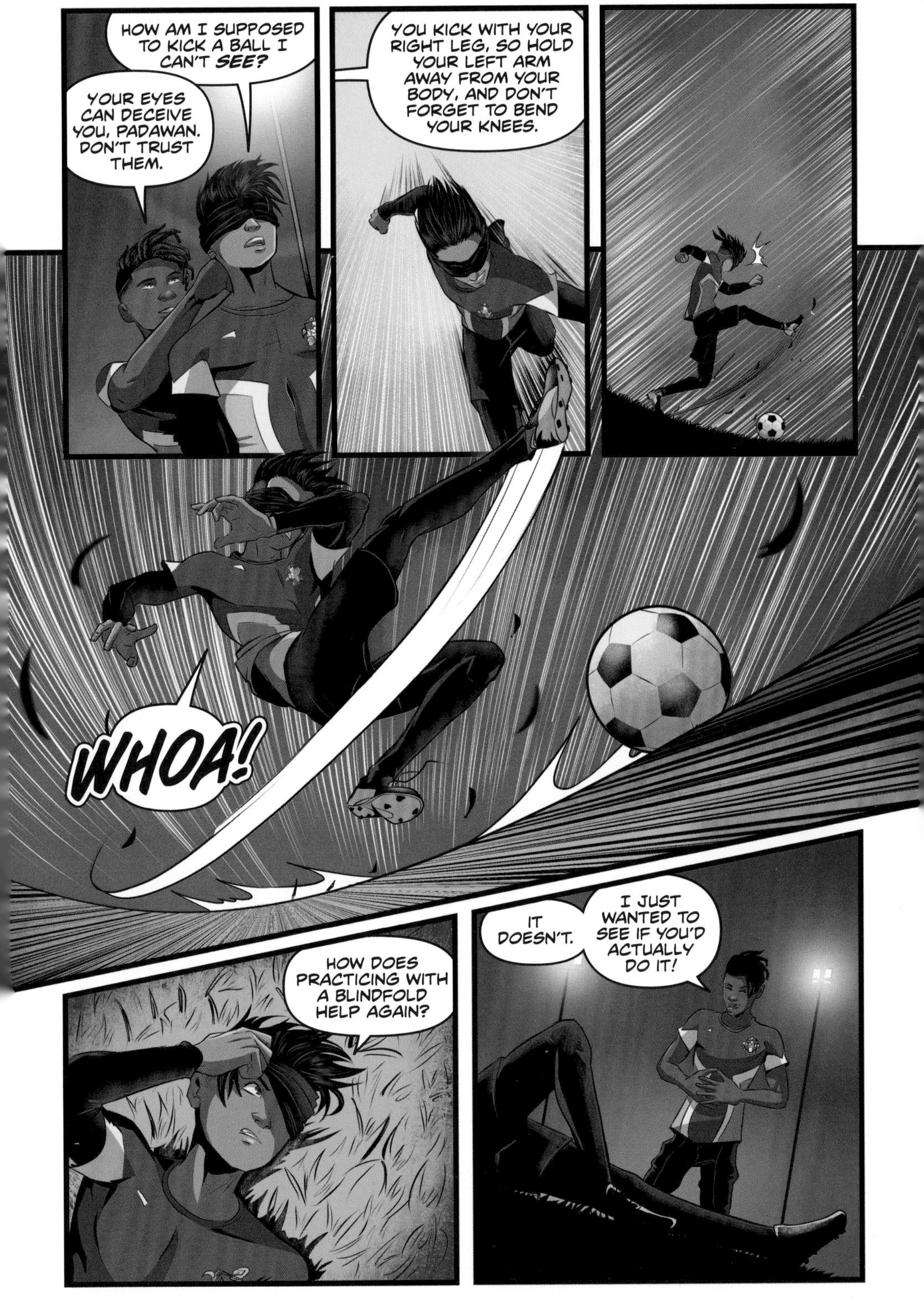
HOW AM I SUPPOSED TO KICK A BALL I CAN'T *SEE?*
YOUR EYES CAN DECEIVE YOU, PADAWAN. DON'T TRUST THEM.
YOU KICK WITH YOUR RIGHT LEG, SO HOLD YOUR LEFT ARM AWAY FROM YOUR BODY, AND DON'T FORGET TO BEND YOUR KNEES.
WHOA!
HOW DOES PRACTICING WITH A BLINDFOLD HELP AGAIN?
IT DOESN'T.
I JUST WANTED TO SEE IF YOU'D ACTUALLY DO IT!

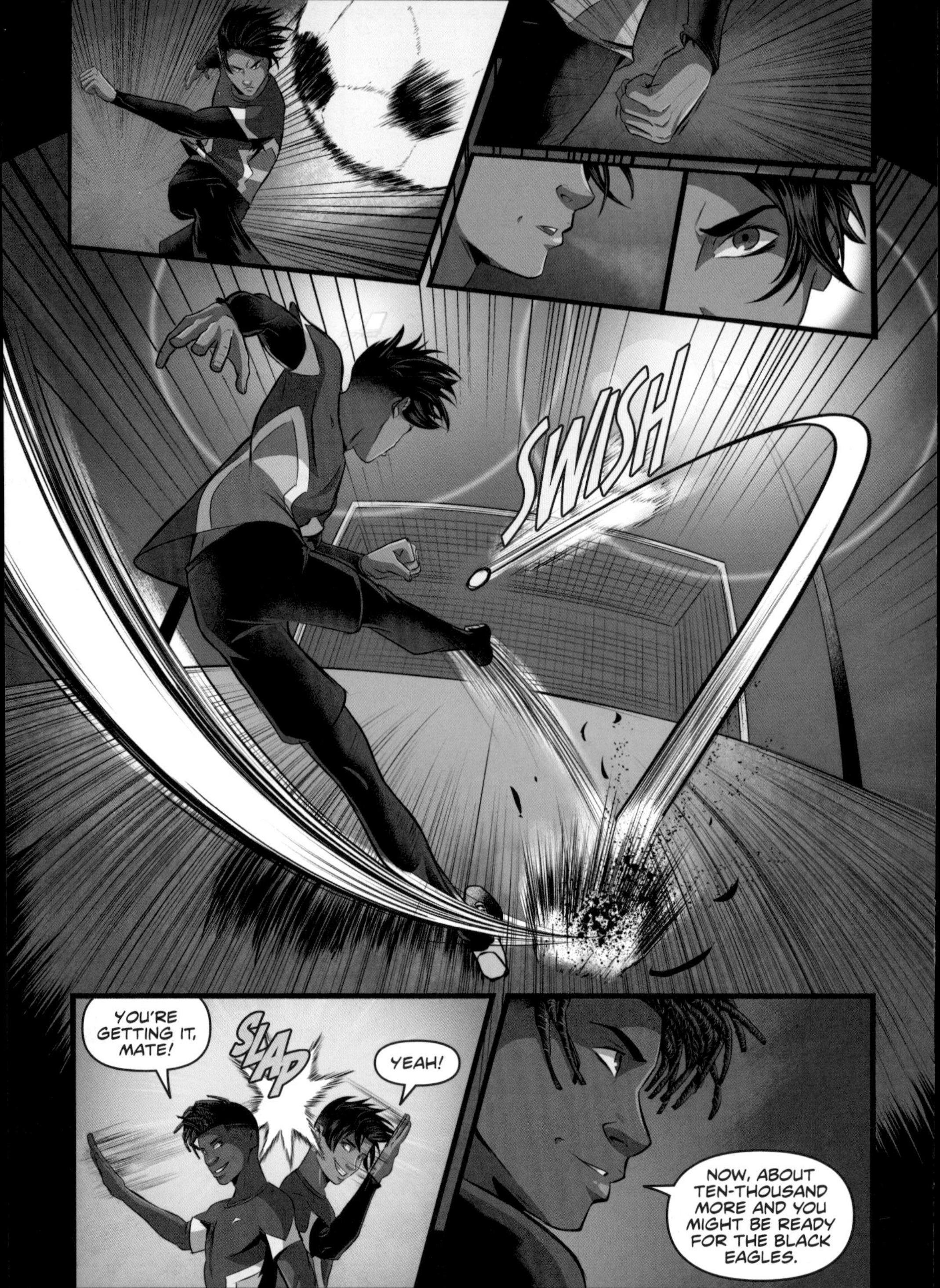
SWISH
YOU'RE GETTING IT, MATE!
SLAP
YEAH!
NOW, ABOUT TEN-THOUSAND MORE AND YOU MIGHT BE READY FOR THE BLACK EAGLES.

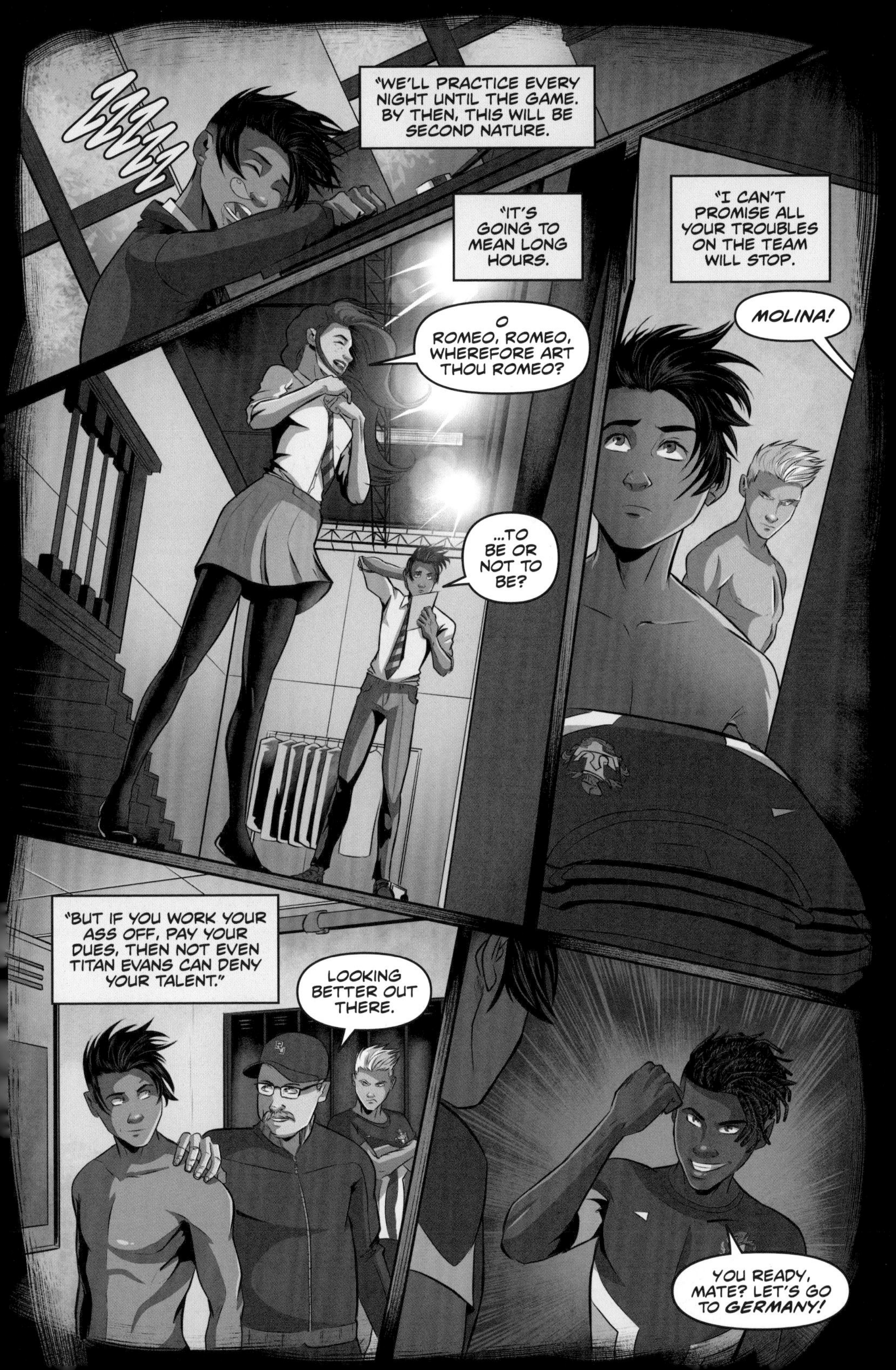

ZZZZZ
"WE'LL PRACTICE EVERY NIGHT UNTIL THE GAME. BY THEN, THIS WILL BE SECOND NATURE.
"IT'S GOING TO MEAN LONG HOURS.
O ROMEO, ROMEO, WHEREFORE ART THOU ROMEO?
...TO BE OR NOT TO BE?
"I CAN'T PROMISE ALL YOUR TROUBLES ON THE TEAM WILL STOP.
MOLINA!
"BUT IF YOU WORK YOUR ASS OFF, PAY YOUR DUES, THEN NOT EVEN TITAN EVANS CAN DENY YOUR TALENT."
LOOKING BETTER OUT THERE.
YOU READY, MATE? LET'S GO TO GERMANY!

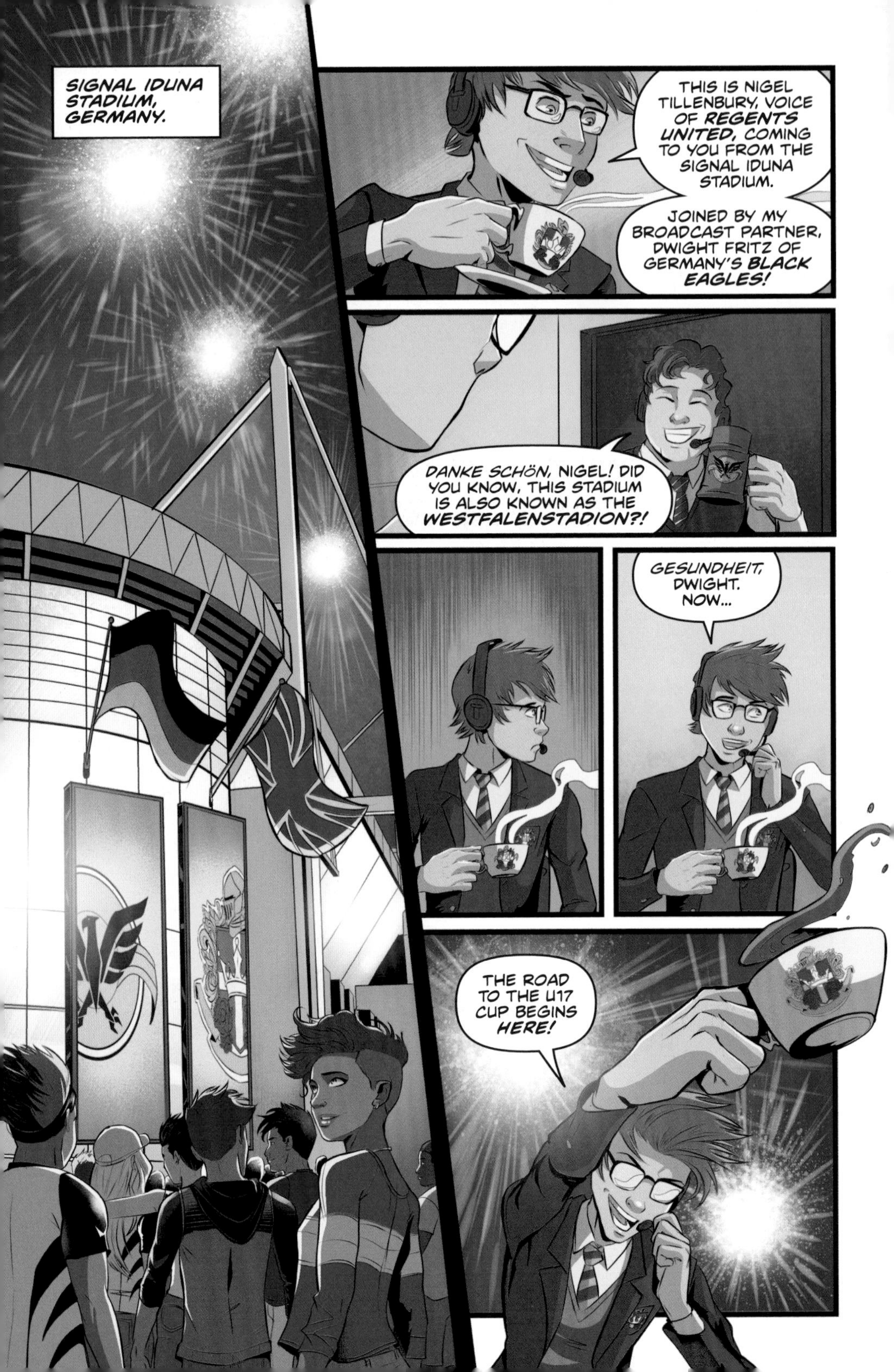
SIGNAL IDUNA STADIUM, GERMANY.
THIS IS NIGEL TILLENBURY, VOICE OF REGENTS UNITED, COMING TO YOU FROM THE SIGNAL IDUNA STADIUM.
JOINED BY MY BROADCAST PARTNER, DWIGHT FRITZ OF GERMANY'S BLACK EAGLES!
DANKE SCHÖN, NIGEL! DID YOU KNOW, THIS STADIUM IS ALSO KNOWN AS THE WESTFALENSTADION?!
GESUNDHEIT, DWIGHT. NOW...
THE ROAD TO THE U17 CUP BEGINS HERE!

THE EAGLES LOOK CONFIDENT ON THEIR HOME TURF, REGENTS UNITED WILL HAVE THEIR HANDS FULL.

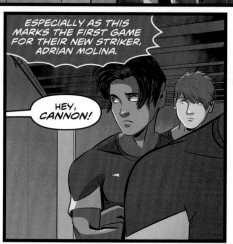

ESPECIALLY AS THIS MARKS THE FIRST GAME FOR THEIR NEW STRIKER, ADRIAN MOLINA.

HEY, CANNON!

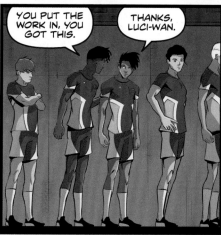

YOU PUT THE WORK IN, YOU GOT THIS.

THANKS, LUCI-WAN.

I CAN'T THANK YOU ENOUGH FOR THE HELP. IF COACH NAMES ANYONE CAPTAIN, IT SHOULD BE *YOU*.

AH, NO WAY MAN. I'M HERE TO PLAY--NOT *POLITIC*.

GOOD.

NICE TO SEE YOU KNOW YOUR PLACE ON THE TEAM, LUCY.

SPEAKING OF, ENJOY RIDING THE BENCH, NUGGET.

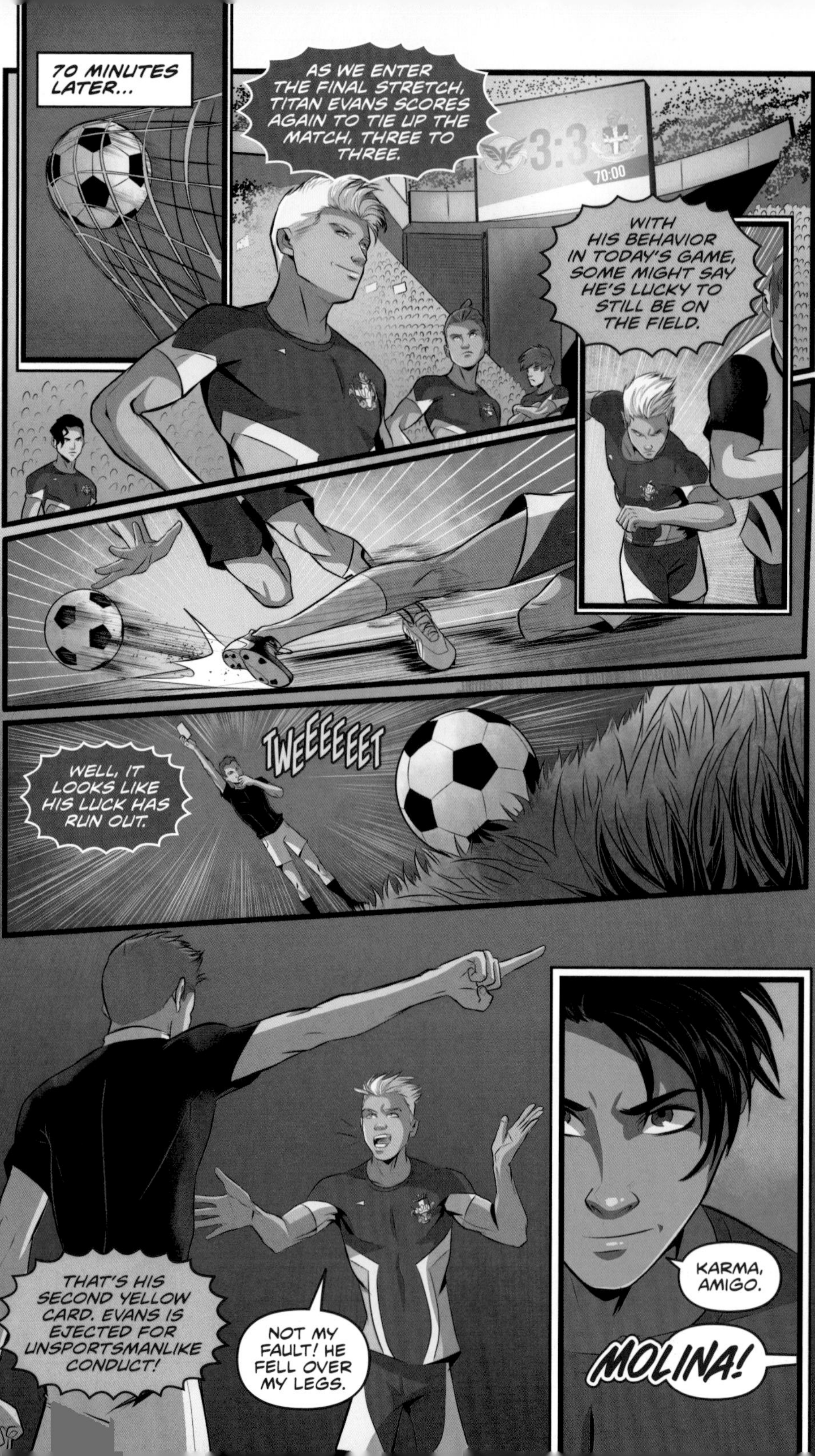
70 MINUTES LATER...
AS WE ENTER THE FINAL STRETCH, TITAN EVANS SCORES AGAIN TO TIE UP THE MATCH, THREE TO THREE.
3:3
70:00
WITH HIS BEHAVIOR IN TODAY'S GAME, SOME MIGHT SAY HE'S LUCKY TO STILL BE ON THE FIELD.
TWEEEEEET
WELL, IT LOOKS LIKE HIS LUCK HAS RUN OUT.
THAT'S HIS SECOND YELLOW CARD. EVANS IS EJECTED FOR UNSPORTSMANLIKE CONDUCT!
NOT MY FAULT! HE FELL OVER MY LEGS.
KARMA, AMIGO.
MOLINA!

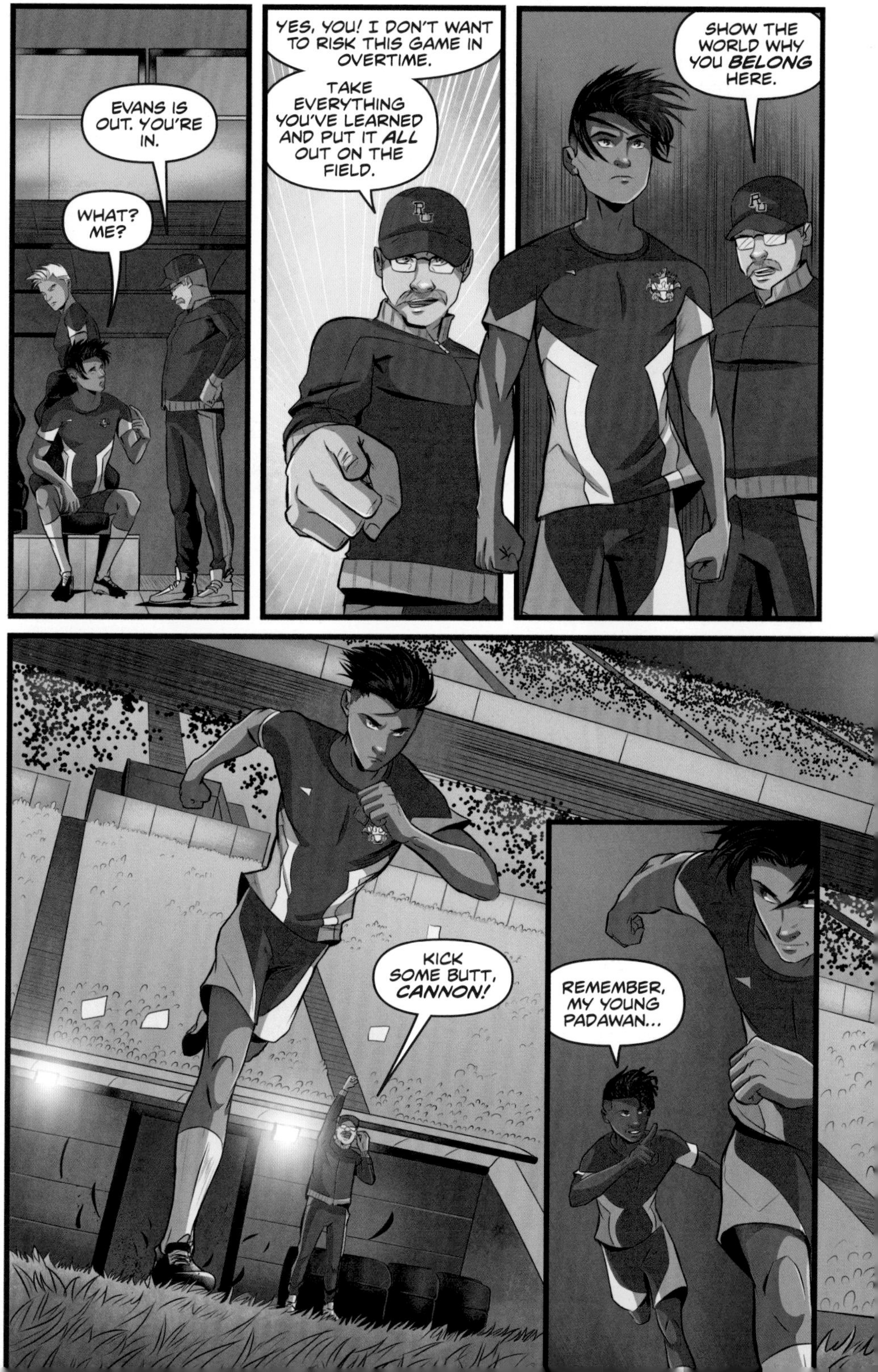
EVANS IS OUT. YOU'RE IN.
WHAT? ME?
YES, YOU! I DON'T WANT TO RISK THIS GAME IN OVERTIME.
TAKE EVERYTHING YOU'VE LEARNED AND PUT IT ALL OUT ON THE FIELD.
SHOW THE WORLD WHY YOU BELONG HERE.
KICK SOME BUTT, CANNON!
REMEMBER, MY YOUNG PADAWAN...

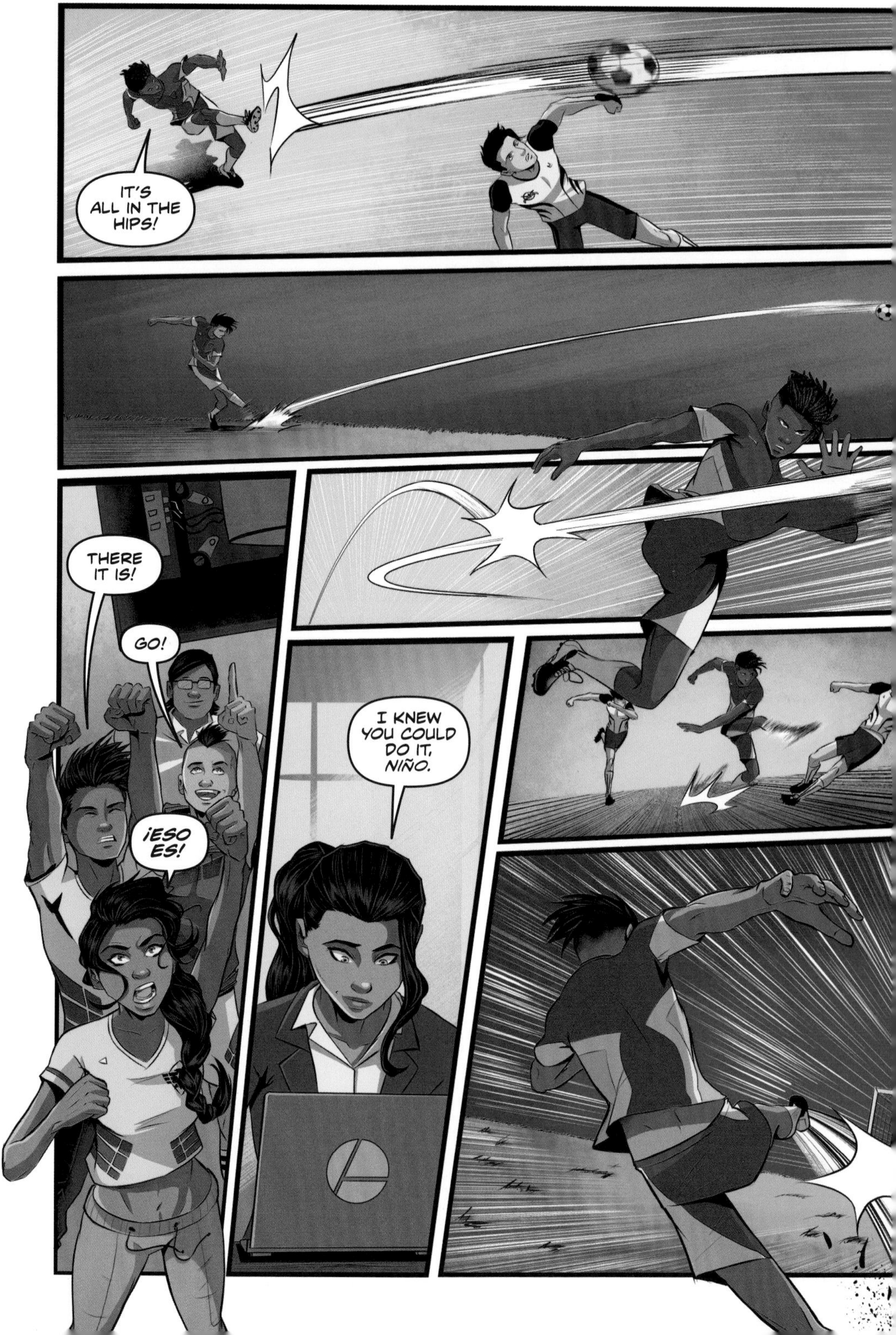
IT'S ALL IN THE HIPS!
THERE IT IS!
GO!
¡ESO ES!
I KNEW YOU COULD DO IT, NIÑO.

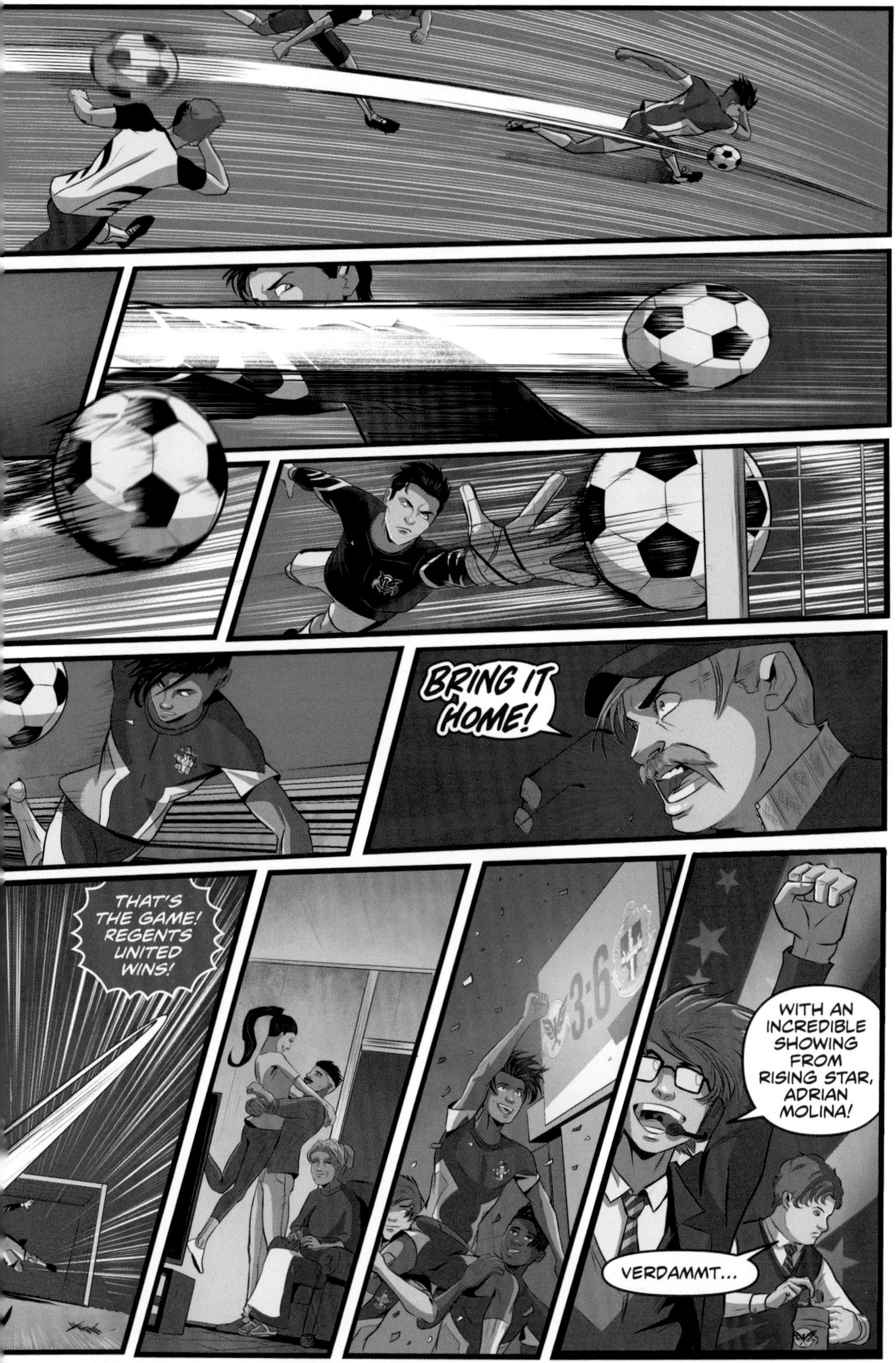
BRING IT HOME!
THAT'S THE GAME! REGENTS UNITED WINS!
3:6
WITH AN INCREDIBLE SHOWING FROM RISING STAR, ADRIAN MOLINA!
VERDAMMT...

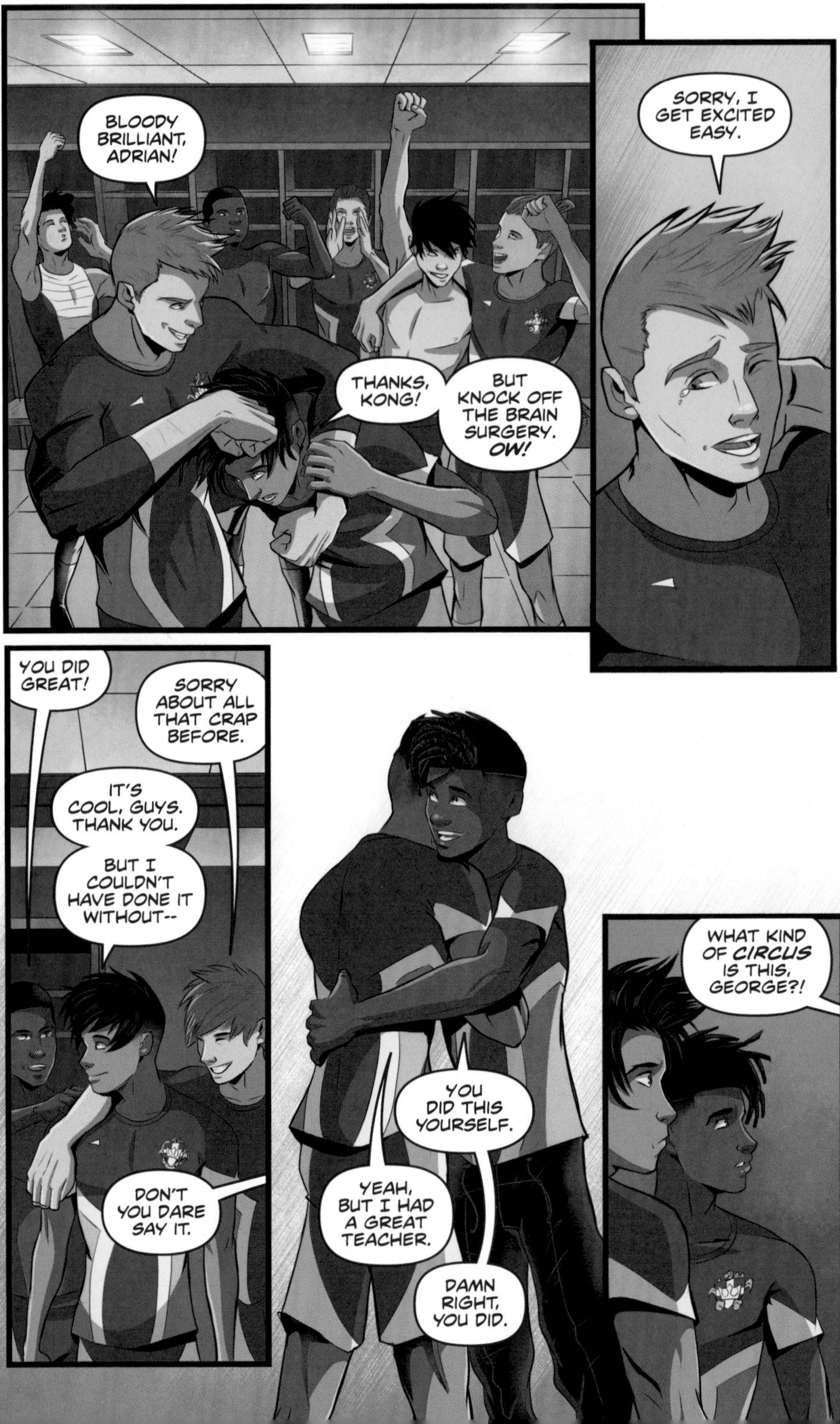
BLOODY BRILLIANT, ADRIAN!
THANKS, KONG!
BUT KNOCK OFF THE BRAIN SURGERY. *OW!*
SORRY, I GET EXCITED EASY.
YOU DID GREAT!
SORRY ABOUT ALL THAT CRAP BEFORE.
IT'S COOL, GUYS. THANK YOU.
BUT I COULDN'T HAVE DONE IT WITHOUT--
DON'T YOU DARE SAY IT.
YOU DID THIS YOURSELF.
YEAH, BUT I HAD A GREAT TEACHER.
DAMN RIGHT, YOU DID.
WHAT KIND OF *CIRCUS* IS THIS, GEORGE?!

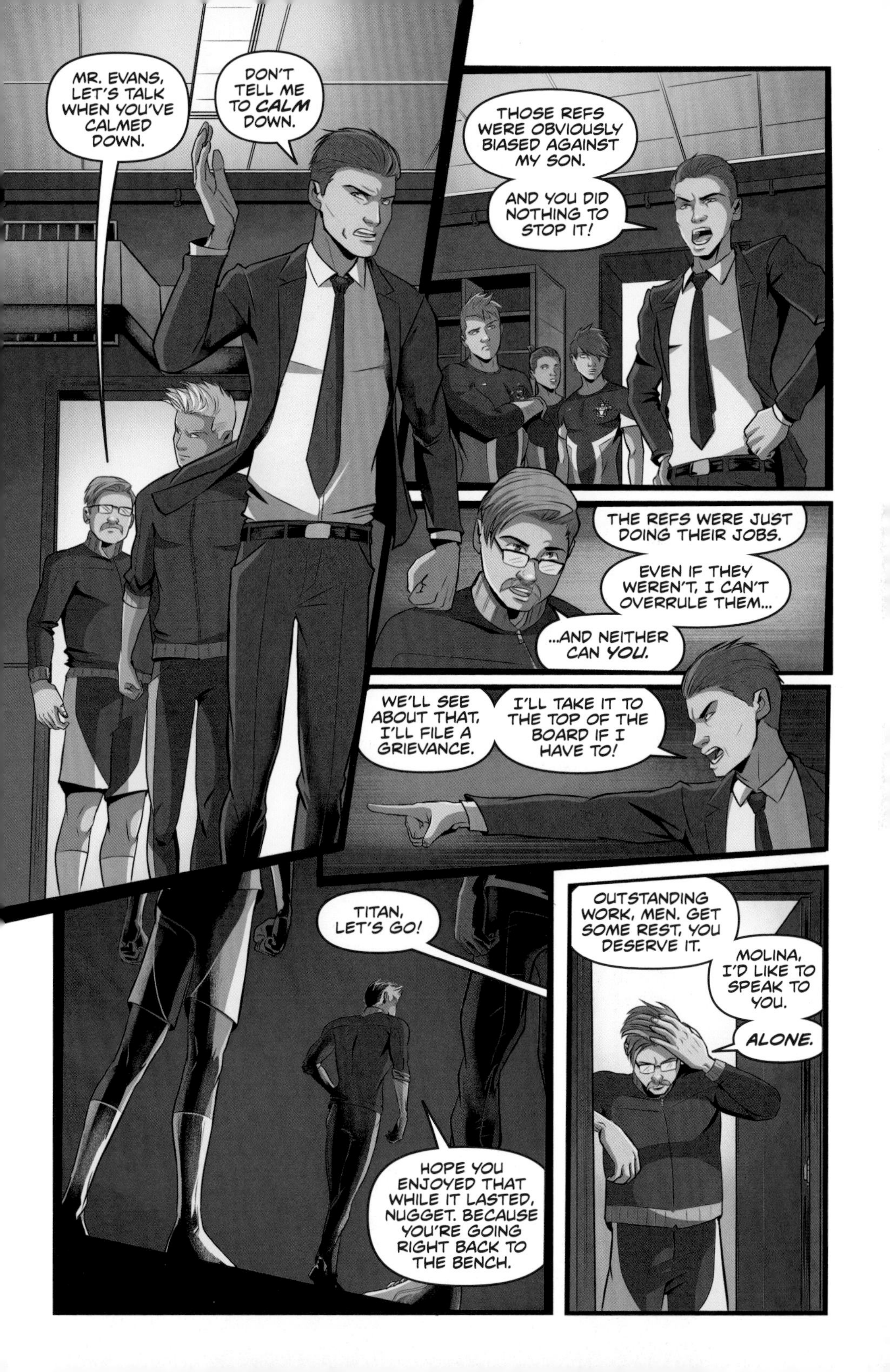
MR. EVANS, LET'S TALK WHEN YOU'VE CALMED DOWN.
DON'T TELL ME TO *CALM* DOWN.
THOSE REFS WERE OBVIOUSLY BIASED AGAINST MY SON.
AND YOU DID NOTHING TO STOP IT!
THE REFS WERE JUST DOING THEIR JOBS.
EVEN IF THEY WEREN'T, I CAN'T OVERRULE THEM...
...AND NEITHER CAN *YOU*.
WE'LL SEE ABOUT THAT, I'LL FILE A GRIEVANCE.
I'LL TAKE IT TO THE TOP OF THE BOARD IF I HAVE TO!
TITAN, LET'S GO!
HOPE YOU ENJOYED THAT WHILE IT LASTED, NUGGET. BECAUSE YOU'RE GOING RIGHT BACK TO THE BENCH.
OUTSTANDING WORK, MEN. GET SOME REST, YOU DESERVE IT.
MOLINA, I'D LIKE TO SPEAK TO YOU.
ALONE.

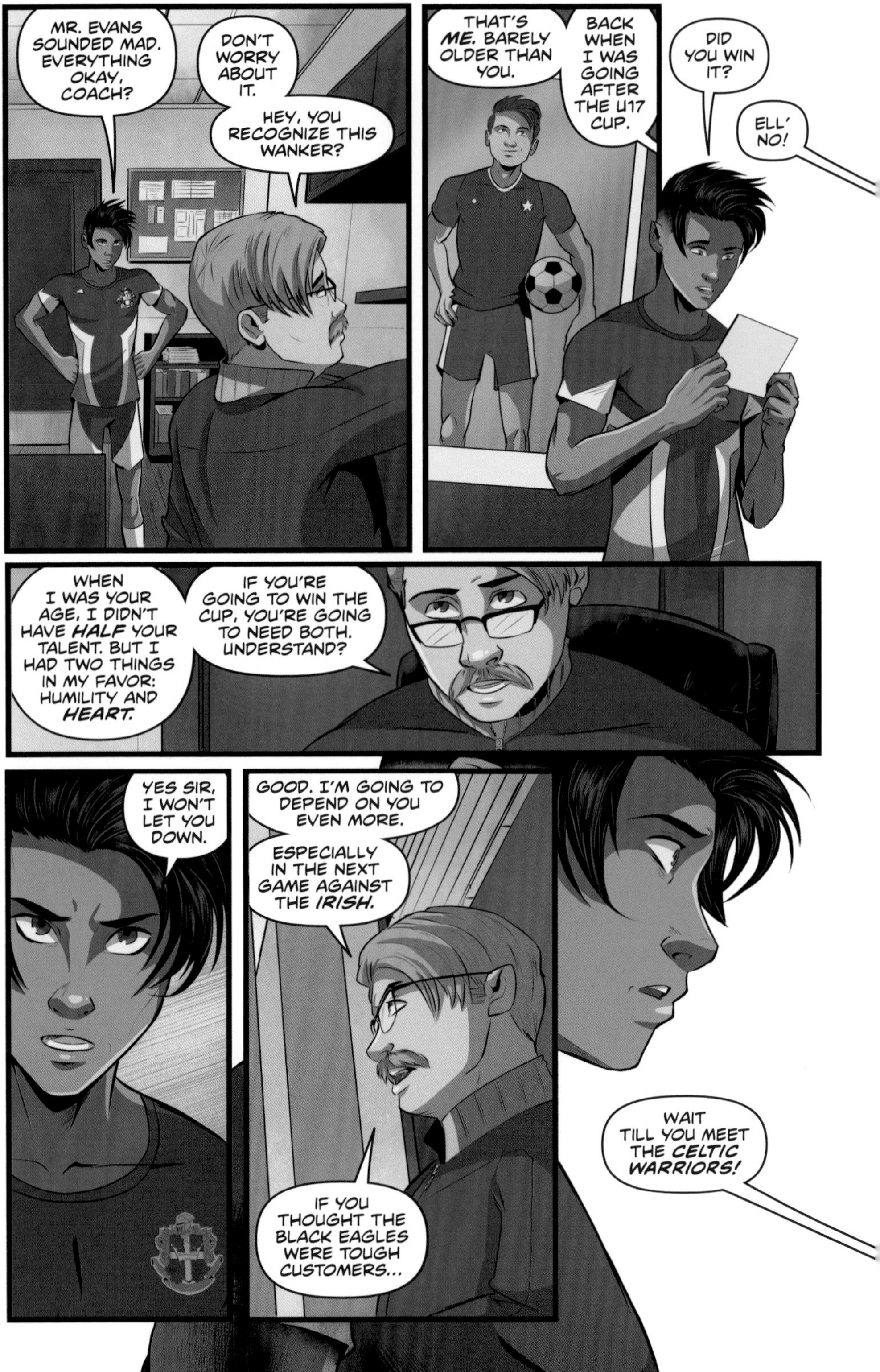
MR. EVANS SOUNDED MAD. EVERYTHING OKAY, COACH?
DON'T WORRY ABOUT IT.
HEY, YOU RECOGNIZE THIS WANKER?
THAT'S ME. BARELY OLDER THAN YOU.
BACK WHEN I WAS GOING AFTER THE U17 CUP.
DID YOU WIN IT?
ELL' NO!
WHEN I WAS YOUR AGE, I DIDN'T HAVE HALF YOUR TALENT. BUT I HAD TWO THINGS IN MY FAVOR: HUMILITY AND HEART.
IF YOU'RE GOING TO WIN THE CUP, YOU'RE GOING TO NEED BOTH. UNDERSTAND?
YES SIR, I WON'T LET YOU DOWN.
GOOD. I'M GOING TO DEPEND ON YOU EVEN MORE.
ESPECIALLY IN THE NEXT GAME AGAINST THE IRISH.
IF YOU THOUGHT THE BLACK EAGLES WERE TOUGH CUSTOMERS...
WAIT TILL YOU MEET THE CELTIC WARRIORS!

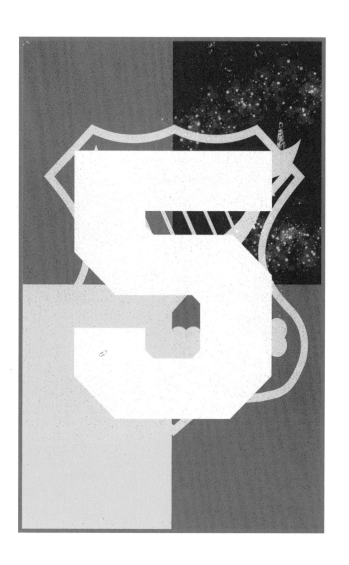

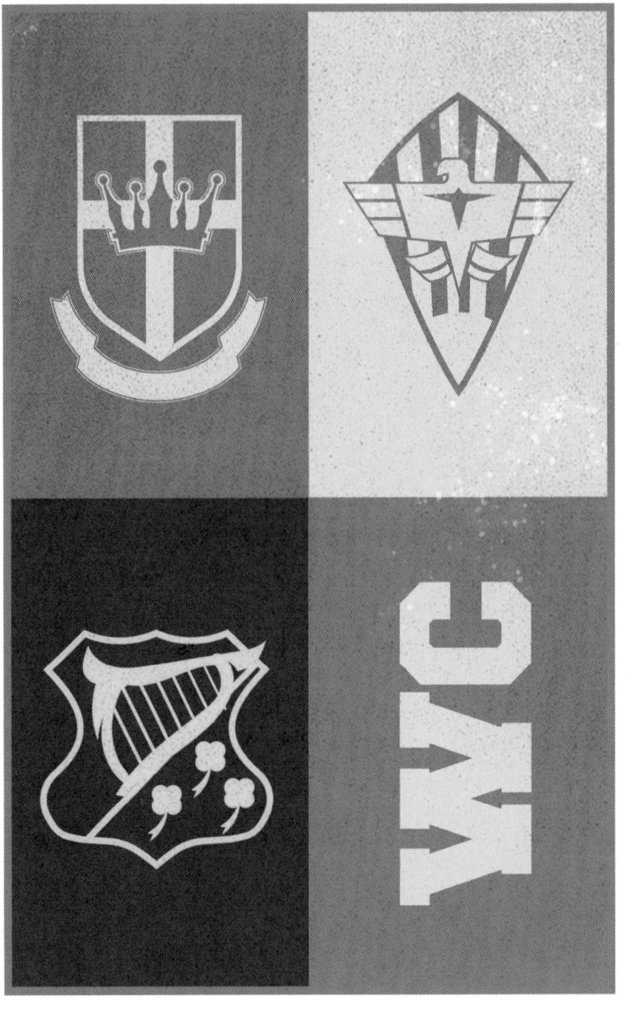
WC

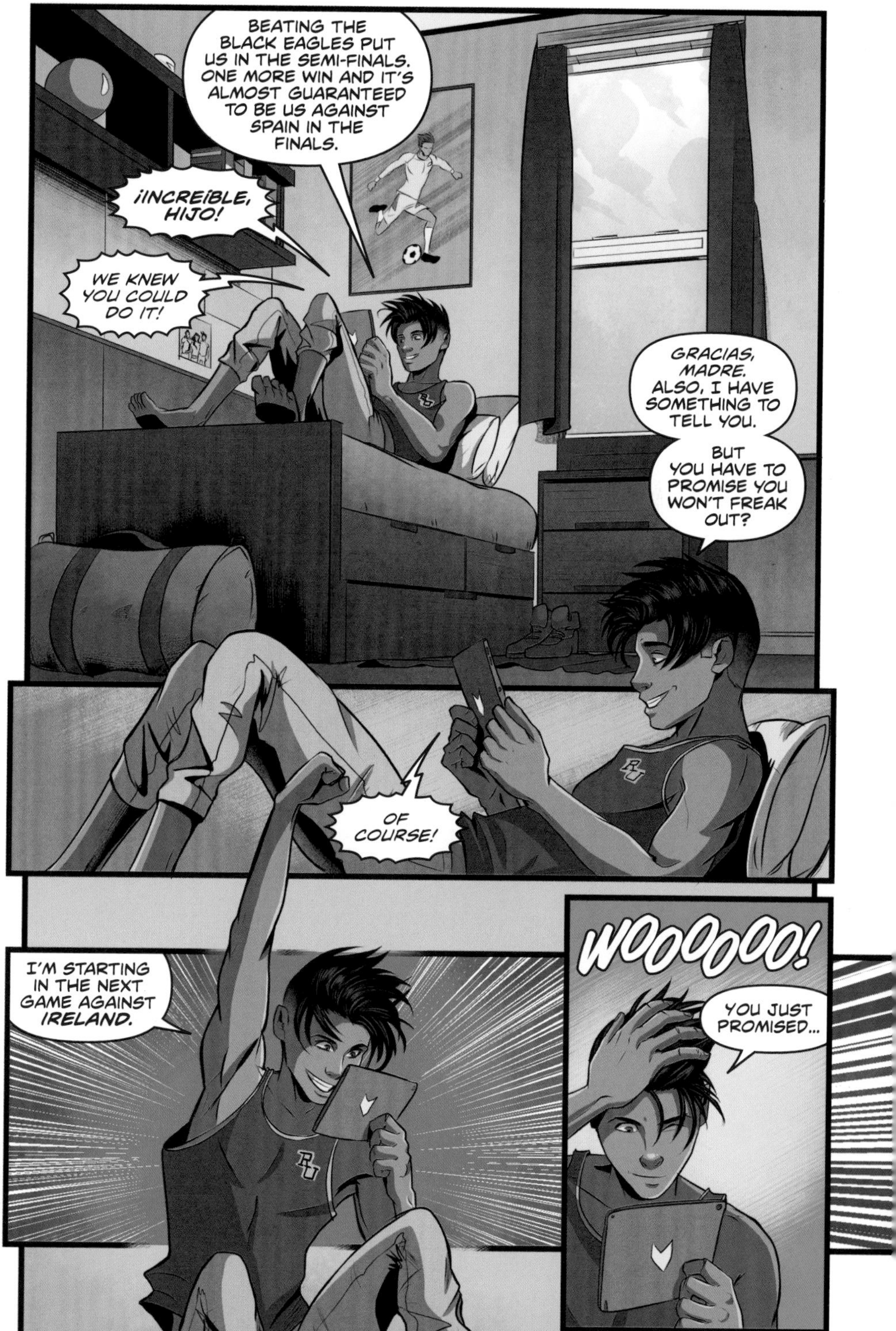
BEATING THE BLACK EAGLES PUT US IN THE SEMI-FINALS. ONE MORE WIN AND IT'S ALMOST GUARANTEED TO BE US AGAINST SPAIN IN THE FINALS.
¡INCREÍBLE, HIJO!
WE KNEW YOU COULD DO IT!
GRACIAS, MADRE. ALSO, I HAVE SOMETHING TO TELL YOU.
BUT YOU HAVE TO PROMISE YOU WON'T FREAK OUT?
OF COURSE!
I'M STARTING IN THE NEXT GAME AGAINST IRELAND.
WOOOOOOO!
YOU JUST PROMISED...

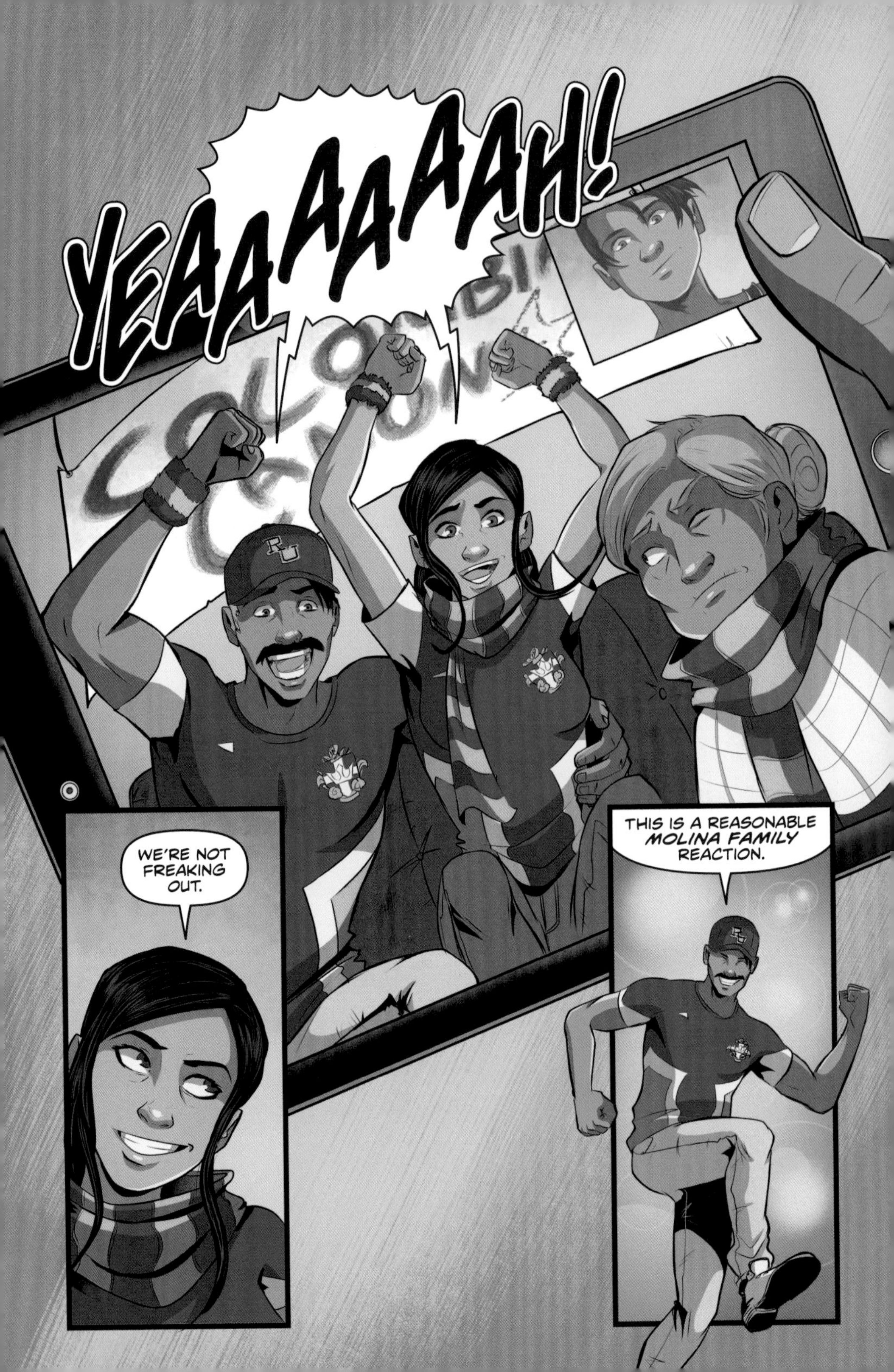
YEAAAAAAH!
WE'RE NOT FREAKING OUT.
THIS IS A REASONABLE *MOLINA FAMILY* REACTION.

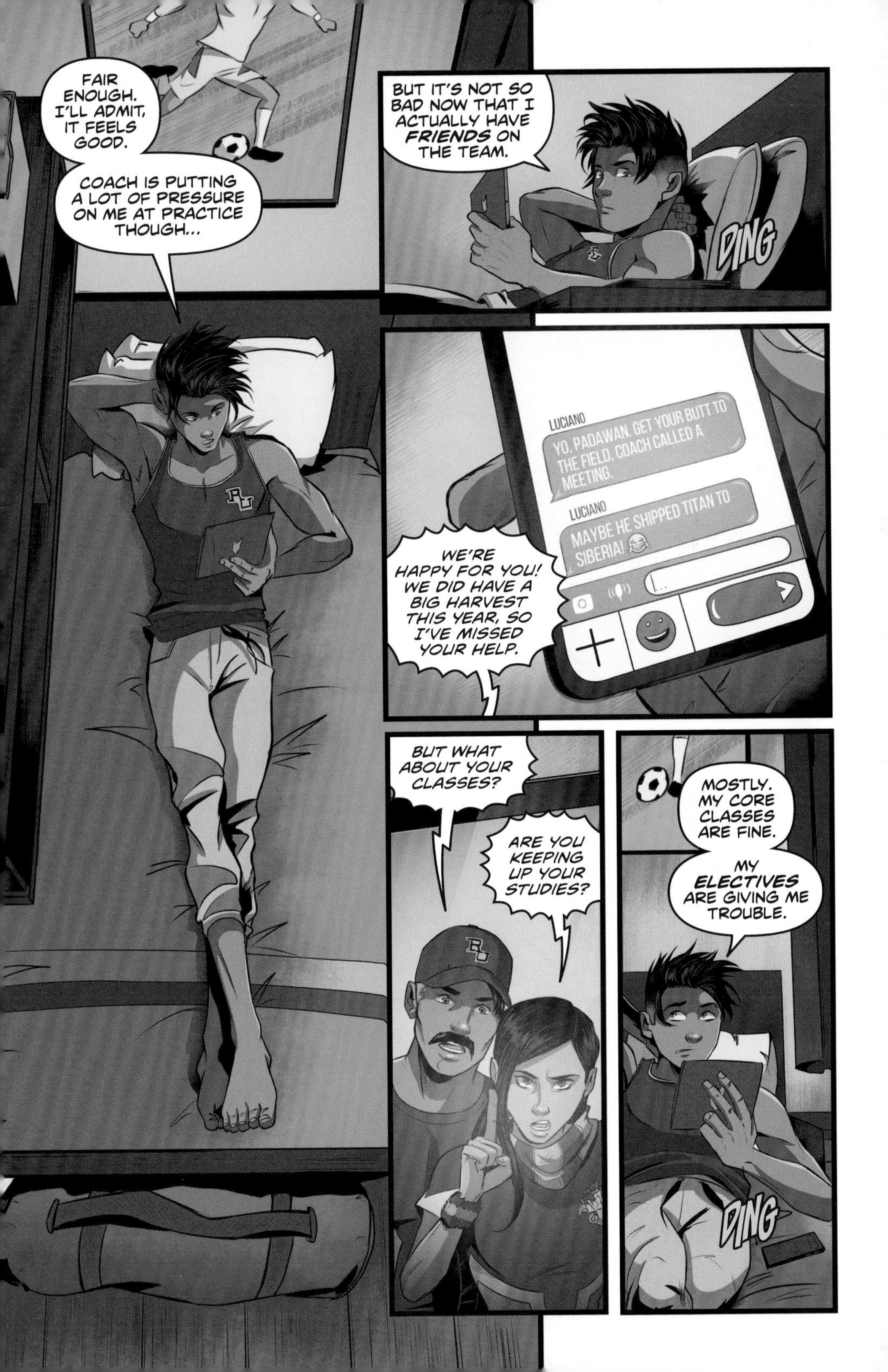
FAIR ENOUGH. I'LL ADMIT, IT FEELS GOOD.
COACH IS PUTTING A LOT OF PRESSURE ON ME AT PRACTICE THOUGH...
BUT IT'S NOT SO BAD NOW THAT I ACTUALLY HAVE FRIENDS ON THE TEAM.
DING
LUCIANO
YO, PADAWAN. GET YOUR BUTT TO THE FIELD, COACH CALLED A MEETING.
LUCIANO
MAYBE HE SHIPPED TITAN TO SIBERIA! 😂
WE'RE HAPPY FOR YOU! WE DID HAVE A BIG HARVEST THIS YEAR, SO I'VE MISSED YOUR HELP.
BUT WHAT ABOUT YOUR CLASSES?
ARE YOU KEEPING UP YOUR STUDIES?
MOSTLY. MY CORE CLASSES ARE FINE.
MY ELECTIVES ARE GIVING ME TROUBLE.
DING

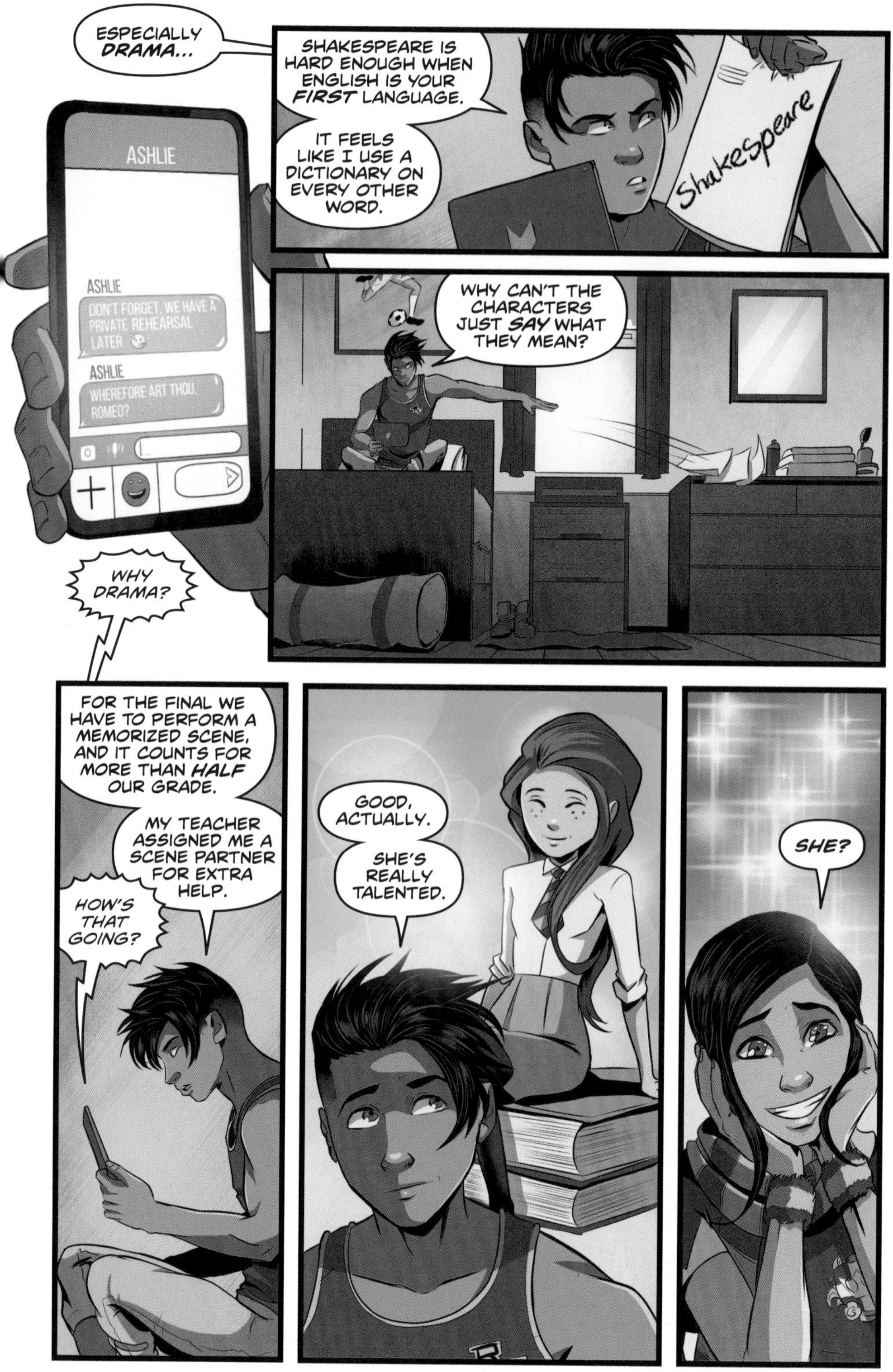
ESPECIALLY DRAMA...
SHAKESPEARE IS HARD ENOUGH WHEN ENGLISH IS YOUR FIRST LANGUAGE.
IT FEELS LIKE I USE A DICTIONARY ON EVERY OTHER WORD.
Shakespeare
ASHLIE
ASHLIE
DON'T FORGET, WE HAVE A PRIVATE REHEARSAL LATER
ASHLIE
WHEREFORE ART THOU, ROMEO?
WHY CAN'T THE CHARACTERS JUST SAY WHAT THEY MEAN?
WHY DRAMA?
FOR THE FINAL WE HAVE TO PERFORM A MEMORIZED SCENE, AND IT COUNTS FOR MORE THAN HALF OUR GRADE.
MY TEACHER ASSIGNED ME A SCENE PARTNER FOR EXTRA HELP.
HOW'S THAT GOING?
GOOD, ACTUALLY.
SHE'S REALLY TALENTED.
SHE?

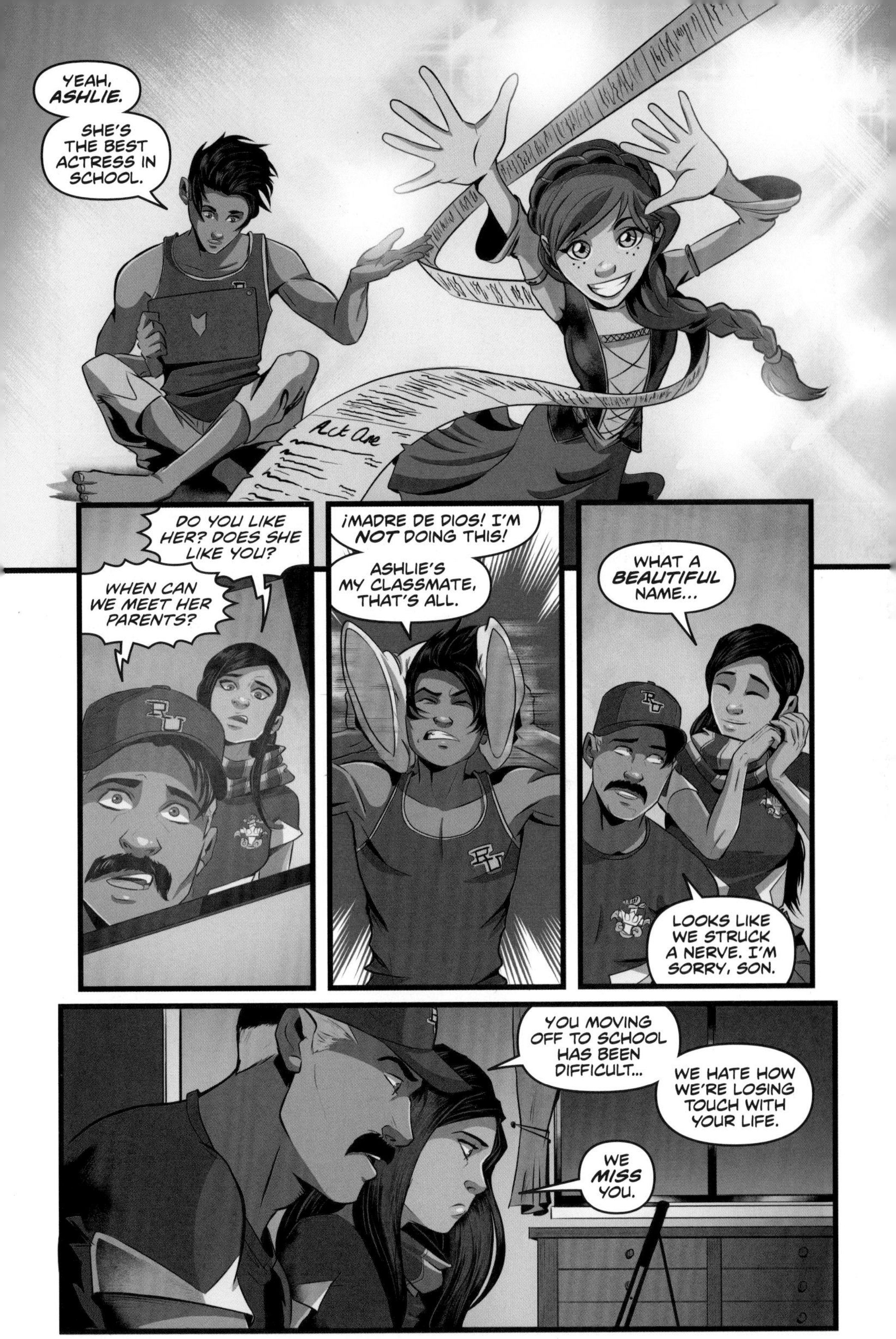
YEAH, ASHLIE.
SHE'S THE BEST ACTRESS IN SCHOOL.
Act One
DO YOU LIKE HER? DOES SHE LIKE YOU?
WHEN CAN WE MEET HER PARENTS?
¡MADRE DE DIOS! I'M NOT DOING THIS!
ASHLIE'S MY CLASSMATE, THAT'S ALL.
WHAT A BEAUTIFUL NAME...
LOOKS LIKE WE STRUCK A NERVE. I'M SORRY, SON.
YOU MOVING OFF TO SCHOOL HAS BEEN DIFFICULT...
WE HATE HOW WE'RE LOSING TOUCH WITH YOUR LIFE.
WE MISS YOU.

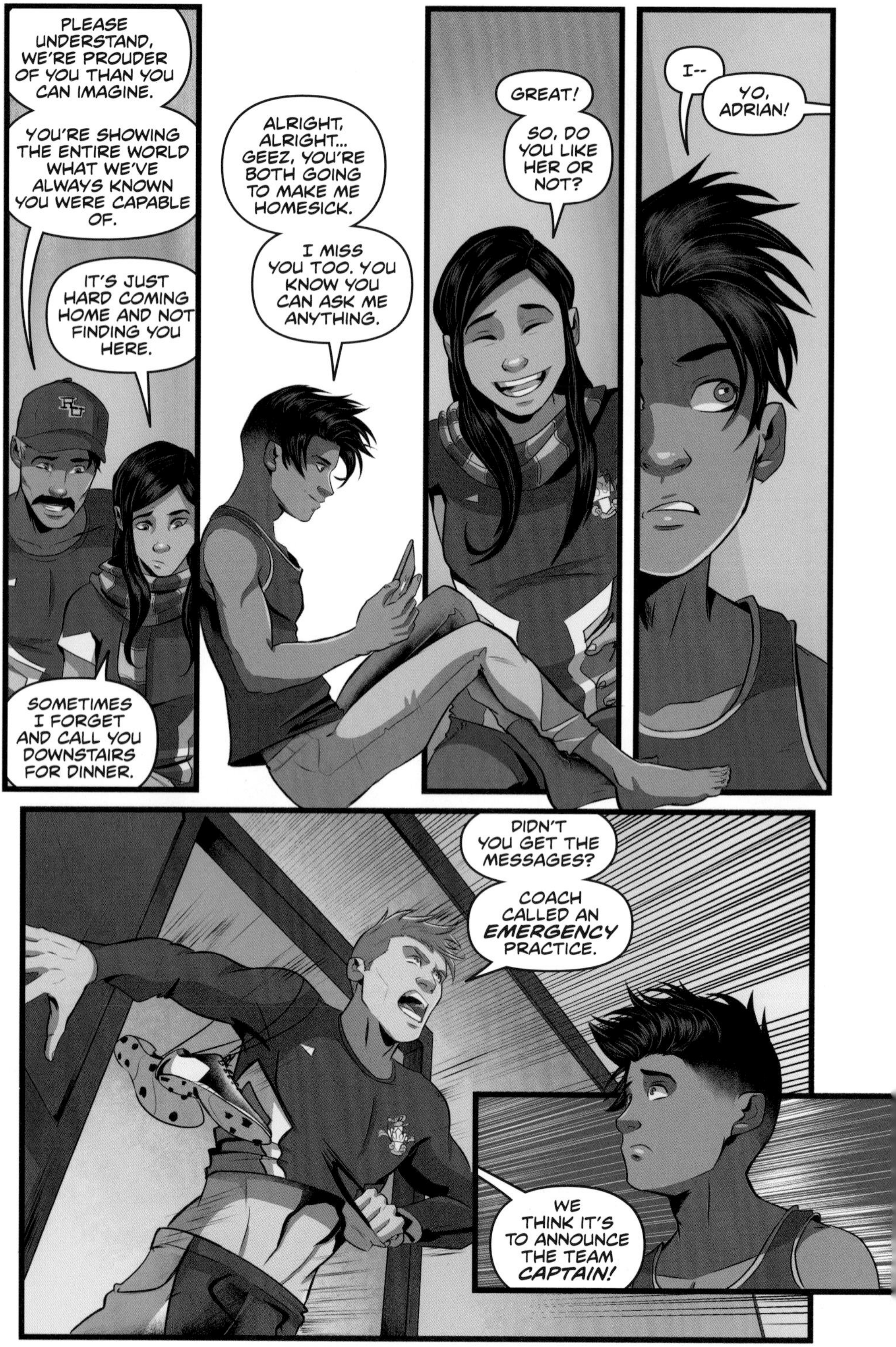
PLEASE UNDERSTAND, WE'RE PROUDER OF YOU THAN YOU CAN IMAGINE.
YOU'RE SHOWING THE ENTIRE WORLD WHAT WE'VE ALWAYS KNOWN YOU WERE CAPABLE OF.
IT'S JUST HARD COMING HOME AND NOT FINDING YOU HERE.
SOMETIMES I FORGET AND CALL YOU DOWNSTAIRS FOR DINNER.
ALRIGHT, ALRIGHT... GEEZ, YOU'RE BOTH GOING TO MAKE ME HOMESICK.
I MISS YOU TOO. YOU KNOW YOU CAN ASK ME ANYTHING.
GREAT!
SO, DO YOU LIKE HER OR NOT?
I--
YO, ADRIAN!
DIDN'T YOU GET THE MESSAGES?
COACH CALLED AN *EMERGENCY* PRACTICE.
WE THINK IT'S TO ANNOUNCE THE TEAM *CAPTAIN!*

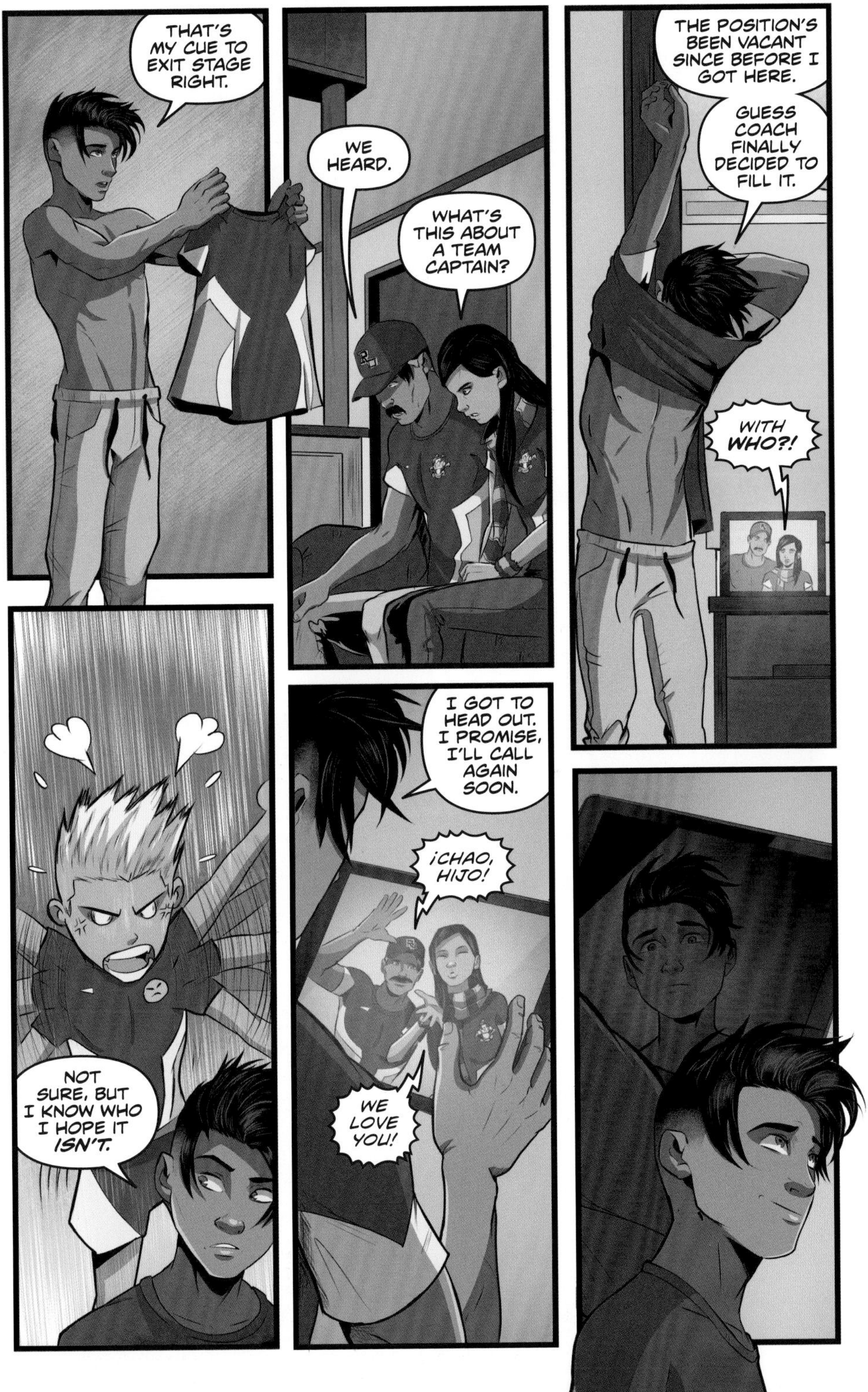
THAT'S MY CUE TO EXIT STAGE RIGHT.
WE HEARD.
WHAT'S THIS ABOUT A TEAM CAPTAIN?
THE POSITION'S BEEN VACANT SINCE BEFORE I GOT HERE.
GUESS COACH FINALLY DECIDED TO FILL IT.
WITH *WHO?!*
NOT SURE, BUT I KNOW WHO I HOPE IT *ISN'T.*
I GOT TO HEAD OUT. I PROMISE, I'LL CALL AGAIN SOON.
¡CHAO, HIJO!
WE LOVE YOU!

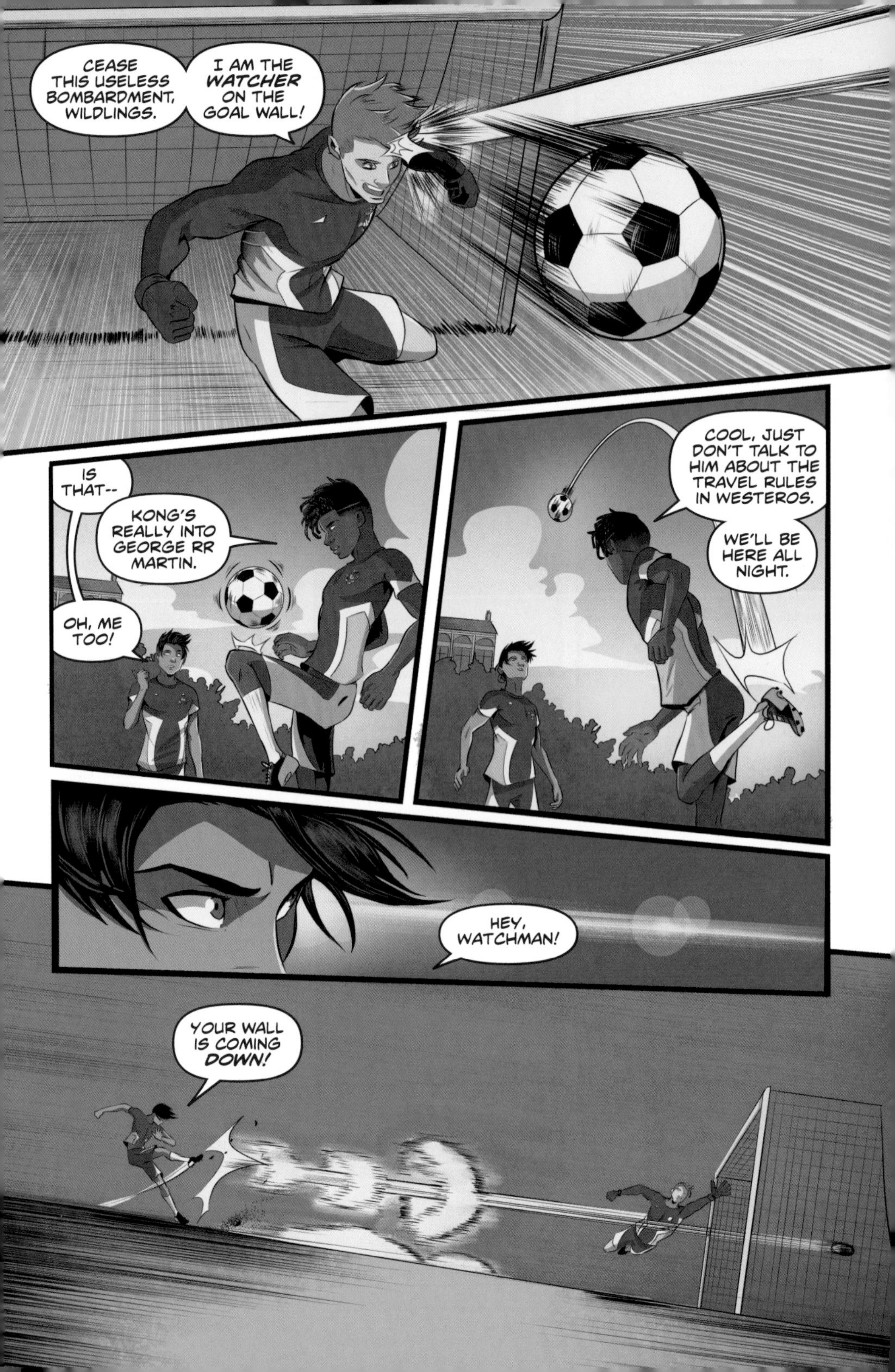
CEASE THIS USELESS BOMBARDMENT, WILDLINGS.
I AM THE *WATCHER* ON THE GOAL WALL!
IS THAT--
KONG'S REALLY INTO GEORGE RR MARTIN.
OH, ME TOO!
COOL, JUST DON'T TALK TO HIM ABOUT THE TRAVEL RULES IN WESTEROS.
WE'LL BE HERE ALL NIGHT.
HEY, WATCHMAN!
YOUR WALL IS COMING *DOWN!*

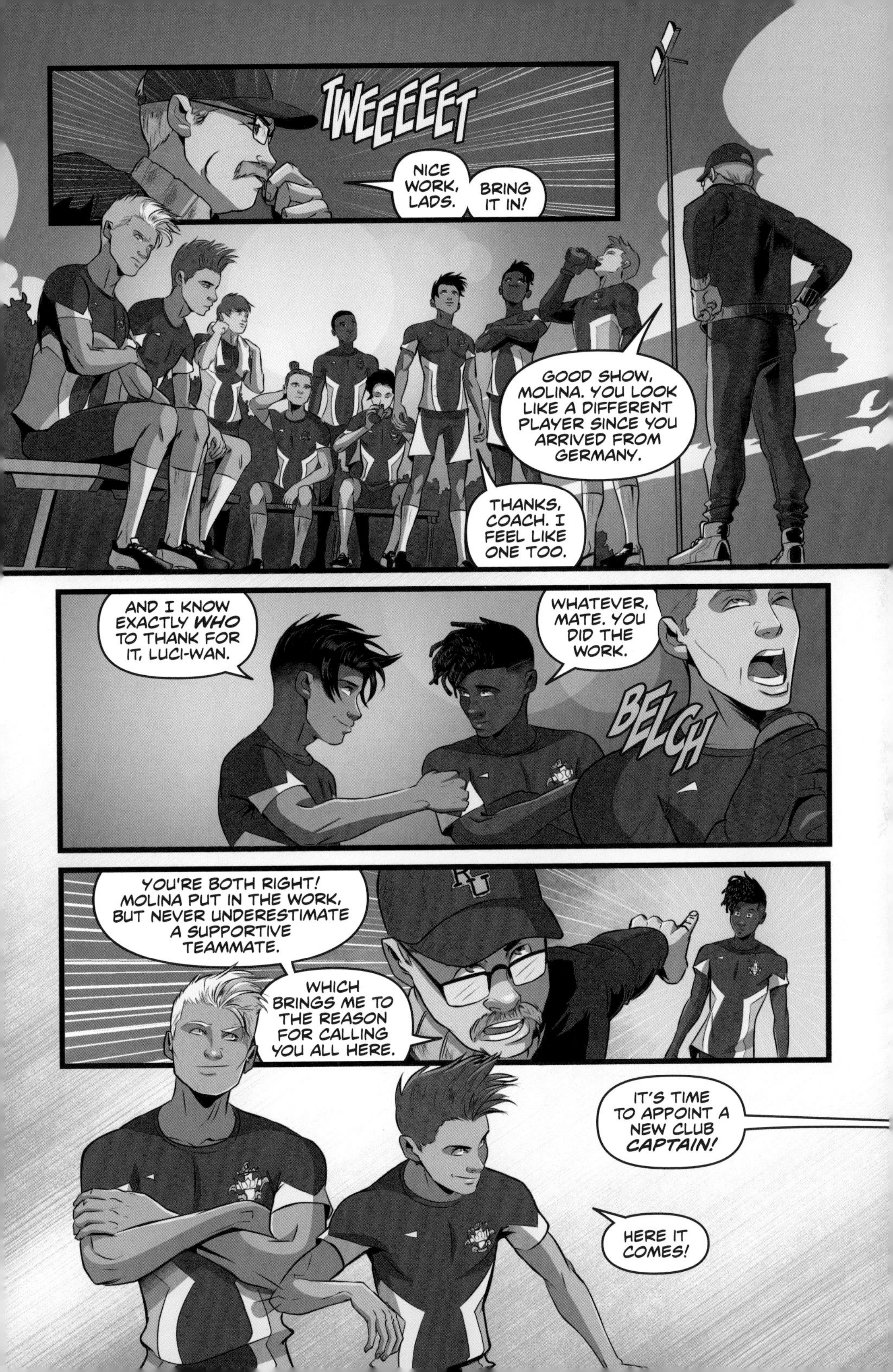
TWEEEEET
NICE WORK, LADS.
BRING IT IN!
GOOD SHOW, MOLINA. YOU LOOK LIKE A DIFFERENT PLAYER SINCE YOU ARRIVED FROM GERMANY.
THANKS, COACH. I FEEL LIKE ONE TOO.
AND I KNOW EXACTLY **WHO** TO THANK FOR IT, LUCI-WAN.
WHATEVER, MATE. YOU DID THE WORK.
BELCH
YOU'RE BOTH RIGHT! MOLINA PUT IN THE WORK, BUT NEVER UNDERESTIMATE A SUPPORTIVE TEAMMATE.
WHICH BRINGS ME TO THE REASON FOR CALLING YOU ALL HERE.
IT'S TIME TO APPOINT A NEW CLUB ***CAPTAIN!***
HERE IT COMES!

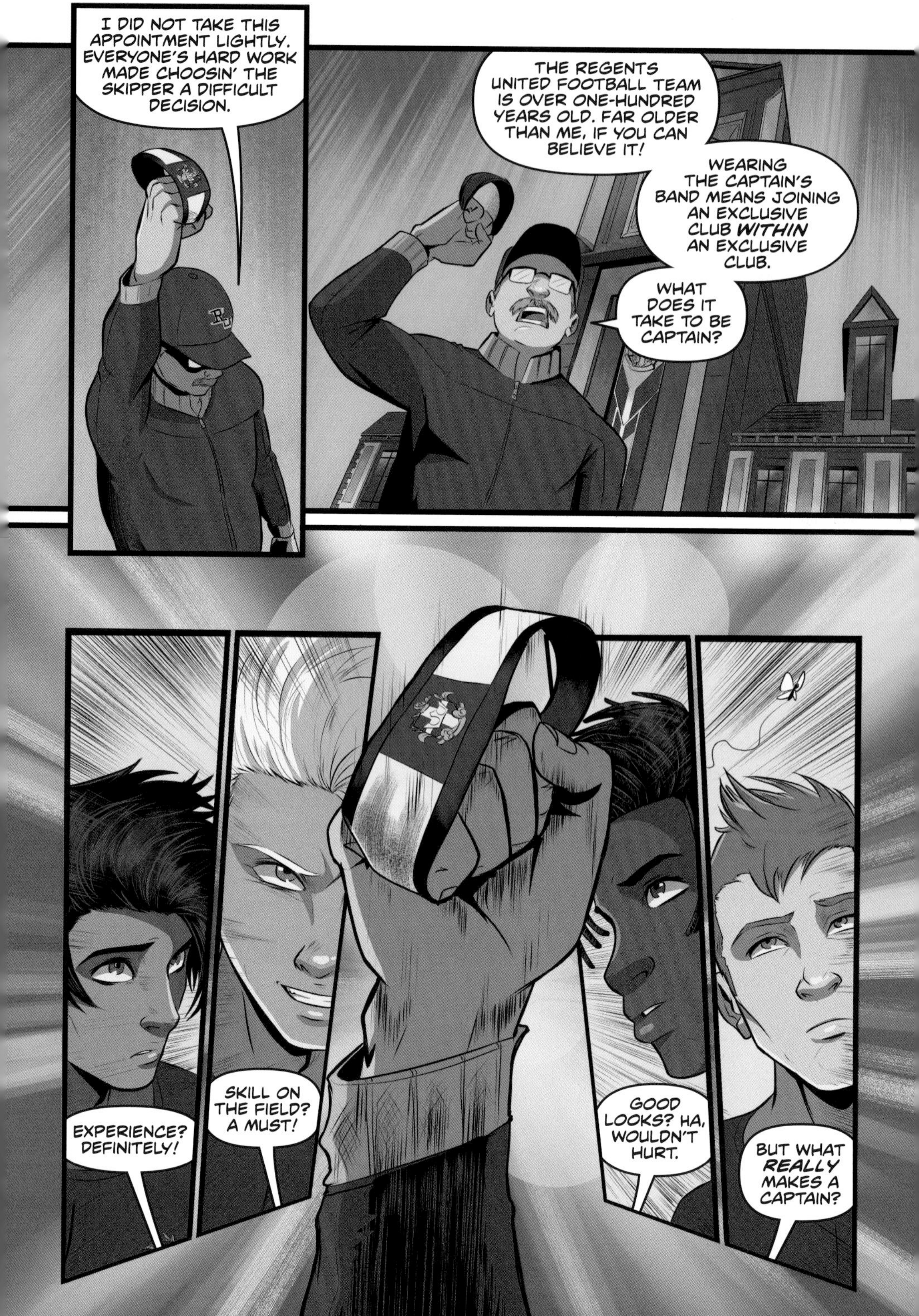
I DID NOT TAKE THIS APPOINTMENT LIGHTLY. EVERYONE'S HARD WORK MADE CHOOSIN' THE SKIPPER A DIFFICULT DECISION.
THE REGENTS UNITED FOOTBALL TEAM IS OVER ONE-HUNDRED YEARS OLD. FAR OLDER THAN ME, IF YOU CAN BELIEVE IT!
WEARING THE CAPTAIN'S BAND MEANS JOINING AN EXCLUSIVE CLUB *WITHIN* AN EXCLUSIVE CLUB.
WHAT DOES IT TAKE TO BE CAPTAIN?
EXPERIENCE? DEFINITELY!
SKILL ON THE FIELD? A MUST!
GOOD LOOKS? HA, WOULDN'T HURT.
BUT WHAT *REALLY* MAKES A CAPTAIN?

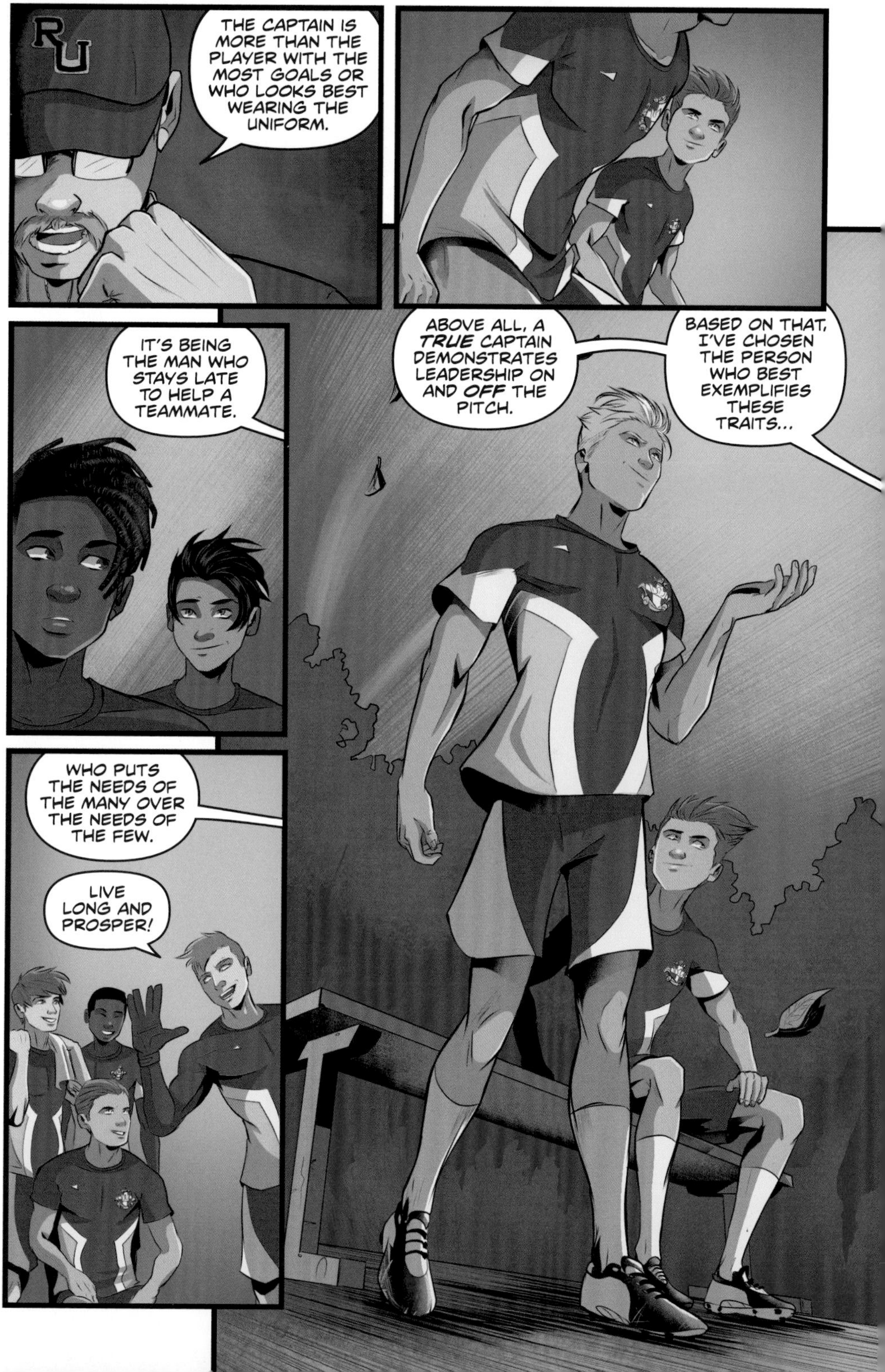
THE CAPTAIN IS MORE THAN THE PLAYER WITH THE MOST GOALS OR WHO LOOKS BEST WEARING THE UNIFORM.
IT'S BEING THE MAN WHO STAYS LATE TO HELP A TEAMMATE.
WHO PUTS THE NEEDS OF THE MANY OVER THE NEEDS OF THE FEW.
LIVE LONG AND PROSPER!
ABOVE ALL, A TRUE CAPTAIN DEMONSTRATES LEADERSHIP ON AND OFF THE PITCH.
BASED ON THAT, I'VE CHOSEN THE PERSON WHO BEST EXEMPLIFIES THESE TRAITS...

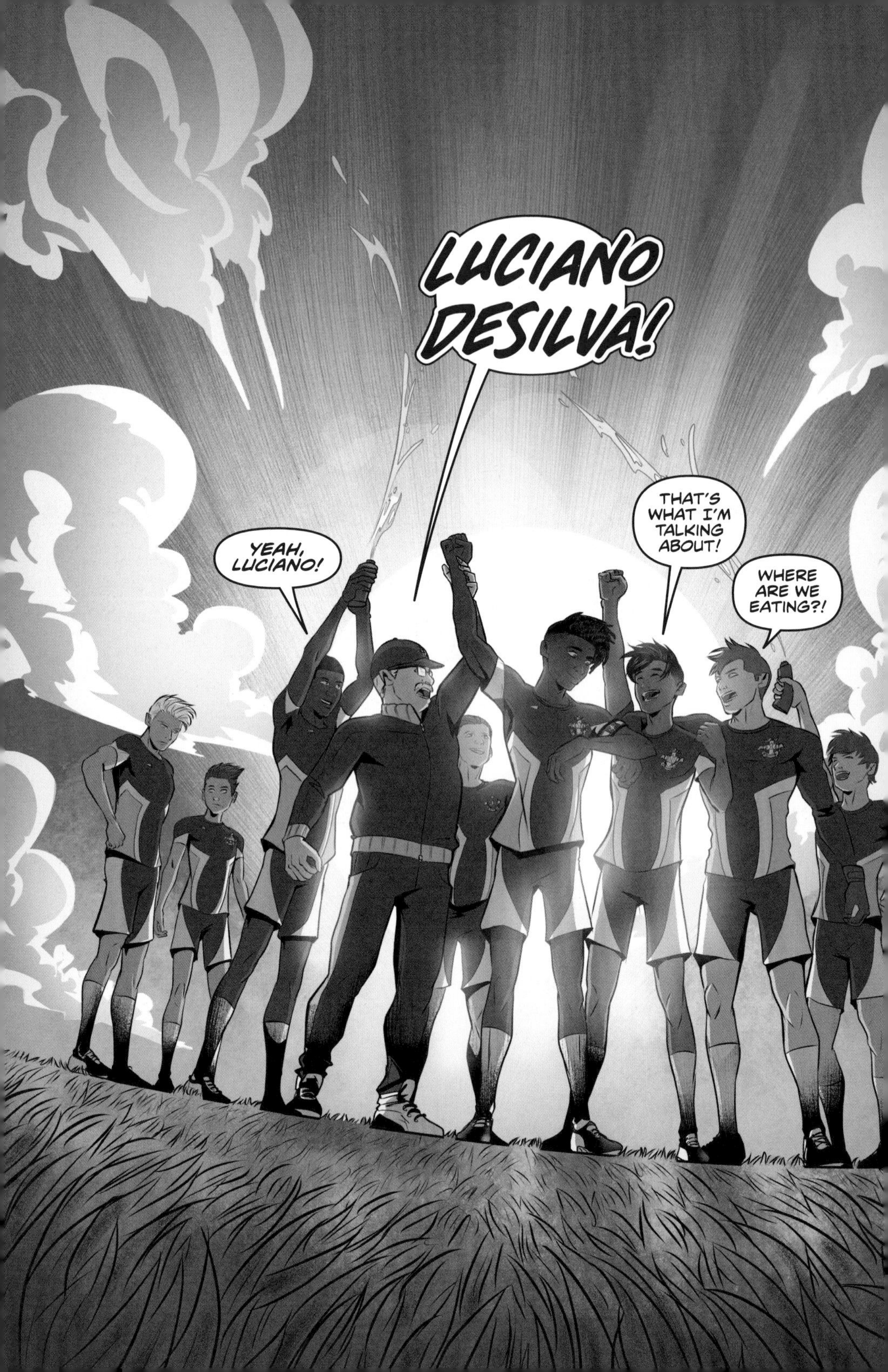
LUCIANO DESILVA!
YEAH, LUCIANO!
THAT'S WHAT I'M TALKING ABOUT!
WHERE ARE WE EATING?!

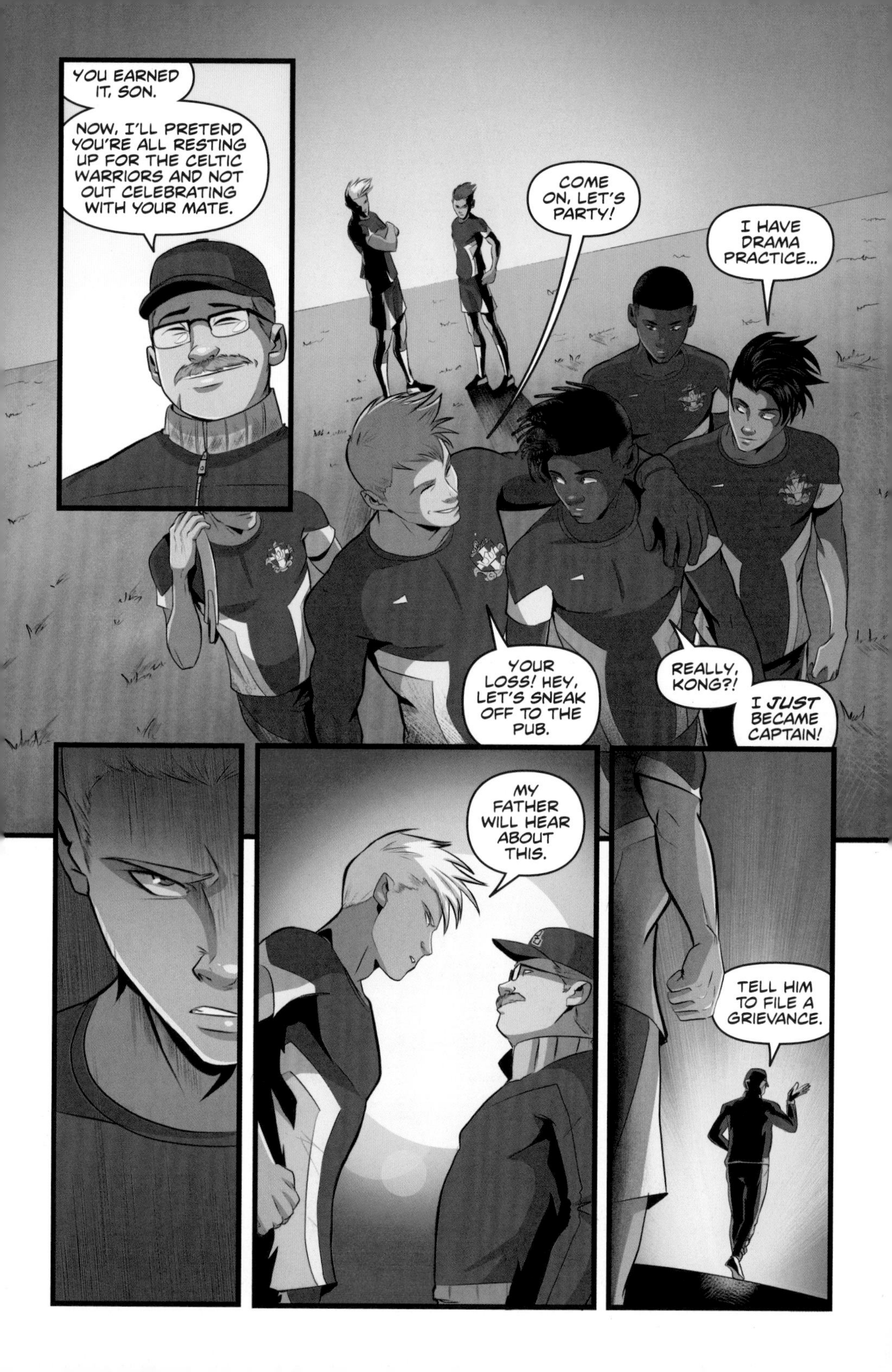

YOU EARNED IT, SON.
NOW, I'LL PRETEND YOU'RE ALL RESTING UP FOR THE CELTIC WARRIORS AND NOT OUT CELEBRATING WITH YOUR MATE.
COME ON, LET'S PARTY!
I HAVE DRAMA PRACTICE...
YOUR LOSS! HEY, LET'S SNEAK OFF TO THE PUB.
REALLY, KONG?!
I JUST BECAME CAPTAIN!
MY FATHER WILL HEAR ABOUT THIS.
TELL HIM TO FILE A GRIEVANCE.

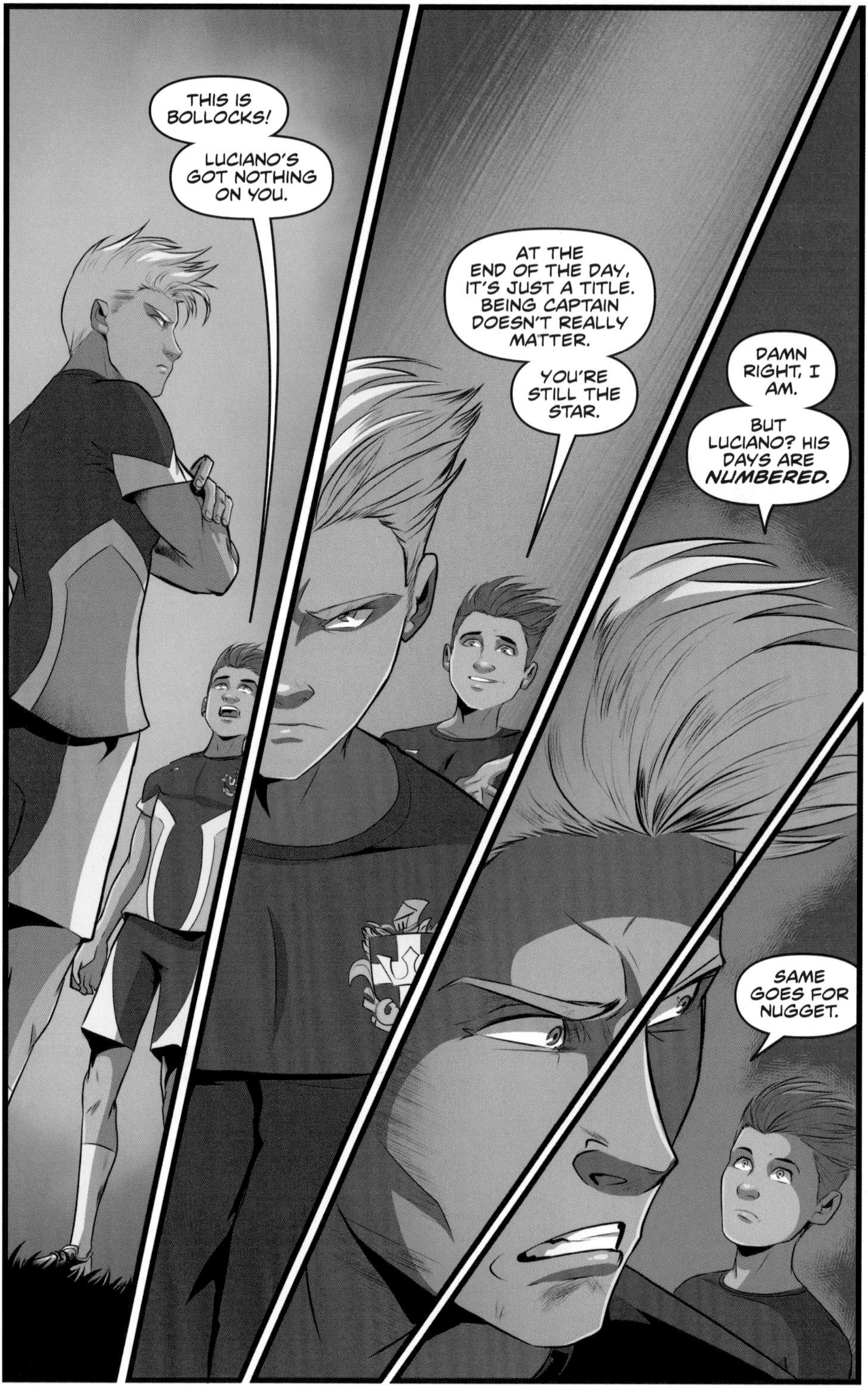
THIS IS BOLLOCKS!
LUCIANO'S GOT NOTHING ON YOU.
AT THE END OF THE DAY, IT'S JUST A TITLE. BEING CAPTAIN DOESN'T REALLY MATTER.
YOU'RE STILL THE STAR.
DAMN RIGHT, I AM.
BUT LUCIANO? HIS DAYS ARE NUMBERED.
SAME GOES FOR NUGGET.

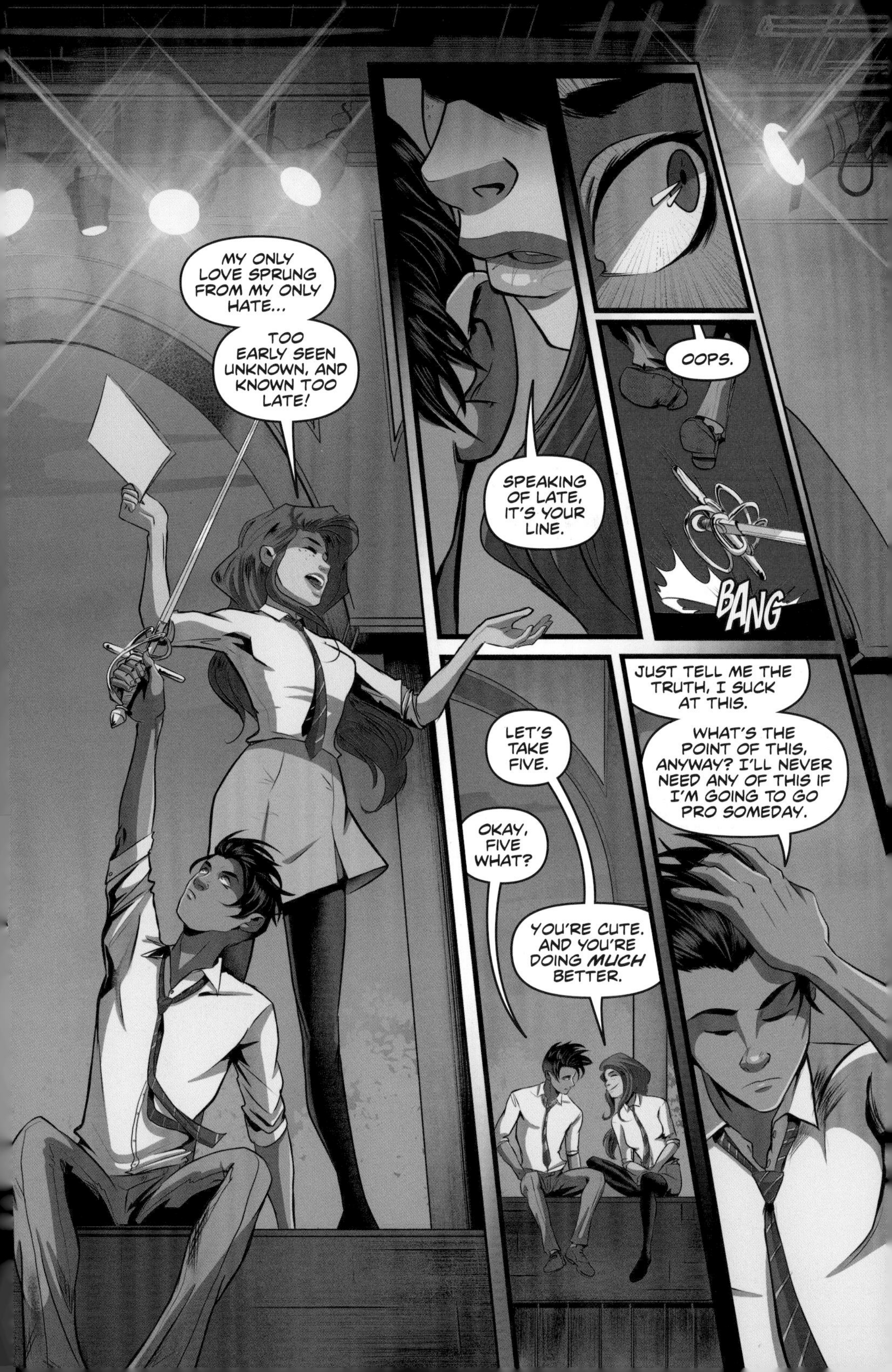
MY ONLY LOVE SPRUNG FROM MY ONLY HATE...
TOO EARLY SEEN UNKNOWN, AND KNOWN TOO LATE!
SPEAKING OF LATE, IT'S YOUR LINE.
OOPS.
BANG
LET'S TAKE FIVE.
OKAY, FIVE WHAT?
YOU'RE CUTE. AND YOU'RE DOING MUCH BETTER.
JUST TELL ME THE TRUTH, I SUCK AT THIS.
WHAT'S THE POINT OF THIS, ANYWAY? I'LL NEVER NEED ANY OF THIS IF I'M GOING TO GO PRO SOMEDAY.

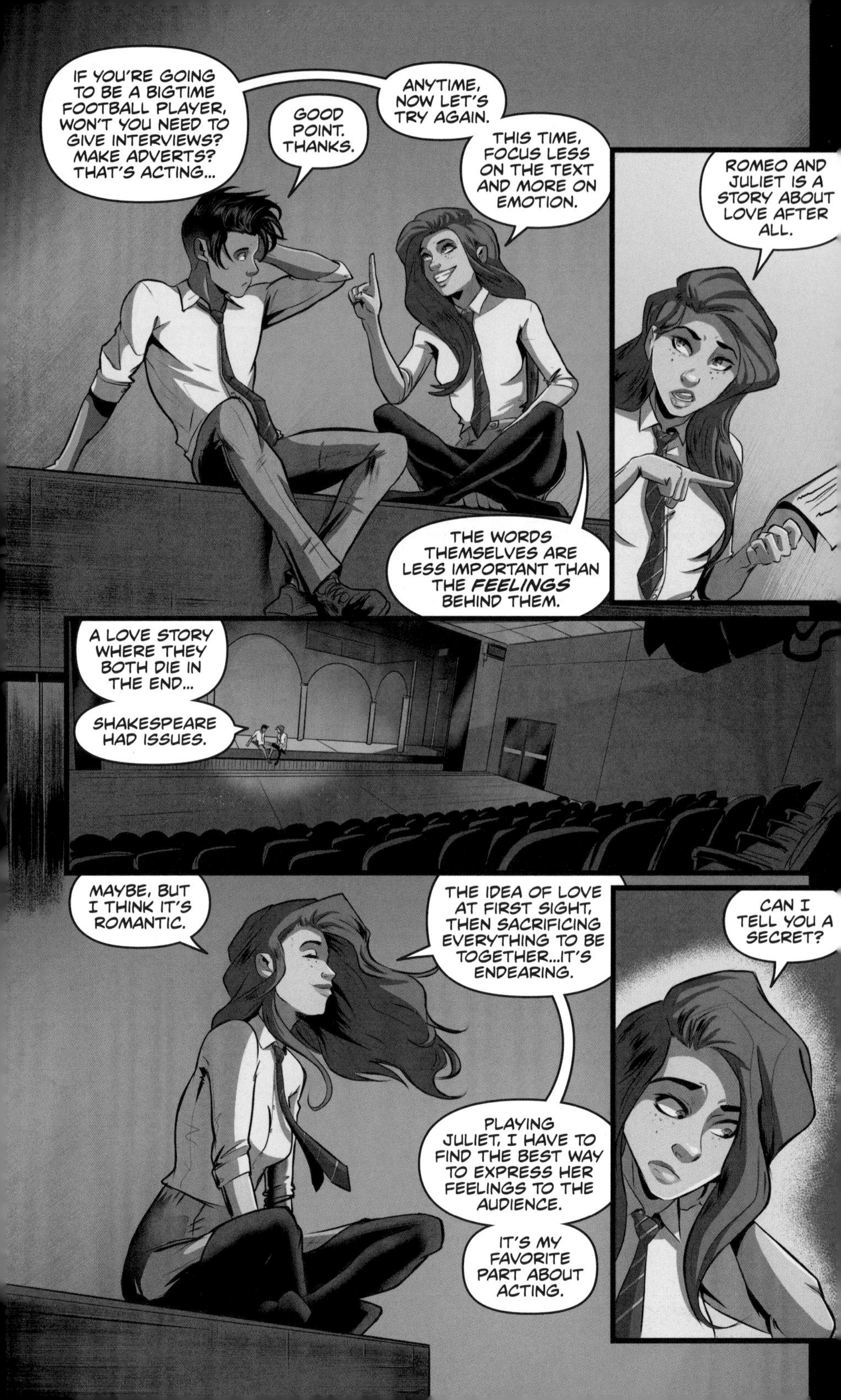
IF YOU'RE GOING TO BE A BIGTIME FOOTBALL PLAYER, WON'T YOU NEED TO GIVE INTERVIEWS? MAKE ADVERTS? THAT'S ACTING...
GOOD POINT. THANKS.
ANYTIME, NOW LET'S TRY AGAIN.
THIS TIME, FOCUS LESS ON THE TEXT AND MORE ON EMOTION.
THE WORDS THEMSELVES ARE LESS IMPORTANT THAN THE FEELINGS BEHIND THEM.
ROMEO AND JULIET IS A STORY ABOUT LOVE AFTER ALL.
A LOVE STORY WHERE THEY BOTH DIE IN THE END...
SHAKESPEARE HAD ISSUES.
MAYBE, BUT I THINK IT'S ROMANTIC.
THE IDEA OF LOVE AT FIRST SIGHT, THEN SACRIFICING EVERYTHING TO BE TOGETHER...IT'S ENDEARING.
PLAYING JULIET, I HAVE TO FIND THE BEST WAY TO EXPRESS HER FEELINGS TO THE AUDIENCE.
IT'S MY FAVORITE PART ABOUT ACTING.
CAN I TELL YOU A SECRET?

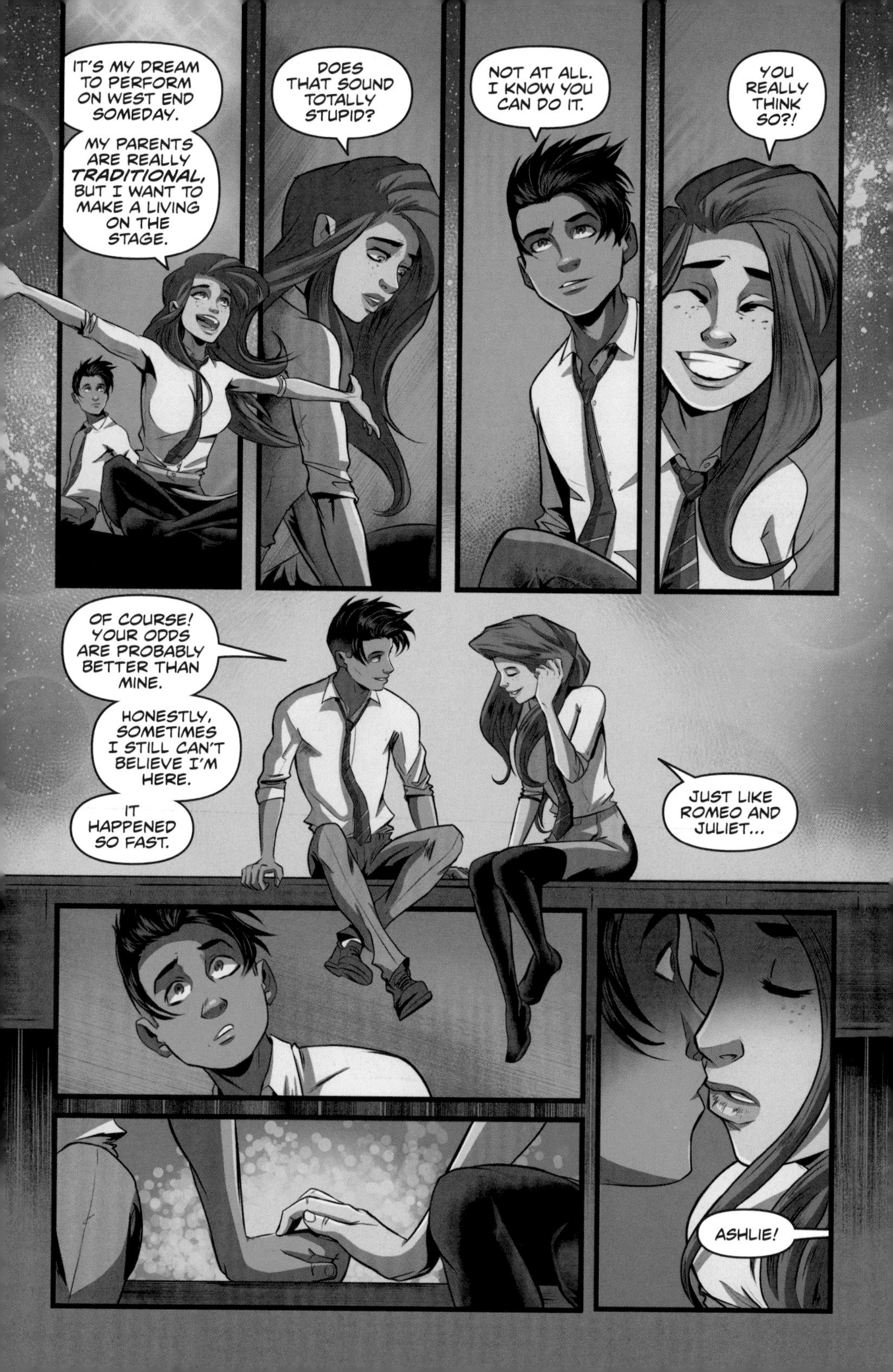
IT'S MY DREAM TO PERFORM ON WEST END SOMEDAY.
MY PARENTS ARE REALLY *TRADITIONAL,* BUT I WANT TO MAKE A LIVING ON THE STAGE.
DOES THAT SOUND TOTALLY STUPID?
NOT AT ALL. I KNOW YOU CAN DO IT.
YOU REALLY THINK SO?!
OF COURSE! YOUR ODDS ARE PROBABLY BETTER THAN MINE.
HONESTLY, SOMETIMES I STILL CAN'T BELIEVE I'M HERE.
IT HAPPENED SO FAST.
JUST LIKE ROMEO AND JULIET...
ASHLIE!

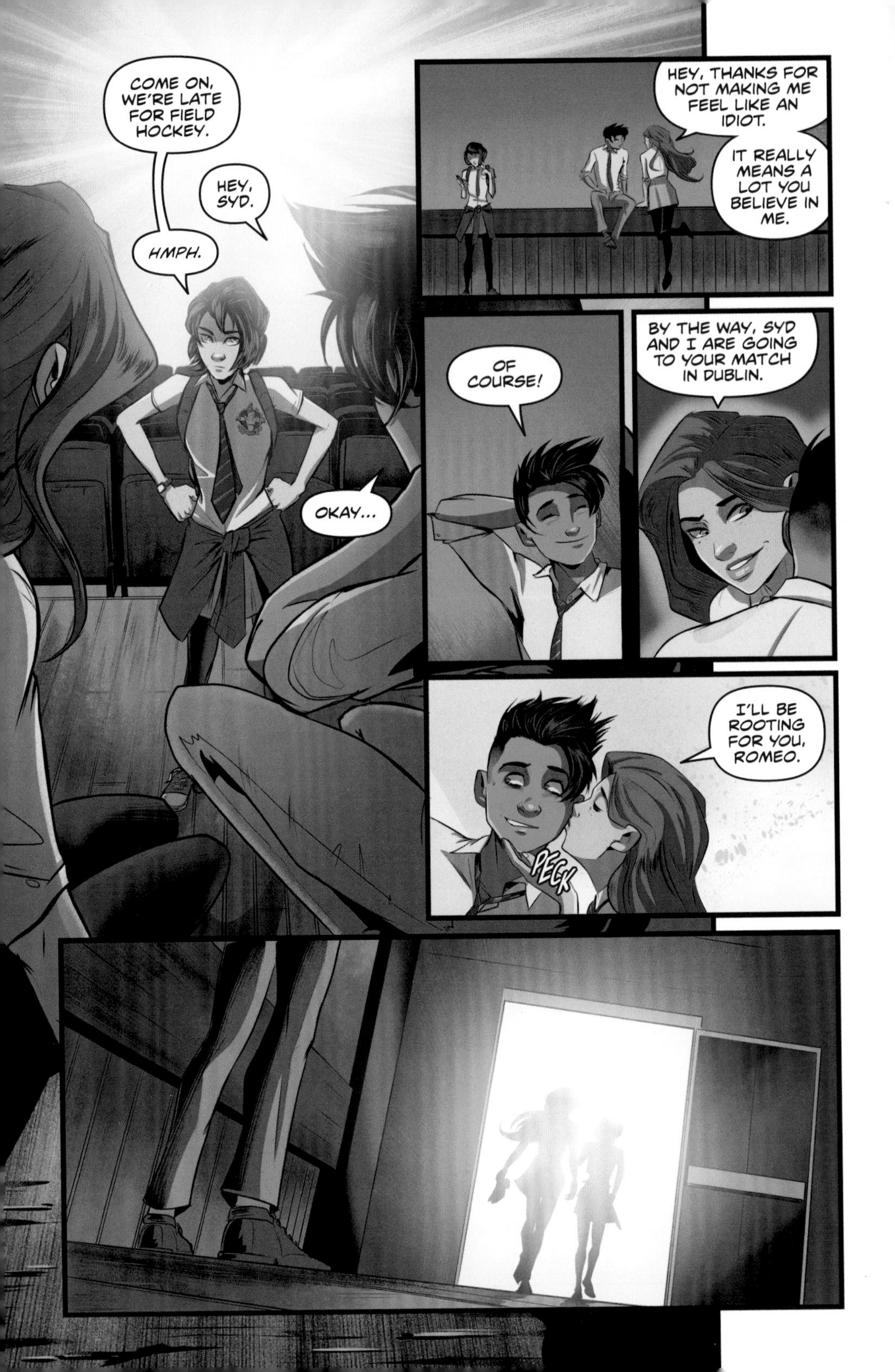
COME ON, WE'RE LATE FOR FIELD HOCKEY.
HEY, SYD.
HMPH.
OKAY...
HEY, THANKS FOR NOT MAKING ME FEEL LIKE AN IDIOT.
IT REALLY MEANS A LOT YOU BELIEVE IN ME.
OF COURSE!
BY THE WAY, SYD AND I ARE GOING TO YOUR MATCH IN DUBLIN.
I'LL BE ROOTING FOR YOU, ROMEO.
PECK

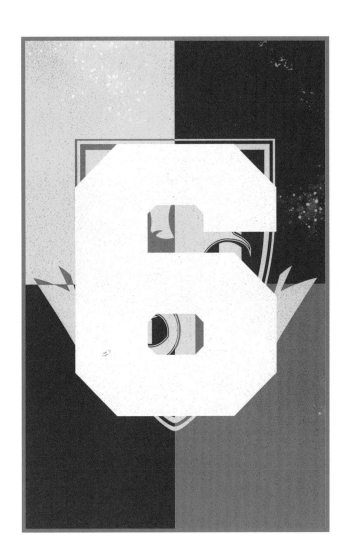

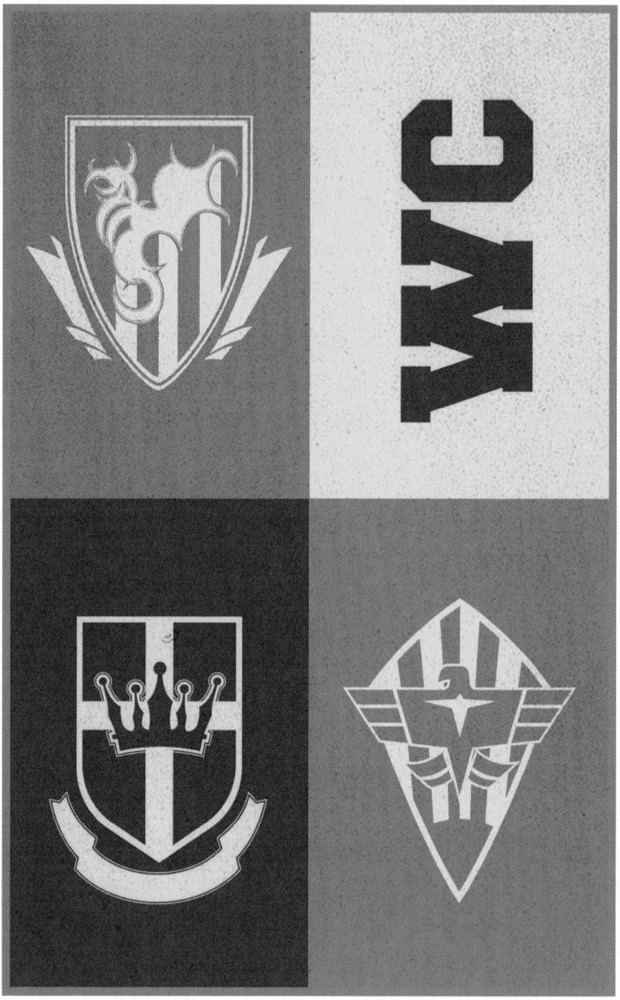
WYC

AVIVA STADIUM, IRELAND.
WELCOME FOOTBALL FANS!
NIGEL TILLENBURY HERE, THE VOICE OF REGENTS UNITED FC.
JOINING ME IS THE CELTIC WARRIORS' FERGAL O'SHAUNESSY!
DIA DHUIT, NIGEL!

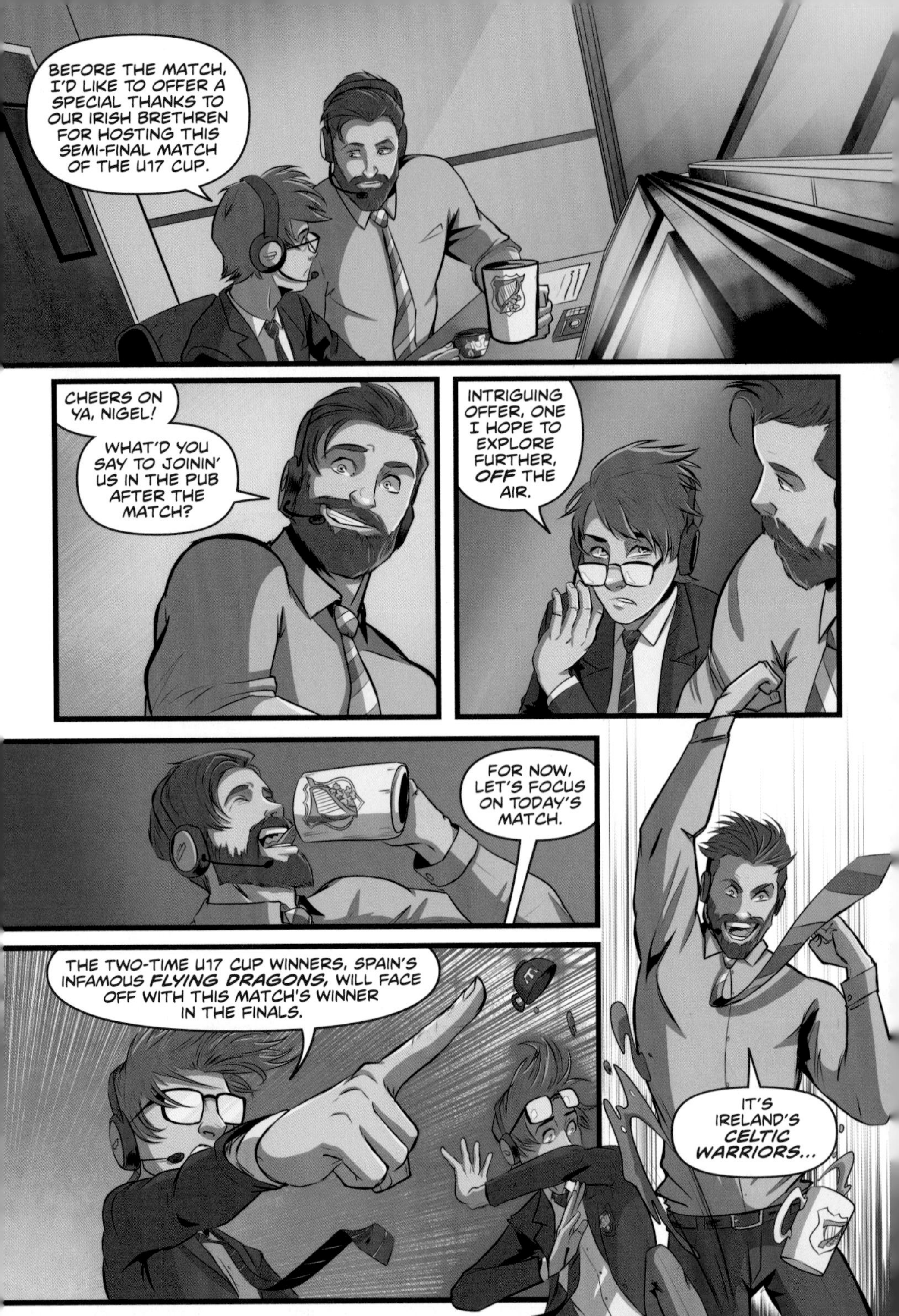
BEFORE THE MATCH, I'D LIKE TO OFFER A SPECIAL THANKS TO OUR IRISH BRETHREN FOR HOSTING THIS SEMI-FINAL MATCH OF THE U17 CUP.
CHEERS ON YA, NIGEL!
WHAT'D YOU SAY TO JOININ' US IN THE PUB AFTER THE MATCH?
INTRIGUING OFFER, ONE I HOPE TO EXPLORE FURTHER, OFF THE AIR.
FOR NOW, LET'S FOCUS ON TODAY'S MATCH.
THE TWO-TIME U17 CUP WINNERS, SPAIN'S INFAMOUS FLYING DRAGONS, WILL FACE OFF WITH THIS MATCH'S WINNER IN THE FINALS.
IT'S IRELAND'S CELTIC WARRIORS...

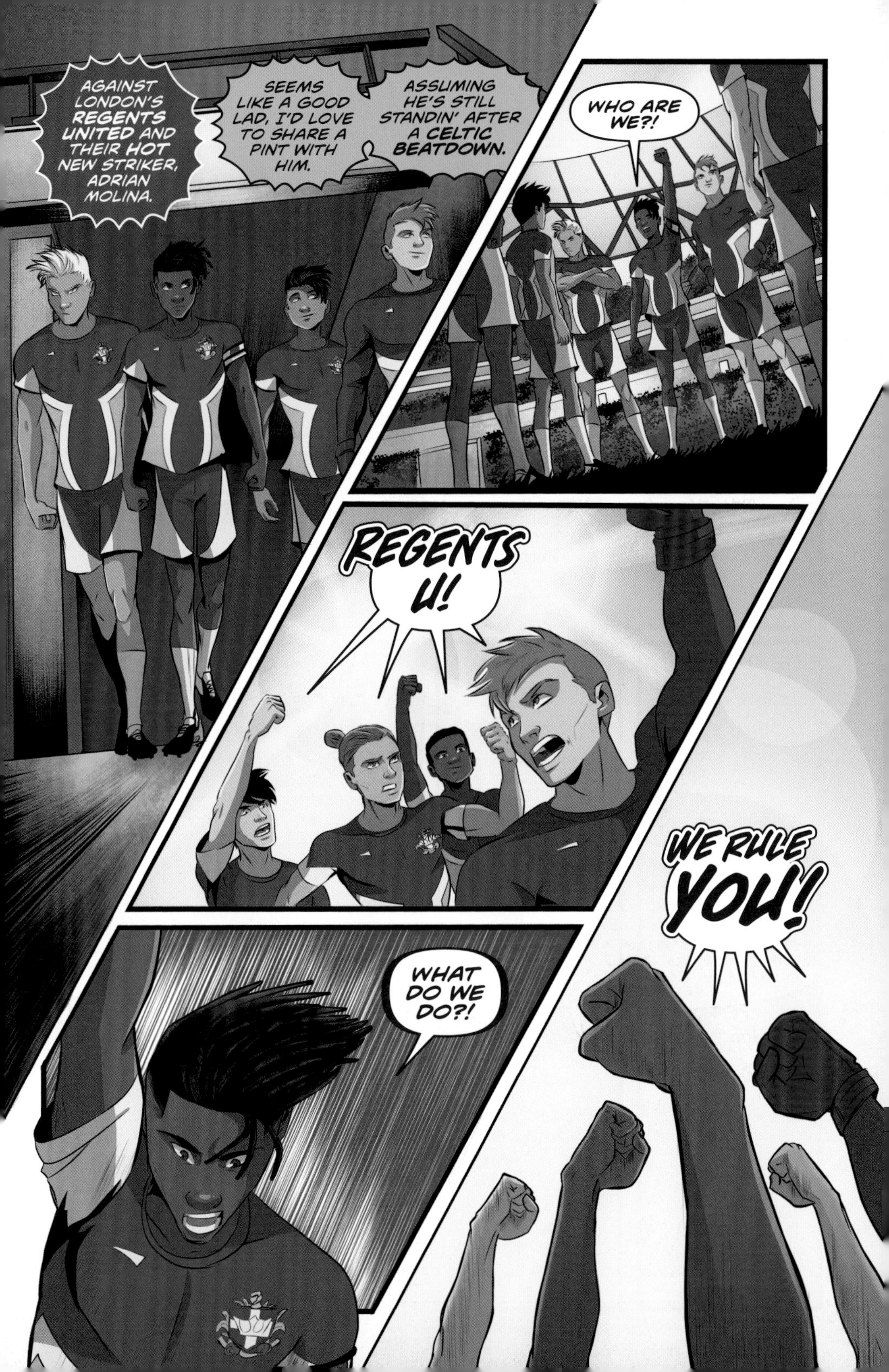
AGAINST LONDON'S REGENTS UNITED AND THEIR HOT NEW STRIKER, ADRIAN MOLINA.
SEEMS LIKE A GOOD LAD, I'D LOVE TO SHARE A PINT WITH HIM.
ASSUMING HE'S STILL STANDIN' AFTER A CELTIC BEATDOWN.
WHO ARE WE?!
REGENTS U!
WHAT DO WE DO?!
WE RULE YOU!

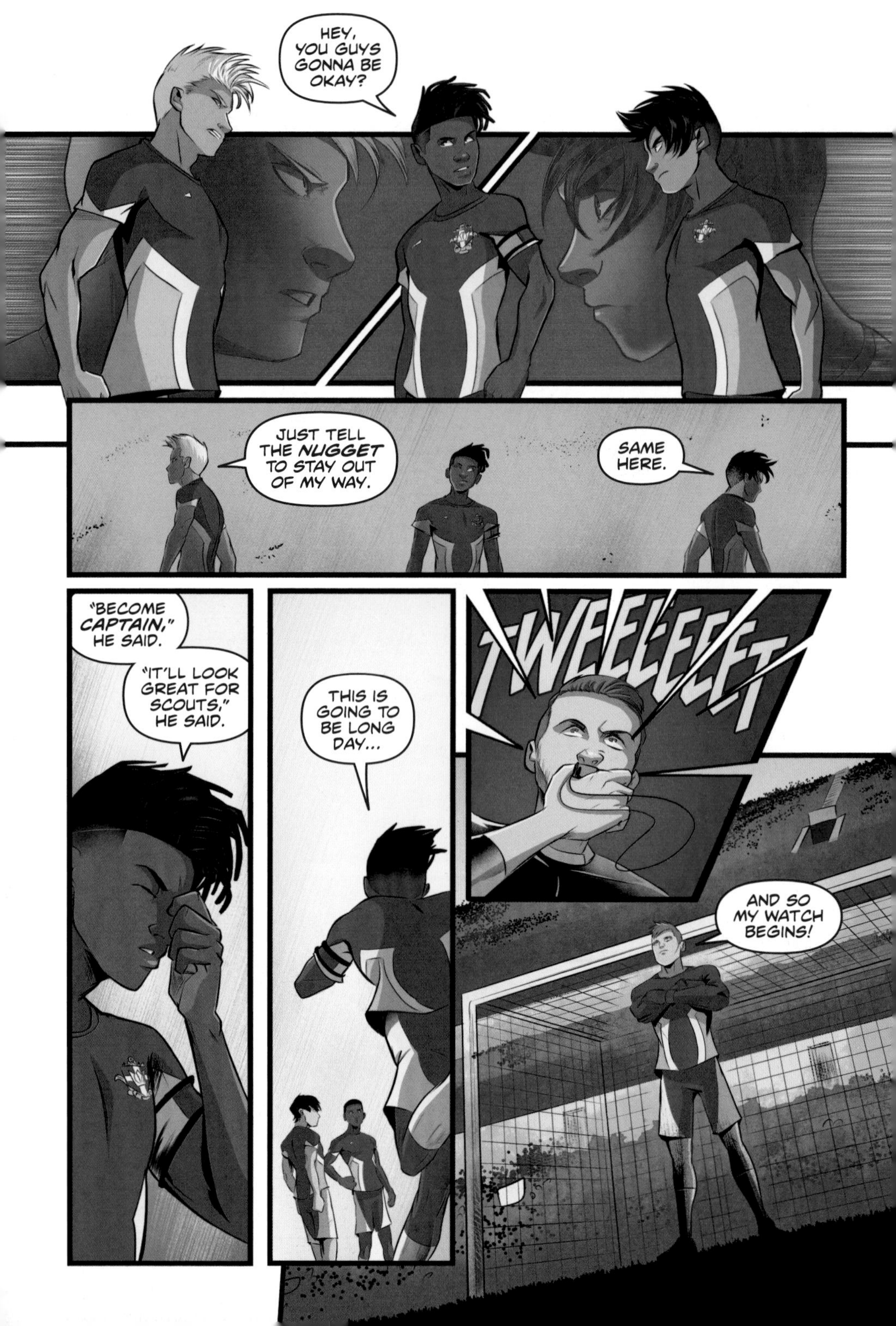
HEY, YOU GUYS GONNA BE OKAY?
JUST TELL THE NUGGET TO STAY OUT OF MY WAY.
SAME HERE.
"BECOME CAPTAIN," HE SAID.
"IT'LL LOOK GREAT FOR SCOUTS," HE SAID.
THIS IS GOING TO BE LONG DAY...
TWEEEEET
AND SO MY WATCH BEGINS!

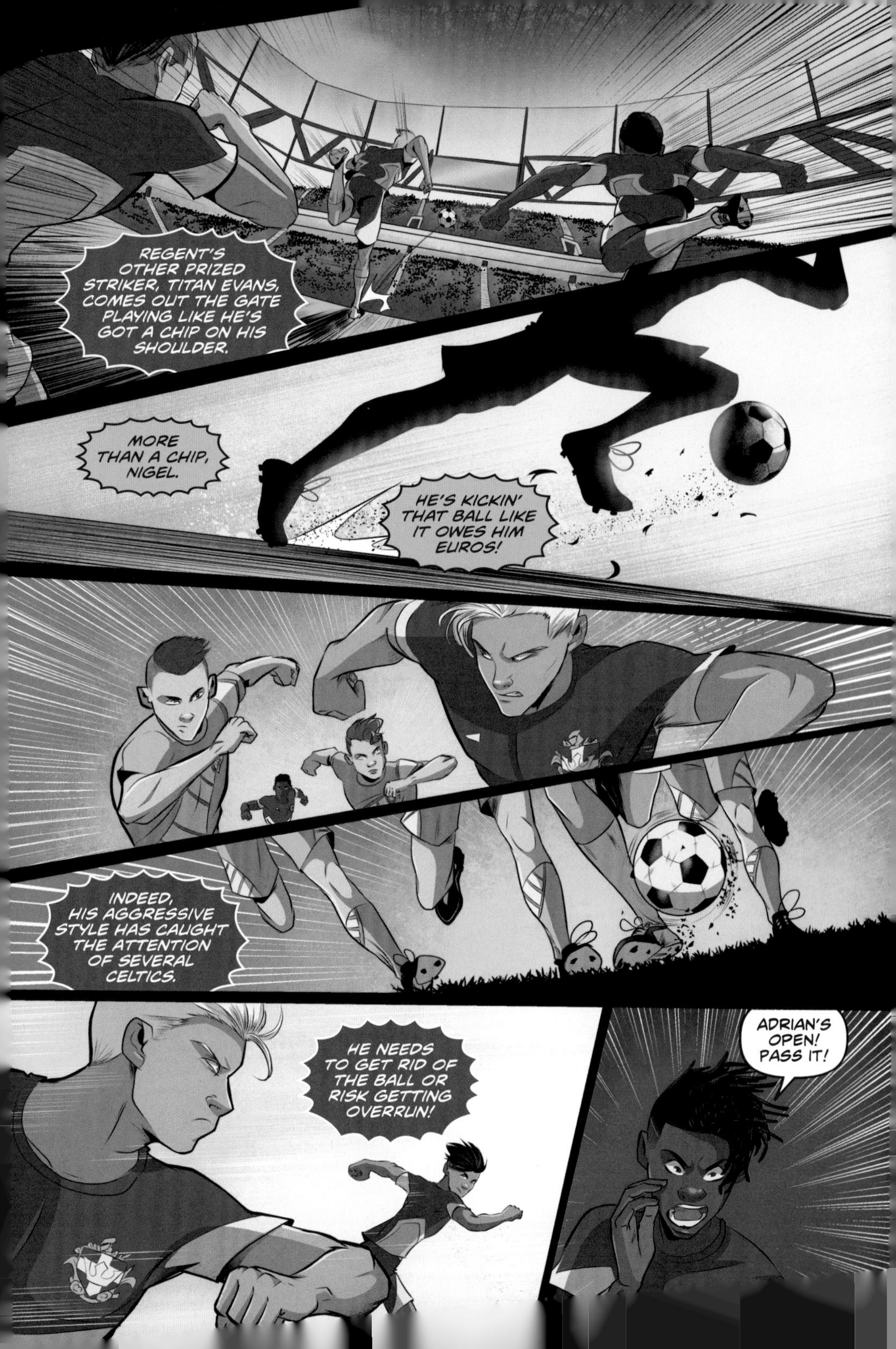
REGENT'S OTHER PRIZED STRIKER, TITAN EVANS, COMES OUT THE GATE PLAYING LIKE HE'S GOT A CHIP ON HIS SHOULDER.
MORE THAN A CHIP, NIGEL.
HE'S KICKIN' THAT BALL LIKE IT OWES HIM EUROS!
INDEED, HIS AGGRESSIVE STYLE HAS CAUGHT THE ATTENTION OF SEVERAL CELTICS.
HE NEEDS TO GET RID OF THE BALL OR RISK GETTING OVERRUN!
ADRIAN'S OPEN! PASS IT!

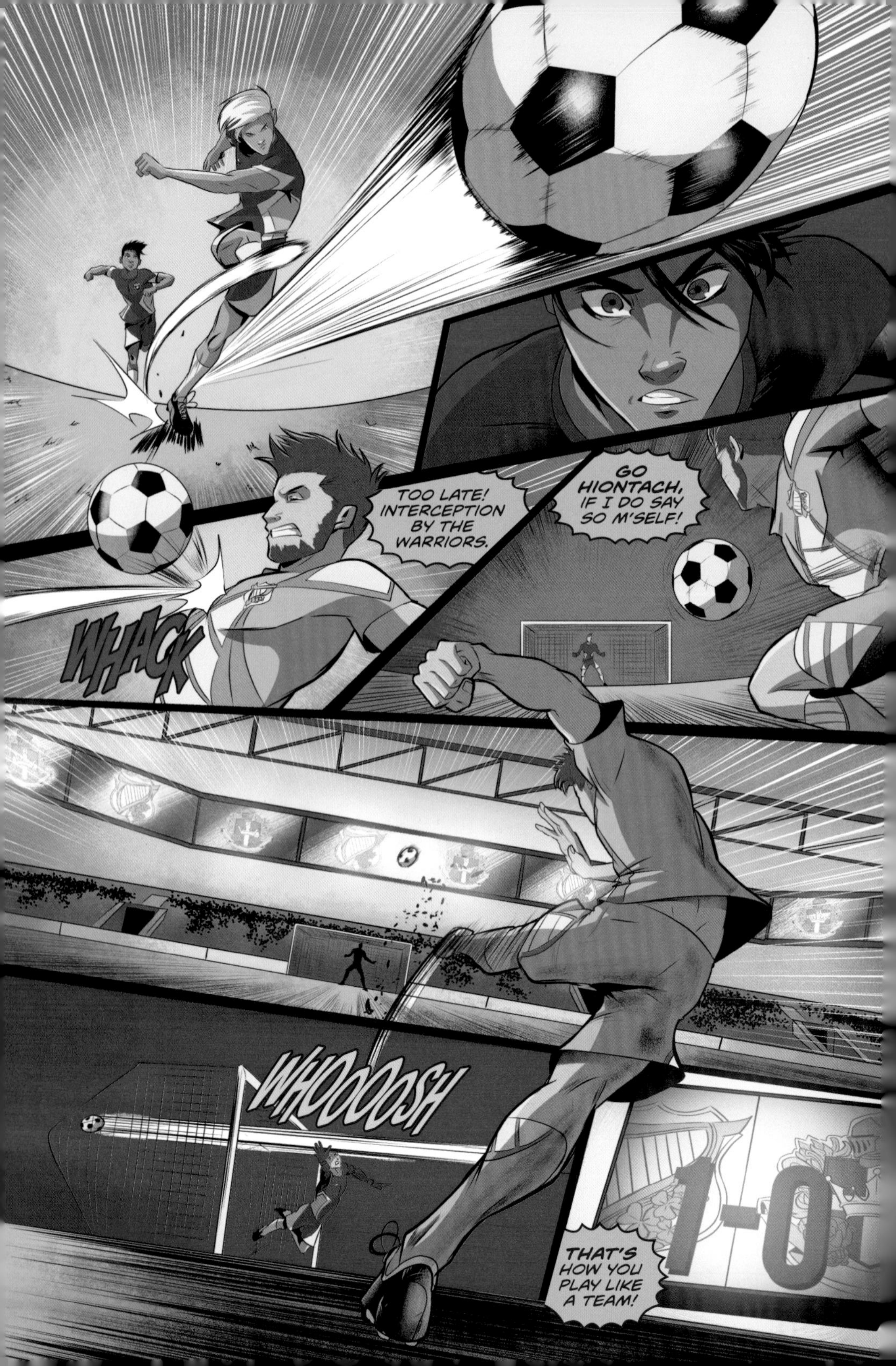
TOO LATE! INTERCEPTION BY THE WARRIORS.
GO HIONTACH, IF I DO SAY SO M'SELF!
WHACK
WHOOOOSH
1-0
THAT'S HOW YOU PLAY LIKE A TEAM!

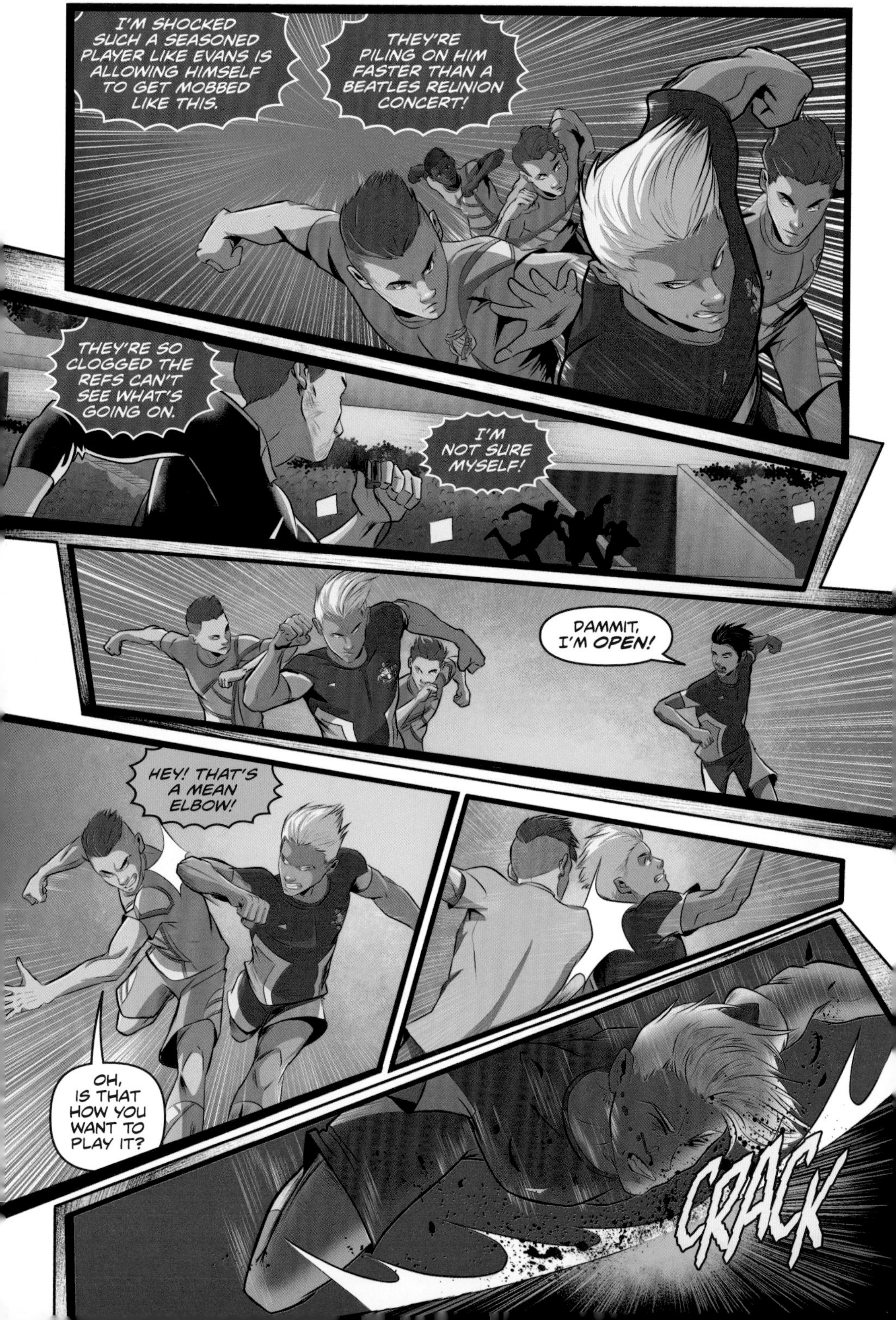
I'M SHOCKED SUCH A SEASONED PLAYER LIKE EVANS IS ALLOWING HIMSELF TO GET MOBBED LIKE THIS.
THEY'RE PILING ON HIM FASTER THAN A BEATLES REUNION CONCERT!
THEY'RE SO CLOGGED THE REFS CAN'T SEE WHAT'S GOING ON.
I'M NOT SURE MYSELF!
DAMMIT, I'M OPEN!
HEY! THAT'S A MEAN ELBOW!
OH, IS THAT HOW YOU WANT TO PLAY IT?
CRACK

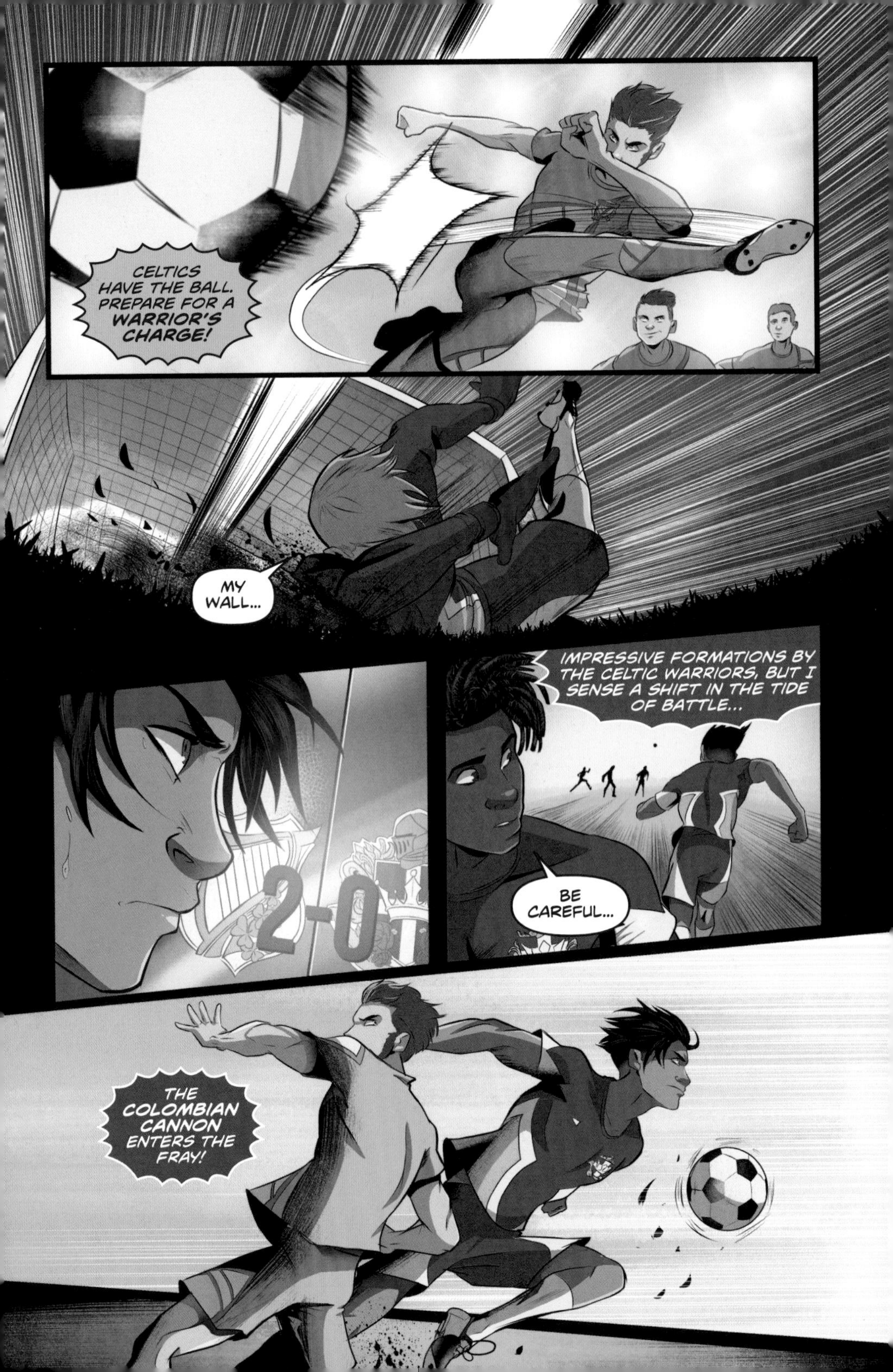
CELTICS HAVE THE BALL. PREPARE FOR A WARRIOR'S CHARGE!
MY WALL...
2-0
IMPRESSIVE FORMATIONS BY THE CELTIC WARRIORS, BUT I SENSE A SHIFT IN THE TIDE OF BATTLE...
BE CAREFUL...
THE COLOMBIAN CANNON ENTERS THE FRAY!

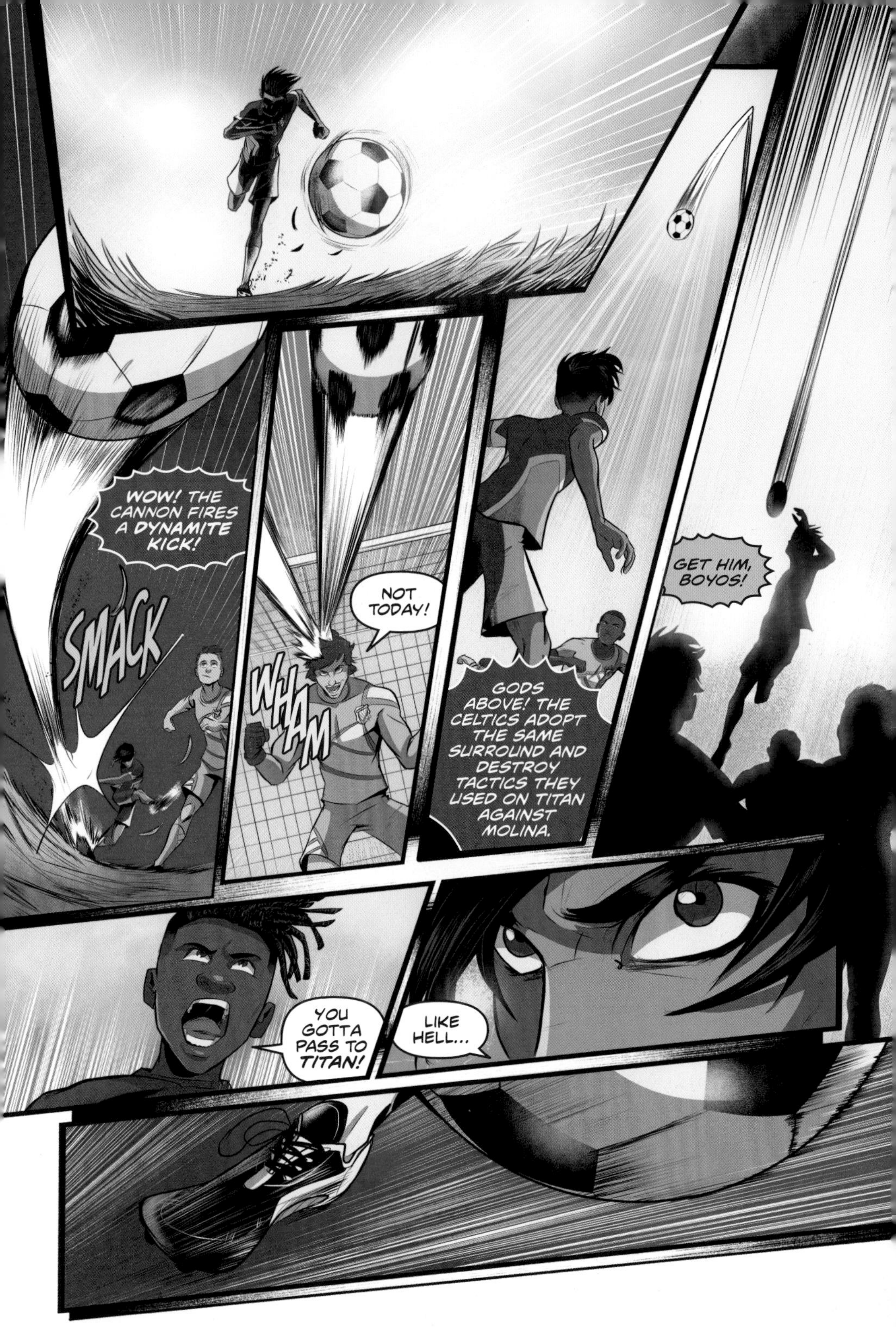
WOW! THE CANNON FIRES A DYNAMITE KICK!
SMACK
NOT TODAY!
WHAM
GODS ABOVE! THE CELTICS ADOPT THE SAME SURROUND AND DESTROY TACTICS THEY USED ON TITAN AGAINST MOLINA.
GET HIM, BOYOS!
YOU GOTTA PASS TO TITAN!
LIKE HELL...

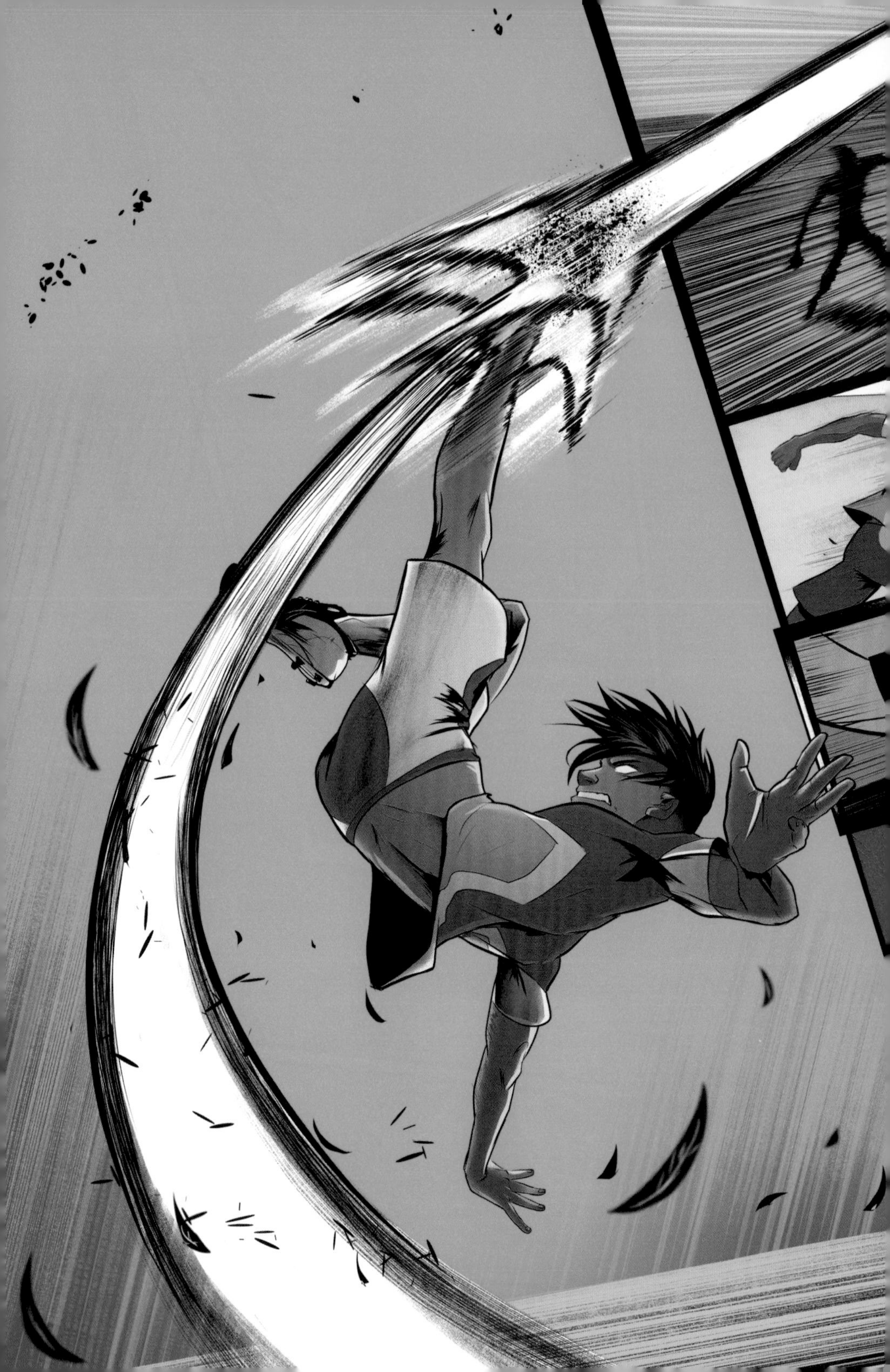

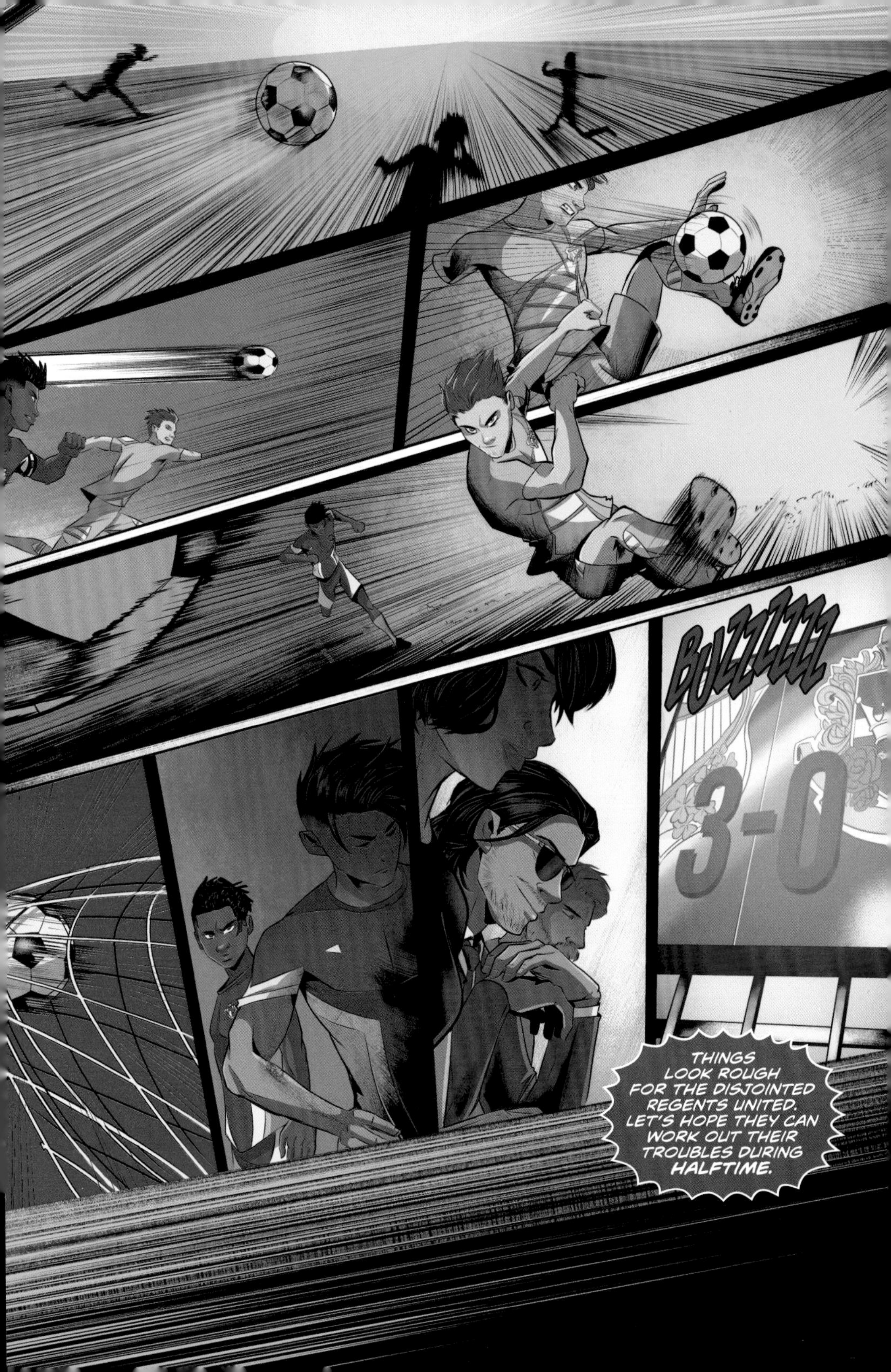
BUZZZZZZ
3-0
THINGS LOOK ROUGH FOR THE DISJOINTED REGENTS UNITED. LET'S HOPE THEY CAN WORK OUT THEIR TROUBLES DURING HALFTIME.

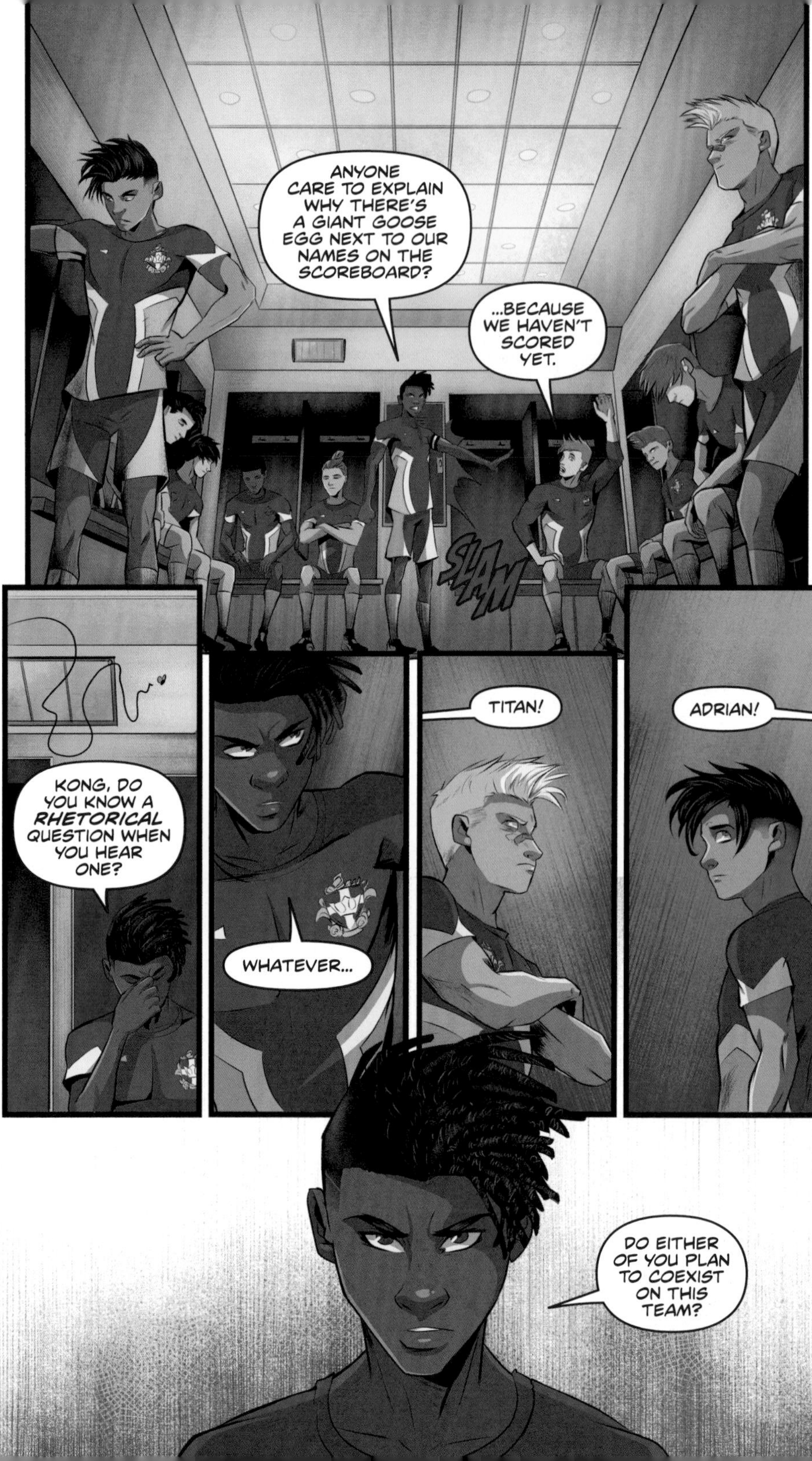
ANYONE CARE TO EXPLAIN WHY THERE'S A GIANT GOOSE EGG NEXT TO OUR NAMES ON THE SCOREBOARD?
...BECAUSE WE HAVEN'T SCORED YET.
SLAM
KONG, DO YOU KNOW A *RHETORICAL* QUESTION WHEN YOU HEAR ONE?
WHATEVER...
TITAN!
ADRIAN!
DO EITHER OF YOU PLAN TO COEXIST ON THIS TEAM?

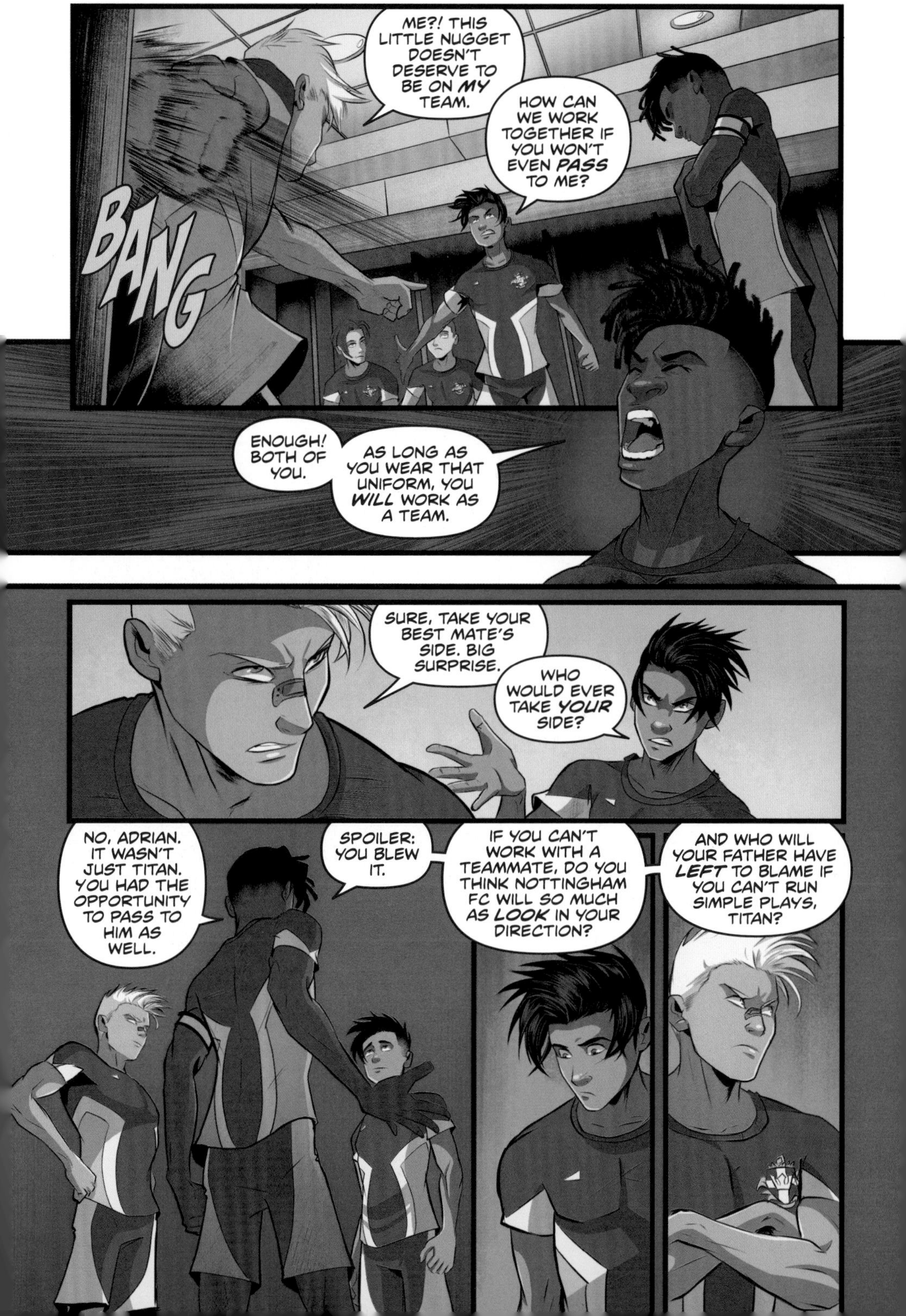

ME?! THIS LITTLE NUGGET DOESN'T DESERVE TO BE ON *MY* TEAM.
HOW CAN WE WORK TOGETHER IF YOU WON'T EVEN *PASS* TO ME?
BANG
ENOUGH! BOTH OF YOU.
AS LONG AS YOU WEAR THAT UNIFORM, YOU *WILL* WORK AS A TEAM.
SURE, TAKE YOUR BEST MATE'S SIDE. BIG SURPRISE.
WHO WOULD EVER TAKE *YOUR* SIDE?
NO, ADRIAN. IT WASN'T JUST TITAN. YOU HAD THE OPPORTUNITY TO PASS TO HIM AS WELL.
SPOILER: YOU BLEW IT.
IF YOU CAN'T WORK WITH A TEAMMATE, DO YOU THINK NOTTINGHAM FC WILL SO MUCH AS *LOOK* IN YOUR DIRECTION?
AND WHO WILL YOUR FATHER HAVE *LEFT* TO BLAME IF YOU CAN'T RUN SIMPLE PLAYS, TITAN?

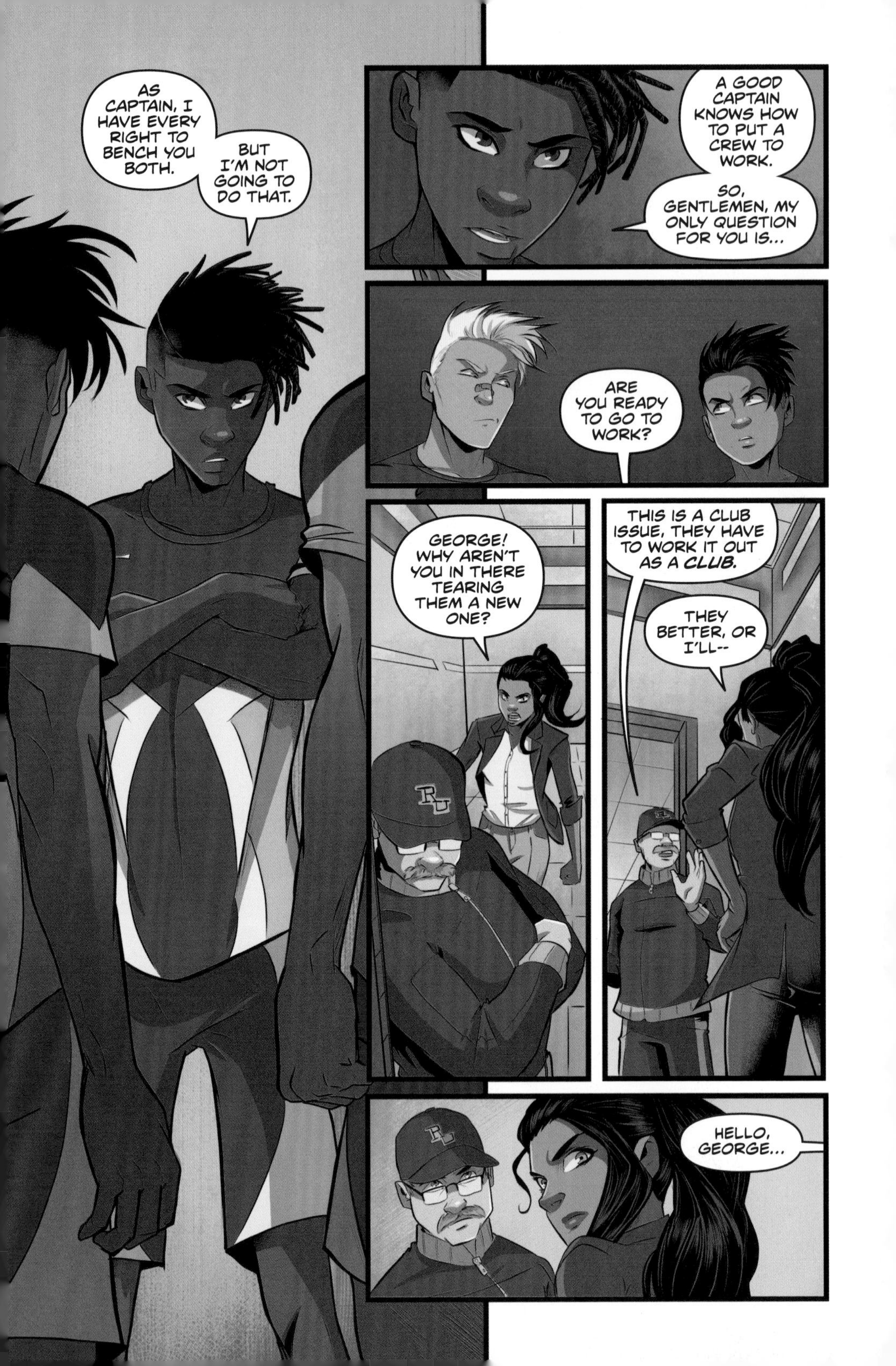
AS CAPTAIN, I HAVE EVERY RIGHT TO BENCH YOU BOTH.
BUT I'M NOT GOING TO DO THAT.
A GOOD CAPTAIN KNOWS HOW TO PUT A CREW TO WORK.
SO, GENTLEMEN, MY ONLY QUESTION FOR YOU IS...
ARE YOU READY TO GO TO WORK?
GEORGE! WHY AREN'T YOU IN THERE TEARING THEM A NEW ONE?
THIS IS A CLUB ISSUE, THEY HAVE TO WORK IT OUT AS A *CLUB*.
THEY BETTER, OR I'LL--
HELLO, GEORGE...

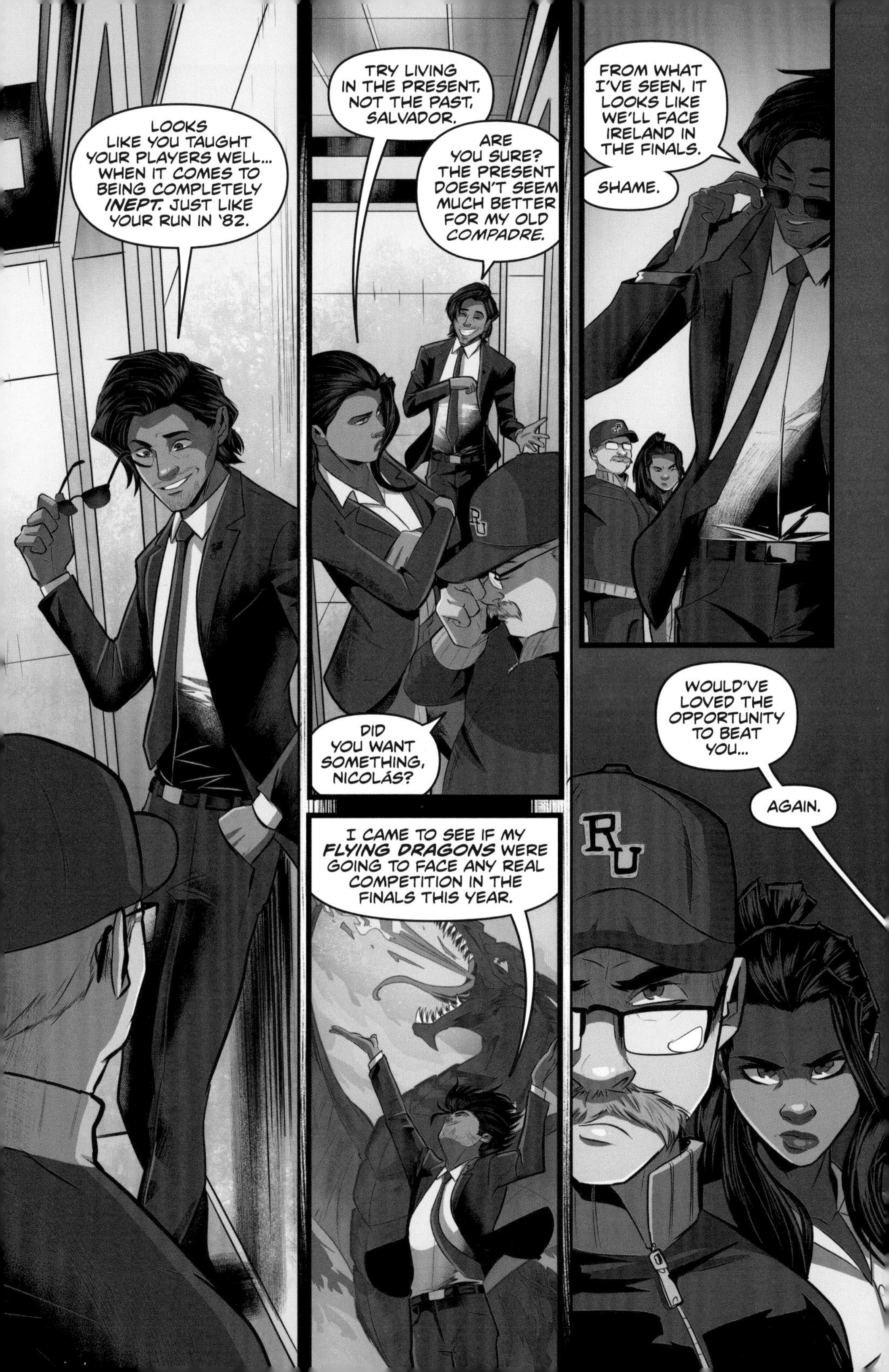
LOOKS LIKE YOU TAUGHT YOUR PLAYERS WELL... WHEN IT COMES TO BEING COMPLETELY *INEPT.* JUST LIKE YOUR RUN IN '82.
TRY LIVING IN THE PRESENT, NOT THE PAST, SALVADOR.
ARE YOU SURE? THE PRESENT DOESN'T SEEM MUCH BETTER FOR MY OLD COMPADRE.
DID YOU WANT SOMETHING, NICOLÁS?
I CAME TO SEE IF MY *FLYING DRAGONS* WERE GOING TO FACE ANY REAL COMPETITION IN THE FINALS THIS YEAR.
FROM WHAT I'VE SEEN, IT LOOKS LIKE WE'LL FACE IRELAND IN THE FINALS.
SHAME.
WOULD'VE LOVED THE OPPORTUNITY TO BEAT YOU...
AGAIN.

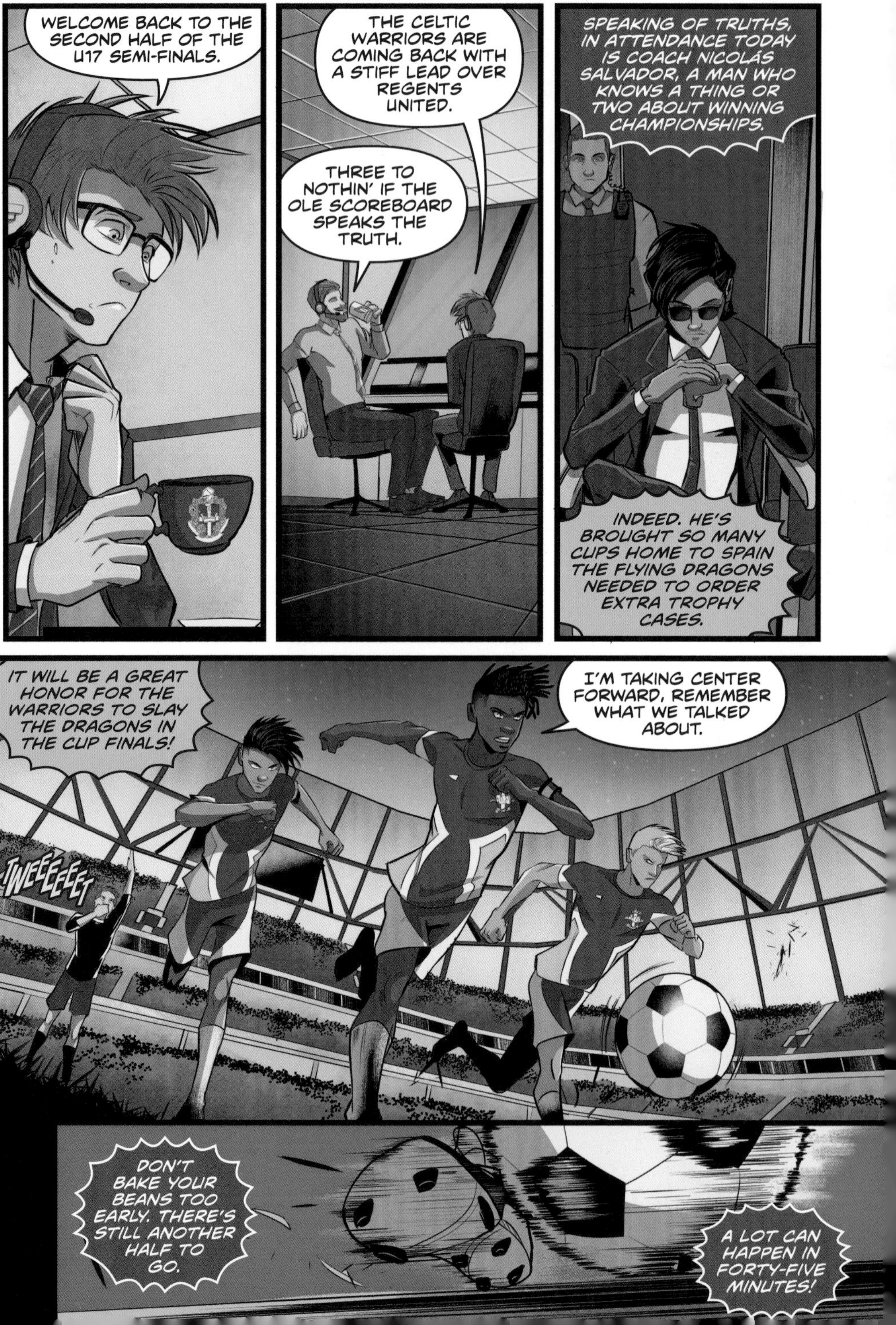
WELCOME BACK TO THE SECOND HALF OF THE U17 SEMI-FINALS.
THE CELTIC WARRIORS ARE COMING BACK WITH A STIFF LEAD OVER REGENTS UNITED.
THREE TO NOTHIN' IF THE OLE SCOREBOARD SPEAKS THE TRUTH.
SPEAKING OF TRUTHS, IN ATTENDANCE TODAY IS COACH NICOLÁS SALVADOR, A MAN WHO KNOWS A THING OR TWO ABOUT WINNING CHAMPIONSHIPS.
INDEED. HE'S BROUGHT SO MANY CUPS HOME TO SPAIN THE FLYING DRAGONS NEEDED TO ORDER EXTRA TROPHY CASES.
IT WILL BE A GREAT HONOR FOR THE WARRIORS TO SLAY THE DRAGONS IN THE CUP FINALS!
I'M TAKING CENTER FORWARD, REMEMBER WHAT WE TALKED ABOUT.
TWEEEEEET
DON'T BAKE YOUR BEANS TOO EARLY. THERE'S STILL ANOTHER HALF TO GO.
A LOT CAN HAPPEN IN FORTY-FIVE MINUTES!

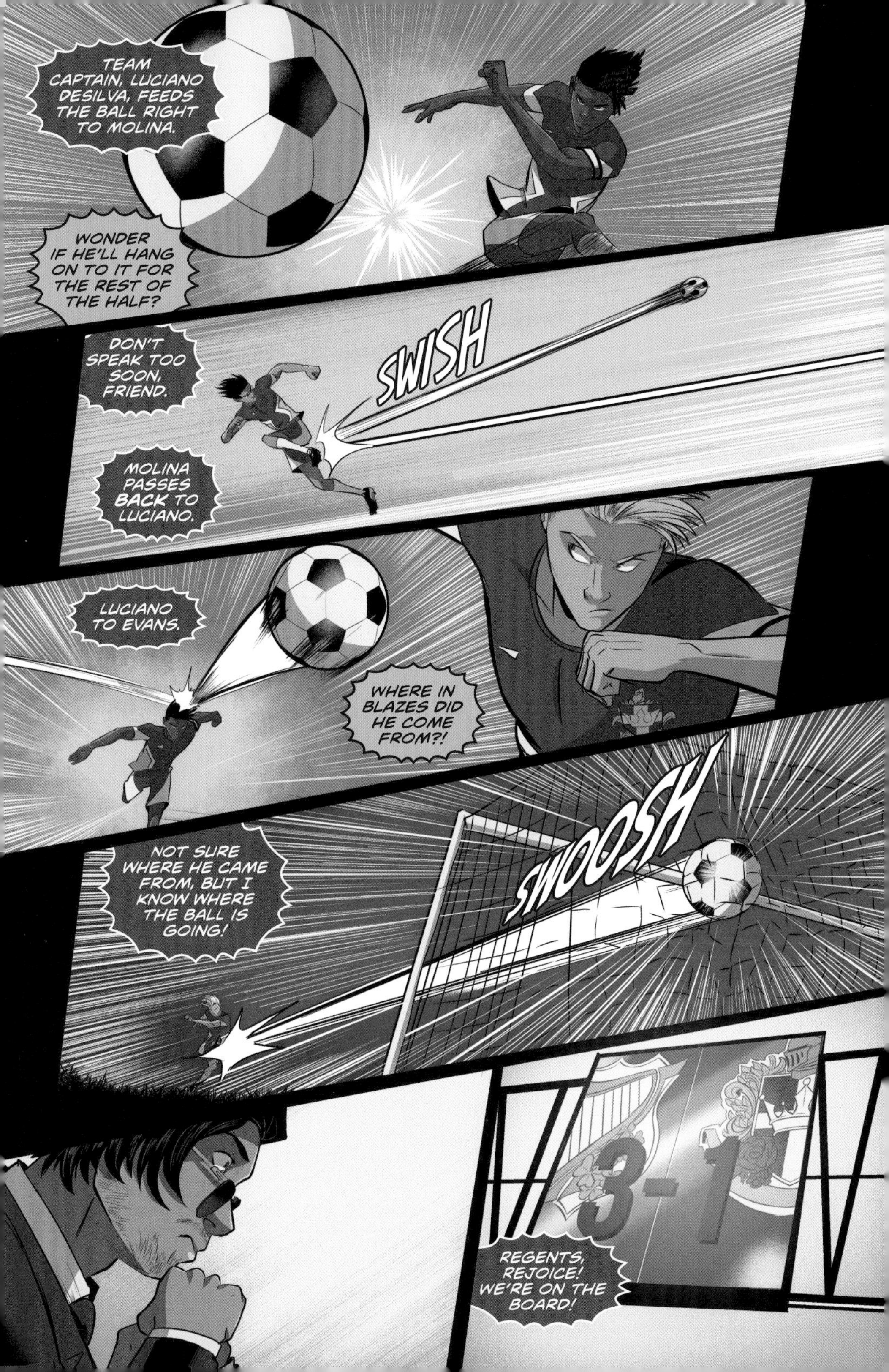
TEAM CAPTAIN, LUCIANO DESILVA, FEEDS THE BALL RIGHT TO MOLINA.
WONDER IF HE'LL HANG ON TO IT FOR THE REST OF THE HALF?
DON'T SPEAK TOO SOON, FRIEND.
SWISH
MOLINA PASSES BACK TO LUCIANO.
LUCIANO TO EVANS.
WHERE IN BLAZES DID HE COME FROM?!
NOT SURE WHERE HE CAME FROM, BUT I KNOW WHERE THE BALL IS GOING!
SWOOSH
3-1
REGENTS, REJOICE! WE'RE ON THE BOARD!

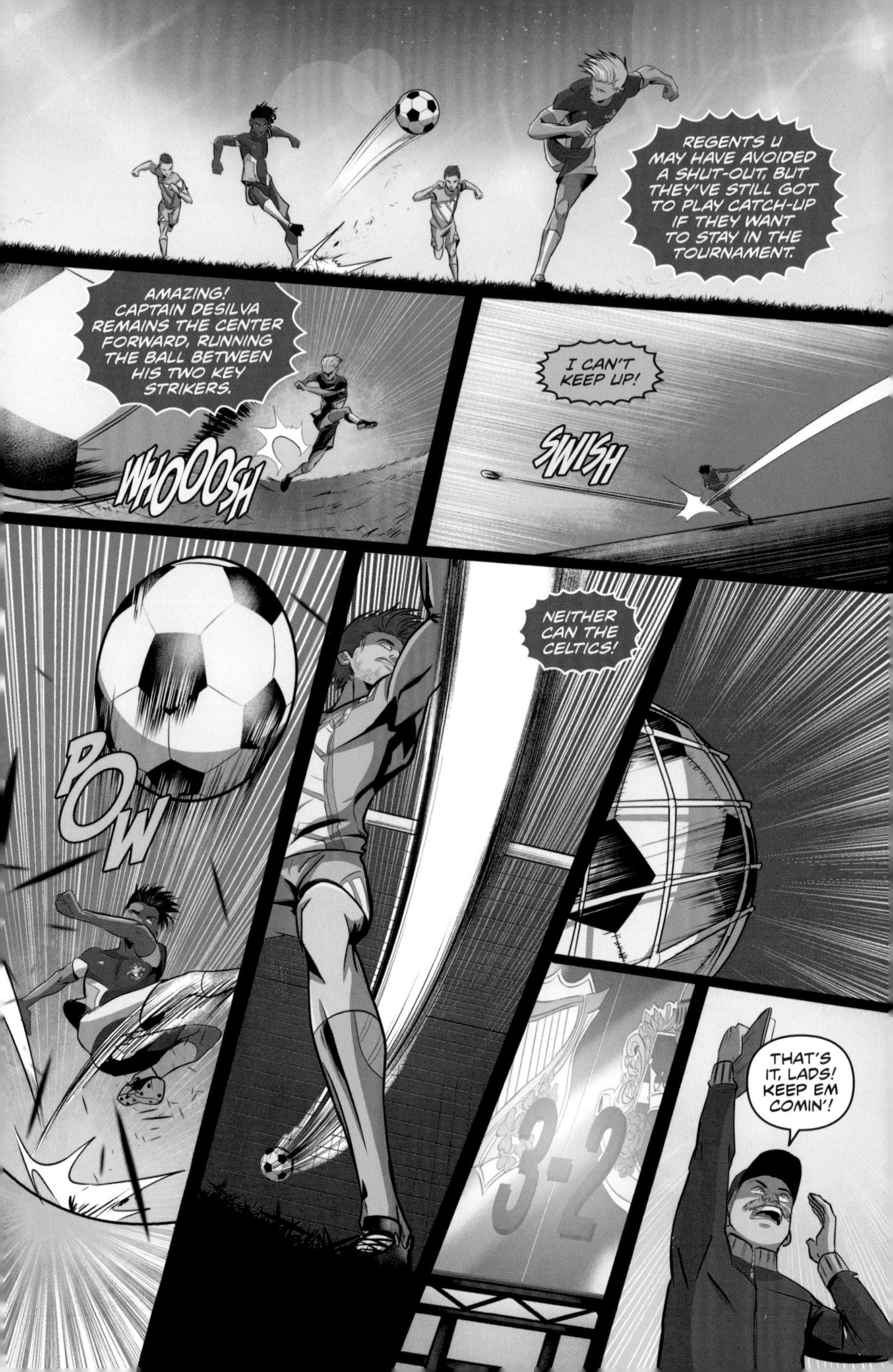
REGENTS U MAY HAVE AVOIDED A SHUT-OUT, BUT THEY'VE STILL GOT TO PLAY CATCH-UP IF THEY WANT TO STAY IN THE TOURNAMENT.
AMAZING! CAPTAIN DESILVA REMAINS THE CENTER FORWARD, RUNNING THE BALL BETWEEN HIS TWO KEY STRIKERS.
WHOOOSH
I CAN'T KEEP UP!
SWISH
POW
NEITHER CAN THE CELTICS!
3-2
THAT'S IT, LADS! KEEP EM COMIN'!

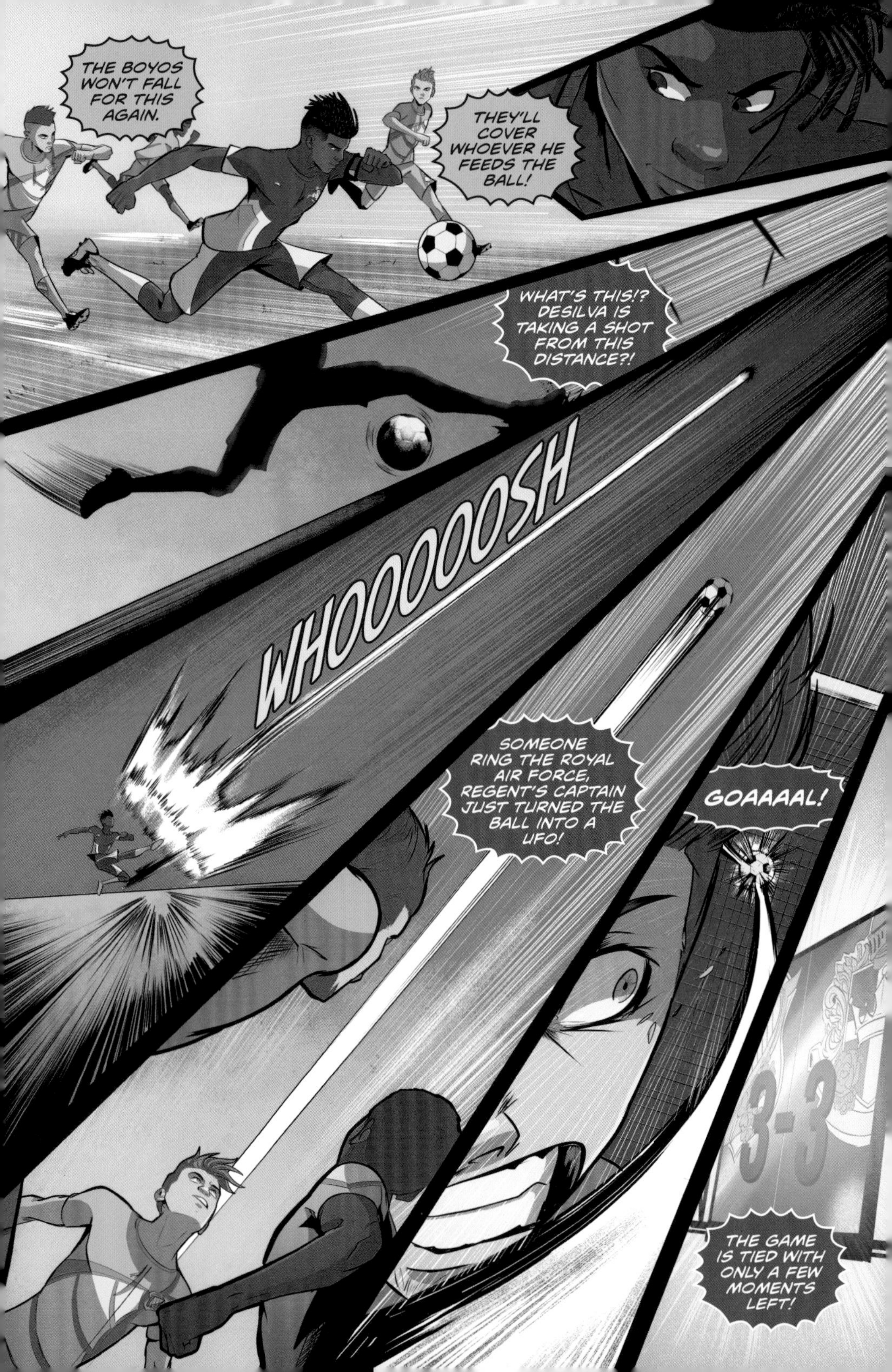
THE BOYOS WON'T FALL FOR THIS AGAIN.
THEY'LL COVER WHOEVER HE FEEDS THE BALL!
WHAT'S THIS!? DESILVA IS TAKING A SHOT FROM THIS DISTANCE?!
WHOOOOOOSH
SOMEONE RING THE ROYAL AIR FORCE, REGENT'S CAPTAIN JUST TURNED THE BALL INTO A UFO!
GOAAAAL!
3-3
THE GAME IS TIED WITH ONLY A FEW MOMENTS LEFT!

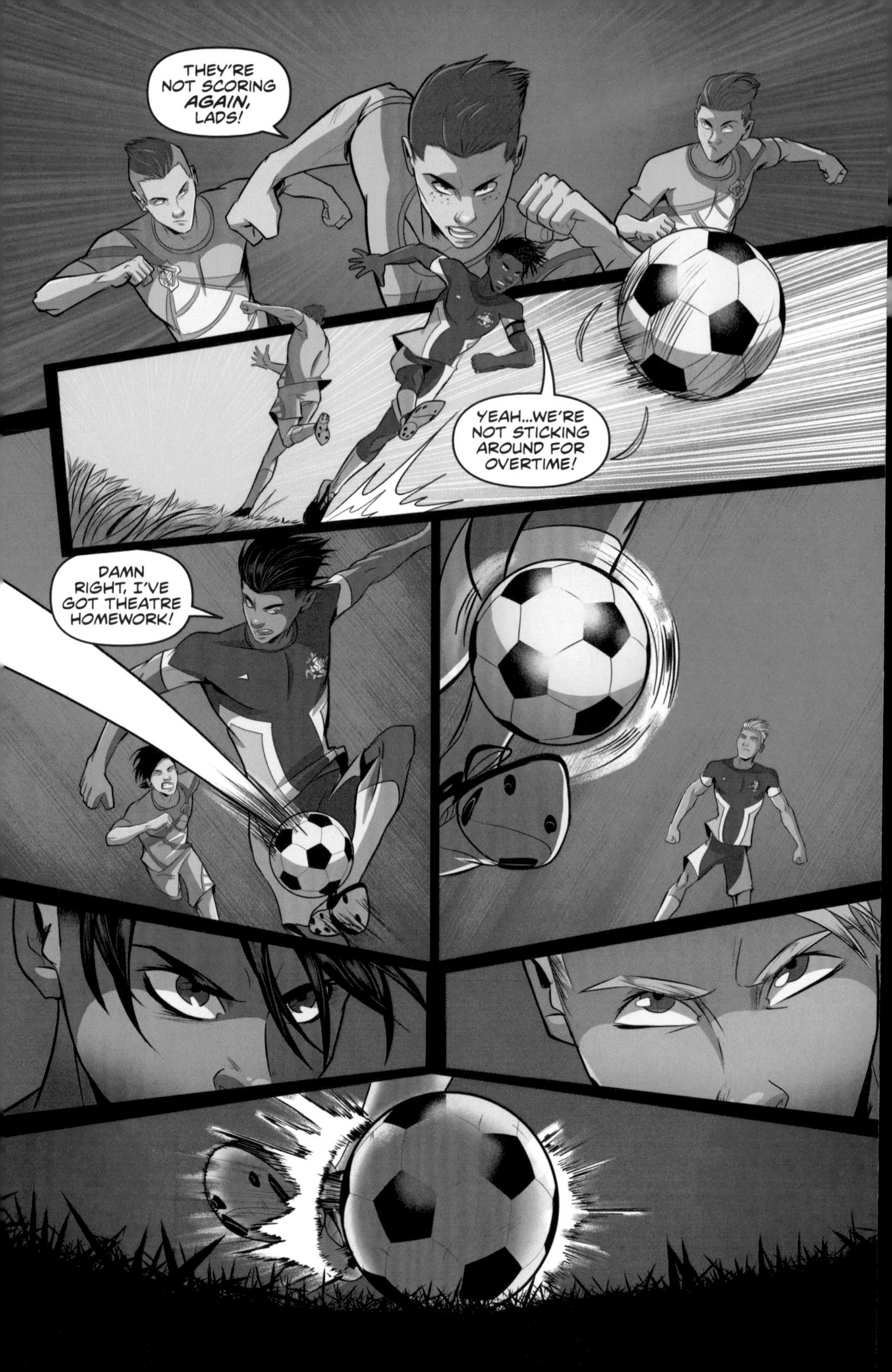
THEY'RE NOT SCORING AGAIN, LADS!
YEAH...WE'RE NOT STICKING AROUND FOR OVERTIME!
DAMN RIGHT, I'VE GOT THEATRE HOMEWORK!

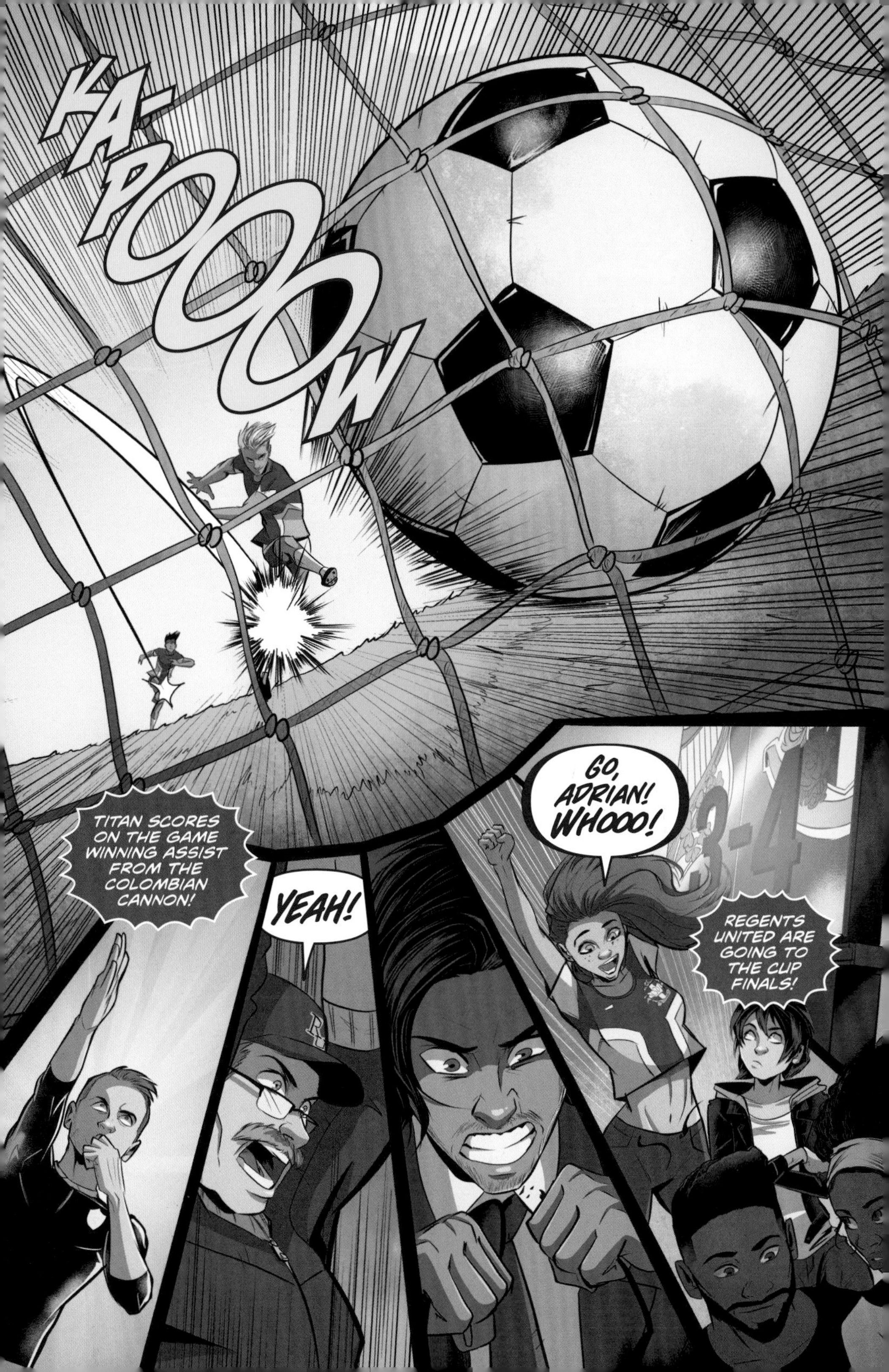
KA-POOOOW
TITAN SCORES ON THE GAME WINNING ASSIST FROM THE COLOMBIAN CANNON!
YEAH!
GO, ADRIAN! WHOOO!
REGENTS UNITED ARE GOING TO THE CUP FINALS!

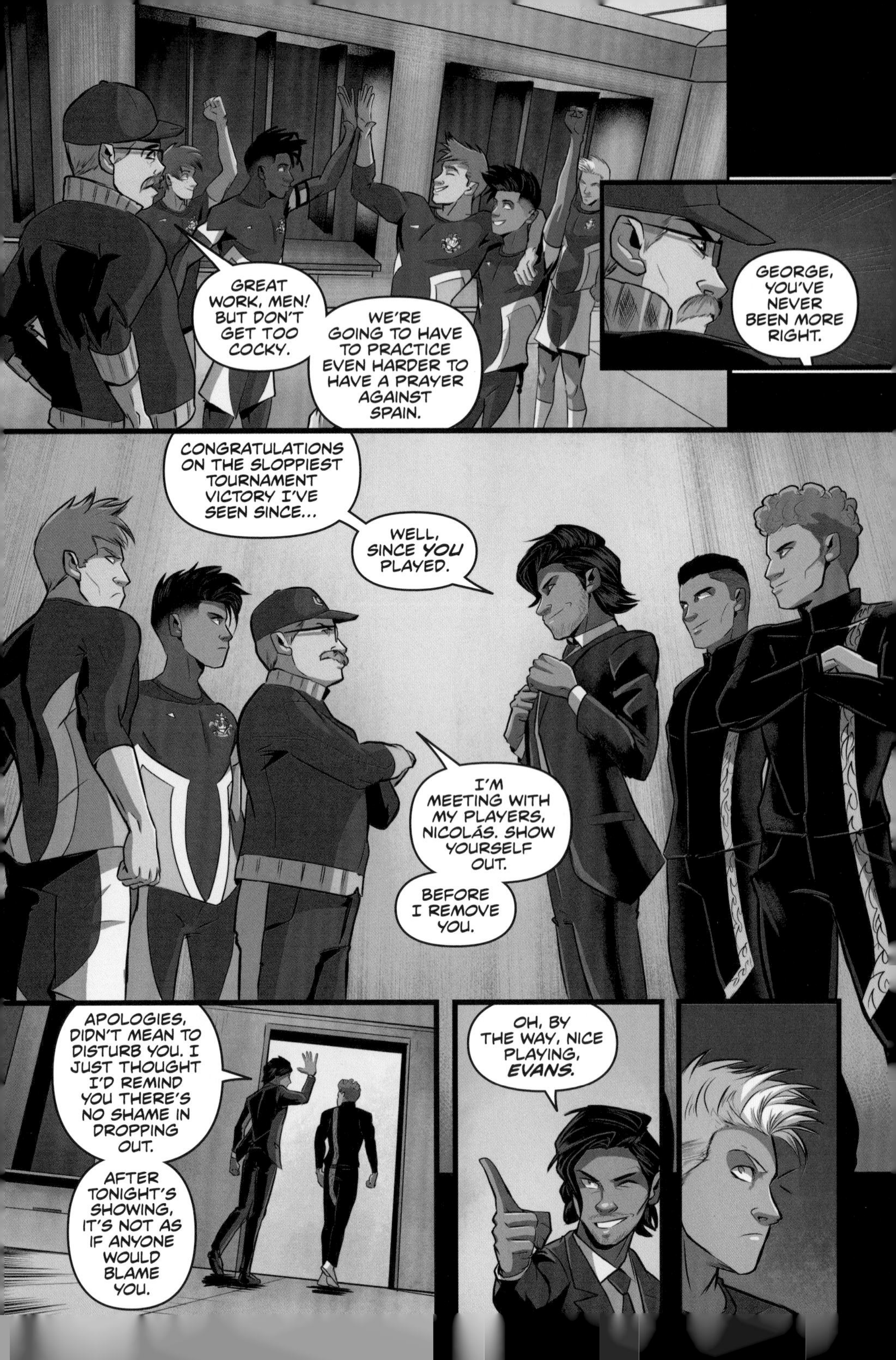
GREAT WORK, MEN! BUT DON'T GET TOO COCKY.
WE'RE GOING TO HAVE TO PRACTICE EVEN HARDER TO HAVE A PRAYER AGAINST SPAIN.
GEORGE, YOU'VE NEVER BEEN MORE RIGHT.
CONGRATULATIONS ON THE SLOPPIEST TOURNAMENT VICTORY I'VE SEEN SINCE...
WELL, SINCE *YOU* PLAYED.
I'M MEETING WITH MY PLAYERS, NICOLÁS. SHOW YOURSELF OUT.
BEFORE I REMOVE YOU.
APOLOGIES, DIDN'T MEAN TO DISTURB YOU. I JUST THOUGHT I'D REMIND YOU THERE'S NO SHAME IN DROPPING OUT.
AFTER TONIGHT'S SHOWING, IT'S NOT AS IF ANYONE WOULD BLAME YOU.
OH, BY THE WAY, NICE PLAYING, *EVANS.*

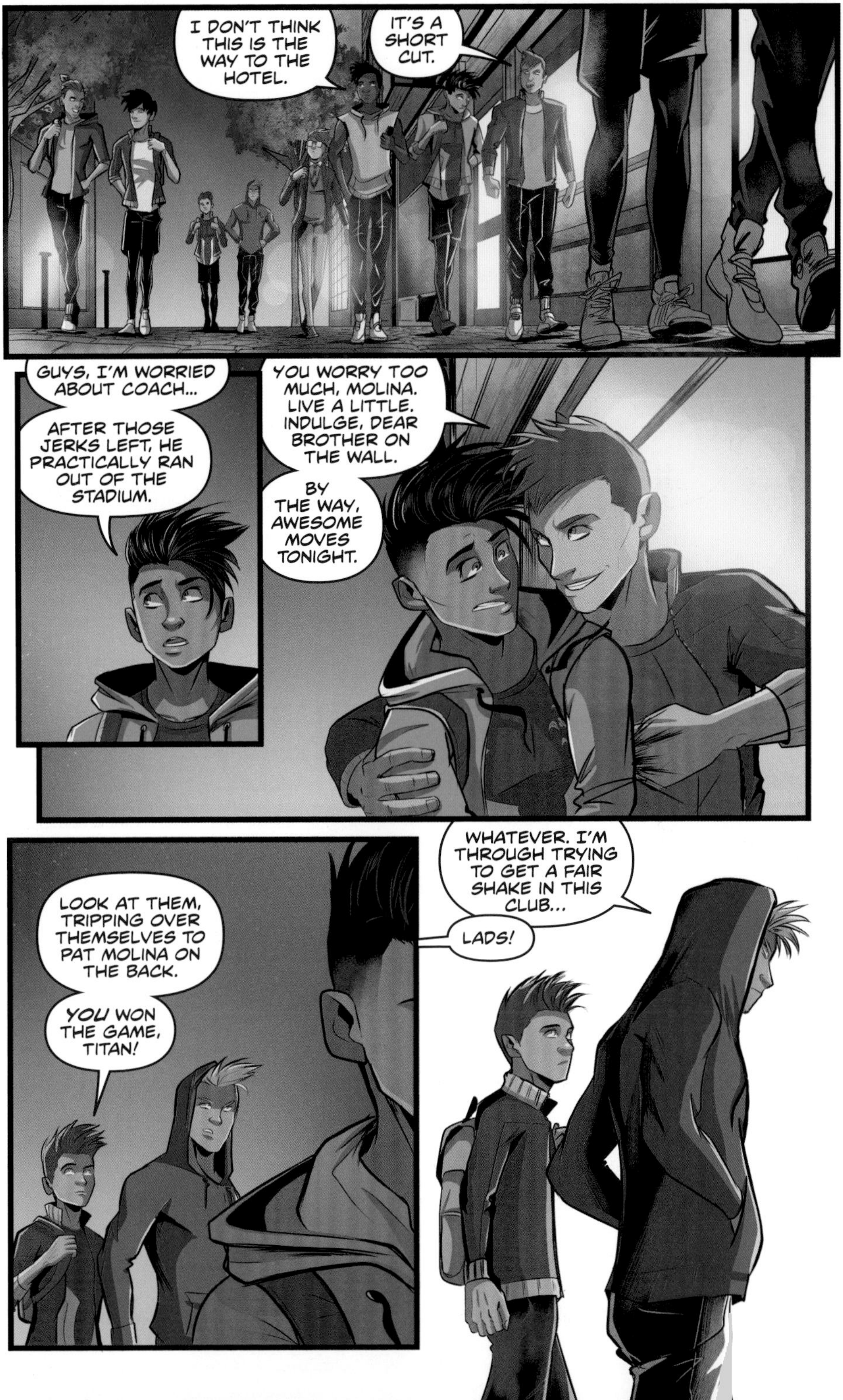
I DON'T THINK THIS IS THE WAY TO THE HOTEL.
IT'S A SHORT CUT.
GUYS, I'M WORRIED ABOUT COACH...
AFTER THOSE JERKS LEFT, HE PRACTICALLY RAN OUT OF THE STADIUM.
YOU WORRY TOO MUCH, MOLINA. LIVE A LITTLE. INDULGE, DEAR BROTHER ON THE WALL.
BY THE WAY, AWESOME MOVES TONIGHT.
LOOK AT THEM, TRIPPING OVER THEMSELVES TO PAT MOLINA ON THE BACK.
YOU WON THE GAME, TITAN!
LADS!
WHATEVER. I'M THROUGH TRYING TO GET A FAIR SHAKE IN THIS CLUB...

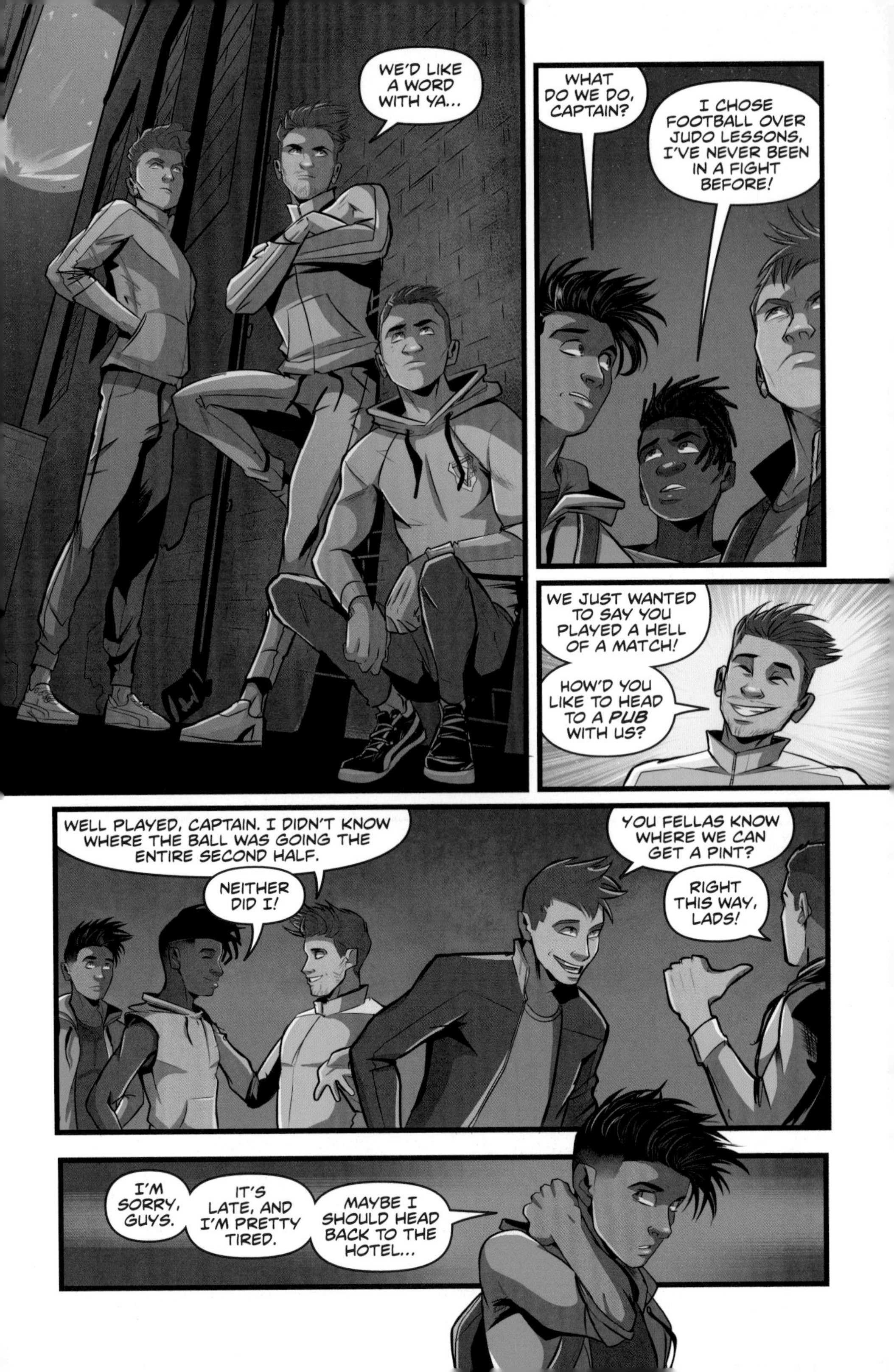
WE'D LIKE A WORD WITH YA...
WHAT DO WE DO, CAPTAIN?
I CHOSE FOOTBALL OVER JUDO LESSONS, I'VE NEVER BEEN IN A FIGHT BEFORE!
WE JUST WANTED TO SAY YOU PLAYED A HELL OF A MATCH!
HOW'D YOU LIKE TO HEAD TO A *PUB* WITH US?
WELL PLAYED, CAPTAIN. I DIDN'T KNOW WHERE THE BALL WAS GOING THE ENTIRE SECOND HALF.
NEITHER DID I!
YOU FELLAS KNOW WHERE WE CAN GET A PINT?
RIGHT THIS WAY, LADS!
I'M SORRY, GUYS.
IT'S LATE, AND I'M PRETTY TIRED.
MAYBE I SHOULD HEAD BACK TO THE HOTEL...

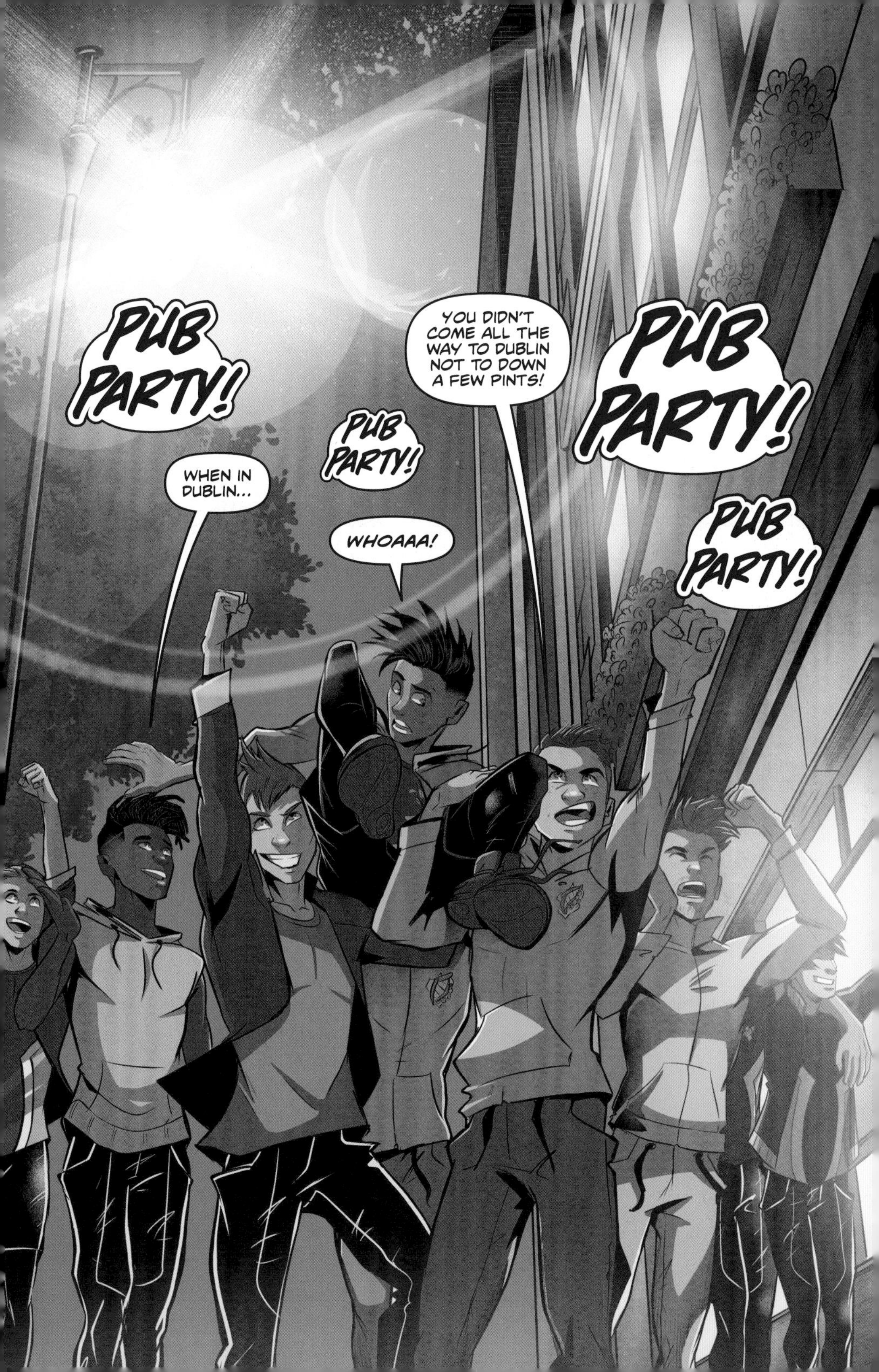
PUB PARTY!
WHEN IN DUBLIN...
PUB PARTY!
WHOAAA!
YOU DIDN'T COME ALL THE WAY TO DUBLIN NOT TO DOWN A FEW PINTS!
PUB PARTY!
PUB PARTY!

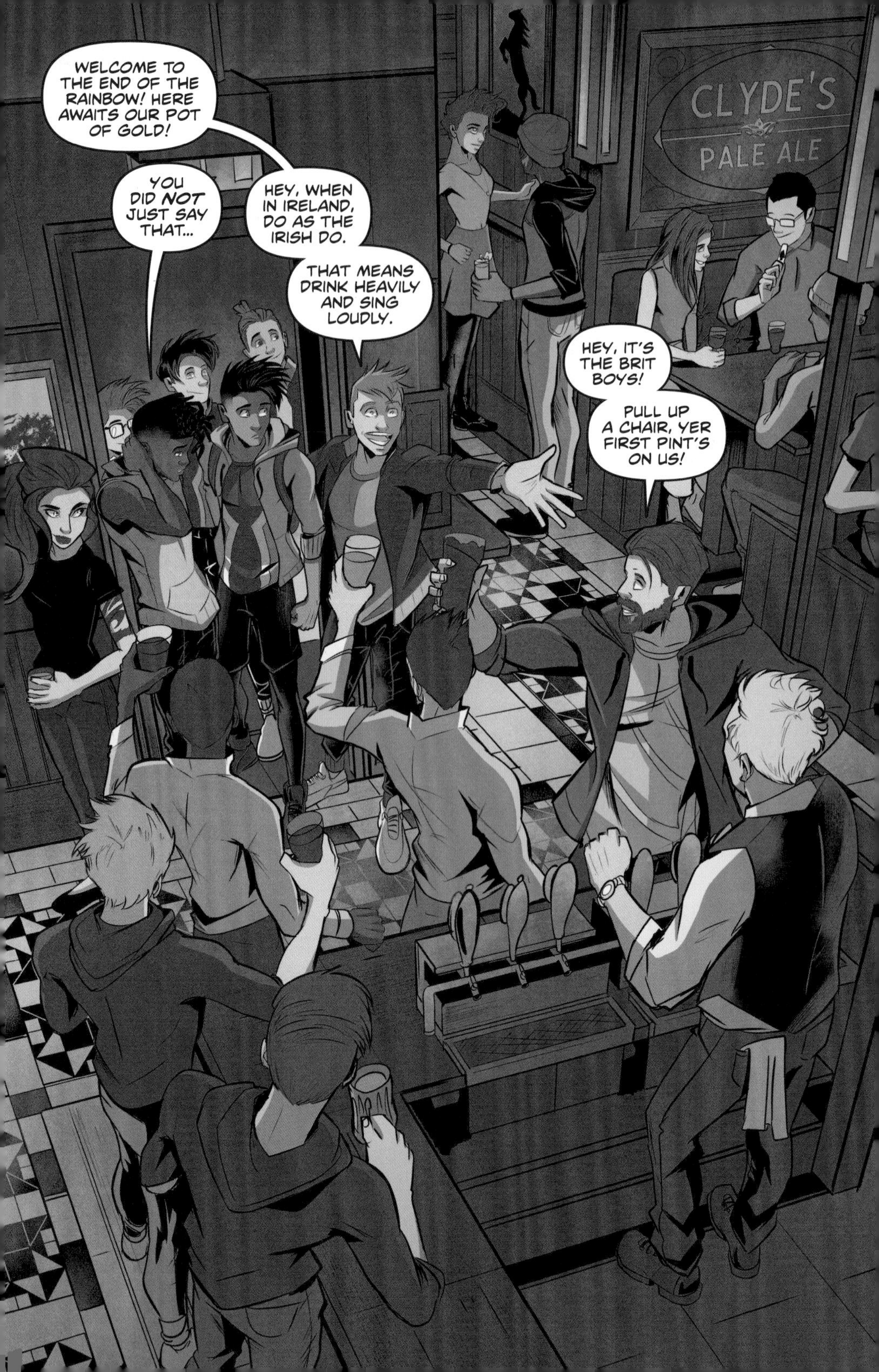
WELCOME TO THE END OF THE RAINBOW! HERE AWAITS OUR POT OF GOLD!
YOU DID **NOT** JUST SAY THAT...
HEY, WHEN IN IRELAND, DO AS THE IRISH DO.
THAT MEANS DRINK HEAVILY AND SING LOUDLY.
CLYDE'S PALE ALE
HEY, IT'S THE BRIT BOYS!
PULL UP A CHAIR, YER FIRST PINT'S ON US!

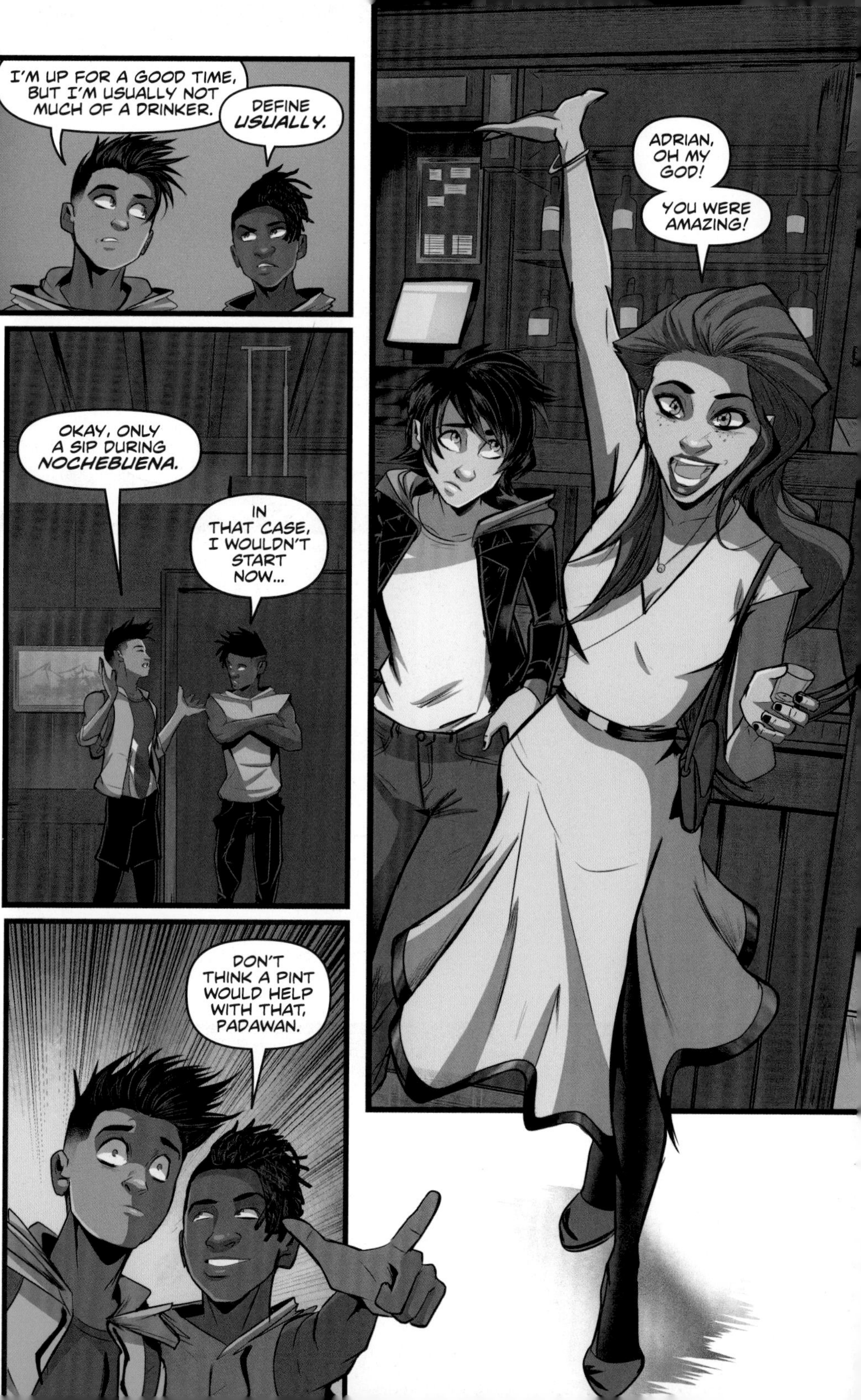
I'M UP FOR A GOOD TIME, BUT I'M USUALLY NOT MUCH OF A DRINKER.
DEFINE *USUALLY.*
OKAY, ONLY A SIP DURING *NOCHEBUENA.*
IN THAT CASE, I WOULDN'T START NOW...
DON'T THINK A PINT WOULD HELP WITH THAT, PADAWAN.
ADRIAN, OH MY GOD!
YOU WERE AMAZING!

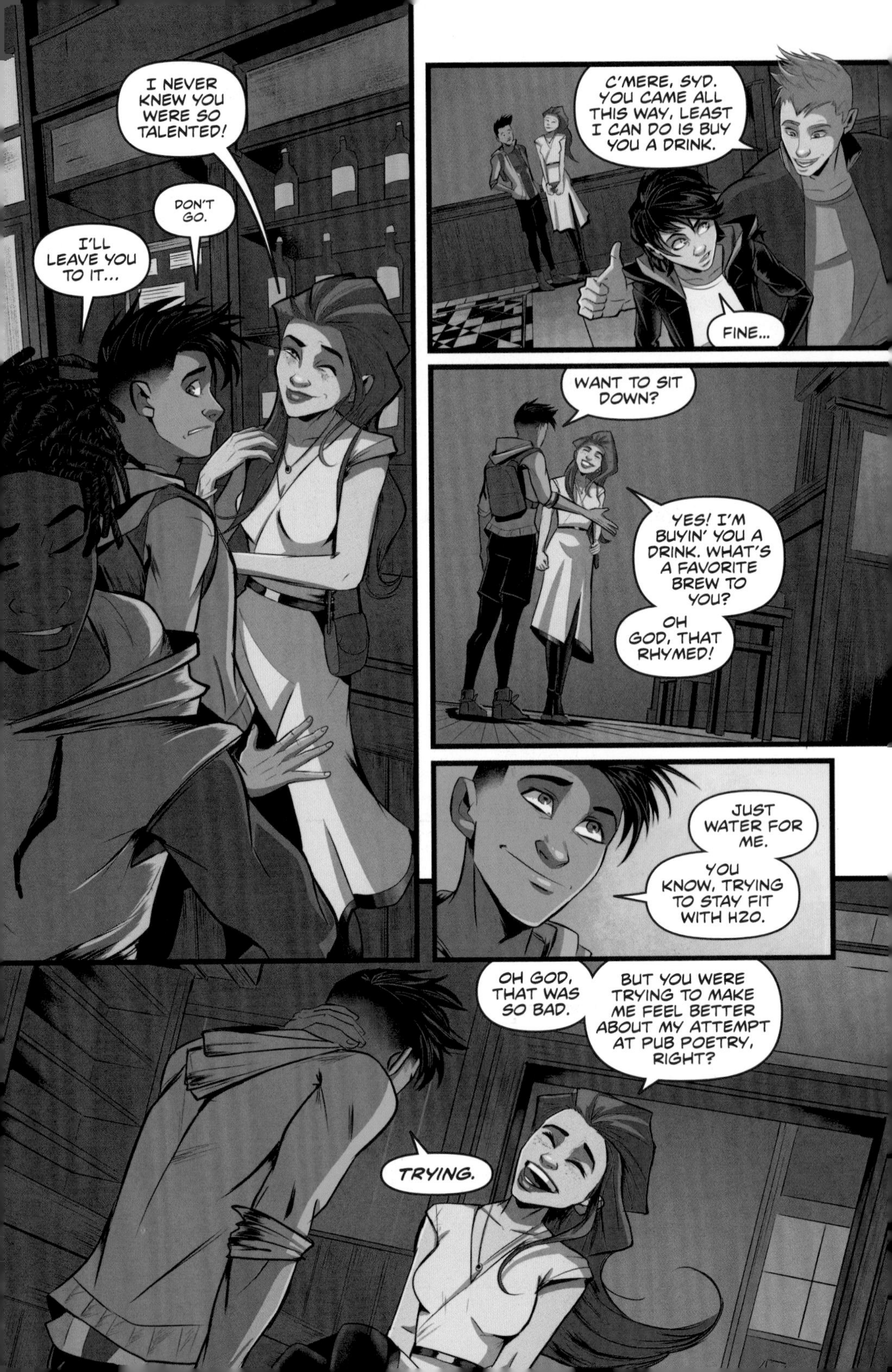

I NEVER KNEW YOU WERE SO TALENTED!
DON'T GO.
I'LL LEAVE YOU TO IT...
C'MERE, SYD. YOU CAME ALL THIS WAY, LEAST I CAN DO IS BUY YOU A DRINK.
FINE...
WANT TO SIT DOWN?
YES! I'M BUYIN' YOU A DRINK. WHAT'S A FAVORITE BREW TO YOU?
OH GOD, THAT RHYMED!
JUST WATER FOR ME.
YOU KNOW, TRYING TO STAY FIT WITH H2O.
OH GOD, THAT WAS SO BAD.
BUT YOU WERE TRYING TO MAKE ME FEEL BETTER ABOUT MY ATTEMPT AT PUB POETRY, RIGHT?
TRYING.

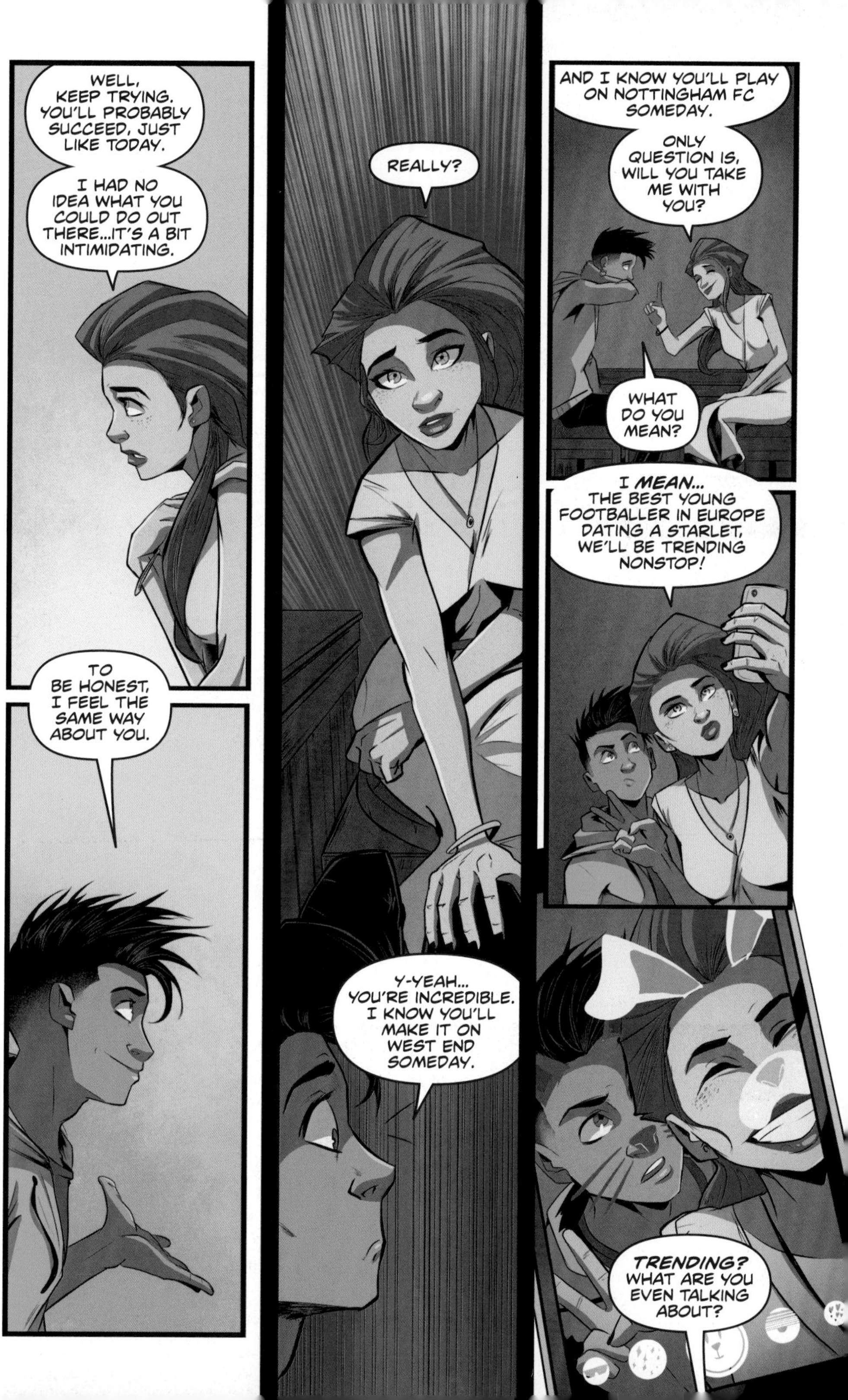
WELL, KEEP TRYING. YOU'LL PROBABLY SUCCEED, JUST LIKE TODAY.
I HAD NO IDEA WHAT YOU COULD DO OUT THERE...IT'S A BIT INTIMIDATING.
TO BE HONEST, I FEEL THE SAME WAY ABOUT YOU.
REALLY?
Y-YEAH... YOU'RE INCREDIBLE. I KNOW YOU'LL MAKE IT ON WEST END SOMEDAY.
AND I KNOW YOU'LL PLAY ON NOTTINGHAM FC SOMEDAY.
ONLY QUESTION IS, WILL YOU TAKE ME WITH YOU?
WHAT DO YOU MEAN?
I *MEAN*... THE BEST YOUNG FOOTBALLER IN EUROPE DATING A STARLET, WE'LL BE TRENDING NONSTOP!
TRENDING? WHAT ARE YOU EVEN TALKING ABOUT?

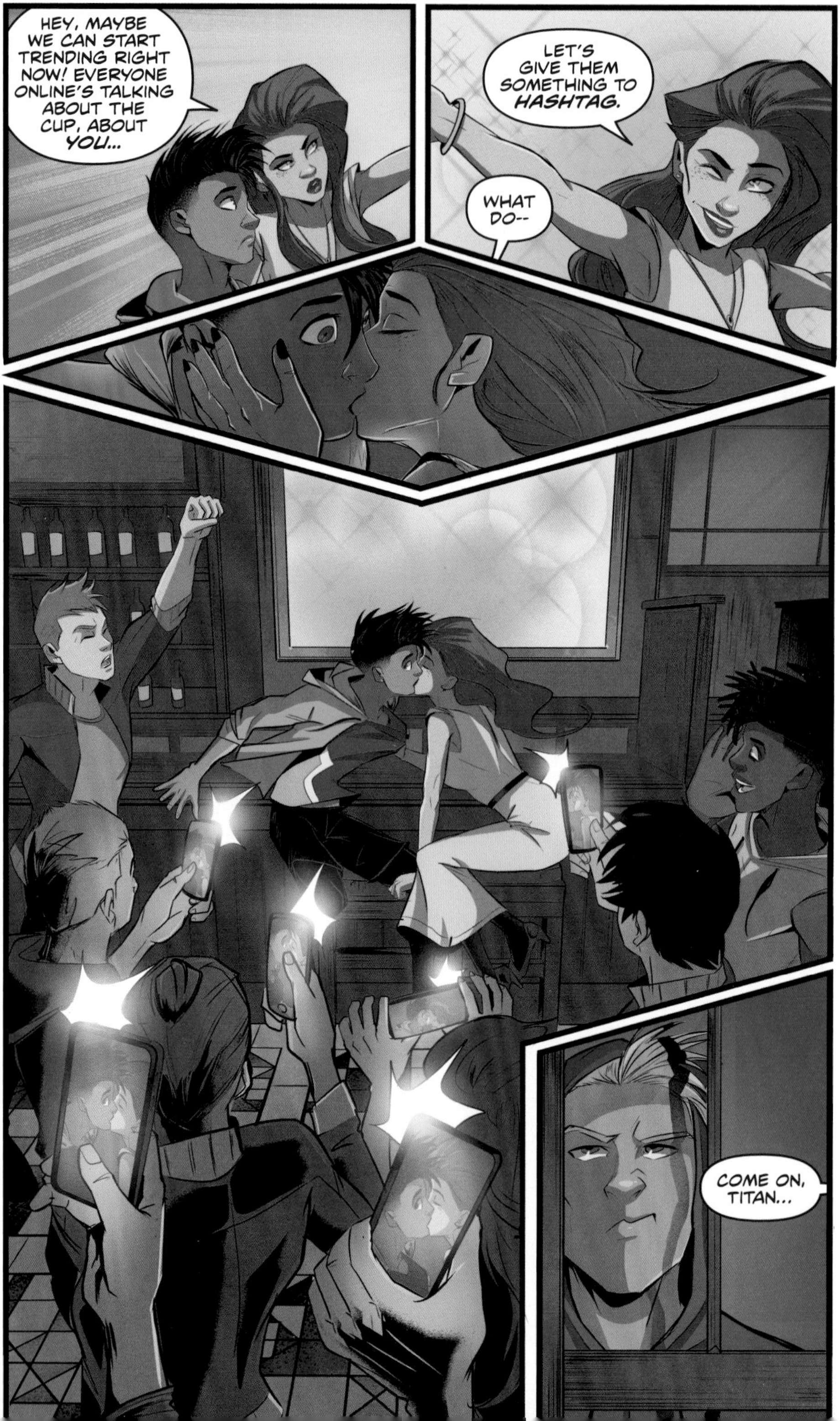
HEY, MAYBE WE CAN START TRENDING RIGHT NOW! EVERYONE ONLINE'S TALKING ABOUT THE CUP, ABOUT YOU...
LET'S GIVE THEM SOMETHING TO HASHTAG.
WHAT DO--
COME ON, TITAN...

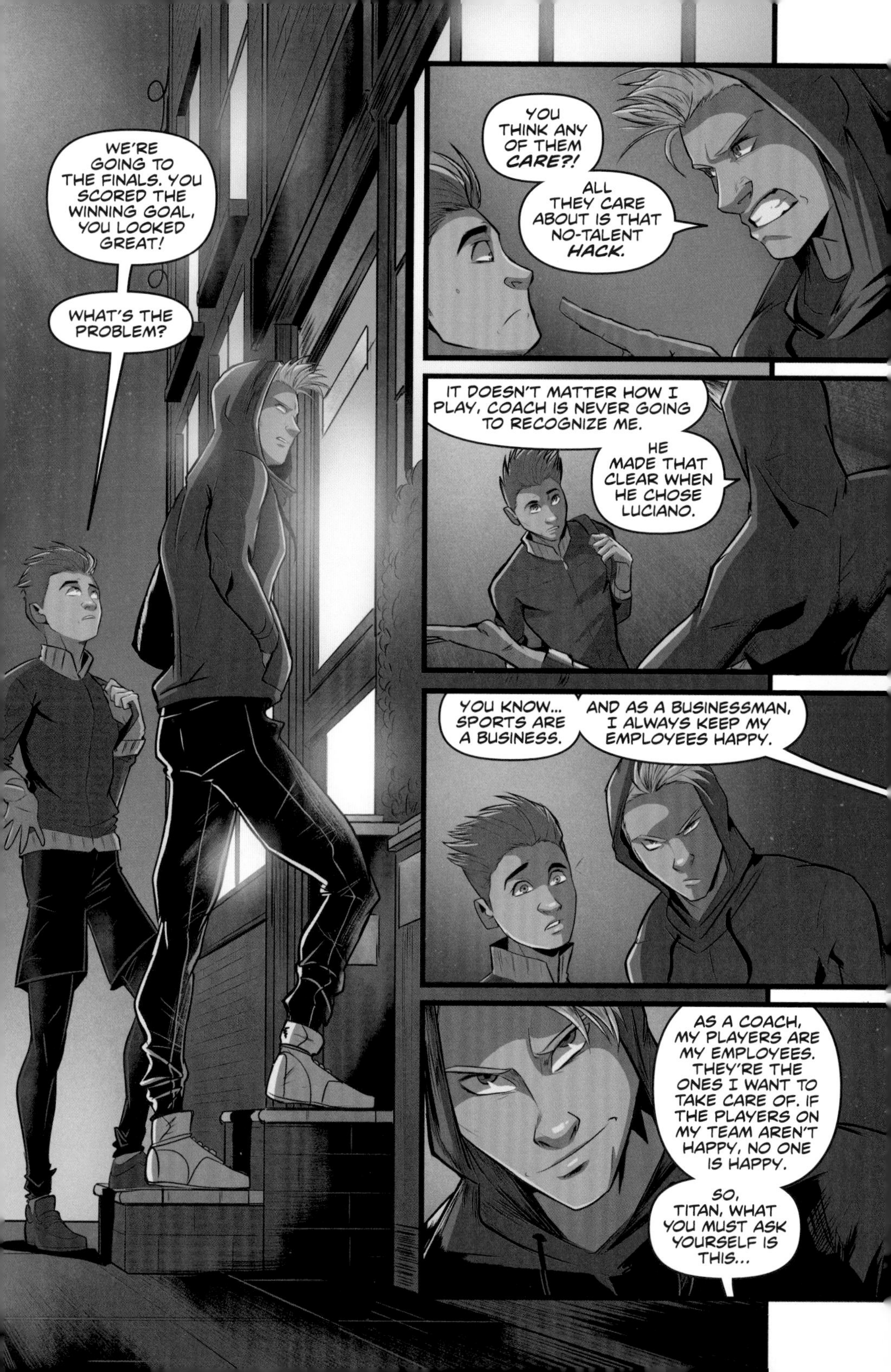
WE'RE GOING TO THE FINALS. YOU SCORED THE WINNING GOAL, YOU LOOKED GREAT!
WHAT'S THE PROBLEM?
YOU THINK ANY OF THEM *CARE?!*
ALL THEY CARE ABOUT IS THAT NO-TALENT *HACK.*
IT DOESN'T MATTER HOW I PLAY, COACH IS NEVER GOING TO RECOGNIZE ME.
HE MADE THAT CLEAR WHEN HE CHOSE LUCIANO.
YOU KNOW... SPORTS ARE A BUSINESS.
AND AS A BUSINESSMAN, I ALWAYS KEEP MY EMPLOYEES HAPPY.
AS A COACH, MY PLAYERS ARE MY EMPLOYEES. THEY'RE THE ONES I WANT TO TAKE CARE OF. IF THE PLAYERS ON MY TEAM AREN'T HAPPY, NO ONE IS HAPPY.
SO, TITAN, WHAT YOU MUST ASK YOURSELF IS THIS...

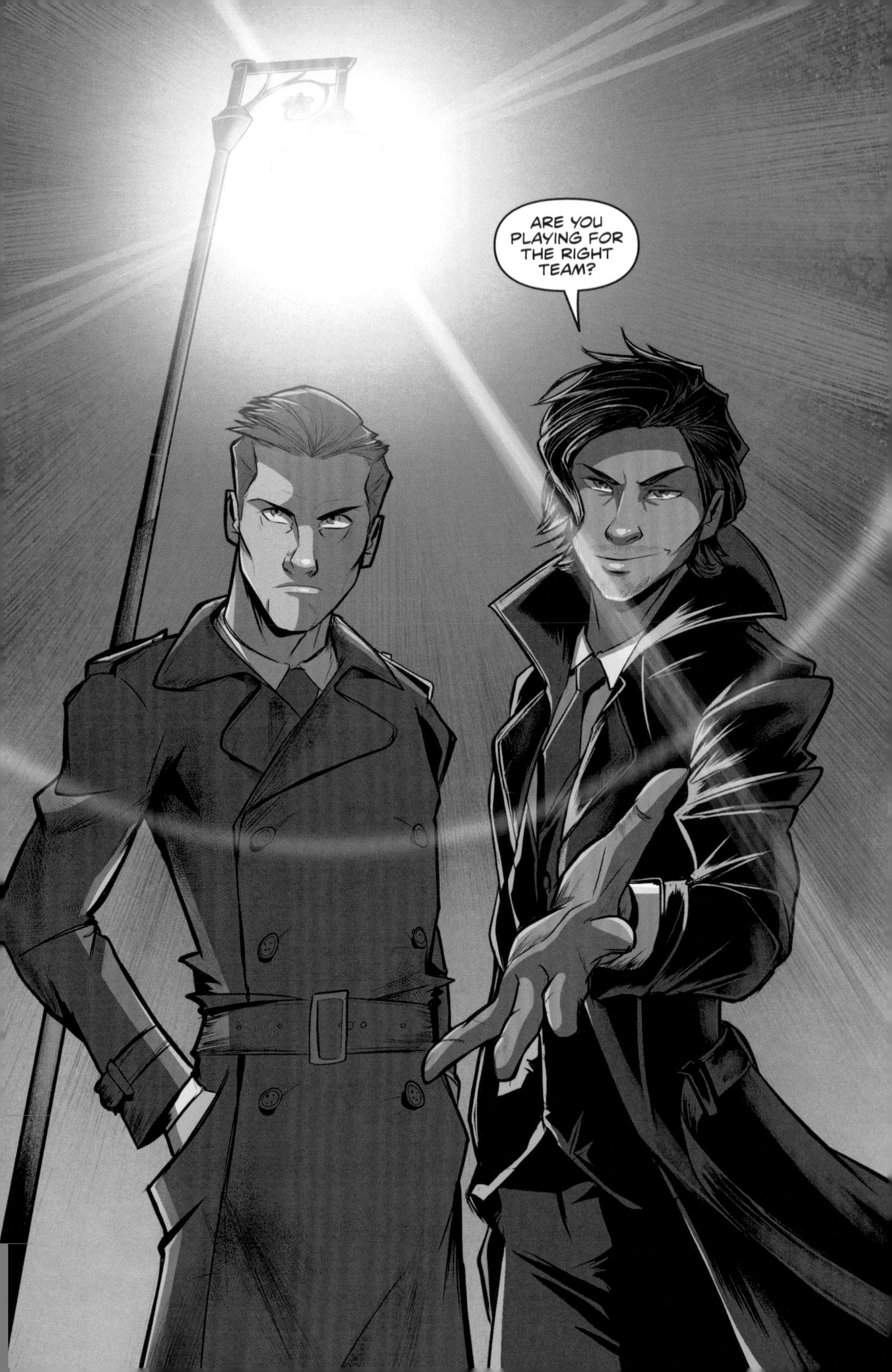
ARE YOU PLAYING FOR THE RIGHT TEAM?

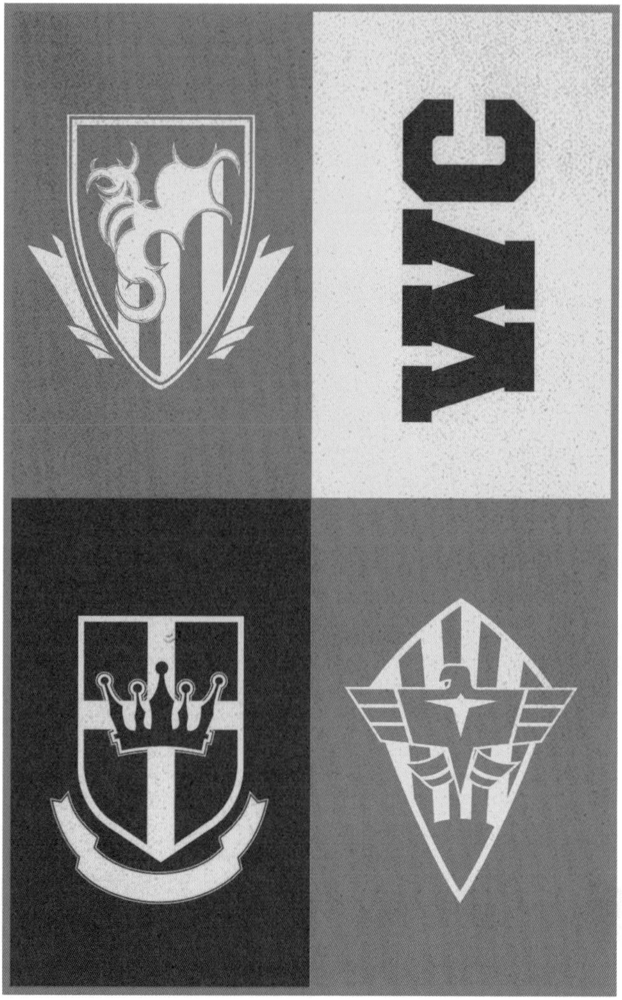
YWC

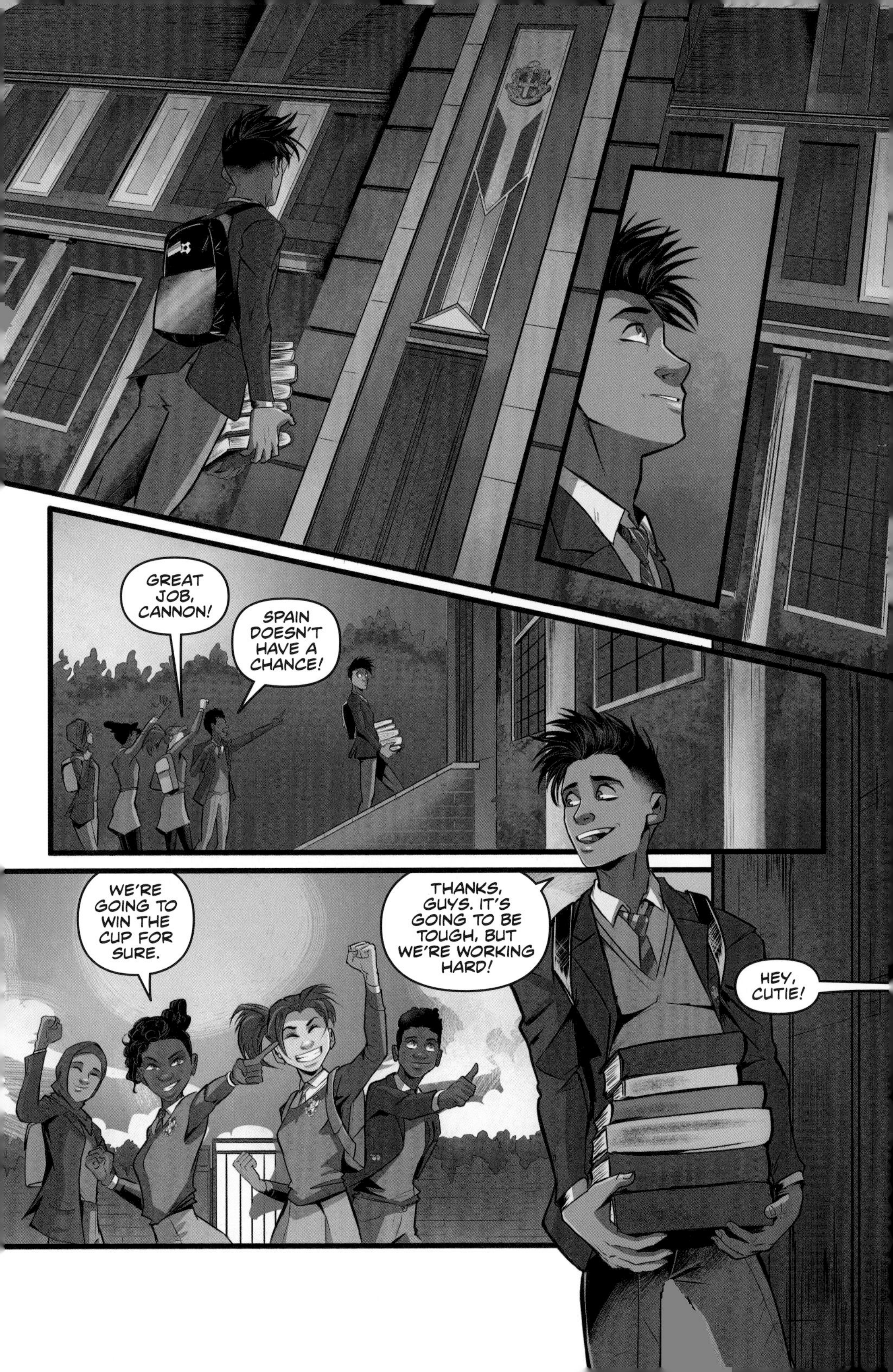
GREAT JOB, CANNON!
SPAIN DOESN'T HAVE A CHANCE!
WE'RE GOING TO WIN THE CUP FOR SURE.
THANKS, GUYS. IT'S GOING TO BE TOUGH, BUT WE'RE WORKING HARD!
HEY, CUTIE!

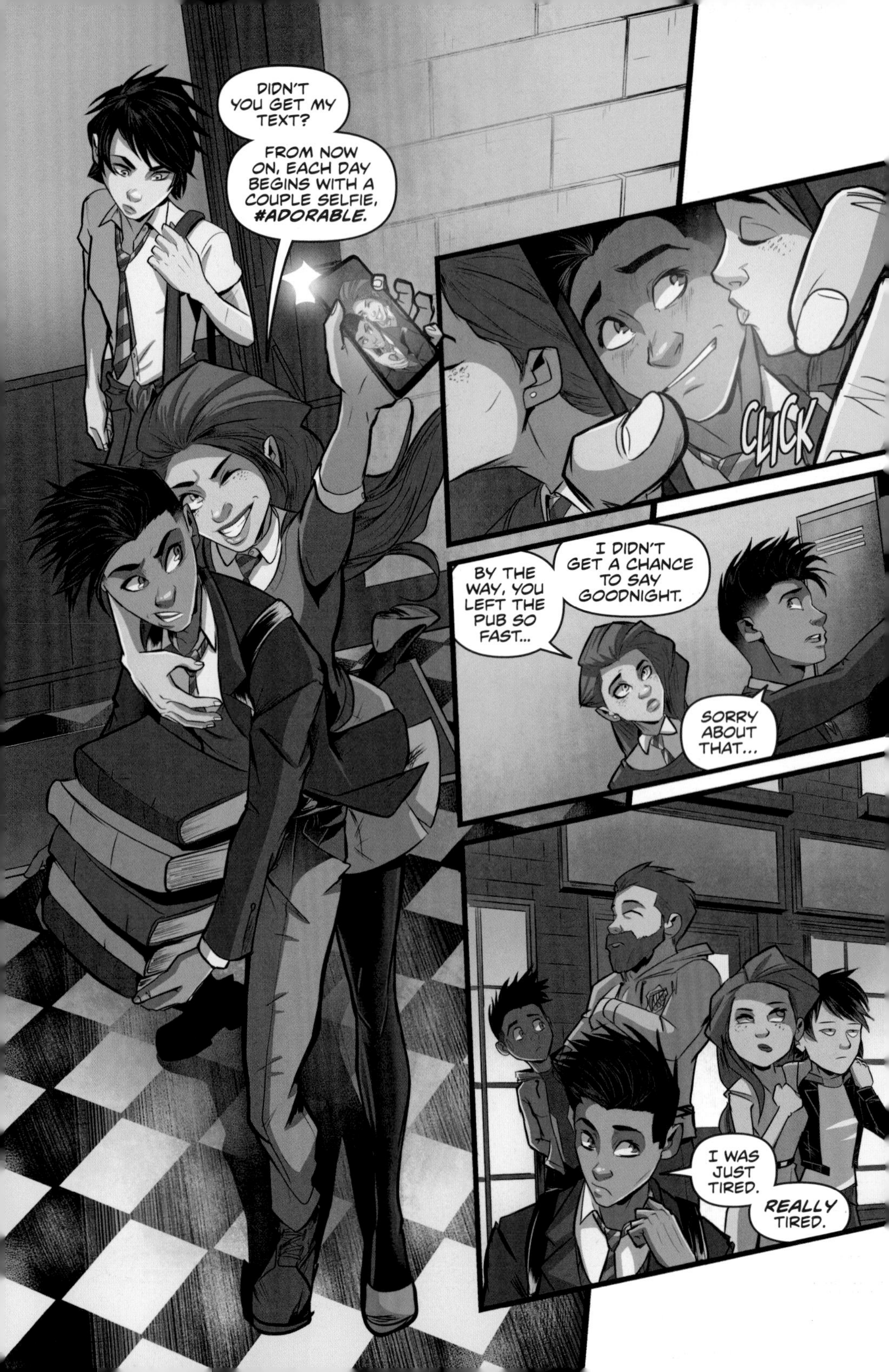
DIDN'T YOU GET MY TEXT?
FROM NOW ON, EACH DAY BEGINS WITH A COUPLE SELFIE, #ADORABLE.
CLICK
BY THE WAY, YOU LEFT THE PUB SO FAST...
I DIDN'T GET A CHANCE TO SAY GOODNIGHT.
SORRY ABOUT THAT...
I WAS JUST TIRED.
REALLY TIRED.

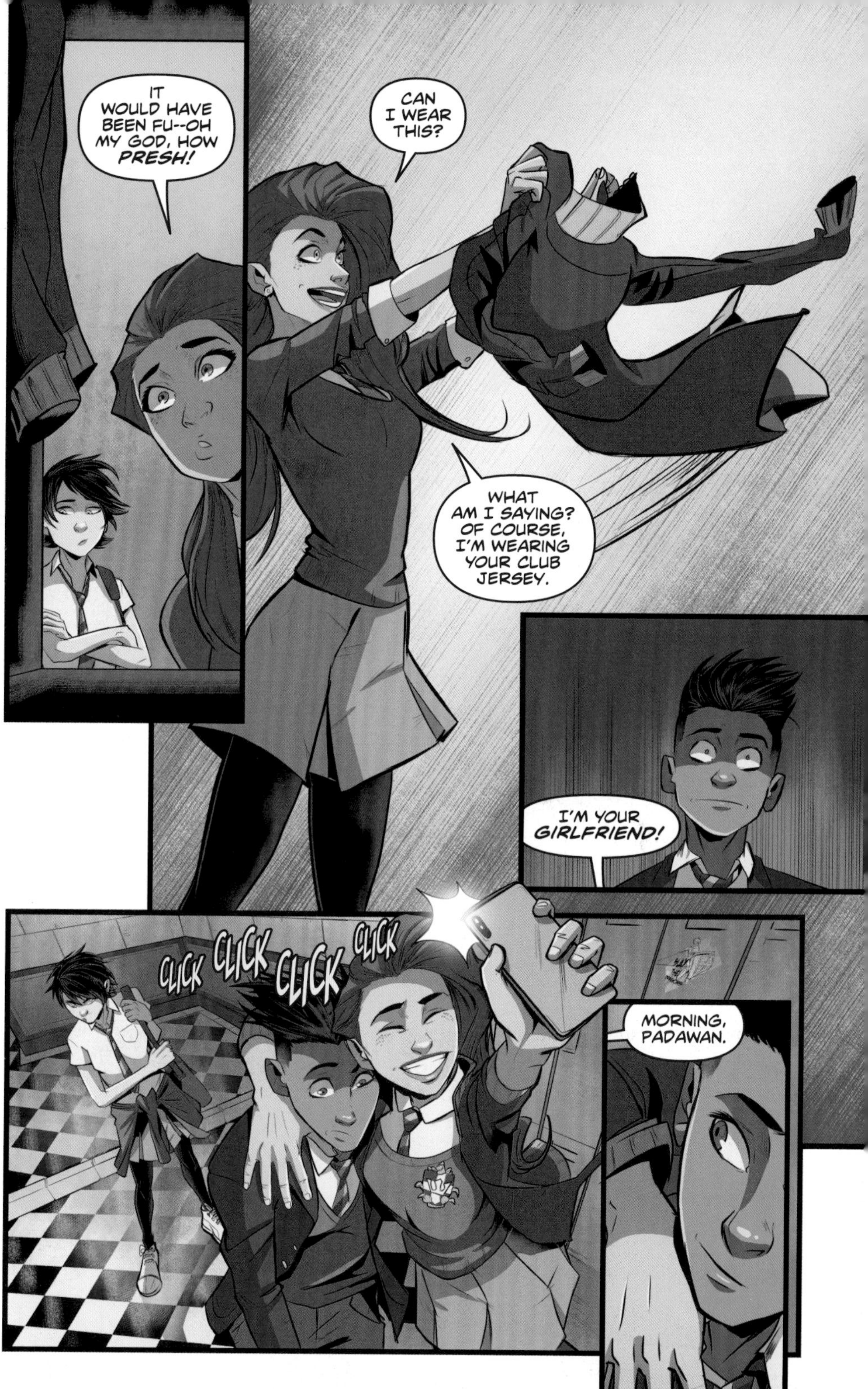
IT WOULD HAVE BEEN FU--OH MY GOD, HOW PRESH!
CAN I WEAR THIS?
WHAT AM I SAYING? OF COURSE, I'M WEARING YOUR CLUB JERSEY.
I'M YOUR GIRLFRIEND!
CLICK CLICK CLICK CLICK
MORNING, PADAWAN.

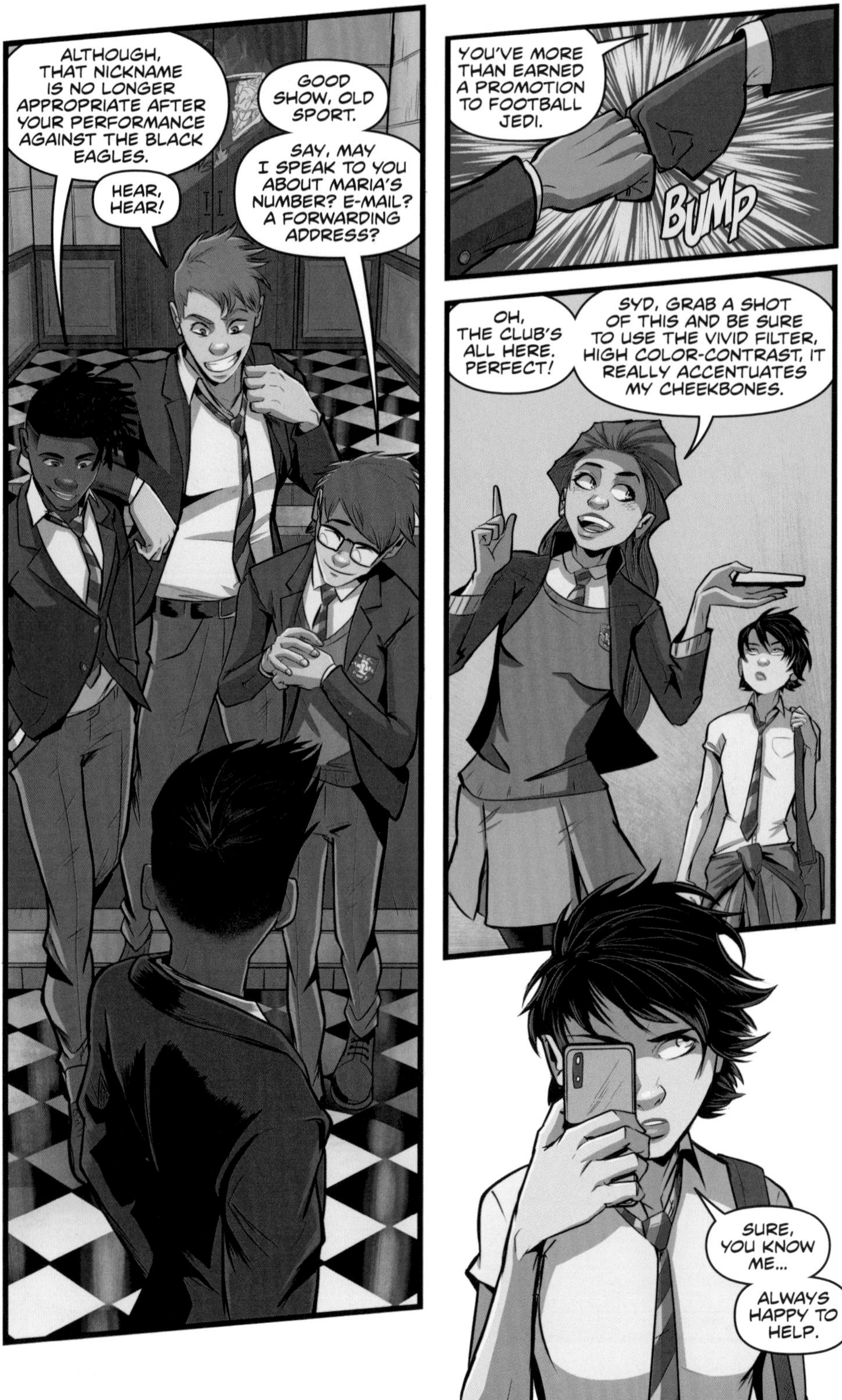
ALTHOUGH, THAT NICKNAME IS NO LONGER APPROPRIATE AFTER YOUR PERFORMANCE AGAINST THE BLACK EAGLES.
HEAR, HEAR!
GOOD SHOW, OLD SPORT.
SAY, MAY I SPEAK TO YOU ABOUT MARIA'S NUMBER? E-MAIL? A FORWARDING ADDRESS?
YOU'VE MORE THAN EARNED A PROMOTION TO FOOTBALL JEDI.
BUMP
OH, THE CLUB'S ALL HERE. PERFECT!
SYD, GRAB A SHOT OF THIS AND BE SURE TO USE THE VIVID FILTER, HIGH COLOR-CONTRAST, IT REALLY ACCENTUATES MY CHEEKBONES.
SURE, YOU KNOW ME...
ALWAYS HAPPY TO HELP.

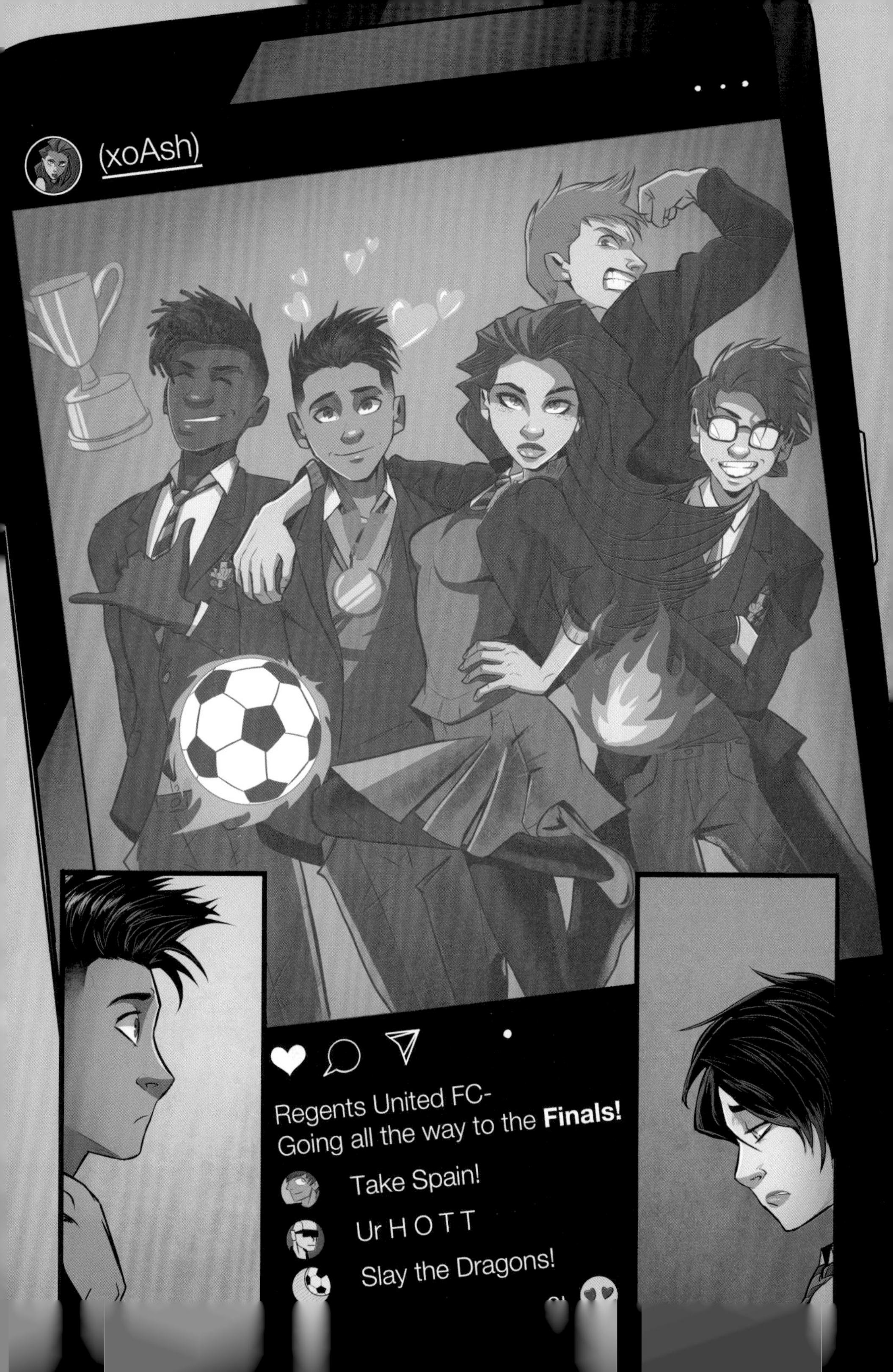
(xoAsh)
Regents United FC-
Going all the way to the **Finals!**
Take Spain!
Ur H O T T
Slay the Dragons!

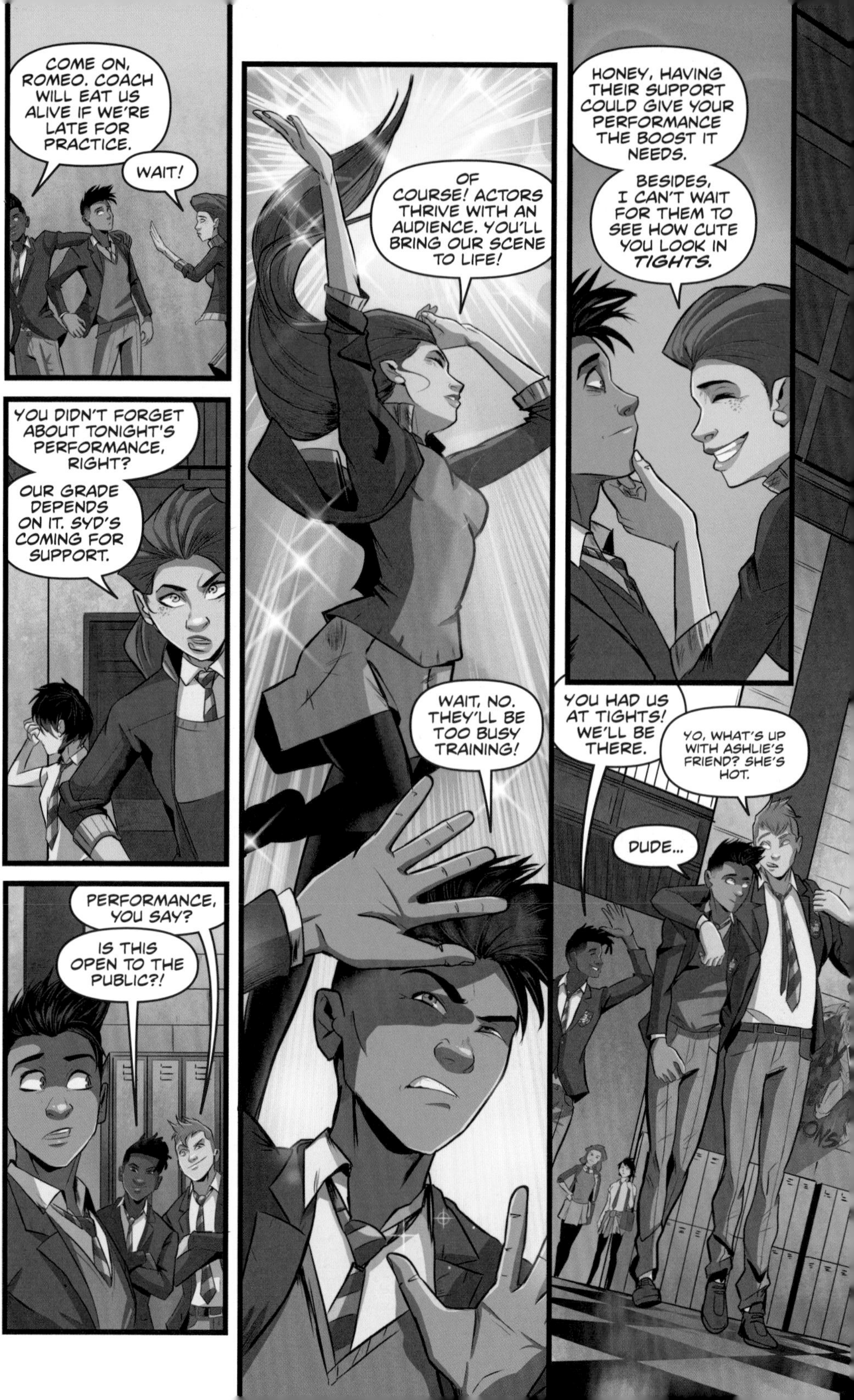
COME ON, ROMEO. COACH WILL EAT US ALIVE IF WE'RE LATE FOR PRACTICE.
WAIT!
YOU DIDN'T FORGET ABOUT TONIGHT'S PERFORMANCE, RIGHT?
OUR GRADE DEPENDS ON IT. SYD'S COMING FOR SUPPORT.
PERFORMANCE, YOU SAY?
IS THIS OPEN TO THE PUBLIC?!
OF COURSE! ACTORS THRIVE WITH AN AUDIENCE. YOU'LL BRING OUR SCENE TO LIFE!
WAIT, NO. THEY'LL BE TOO BUSY TRAINING!
HONEY, HAVING THEIR SUPPORT COULD GIVE YOUR PERFORMANCE THE BOOST IT NEEDS.
BESIDES, I CAN'T WAIT FOR THEM TO SEE HOW CUTE YOU LOOK IN *TIGHTS.*
YOU HAD US AT TIGHTS! WE'LL BE THERE.
YO, WHAT'S UP WITH ASHLIE'S FRIEND? SHE'S HOT.
DUDE...

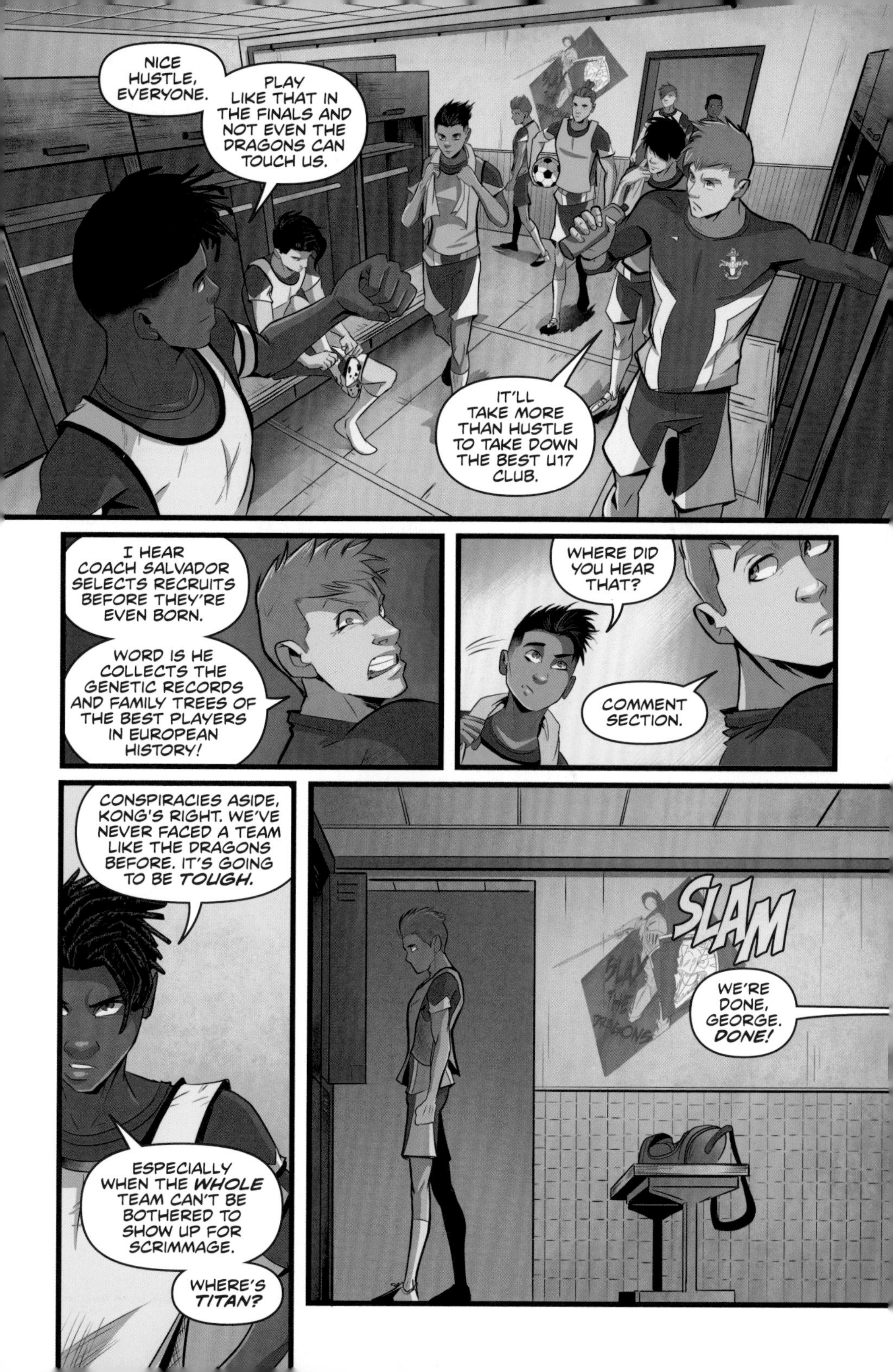
NICE HUSTLE, EVERYONE.
PLAY LIKE THAT IN THE FINALS AND NOT EVEN THE DRAGONS CAN TOUCH US.
IT'LL TAKE MORE THAN HUSTLE TO TAKE DOWN THE BEST U17 CLUB.
I HEAR COACH SALVADOR SELECTS RECRUITS BEFORE THEY'RE EVEN BORN.
WORD IS HE COLLECTS THE GENETIC RECORDS AND FAMILY TREES OF THE BEST PLAYERS IN EUROPEAN HISTORY!
WHERE DID YOU HEAR THAT?
COMMENT SECTION.
CONSPIRACIES ASIDE, KONG'S RIGHT. WE'VE NEVER FACED A TEAM LIKE THE DRAGONS BEFORE. IT'S GOING TO BE *TOUGH*.
ESPECIALLY WHEN THE *WHOLE* TEAM CAN'T BE BOTHERED TO SHOW UP FOR SCRIMMAGE.
WHERE'S *TITAN*?
SLAM
SLAY THE DRAGONS
WE'RE DONE, GEORGE. *DONE!*

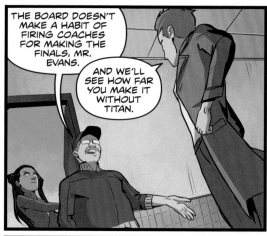

INFORM THE BOARD TO NOT EXPECT ANOTHER CHECK, ASSUMING THEY DON'T *FIRE* YOU.

WE'RE OUT OF THIS DUMP!

THE BOARD DOESN'T MAKE A HABIT OF FIRING COACHES FOR MAKING THE FINALS, MR. EVANS.

AND WE'LL SEE HOW FAR YOU MAKE IT WITHOUT TITAN.

TITAN'S ALWAYS BEEN A VALUED MEMBER OF THE CLUB, RICHARD.

IF YOU'D APPROACH THIS RATIONALLY--

RATIONALITY HAS LEFT THIS BUILDING A LONG TIME AGO, OLIVIA.

WHEN YOU DECIDED *THIS ONE* WAS A PRIORITY OVER MY SON!

TITAN, GET YOUR THINGS. WE'RE LEAVING.

NOW!

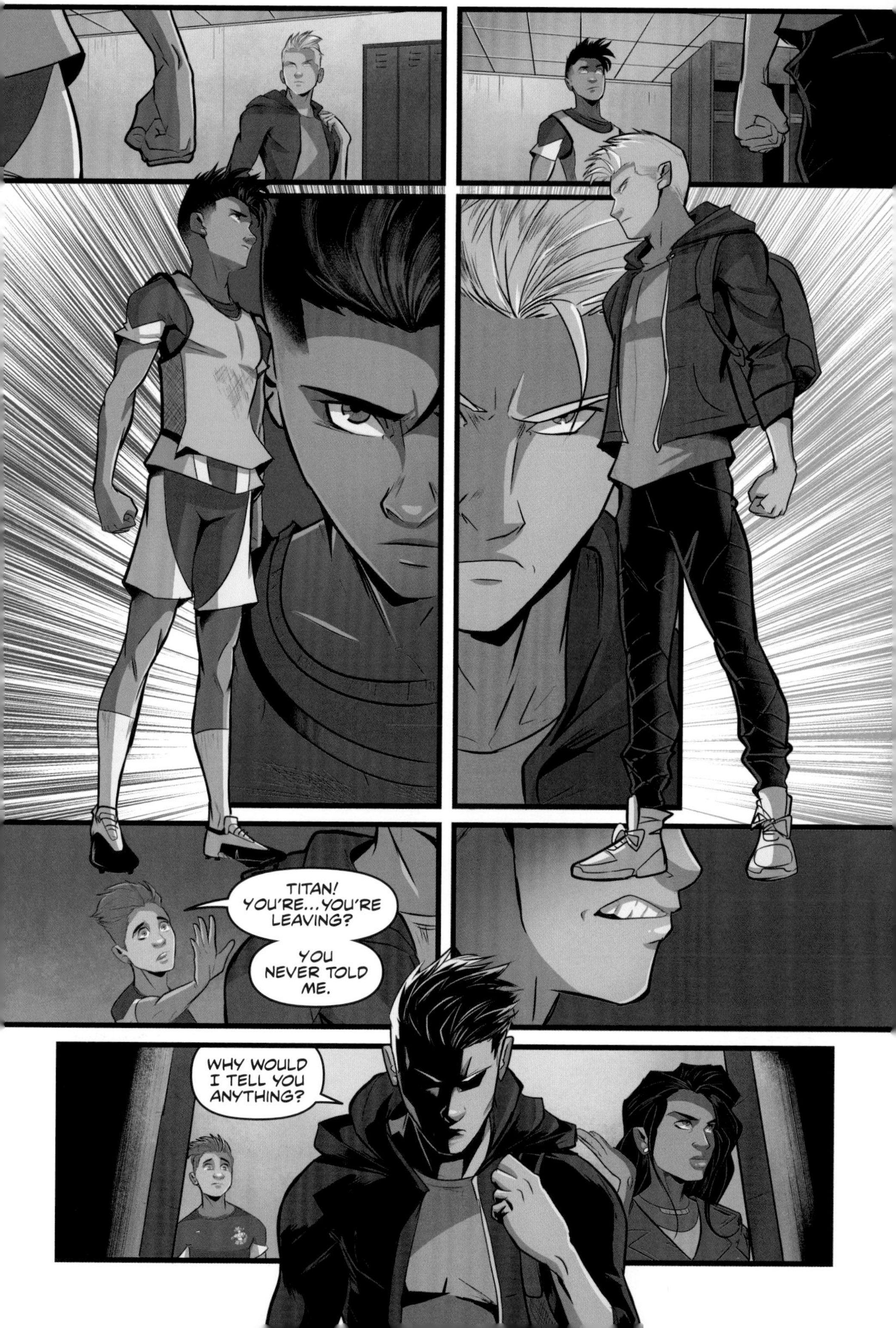
TITAN! YOU'RE...YOU'RE LEAVING?
YOU NEVER TOLD ME.
WHY WOULD I TELL YOU ANYTHING?

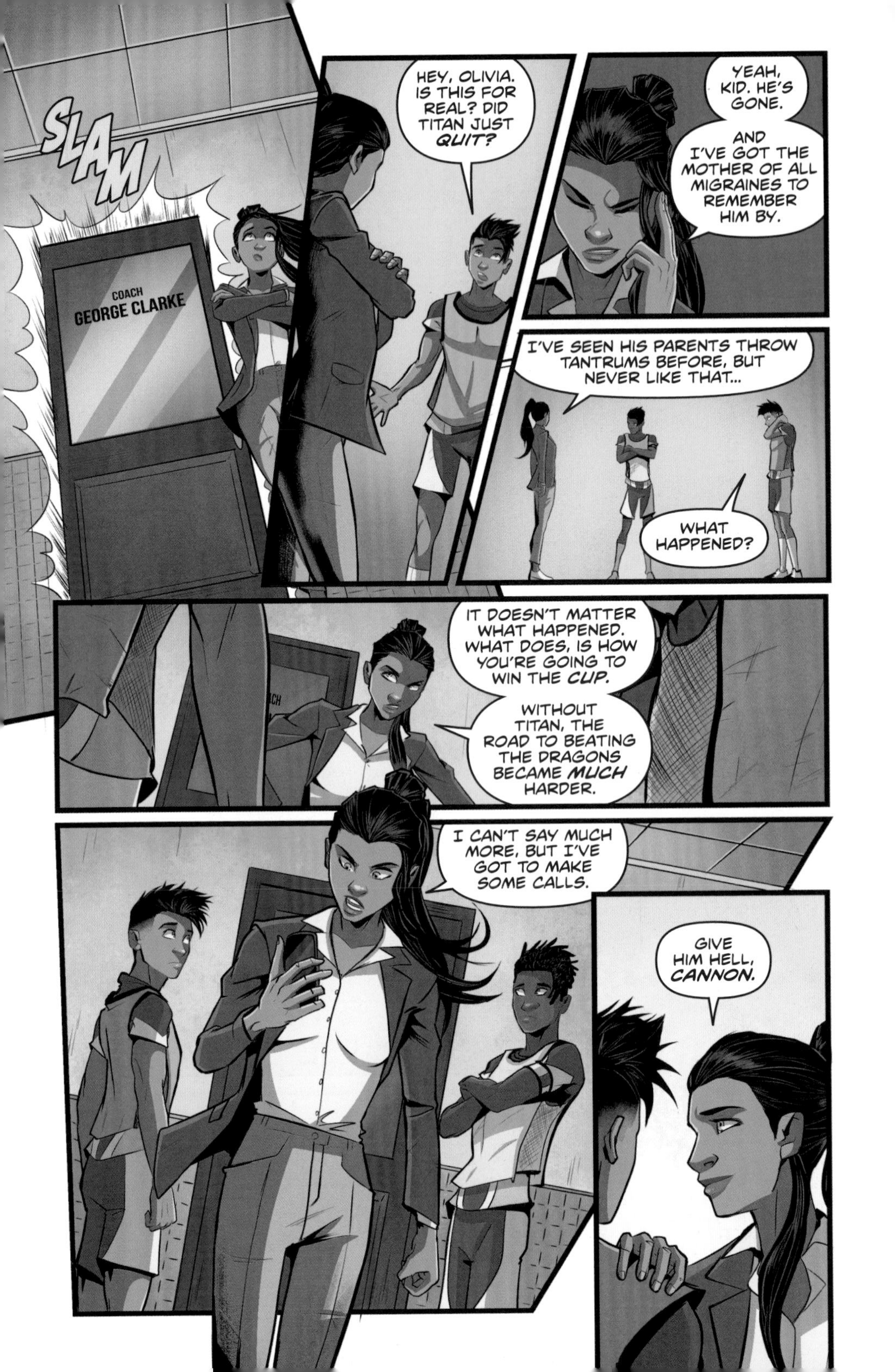
SLAM
COACH
GEORGE CLARKE
HEY, OLIVIA. IS THIS FOR REAL? DID TITAN JUST *QUIT?*
YEAH, KID. HE'S GONE.
AND I'VE GOT THE MOTHER OF ALL MIGRAINES TO REMEMBER HIM BY.
I'VE SEEN HIS PARENTS THROW TANTRUMS BEFORE, BUT NEVER LIKE THAT...
WHAT HAPPENED?
IT DOESN'T MATTER WHAT HAPPENED. WHAT DOES, IS HOW YOU'RE GOING TO WIN THE *CUP*.
WITHOUT TITAN, THE ROAD TO BEATING THE DRAGONS BECAME ***MUCH*** HARDER.
I CAN'T SAY MUCH MORE, BUT I'VE GOT TO MAKE SOME CALLS.
GIVE HIM HELL, ***CANNON.***

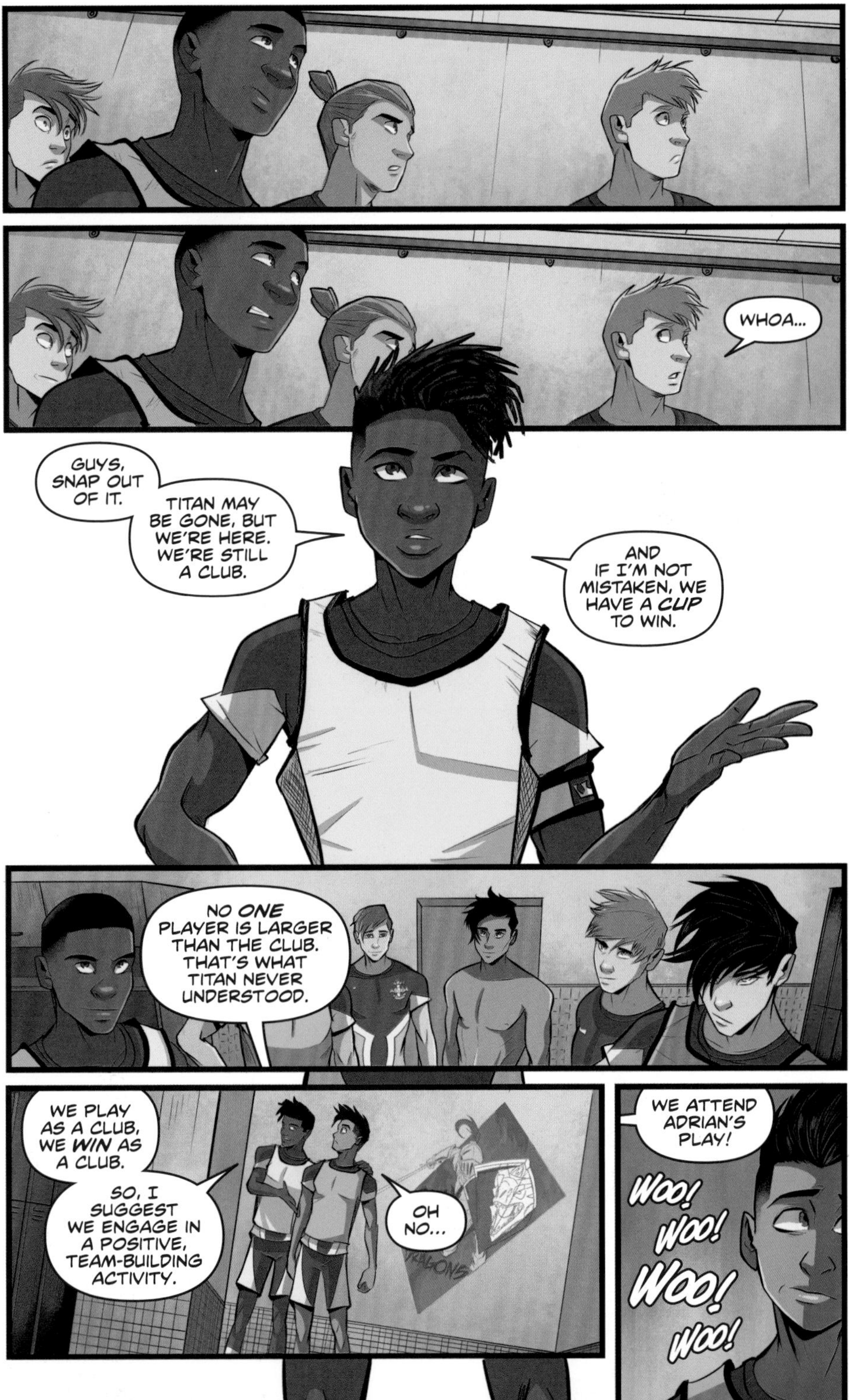
WHOA...
GUYS, SNAP OUT OF IT.
TITAN MAY BE GONE, BUT WE'RE HERE. WE'RE STILL A CLUB.
AND IF I'M NOT MISTAKEN, WE HAVE A CUP TO WIN.
NO ONE PLAYER IS LARGER THAN THE CLUB. THAT'S WHAT TITAN NEVER UNDERSTOOD.
WE PLAY AS A CLUB, WE WIN AS A CLUB.
SO, I SUGGEST WE ENGAGE IN A POSITIVE, TEAM-BUILDING ACTIVITY.
OH NO...
WE ATTEND ADRIAN'S PLAY!
WOO!
WOO!
WOO!
WOO!

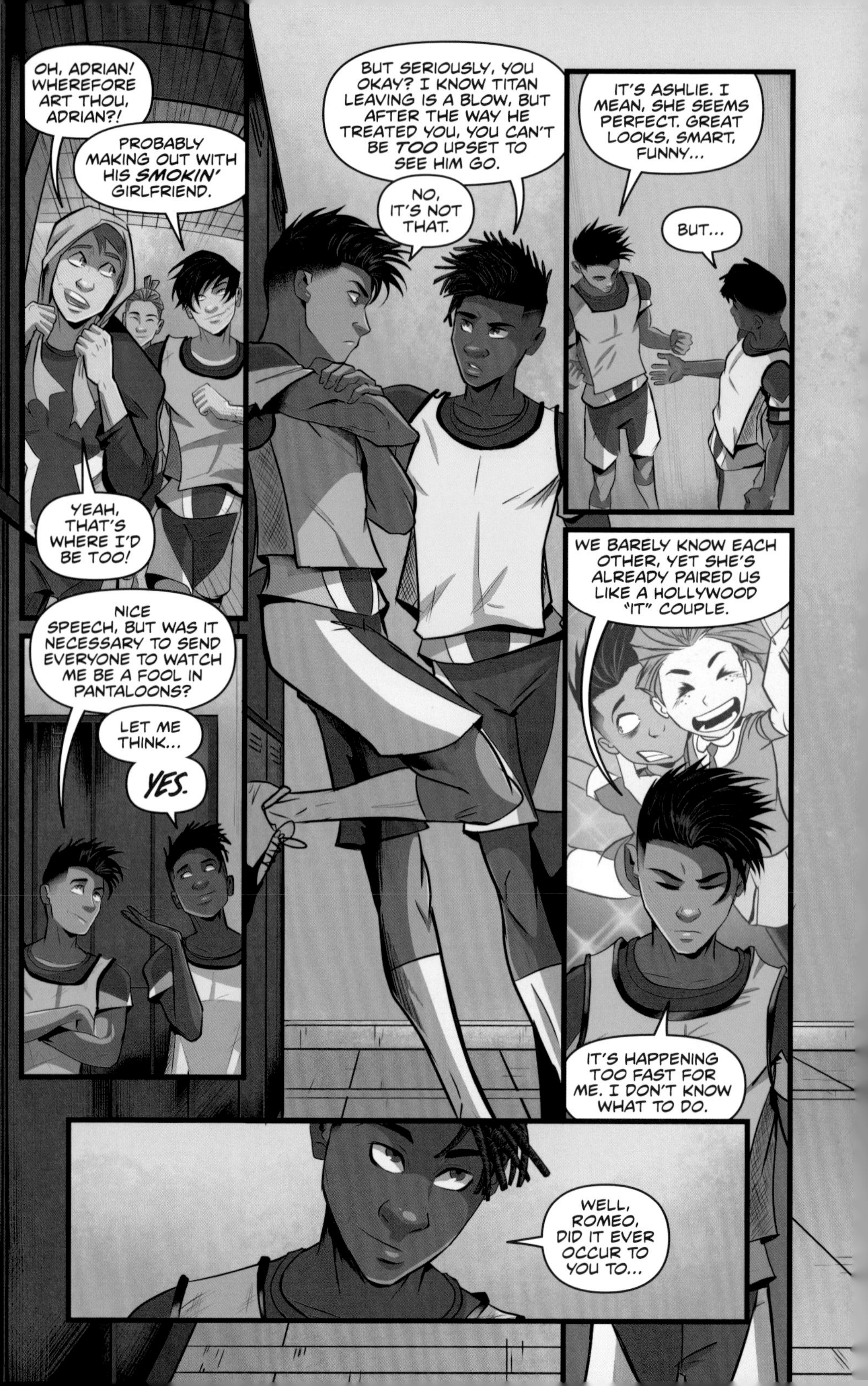
OH, ADRIAN! WHEREFORE ART THOU, ADRIAN?!
PROBABLY MAKING OUT WITH HIS *SMOKIN'* GIRLFRIEND.
YEAH, THAT'S WHERE I'D BE TOO!
NICE SPEECH, BUT WAS IT NECESSARY TO SEND EVERYONE TO WATCH ME BE A FOOL IN PANTALOONS?
LET ME THINK...
YES.
BUT SERIOUSLY, YOU OKAY? I KNOW TITAN LEAVING IS A BLOW, BUT AFTER THE WAY HE TREATED YOU, YOU CAN'T BE *TOO* UPSET TO SEE HIM GO.
NO, IT'S NOT THAT.
IT'S ASHLIE. I MEAN, SHE SEEMS PERFECT. GREAT LOOKS, SMART, FUNNY...
BUT...
WE BARELY KNOW EACH OTHER, YET SHE'S ALREADY PAIRED US LIKE A HOLLYWOOD "IT" COUPLE.
IT'S HAPPENING TOO FAST FOR ME. I DON'T KNOW WHAT TO DO.
WELL, ROMEO, DID IT EVER OCCUR TO YOU TO...

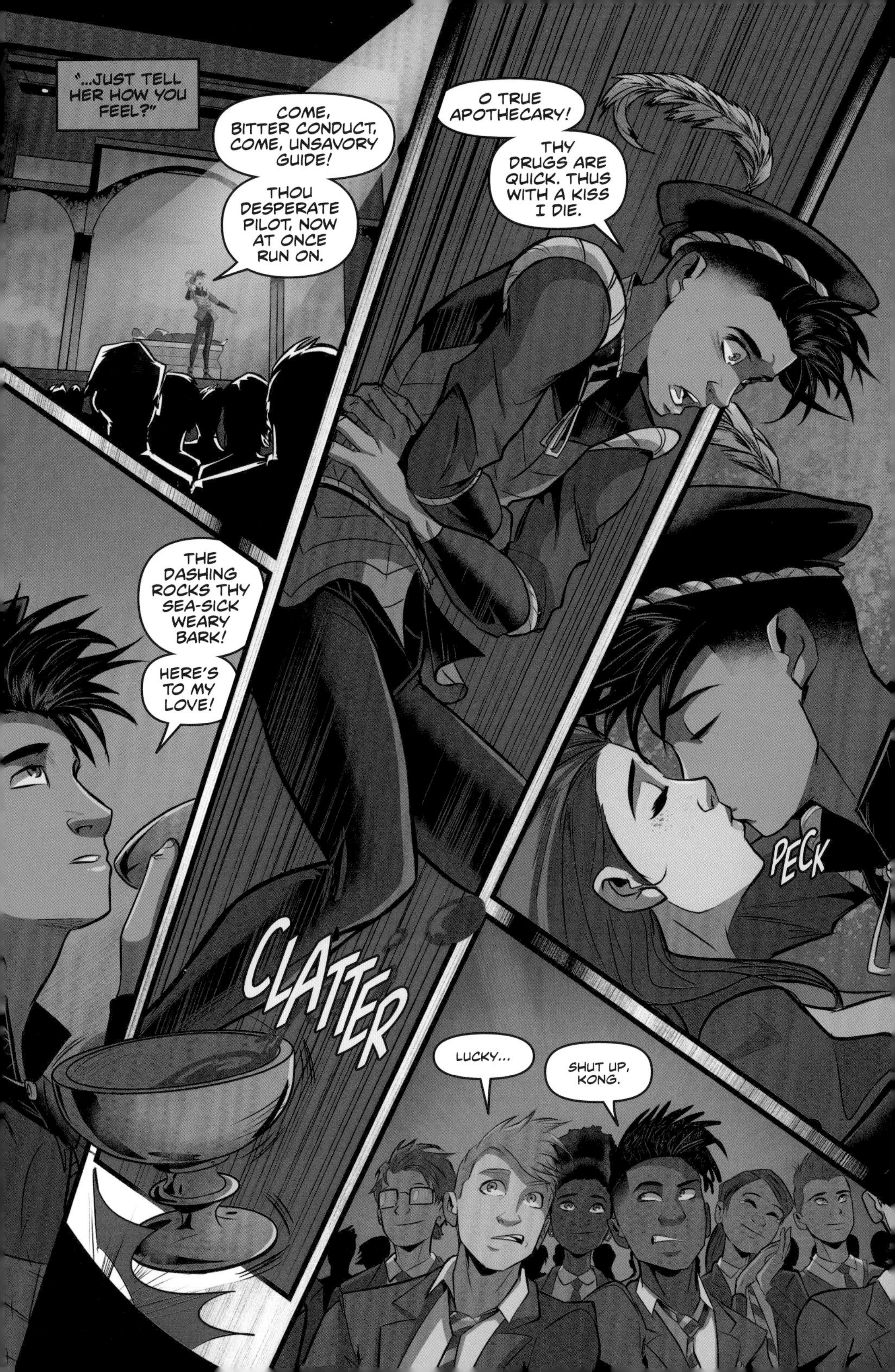
"...JUST TELL HER HOW YOU FEEL?"
COME, BITTER CONDUCT, COME, UNSAVORY GUIDE!
THOU DESPERATE PILOT, NOW AT ONCE RUN ON.
THE DASHING ROCKS THY SEA-SICK WEARY BARK!
HERE'S TO MY LOVE!
O TRUE APOTHECARY!
THY DRUGS ARE QUICK. THUS WITH A KISS I DIE.
CLATTER
PECK
LUCKY...
SHUT UP, KONG.

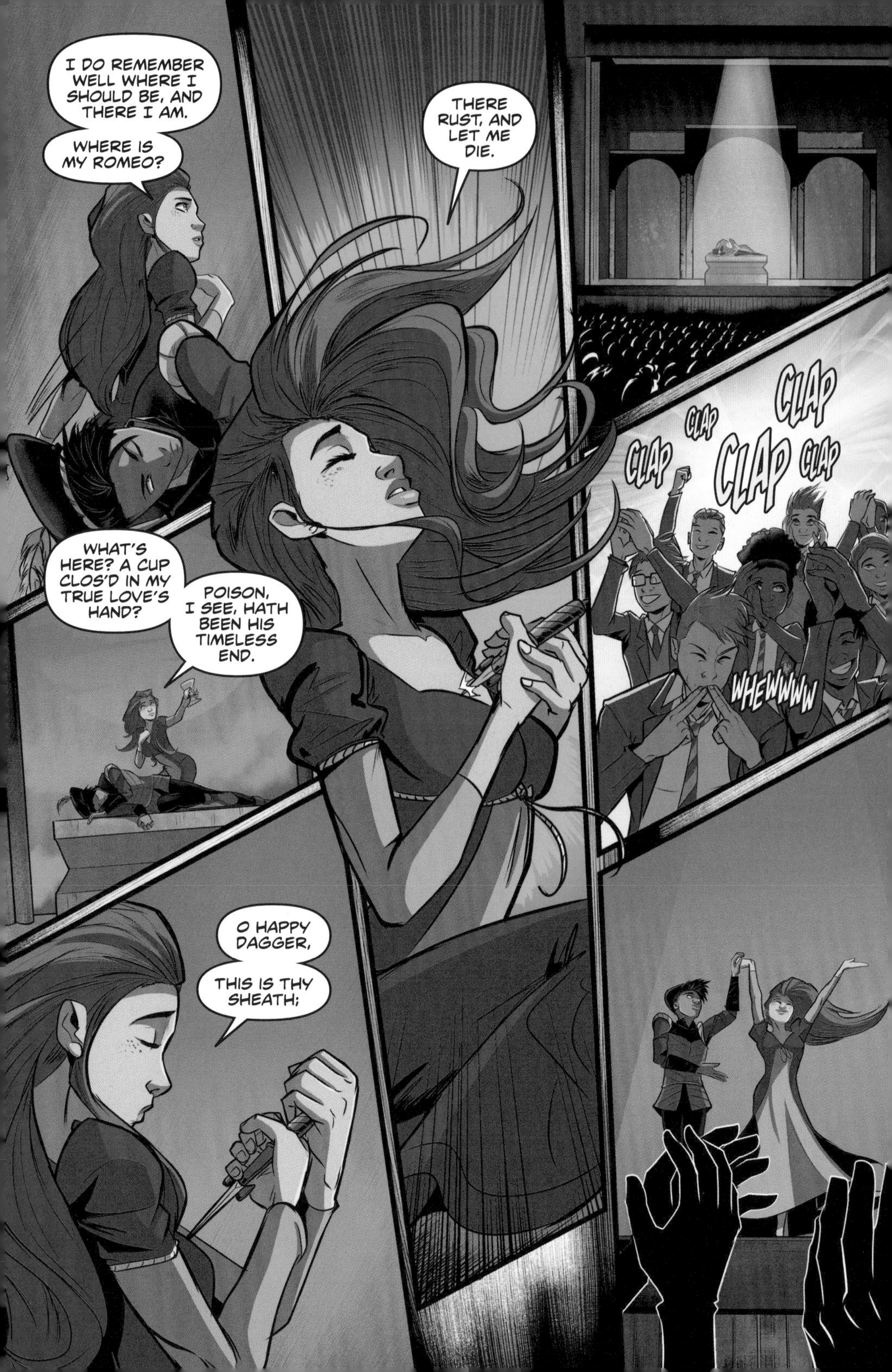
I DO REMEMBER WELL WHERE I SHOULD BE, AND THERE I AM.
WHERE IS MY ROMEO?
THERE RUST, AND LET ME DIE.
WHAT'S HERE? A CUP CLOS'D IN MY TRUE LOVE'S HAND?
POISON, I SEE, HATH BEEN HIS TIMELESS END.
CLAP
CLAP
CLAP
CLAP
CLAP
WHEWWWW
O HAPPY DAGGER,
THIS IS THY SHEATH;

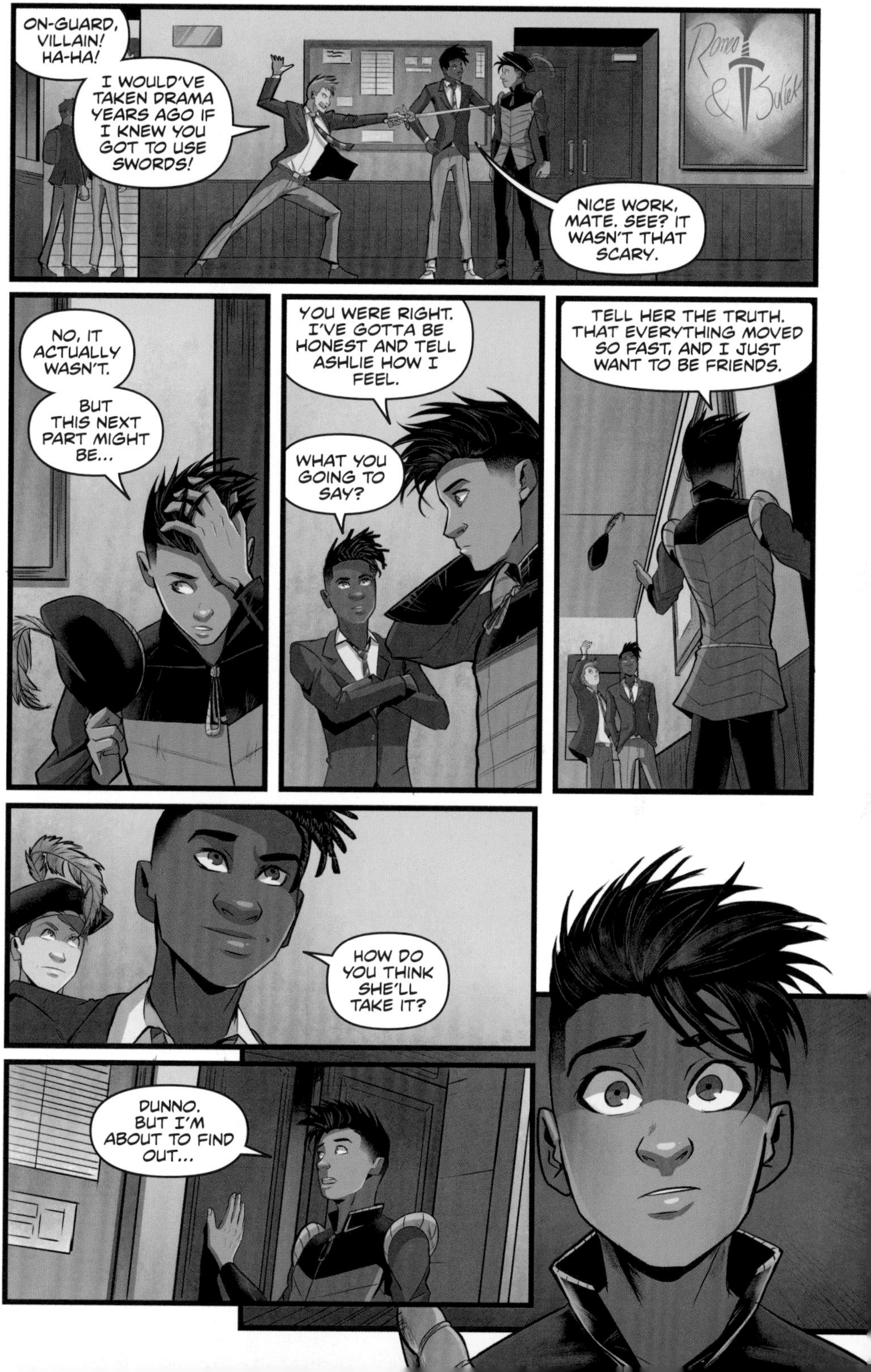
ON-GUARD, VILLAIN! HA-HA!
I WOULD'VE TAKEN DRAMA YEARS AGO IF I KNEW YOU GOT TO USE SWORDS!
Romeo & Juliet
NICE WORK, MATE. SEE? IT WASN'T THAT SCARY.
NO, IT ACTUALLY WASN'T.
BUT THIS NEXT PART MIGHT BE...
YOU WERE RIGHT. I'VE GOTTA BE HONEST AND TELL ASHLIE HOW I FEEL.
WHAT YOU GOING TO SAY?
TELL HER THE TRUTH. THAT EVERYTHING MOVED SO FAST, AND I JUST WANT TO BE FRIENDS.
HOW DO YOU THINK SHE'LL TAKE IT?
DUNNO. BUT I'M ABOUT TO FIND OUT...

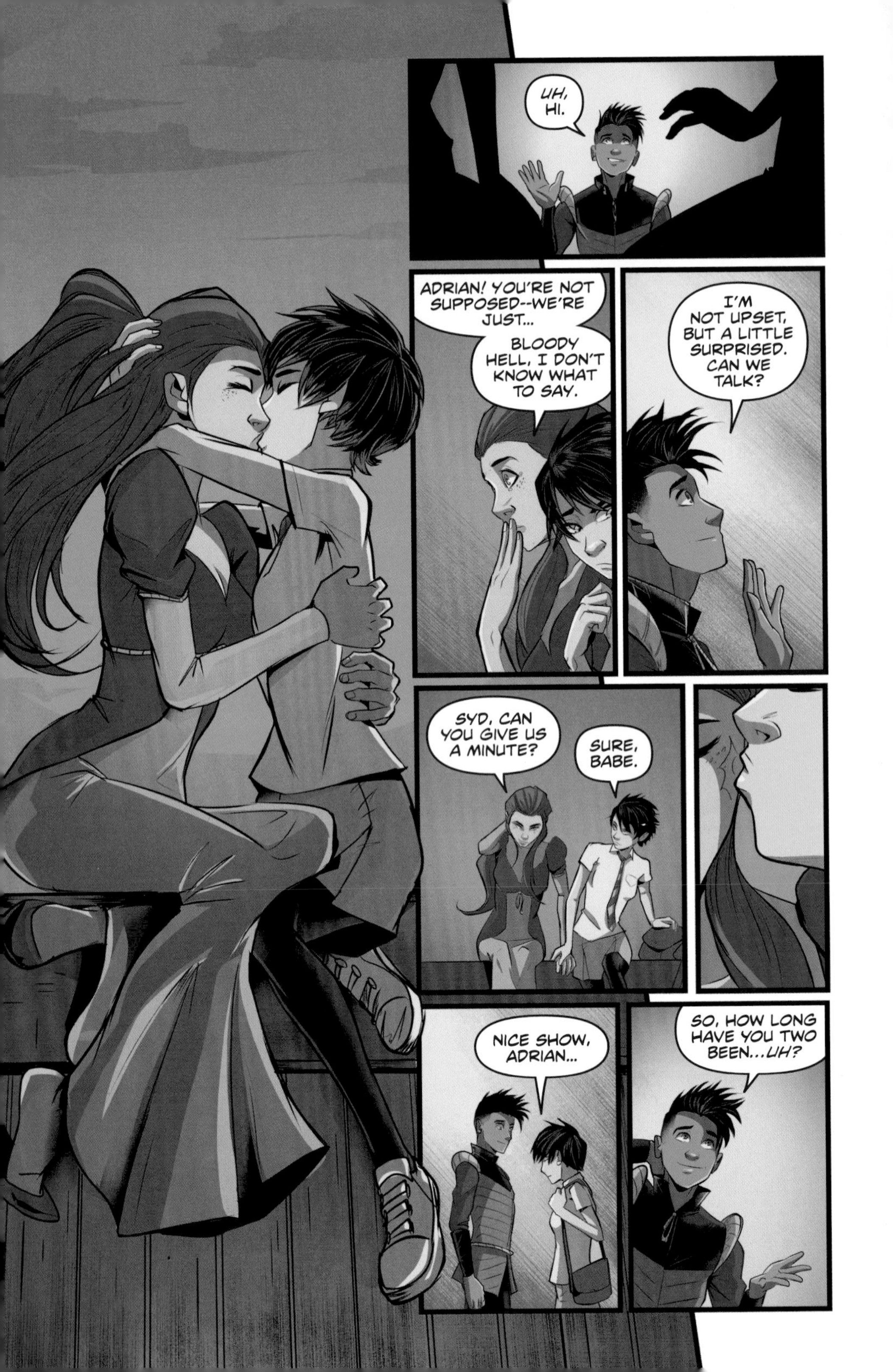
UH, HI.
ADRIAN! YOU'RE NOT SUPPOSED--WE'RE JUST...
BLOODY HELL, I DON'T KNOW WHAT TO SAY.
I'M NOT UPSET, BUT A LITTLE SURPRISED. CAN WE TALK?
SYD, CAN YOU GIVE US A MINUTE?
SURE, BABE.
NICE SHOW, ADRIAN...
SO, HOW LONG HAVE YOU TWO BEEN...*UH*?

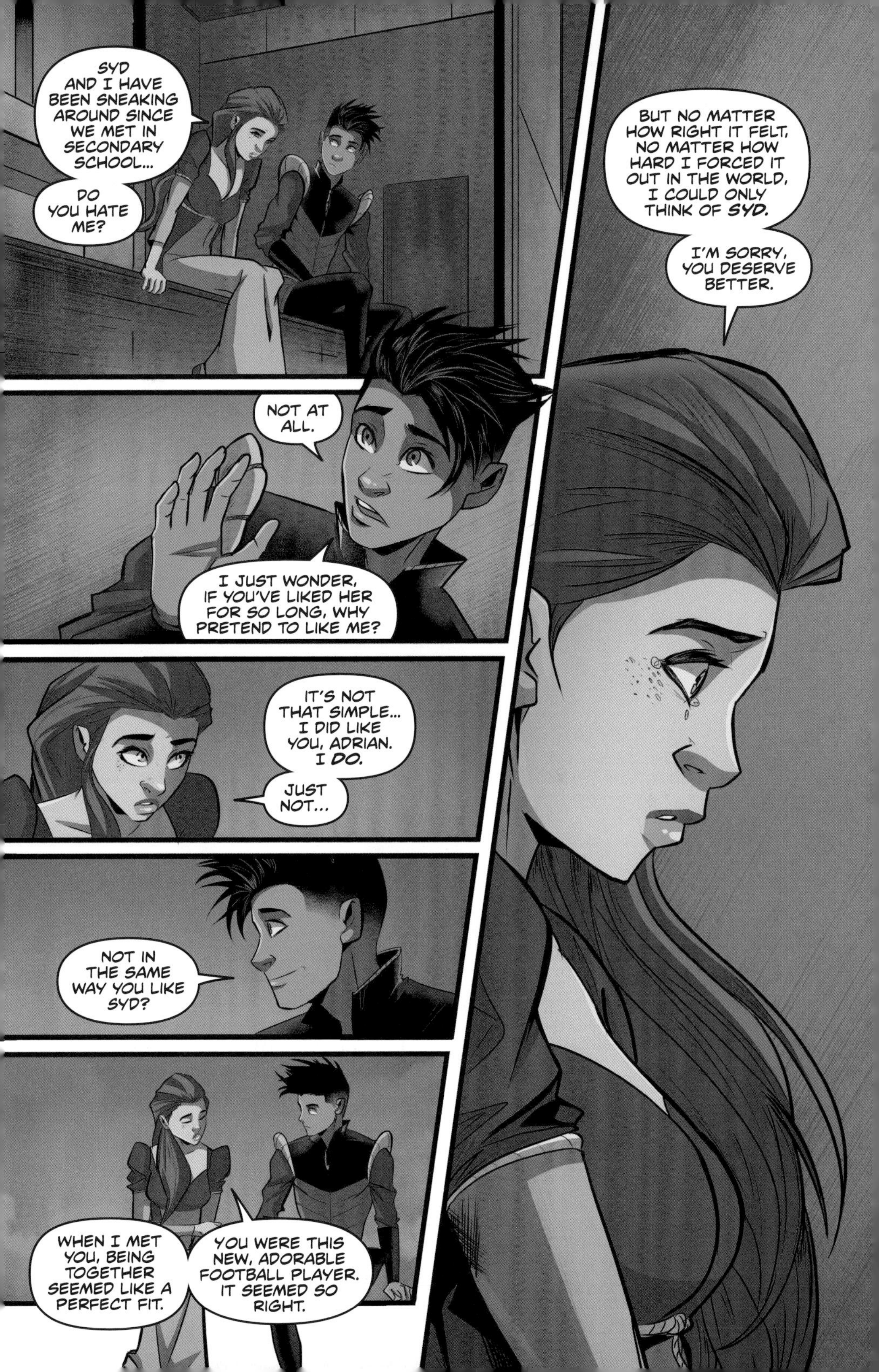
SYD AND I HAVE BEEN SNEAKING AROUND SINCE WE MET IN SECONDARY SCHOOL...
DO YOU HATE ME?
NOT AT ALL.
I JUST WONDER, IF YOU'VE LIKED HER FOR SO LONG, WHY PRETEND TO LIKE ME?
IT'S NOT THAT SIMPLE... I DID LIKE YOU, ADRIAN. I *DO*.
JUST NOT...
NOT IN THE SAME WAY YOU LIKE SYD?
WHEN I MET YOU, BEING TOGETHER SEEMED LIKE A PERFECT FIT.
YOU WERE THIS NEW, ADORABLE FOOTBALL PLAYER. IT SEEMED SO RIGHT.
BUT NO MATTER HOW RIGHT IT FELT, NO MATTER HOW HARD I FORCED IT OUT IN THE WORLD, I COULD ONLY THINK OF ***SYD***.
I'M SORRY, YOU DESERVE BETTER.

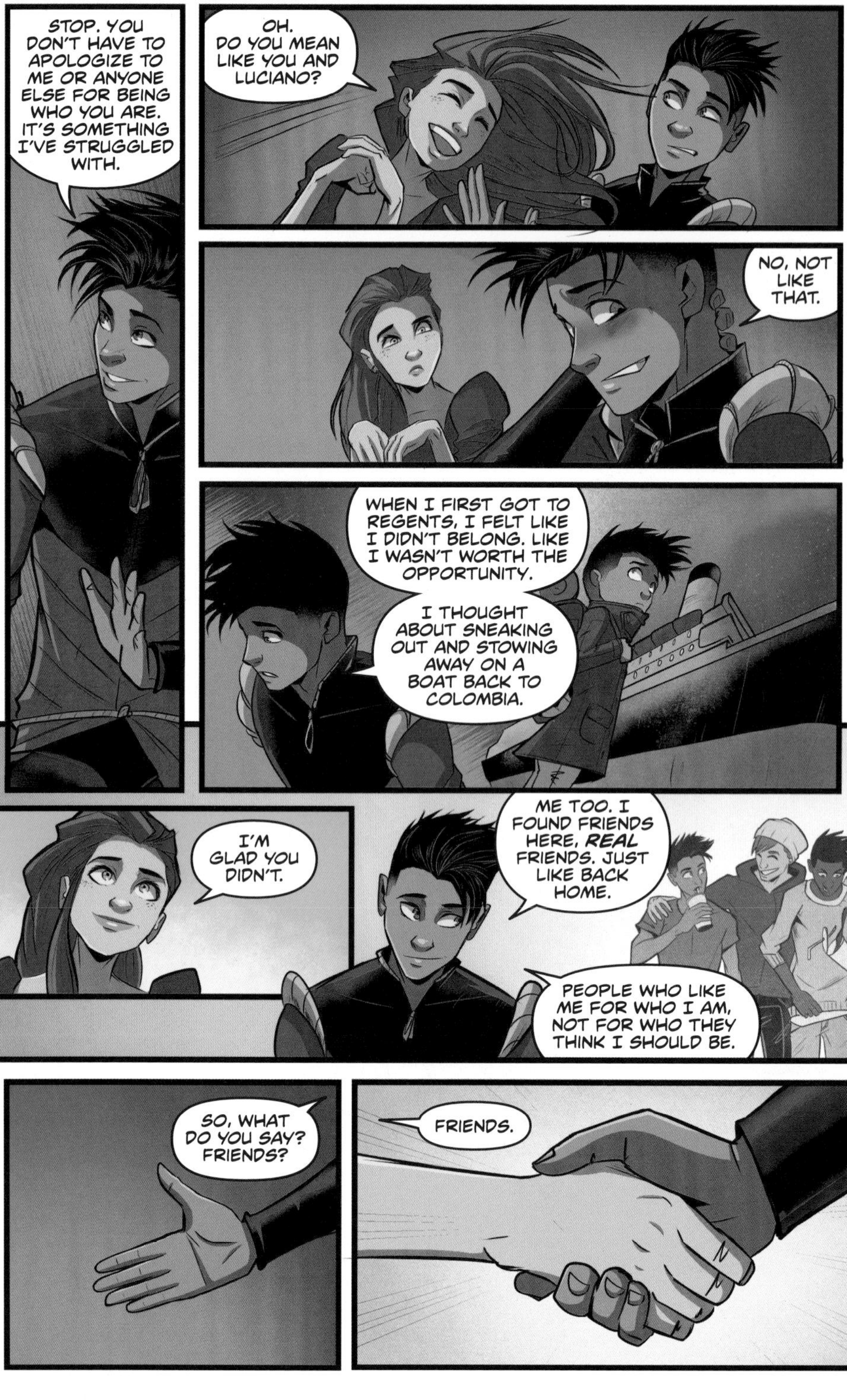
STOP. YOU DON'T HAVE TO APOLOGIZE TO ME OR ANYONE ELSE FOR BEING WHO YOU ARE. IT'S SOMETHING I'VE STRUGGLED WITH.
OH. DO YOU MEAN LIKE YOU AND LUCIANO?
NO, NOT LIKE THAT.
WHEN I FIRST GOT TO REGENTS, I FELT LIKE I DIDN'T BELONG. LIKE I WASN'T WORTH THE OPPORTUNITY.
I THOUGHT ABOUT SNEAKING OUT AND STOWING AWAY ON A BOAT BACK TO COLOMBIA.
I'M GLAD YOU DIDN'T.
ME TOO. I FOUND FRIENDS HERE, *REAL* FRIENDS. JUST LIKE BACK HOME.
PEOPLE WHO LIKE ME FOR WHO I AM, NOT FOR WHO THEY THINK I SHOULD BE.
SO, WHAT DO YOU SAY? FRIENDS?
FRIENDS.

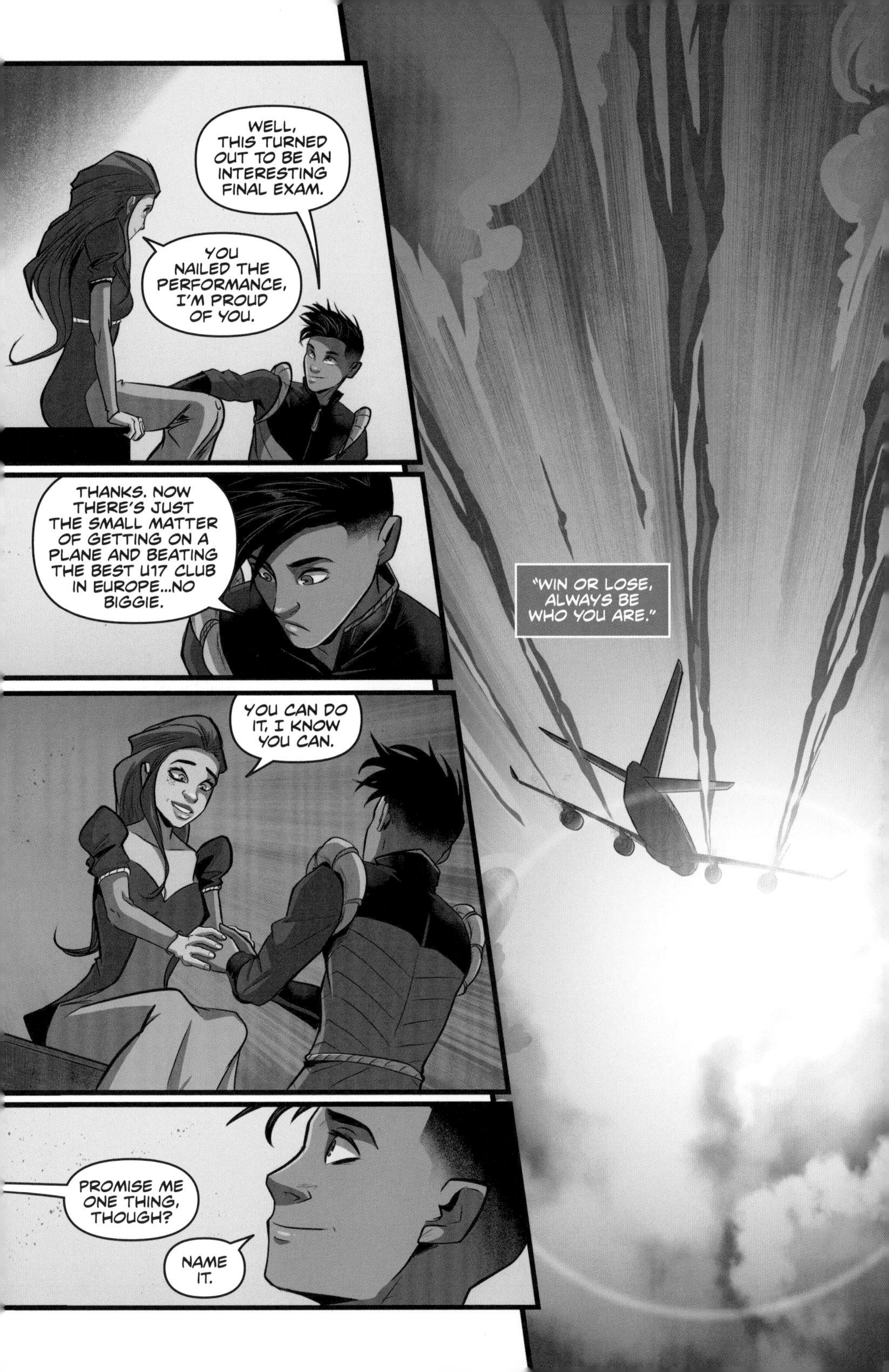
WELL, THIS TURNED OUT TO BE AN INTERESTING FINAL EXAM.
YOU NAILED THE PERFORMANCE, I'M PROUD OF YOU.
THANKS. NOW THERE'S JUST THE SMALL MATTER OF GETTING ON A PLANE AND BEATING THE BEST U17 CLUB IN EUROPE...NO BIGGIE.
YOU CAN DO IT, I KNOW YOU CAN.
PROMISE ME ONE THING, THOUGH?
NAME IT.
"WIN OR LOSE, ALWAYS BE WHO YOU ARE."

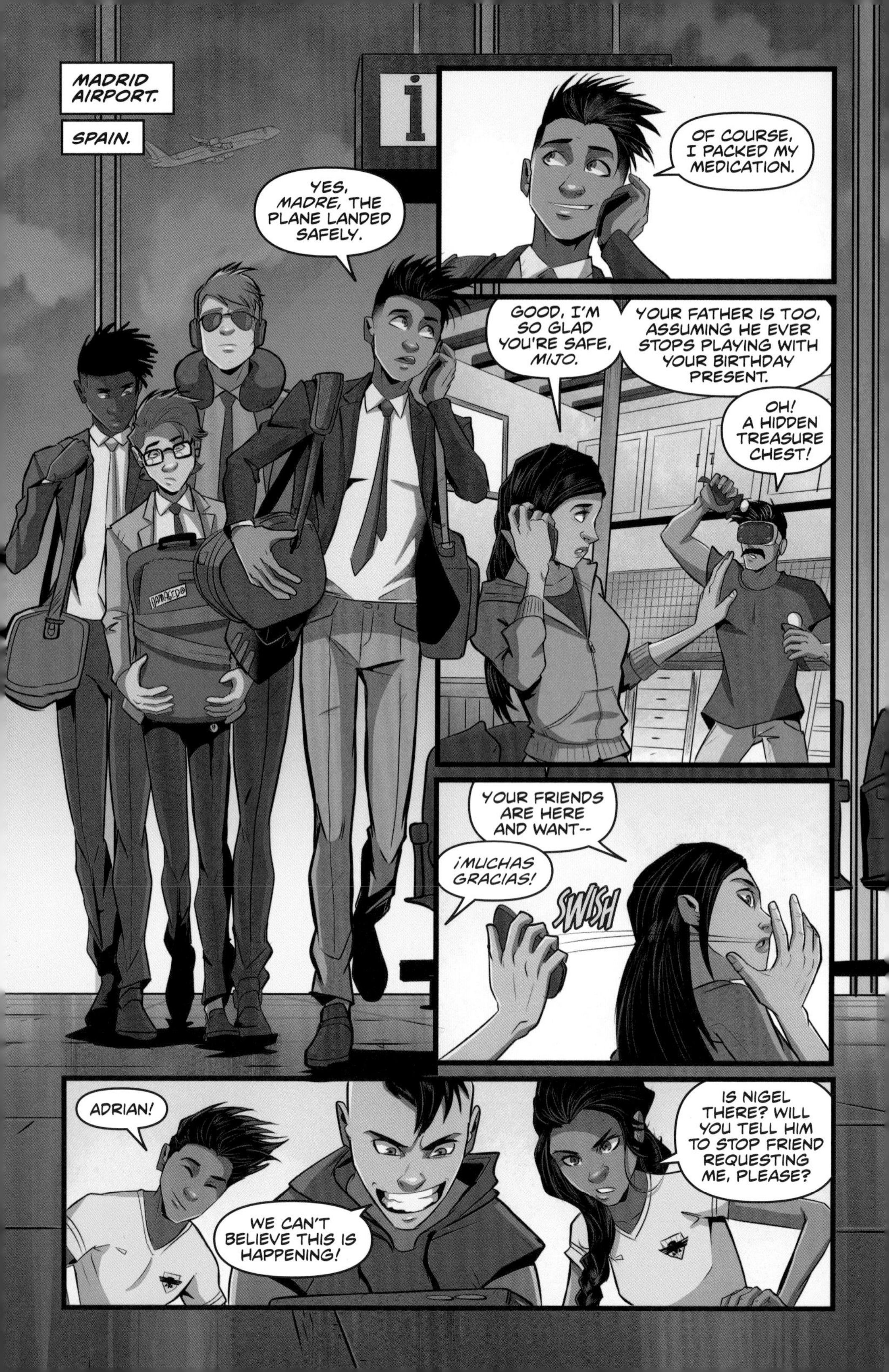
MADRID AIRPORT.
SPAIN.
YES, MADRE, THE PLANE LANDED SAFELY.
OF COURSE, I PACKED MY MEDICATION.
DAMAGED
GOOD, I'M SO GLAD YOU'RE SAFE, MIJO.
YOUR FATHER IS TOO, ASSUMING HE EVER STOPS PLAYING WITH YOUR BIRTHDAY PRESENT.
OH! A HIDDEN TREASURE CHEST!
YOUR FRIENDS ARE HERE AND WANT--
¡MUCHAS GRACIAS!
SWISH
ADRIAN!
WE CAN'T BELIEVE THIS IS HAPPENING!
IS NIGEL THERE? WILL YOU TELL HIM TO STOP FRIEND REQUESTING ME, PLEASE?

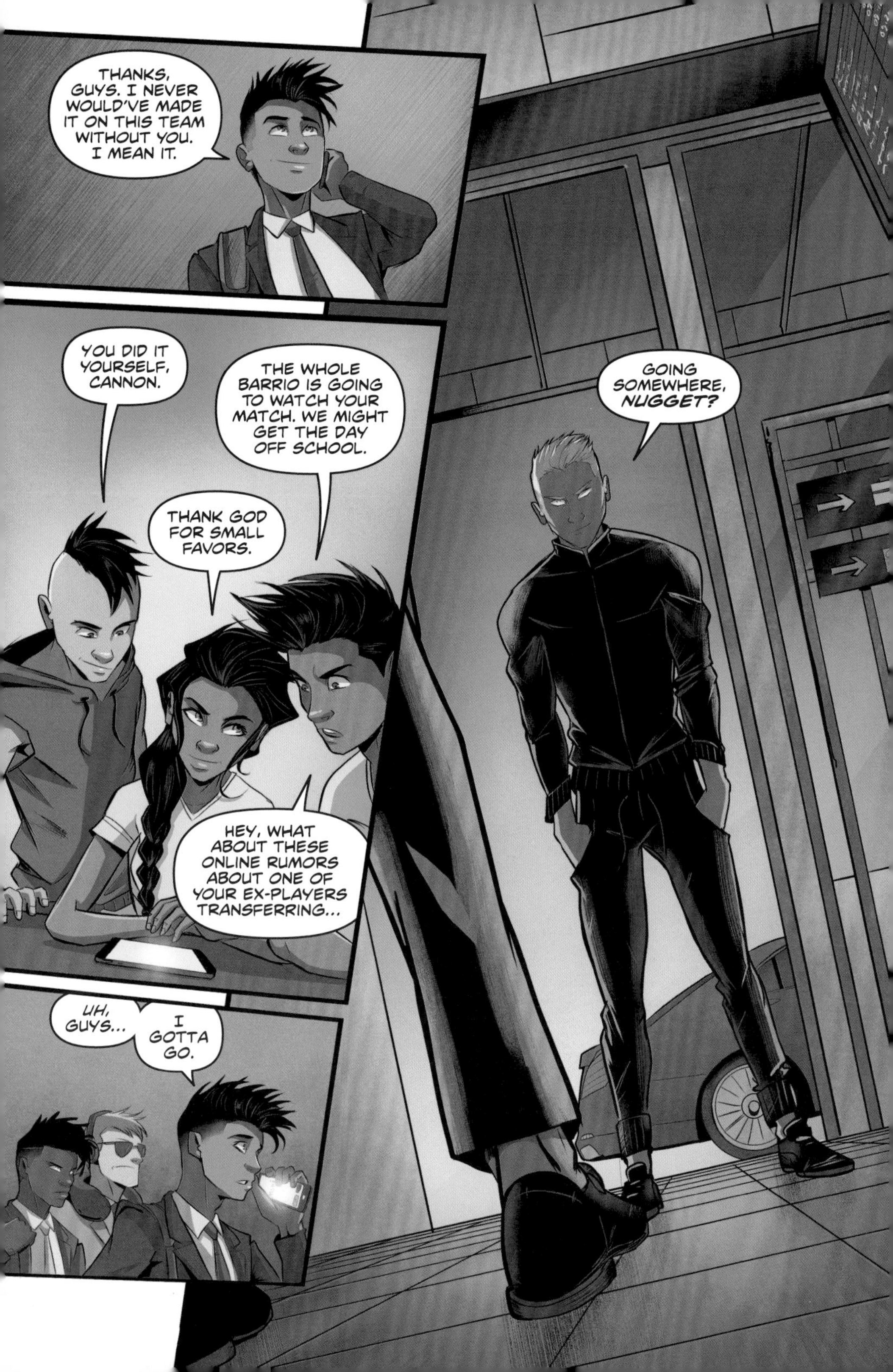
THANKS, GUYS. I NEVER WOULD'VE MADE IT ON THIS TEAM WITHOUT YOU. I MEAN IT.
YOU DID IT YOURSELF, CANNON.
THE WHOLE BARRIO IS GOING TO WATCH YOUR MATCH. WE MIGHT GET THE DAY OFF SCHOOL.
THANK GOD FOR SMALL FAVORS.
HEY, WHAT ABOUT THESE ONLINE RUMORS ABOUT ONE OF YOUR EX-PLAYERS TRANSFERRING...
UH, GUYS...
I GOTTA GO.
GOING SOMEWHERE, *NUGGET?*

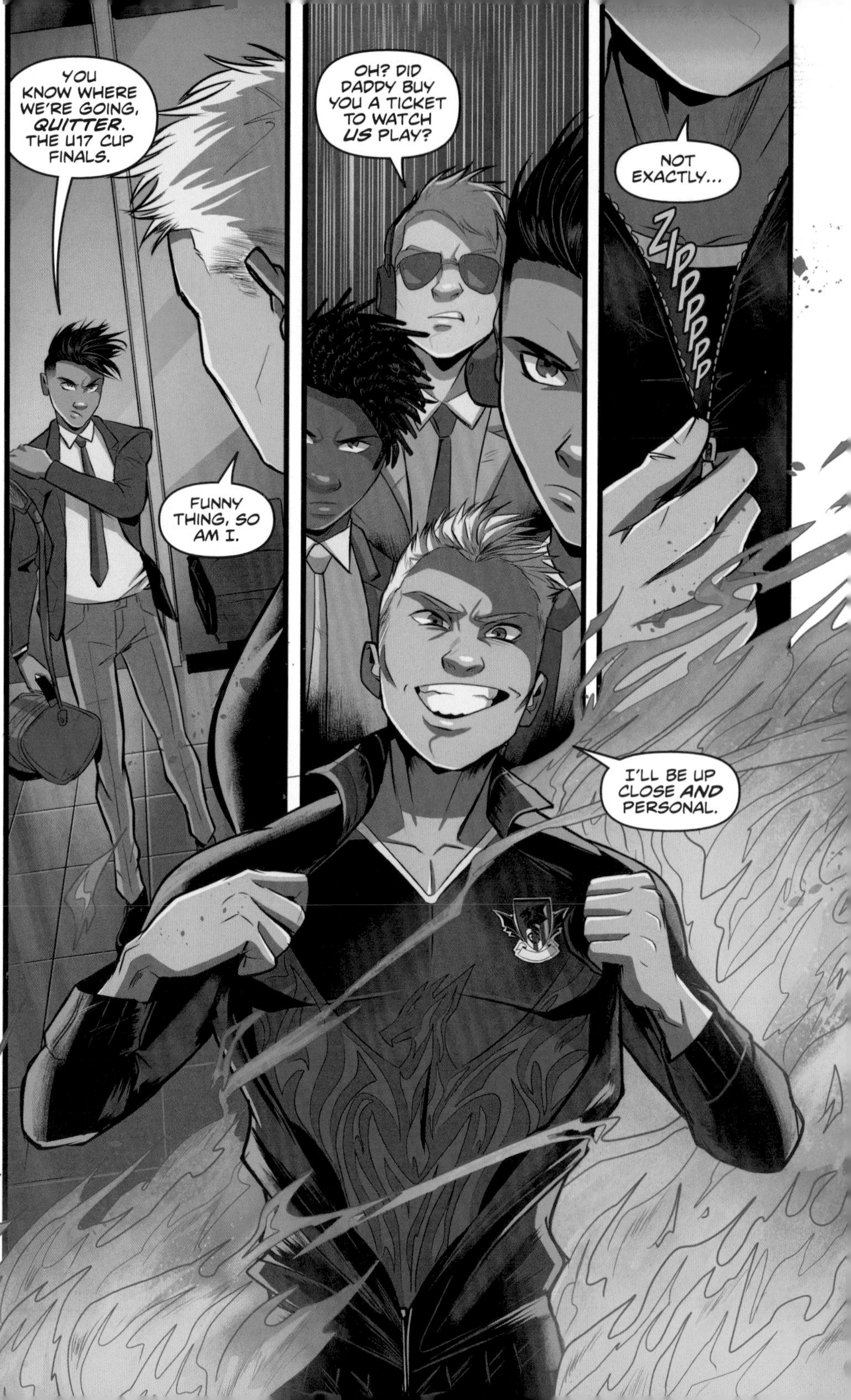
YOU KNOW WHERE WE'RE GOING, QUITTER. THE U17 CUP FINALS.
OH? DID DADDY BUY YOU A TICKET TO WATCH US PLAY?
NOT EXACTLY...
ZIPPPPP
FUNNY THING, SO AM I.
I'LL BE UP CLOSE AND PERSONAL.

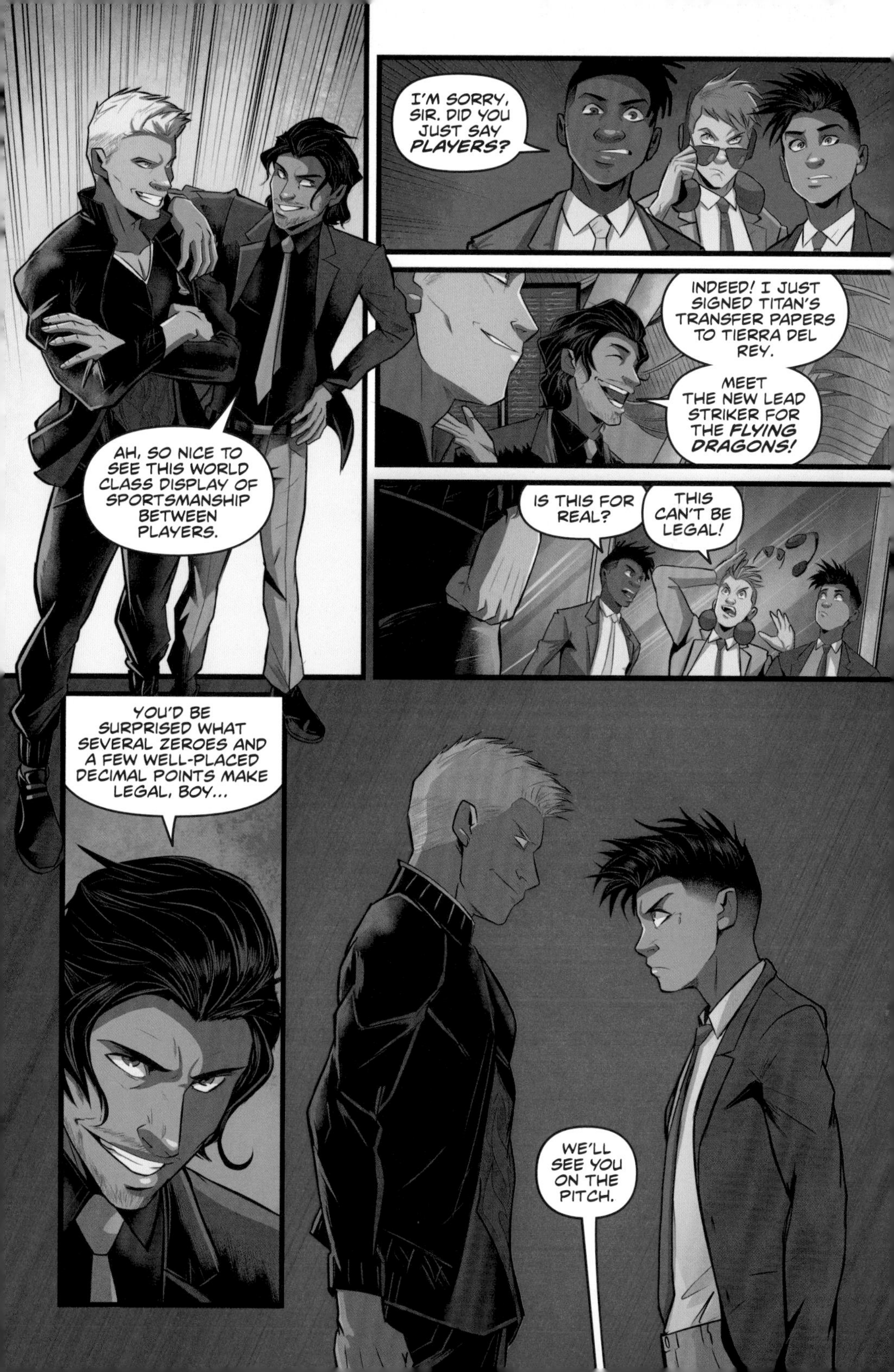
AH, SO NICE TO SEE THIS WORLD CLASS DISPLAY OF SPORTSMANSHIP BETWEEN PLAYERS.
I'M SORRY, SIR. DID YOU JUST SAY *PLAYERS?*
INDEED! I JUST SIGNED TITAN'S TRANSFER PAPERS TO TIERRA DEL REY.
MEET THE NEW LEAD STRIKER FOR THE *FLYING DRAGONS!*
IS THIS FOR REAL?
THIS CAN'T BE LEGAL!
YOU'D BE SURPRISED WHAT SEVERAL ZEROES AND A FEW WELL-PLACED DECIMAL POINTS MAKE LEGAL, BOY...
WE'LL SEE YOU ON THE PITCH.

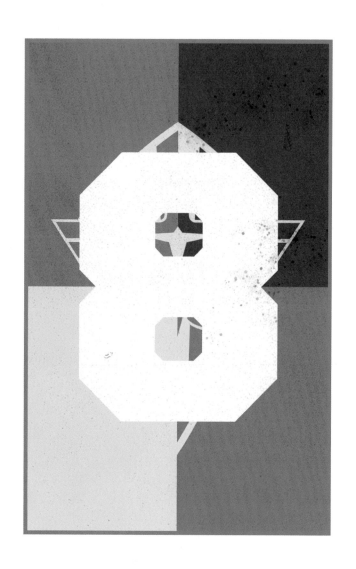

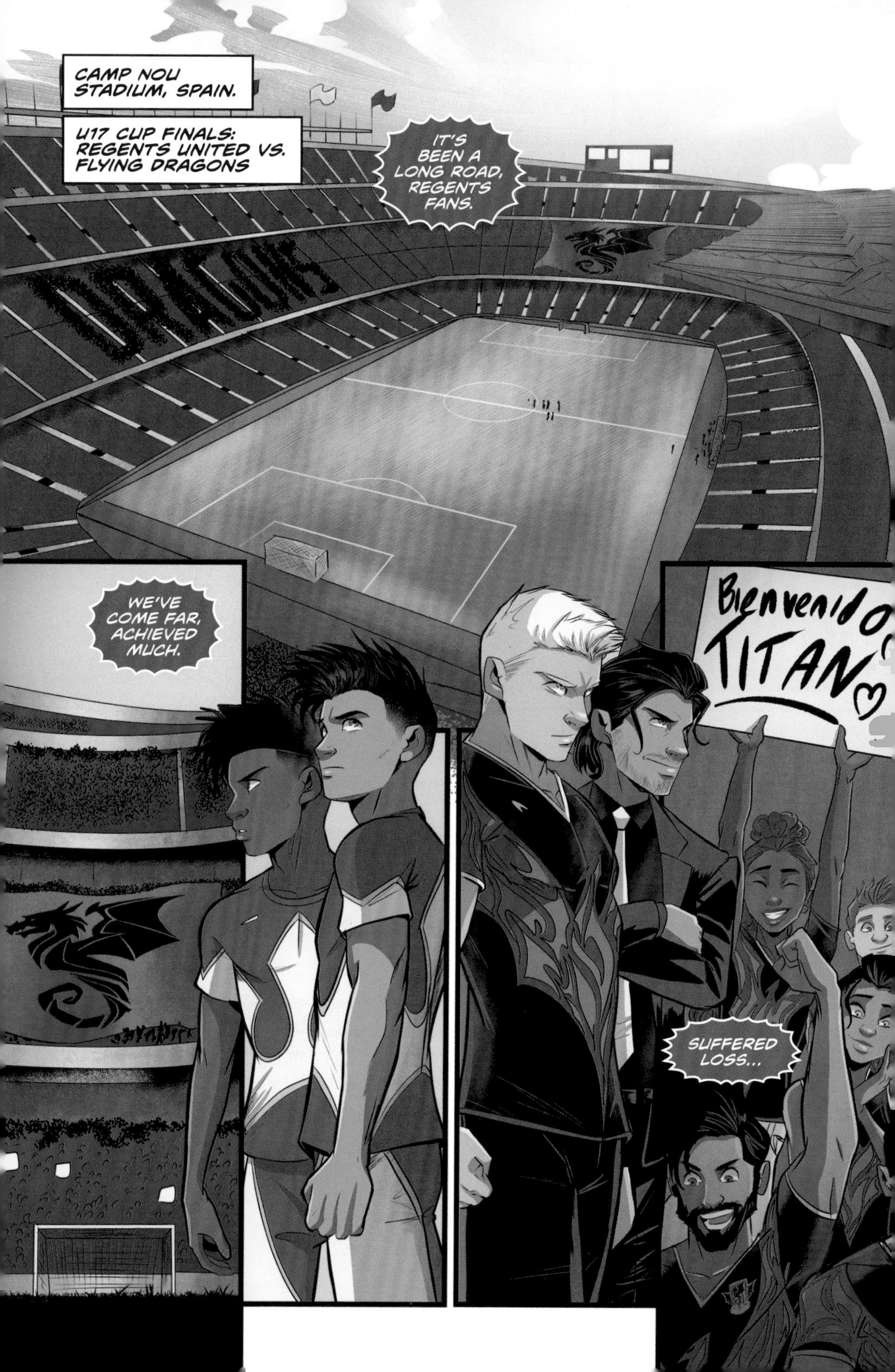
CAMP NOU STADIUM, SPAIN.
U17 CUP FINALS: REGENTS UNITED VS. FLYING DRAGONS
IT'S BEEN A LONG ROAD, REGENTS FANS.
WE'VE COME FAR, ACHIEVED MUCH.
Bienvenido TITAN
SUFFERED LOSS...

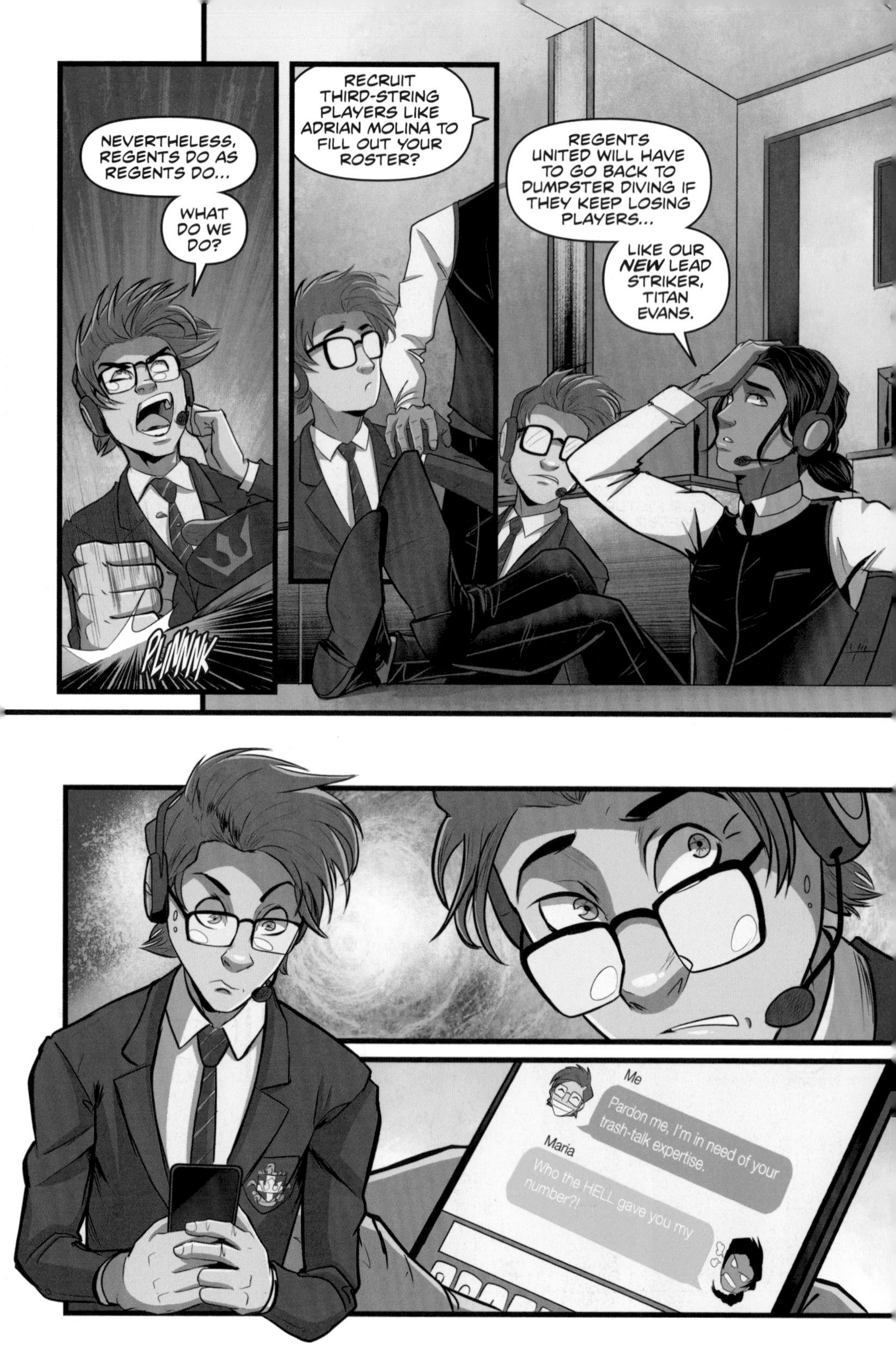
NEVERTHELESS, REGENTS DO AS REGENTS DO...
WHAT DO WE DO?
PLINNNK
RECRUIT THIRD-STRING PLAYERS LIKE ADRIAN MOLINA TO FILL OUT YOUR ROSTER?
REGENTS UNITED WILL HAVE TO GO BACK TO DUMPSTER DIVING IF THEY KEEP LOSING PLAYERS...
LIKE OUR NEW LEAD STRIKER, TITAN EVANS.
Me
Pardon me, I'm in need of your trash-talk expertise.
Maria
Who the HELL gave you my number?!

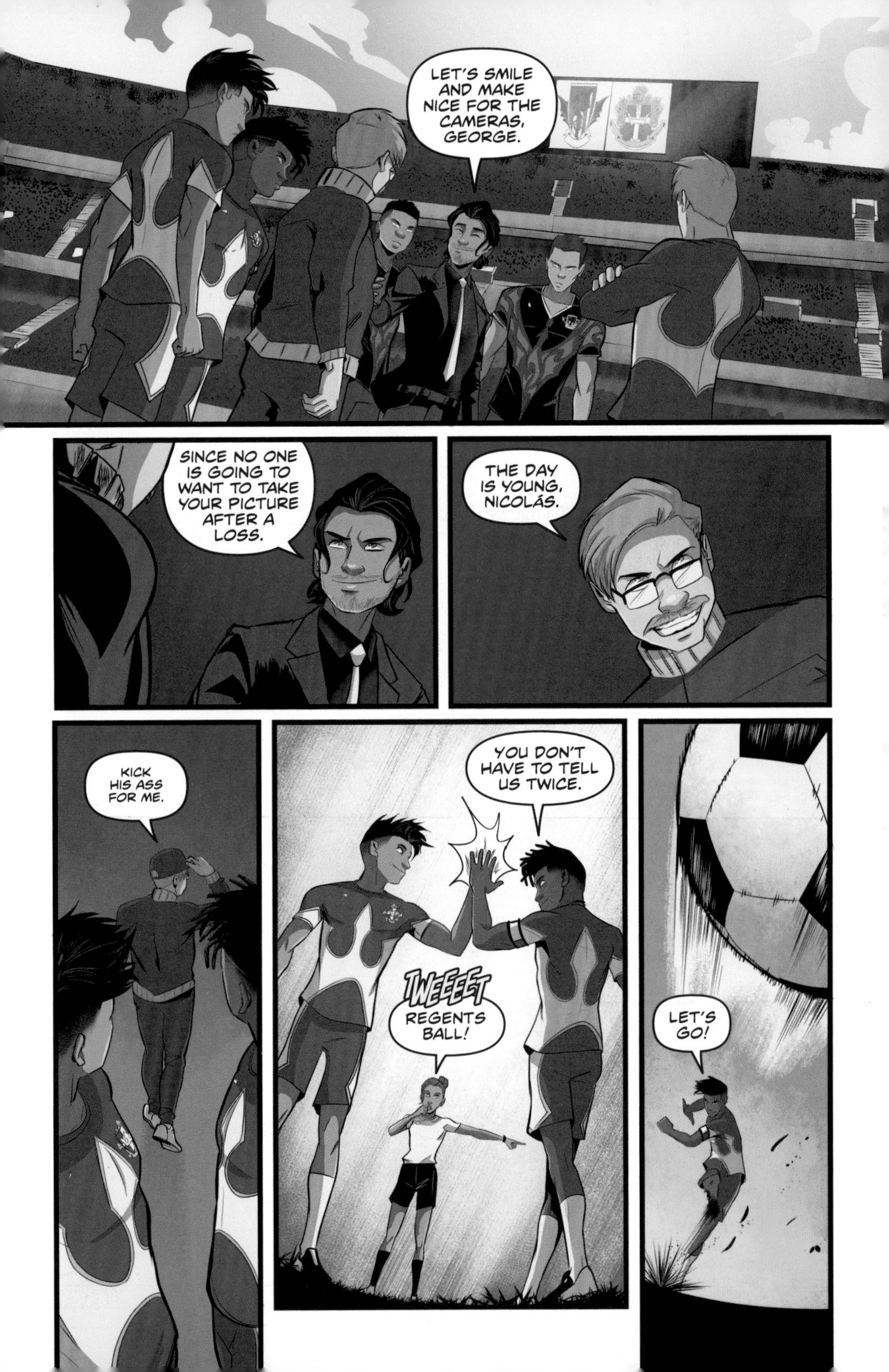
LET'S SMILE AND MAKE NICE FOR THE CAMERAS, GEORGE.
SINCE NO ONE IS GOING TO WANT TO TAKE YOUR PICTURE AFTER A LOSS.
THE DAY IS YOUNG, NICOLÁS.
KICK HIS ASS FOR ME.
YOU DON'T HAVE TO TELL US TWICE.
TWEEEET
REGENTS BALL!
LET'S GO!

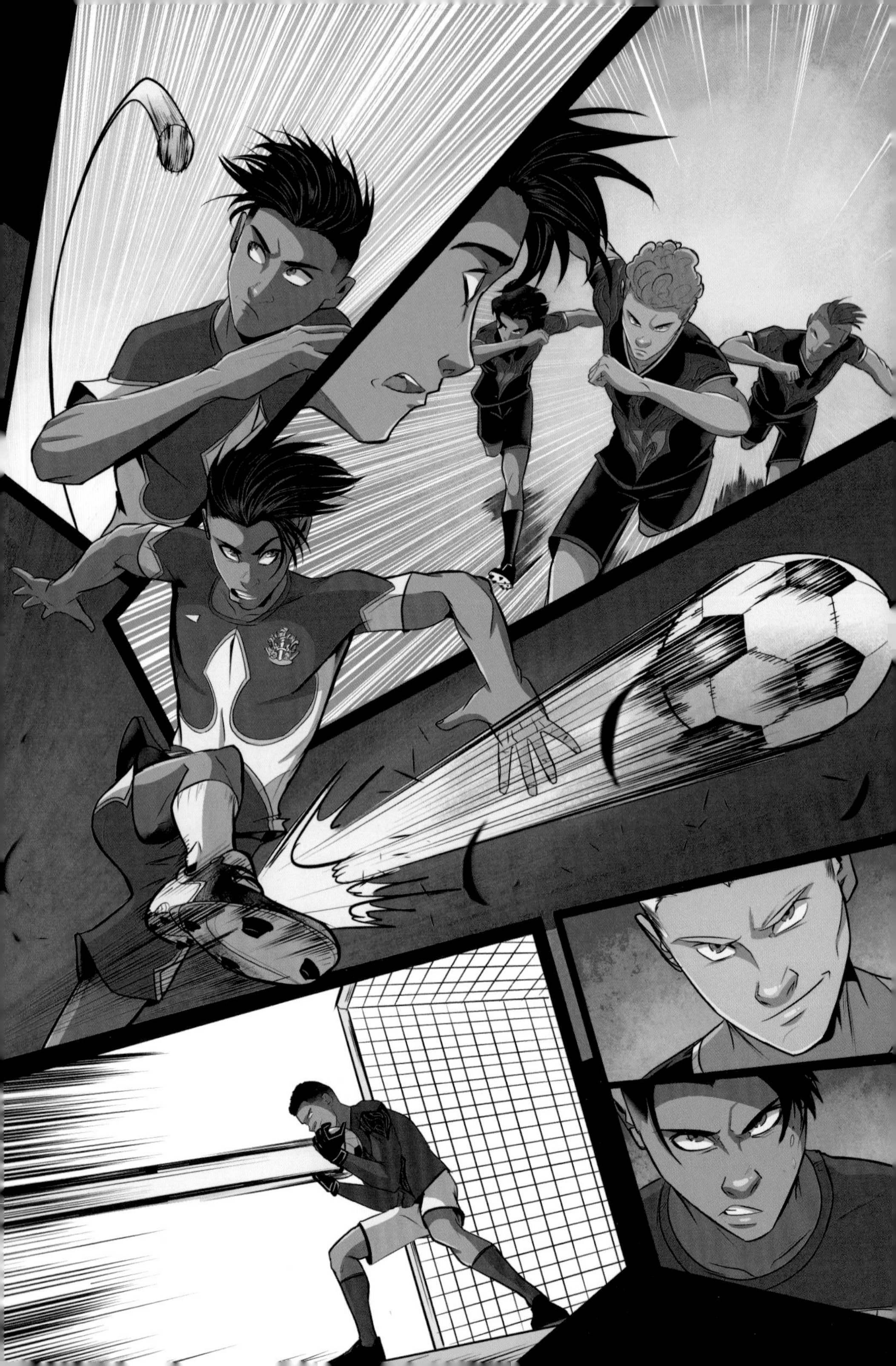

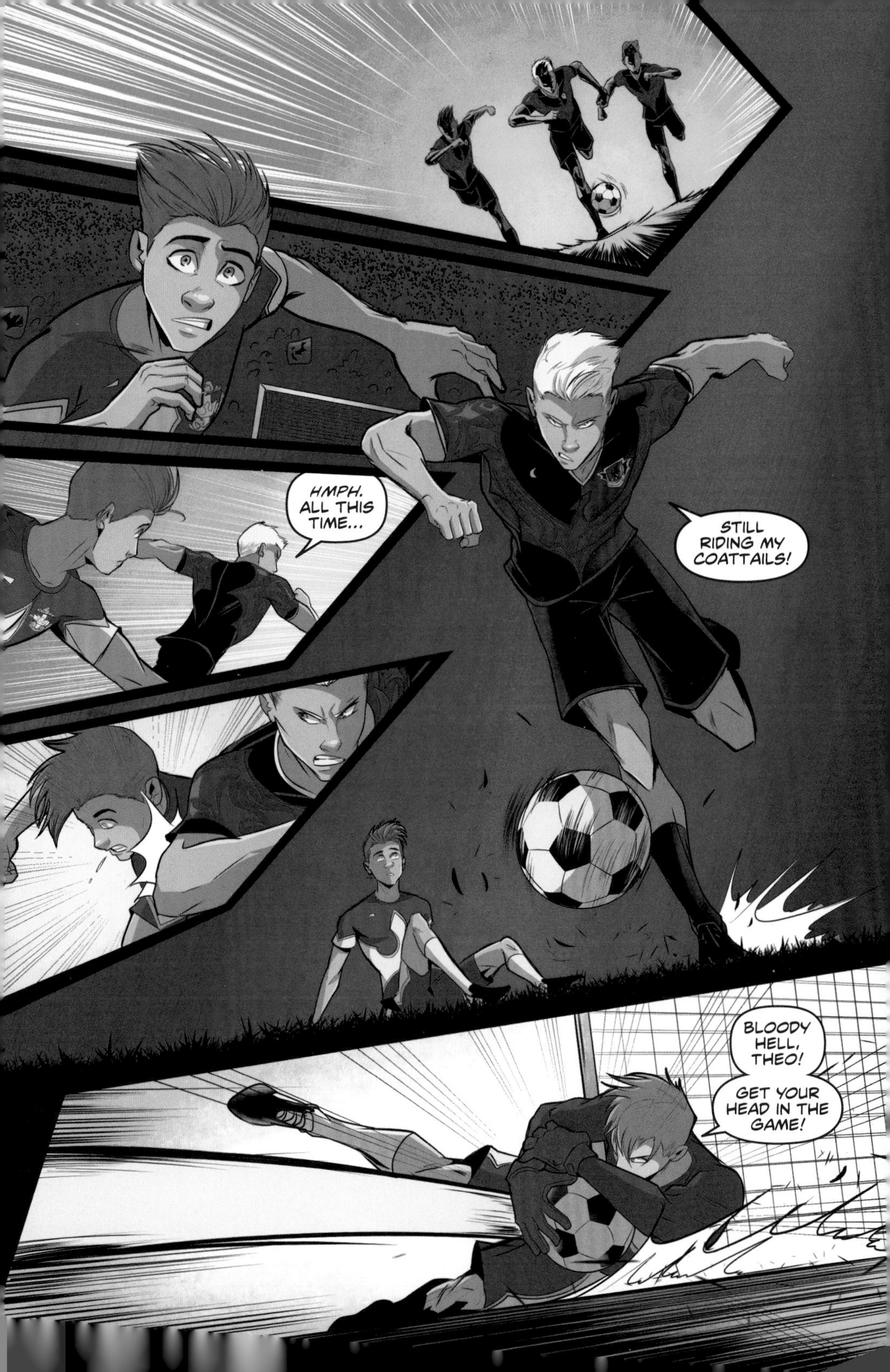
HMPH. ALL THIS TIME...
STILL RIDING MY COATTAILS!
BLOODY HELL, THEO!
GET YOUR HEAD IN THE GAME!

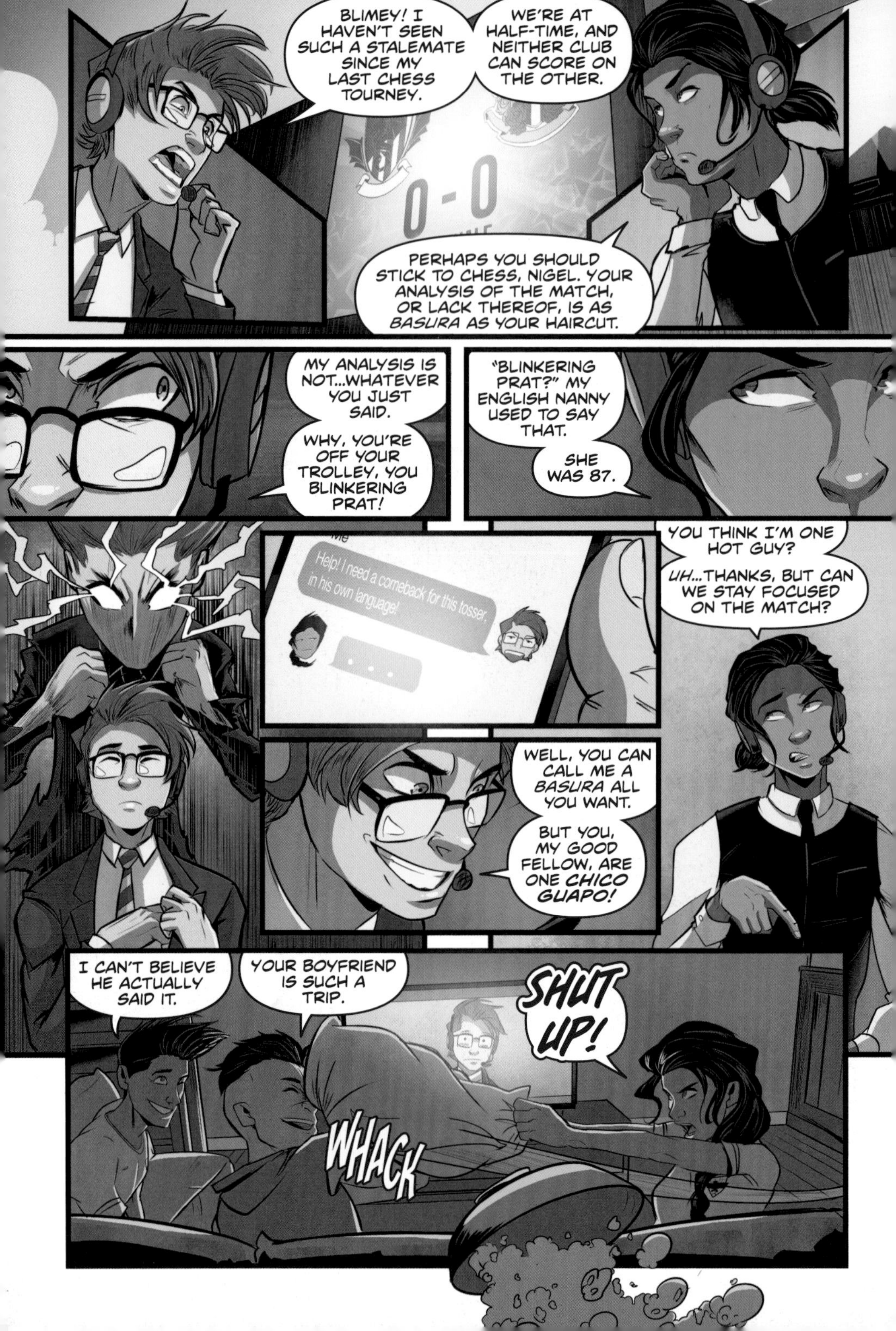
BLIMEY! I HAVEN'T SEEN SUCH A STALEMATE SINCE MY LAST CHESS TOURNEY.
WE'RE AT HALF-TIME, AND NEITHER CLUB CAN SCORE ON THE OTHER.
0 - 0
PERHAPS YOU SHOULD STICK TO CHESS, NIGEL. YOUR ANALYSIS OF THE MATCH, OR LACK THEREOF, IS AS *BASURA* AS YOUR HAIRCUT.
MY ANALYSIS IS NOT...WHATEVER YOU JUST SAID.
WHY, YOU'RE OFF YOUR TROLLEY, YOU BLINKERING PRAT!
"BLINKERING PRAT?" MY ENGLISH NANNY USED TO SAY THAT.
SHE WAS 87.
Help! I need a comeback for this tosser, in his own language!
WELL, YOU CAN CALL ME A *BASURA* ALL YOU WANT.
BUT YOU, MY GOOD FELLOW, ARE ONE *CHICO GUAPO*!
YOU THINK I'M ONE HOT GUY?
UH...THANKS, BUT CAN WE STAY FOCUSED ON THE MATCH?
I CAN'T BELIEVE HE ACTUALLY SAID IT.
YOUR BOYFRIEND IS SUCH A TRIP.
SHUT UP!
WHACK

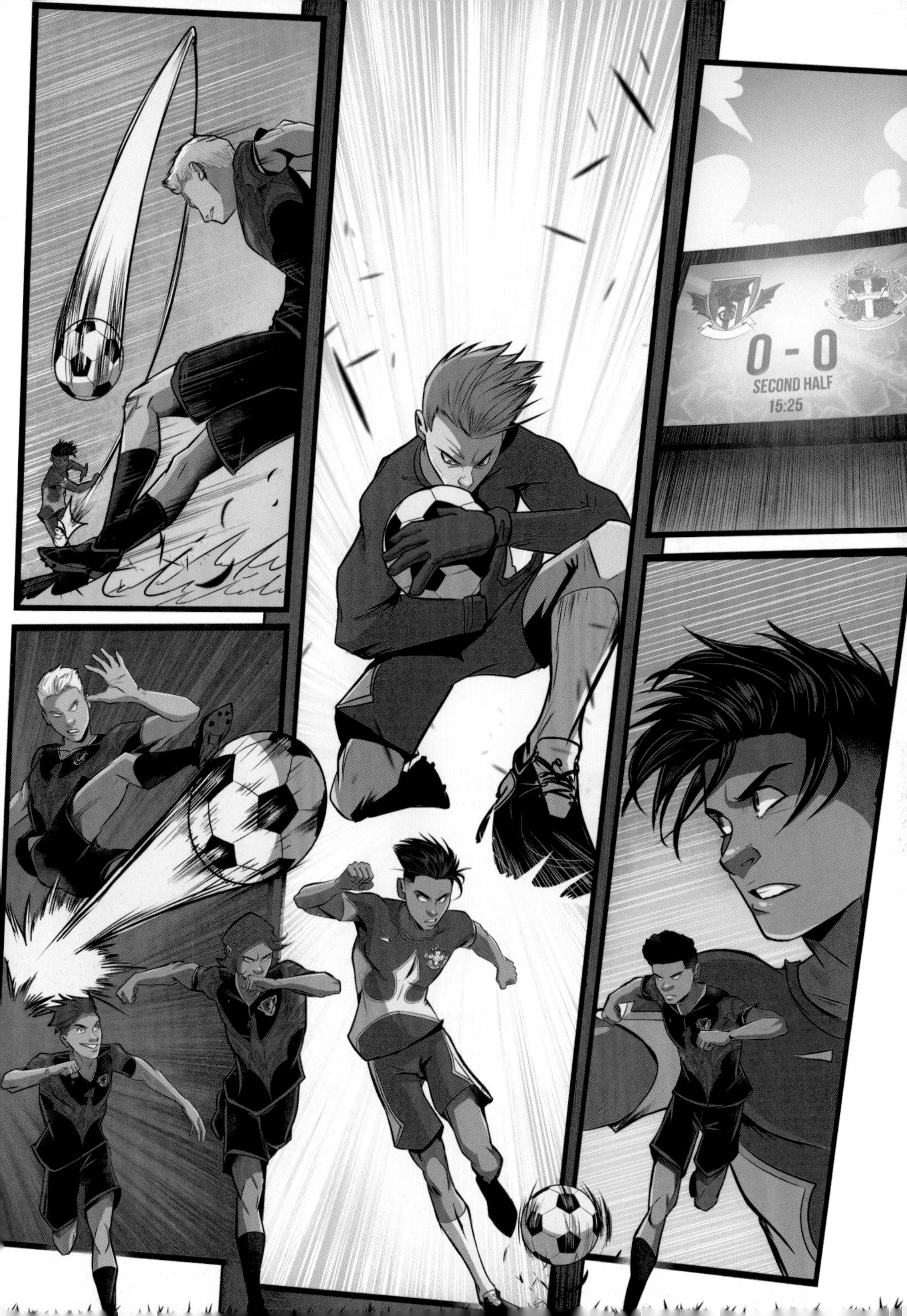
0 - 0
SECOND HALF
15:25

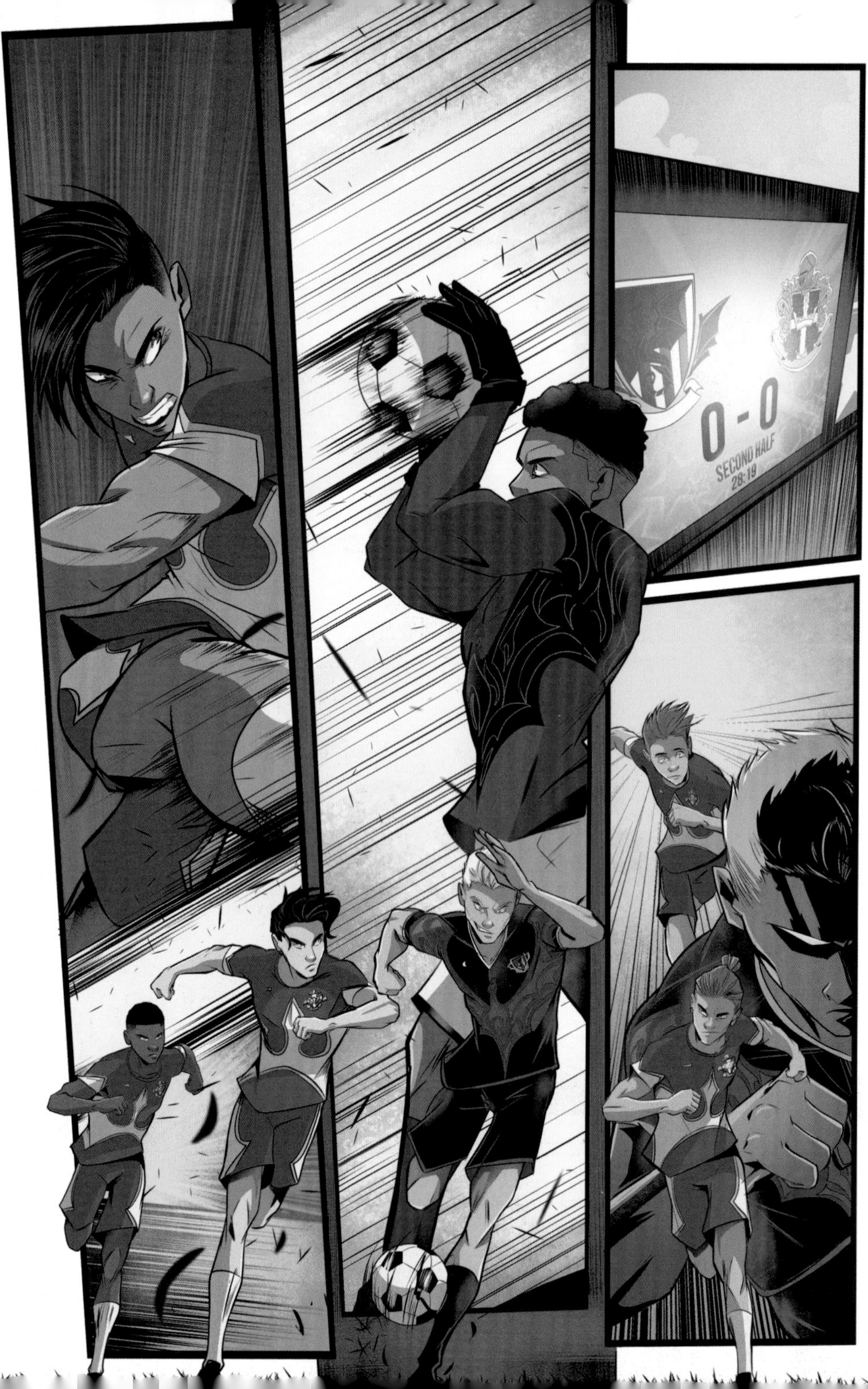
0 - 0
SECOND HALF
28:19

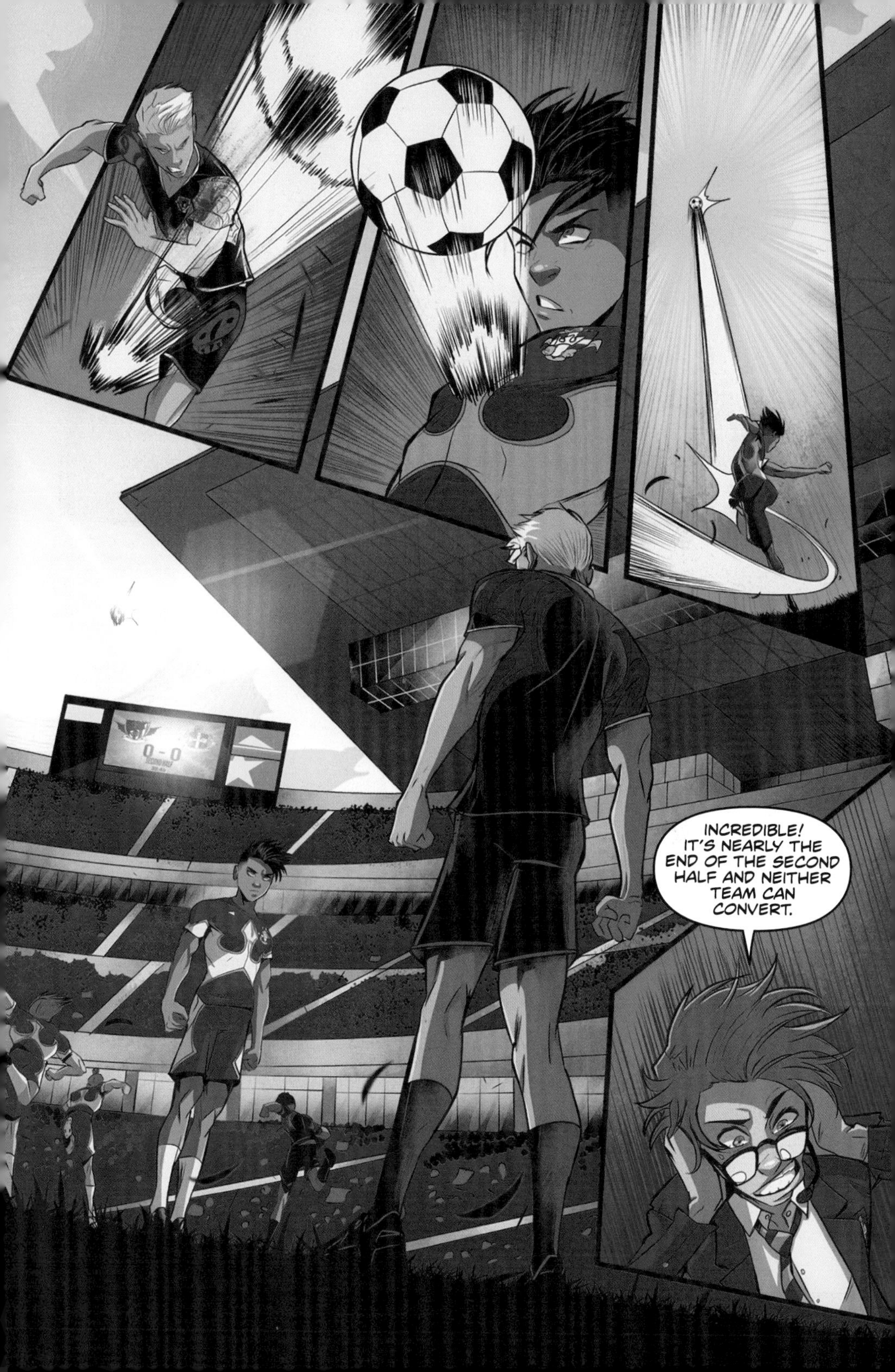
INCREDIBLE! IT'S NEARLY THE END OF THE SECOND HALF AND NEITHER TEAM CAN CONVERT.

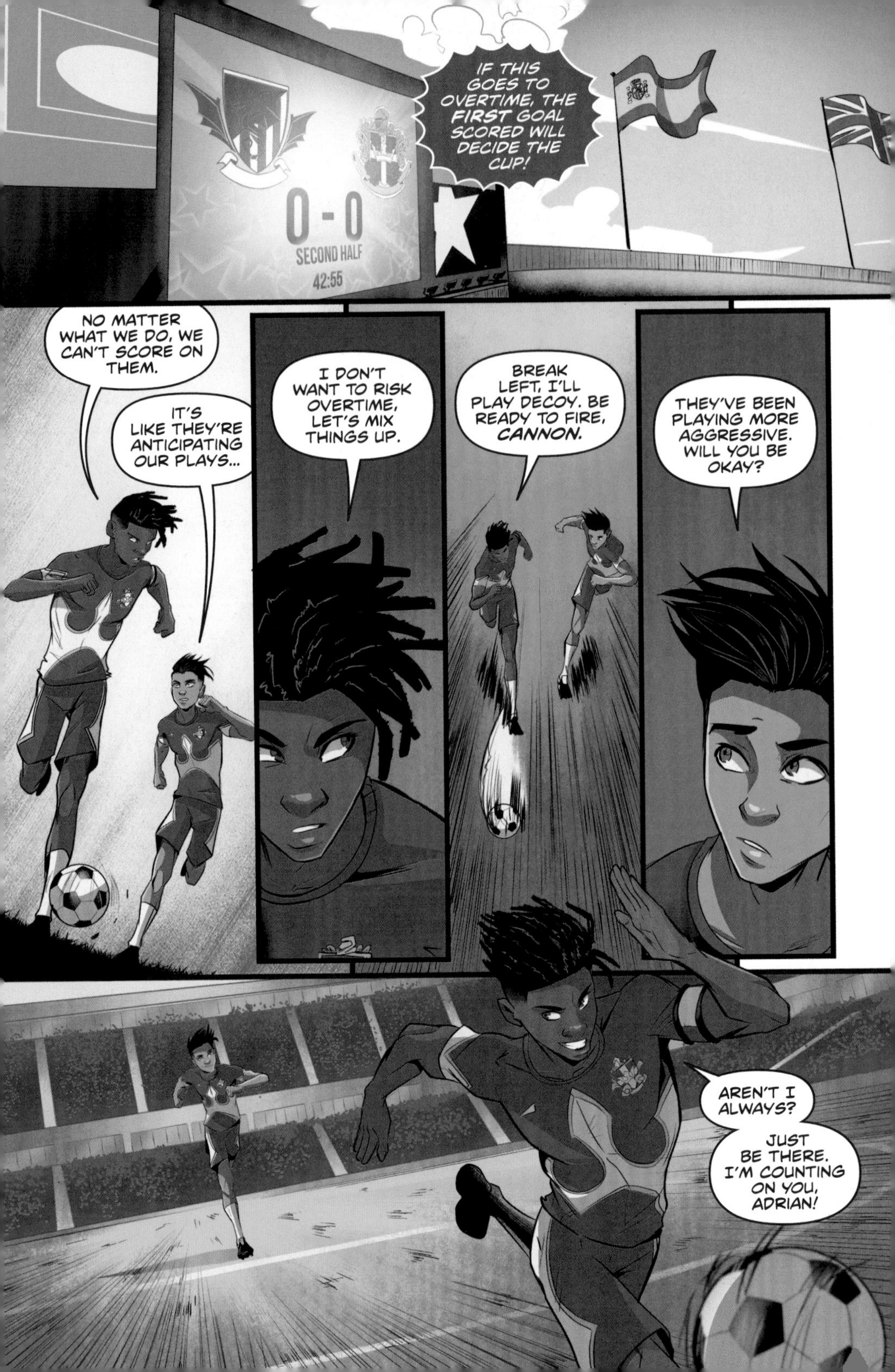
0 - 0
SECOND HALF
42:55
IF THIS GOES TO OVERTIME, THE FIRST GOAL SCORED WILL DECIDE THE CUP!
NO MATTER WHAT WE DO, WE CAN'T SCORE ON THEM.
IT'S LIKE THEY'RE ANTICIPATING OUR PLAYS...
I DON'T WANT TO RISK OVERTIME, LET'S MIX THINGS UP.
BREAK LEFT, I'LL PLAY DECOY. BE READY TO FIRE, CANNON.
THEY'VE BEEN PLAYING MORE AGGRESSIVE. WILL YOU BE OKAY?
AREN'T I ALWAYS?
JUST BE THERE. I'M COUNTING ON YOU, ADRIAN!

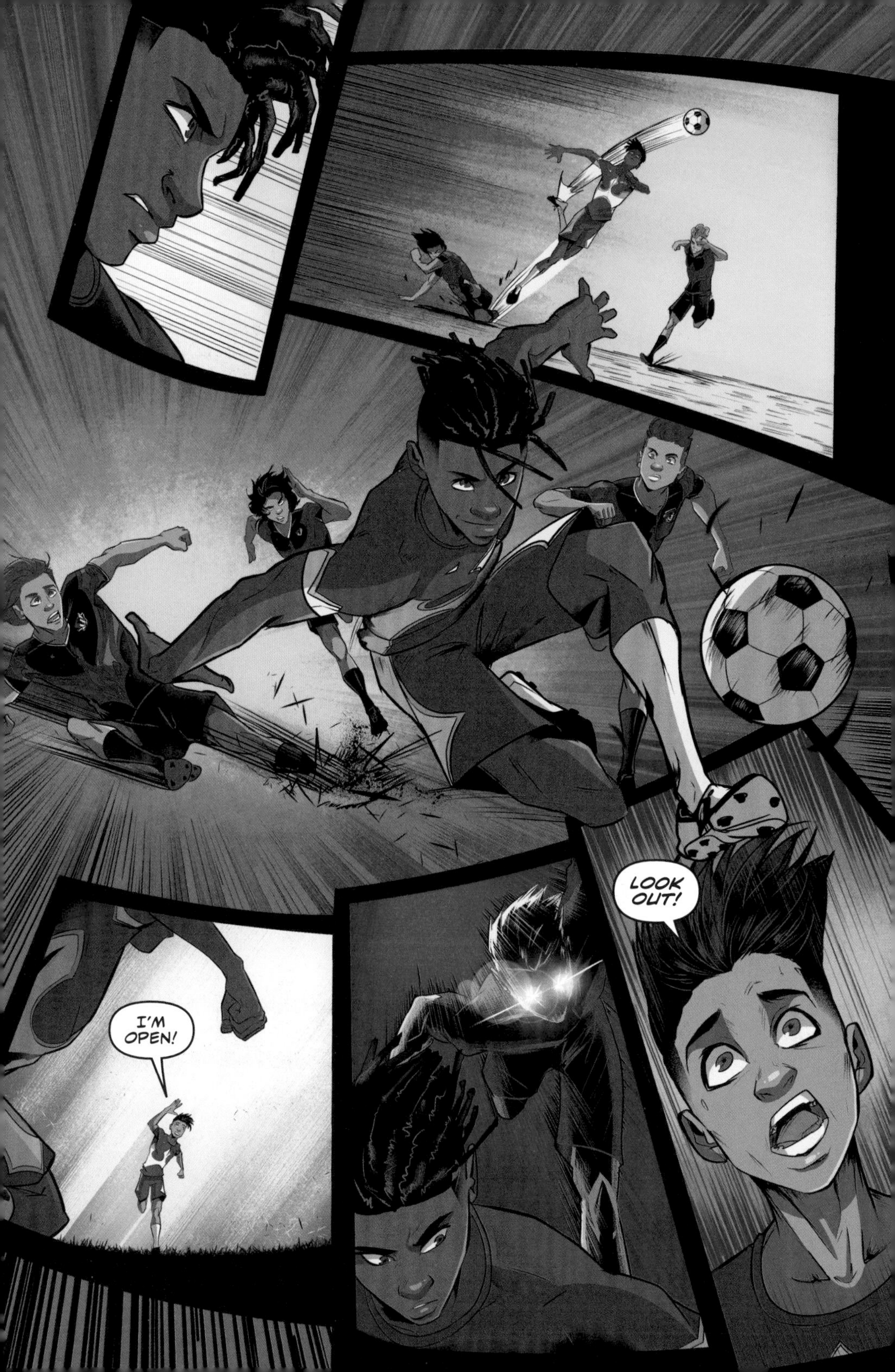
LOOK OUT!
I'M OPEN!

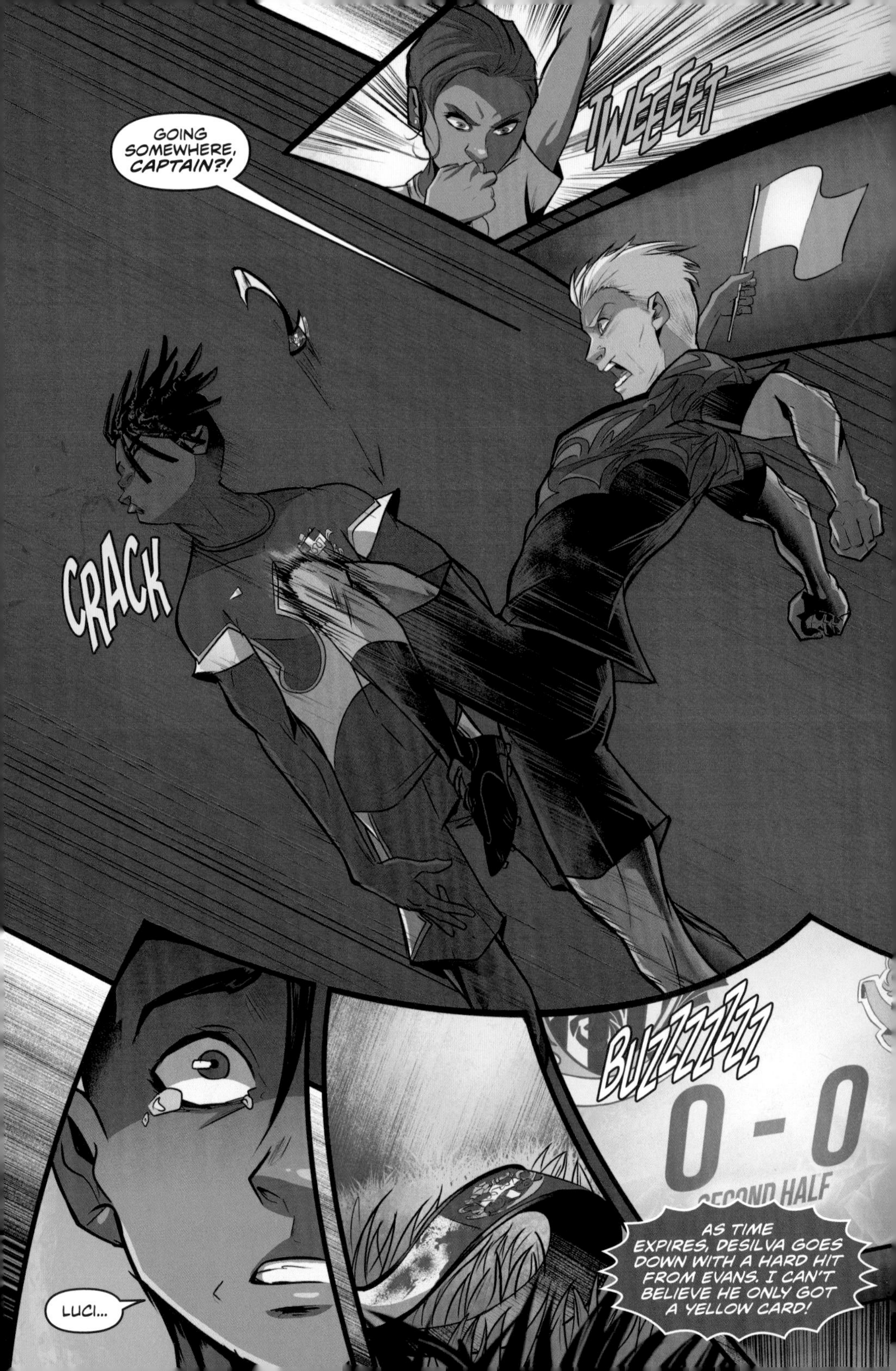
GOING SOMEWHERE, CAPTAIN?!
TWEEEET
CRACK
LUCI...
BUZZZZZZ
0 - 0
SECOND HALF
AS TIME EXPIRES, DESILVA GOES DOWN WITH A HARD HIT FROM EVANS. I CAN'T BELIEVE HE ONLY GOT A YELLOW CARD!

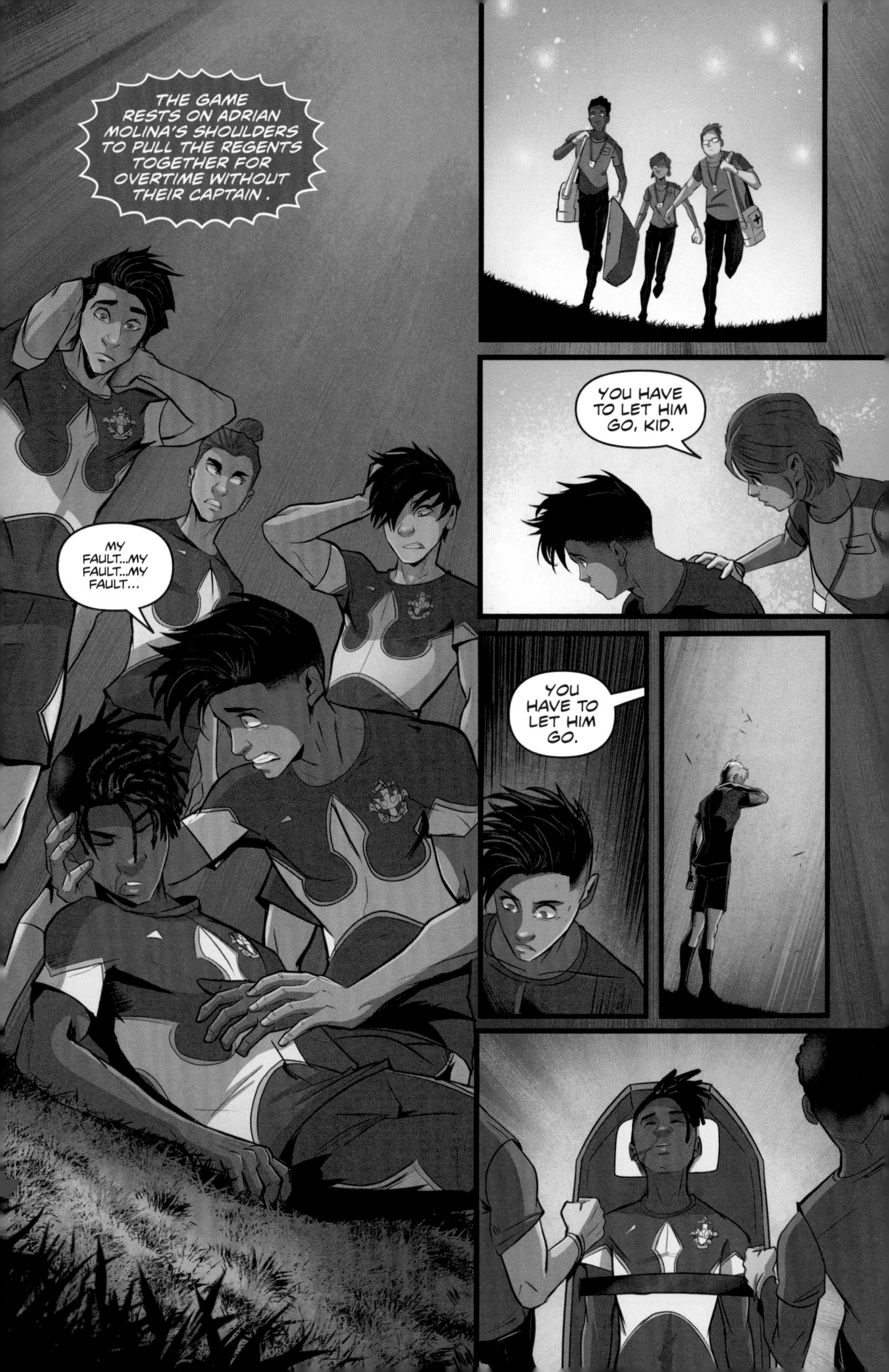
THE GAME RESTS ON ADRIAN MOLINA'S SHOULDERS TO PULL THE REGENTS TOGETHER FOR OVERTIME WITHOUT THEIR CAPTAIN.
MY FAULT...MY FAULT...MY FAULT...
YOU HAVE TO LET HIM GO, KID.
YOU HAVE TO LET HIM GO.

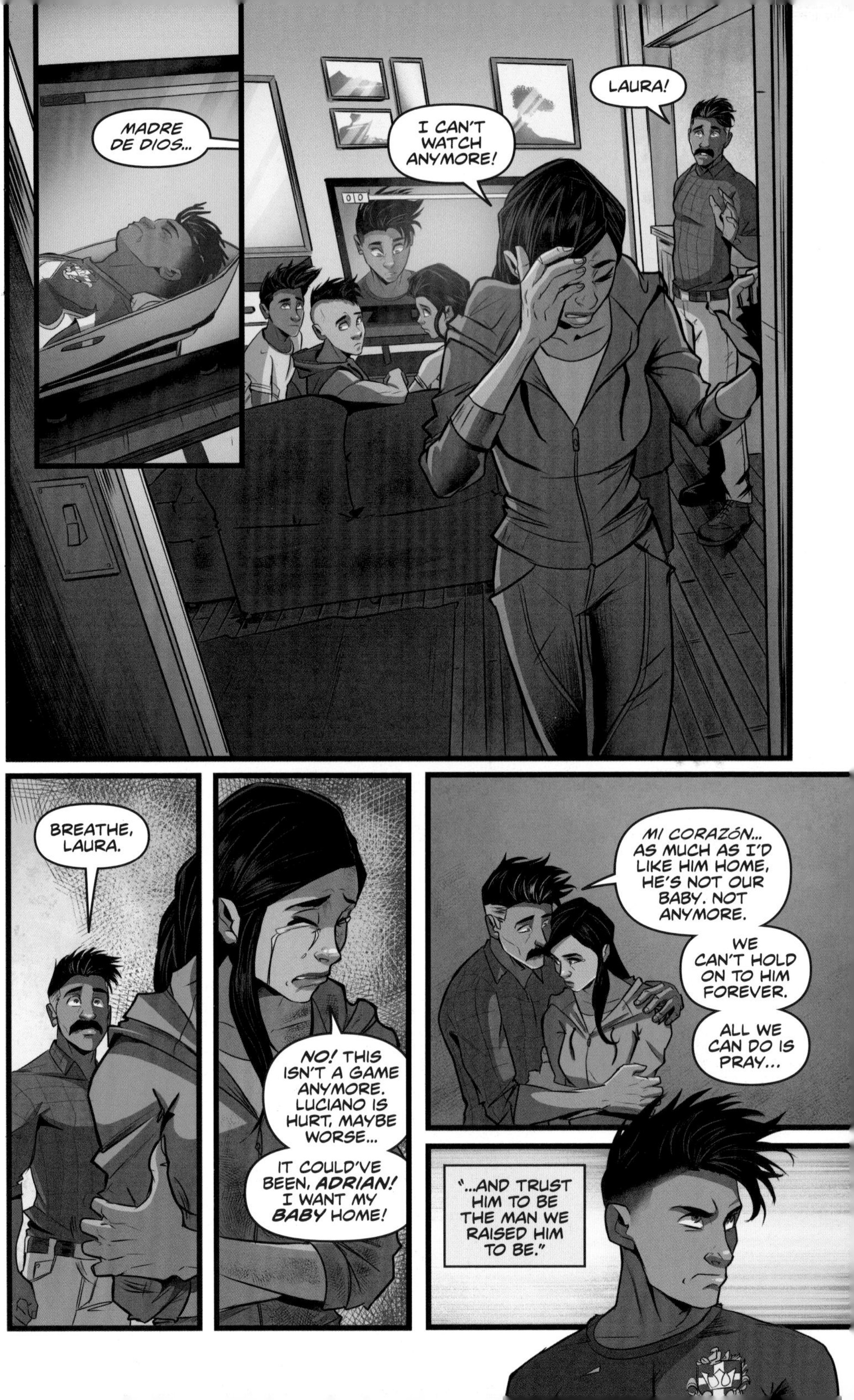
MADRE DE DIOS...
I CAN'T WATCH ANYMORE!
LAURA!
BREATHE, LAURA.
NO! THIS ISN'T A GAME ANYMORE. LUCIANO IS HURT, MAYBE WORSE...
IT COULD'VE BEEN, ADRIAN! I WANT MY BABY HOME!
MI CORAZÓN... AS MUCH AS I'D LIKE HIM HOME, HE'S NOT OUR BABY. NOT ANYMORE.
WE CAN'T HOLD ON TO HIM FOREVER.
ALL WE CAN DO IS PRAY...
"...AND TRUST HIM TO BE THE MAN WE RAISED HIM TO BE."

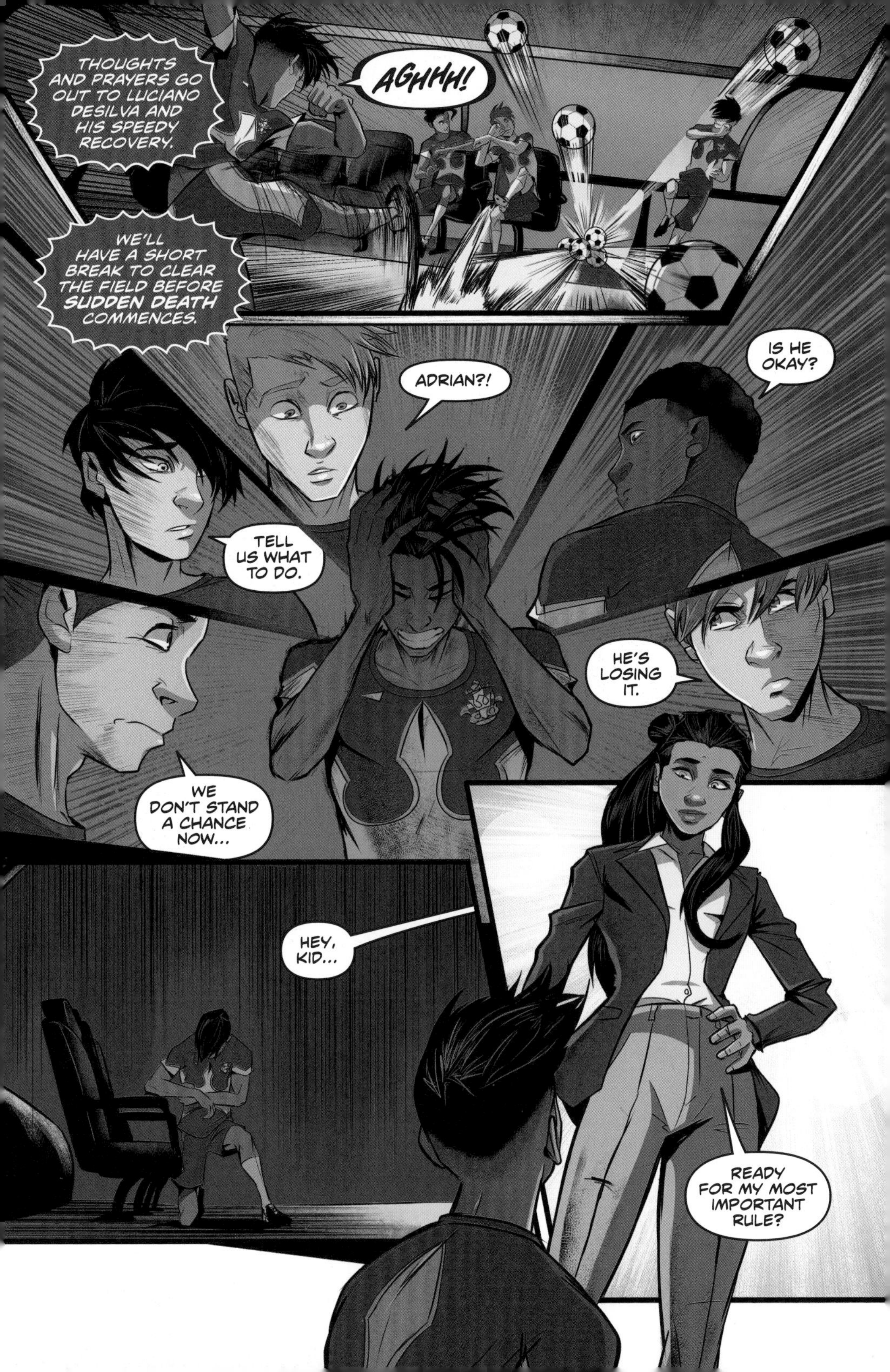
THOUGHTS AND PRAYERS GO OUT TO LUCIANO DESILVA AND HIS SPEEDY RECOVERY.
AGHHH!
WE'LL HAVE A SHORT BREAK TO CLEAR THE FIELD BEFORE **SUDDEN DEATH** COMMENCES.
ADRIAN?!
IS HE OKAY?
TELL US WHAT TO DO.
HE'S LOSING IT.
WE DON'T STAND A CHANCE NOW...
HEY, KID...
READY FOR MY MOST IMPORTANT RULE?

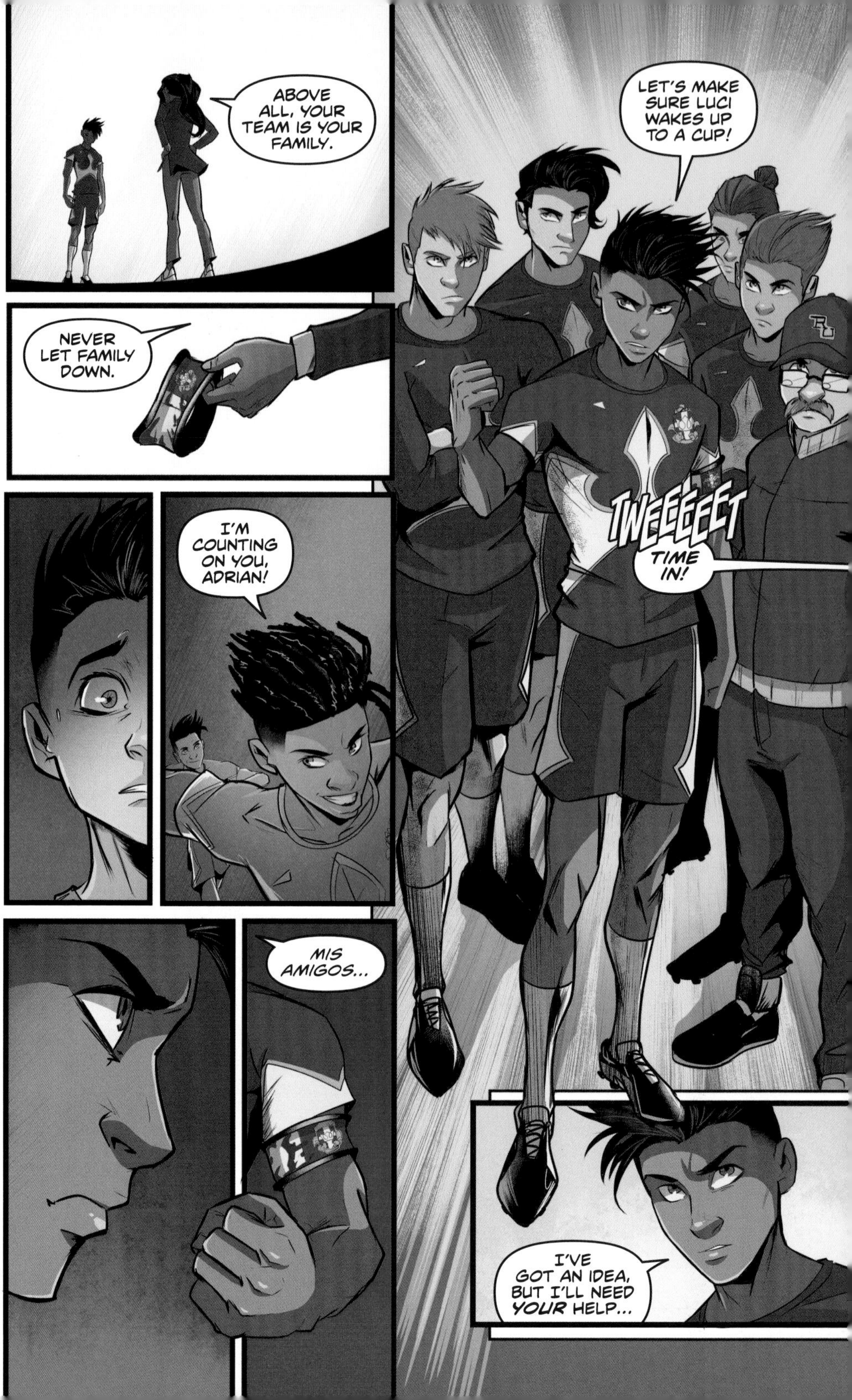
ABOVE ALL, YOUR TEAM IS YOUR FAMILY.
NEVER LET FAMILY DOWN.
I'M COUNTING ON YOU, ADRIAN!
MIS AMIGOS...
LET'S MAKE SURE LUCI WAKES UP TO A CUP!
TWEEEEEEET
TIME IN!
I'VE GOT AN IDEA, BUT I'LL NEED *YOUR* HELP...

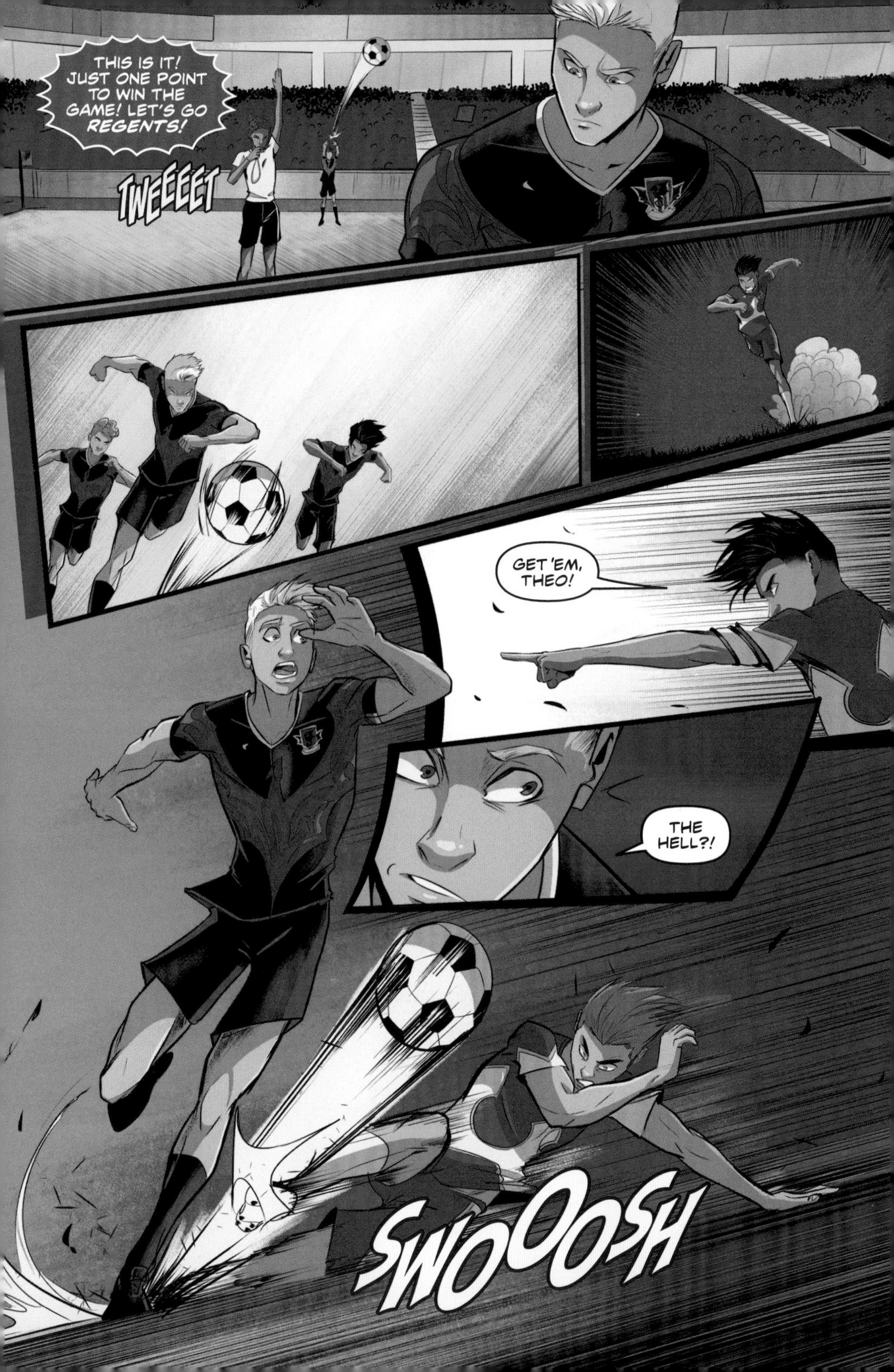
THIS IS IT! JUST ONE POINT TO WIN THE GAME! LET'S GO *REGENTS!*
TWEEEEET
GET 'EM, THEO!
THE HELL?!
SWOOOSH

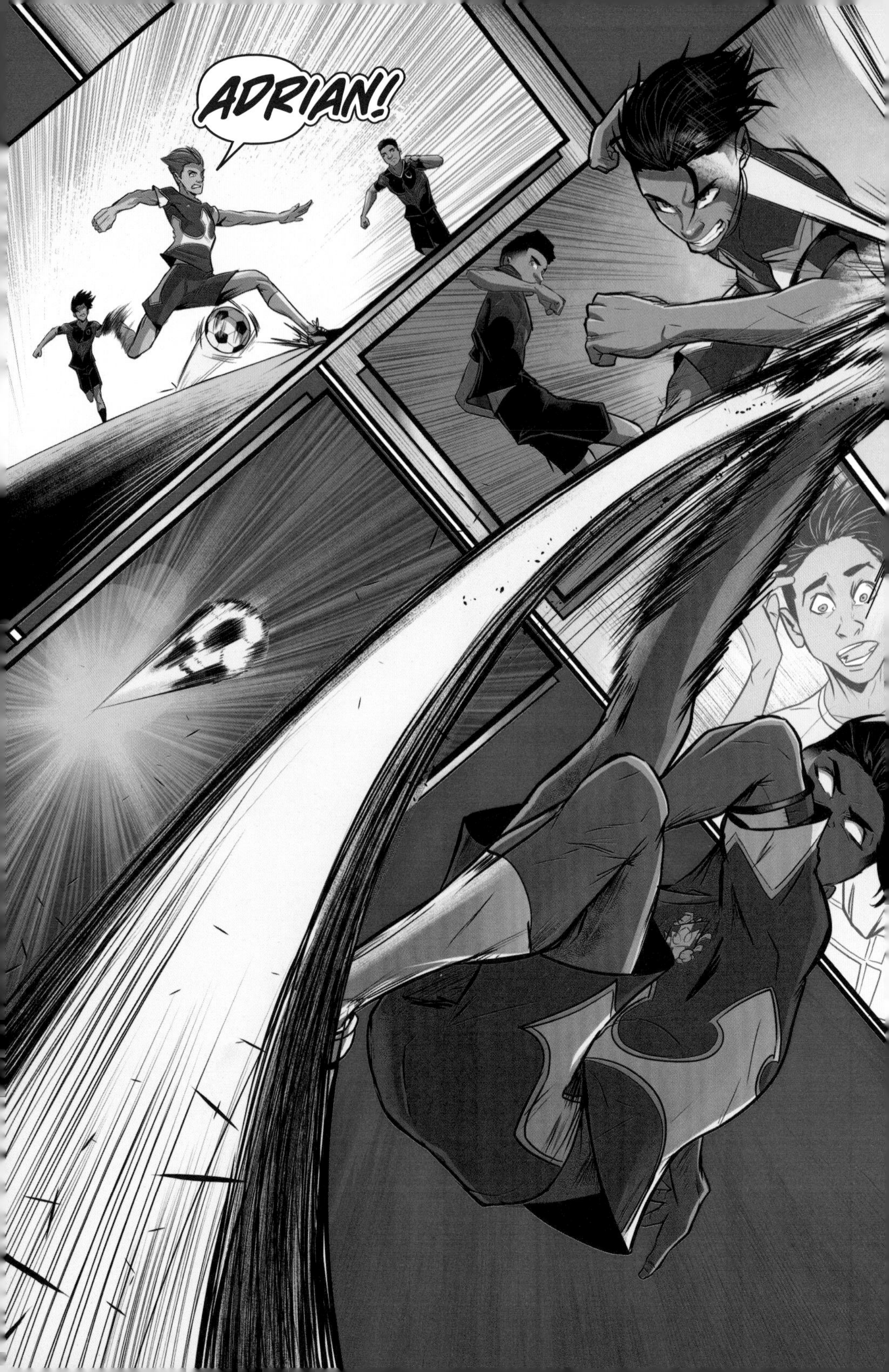
ADRIAN!

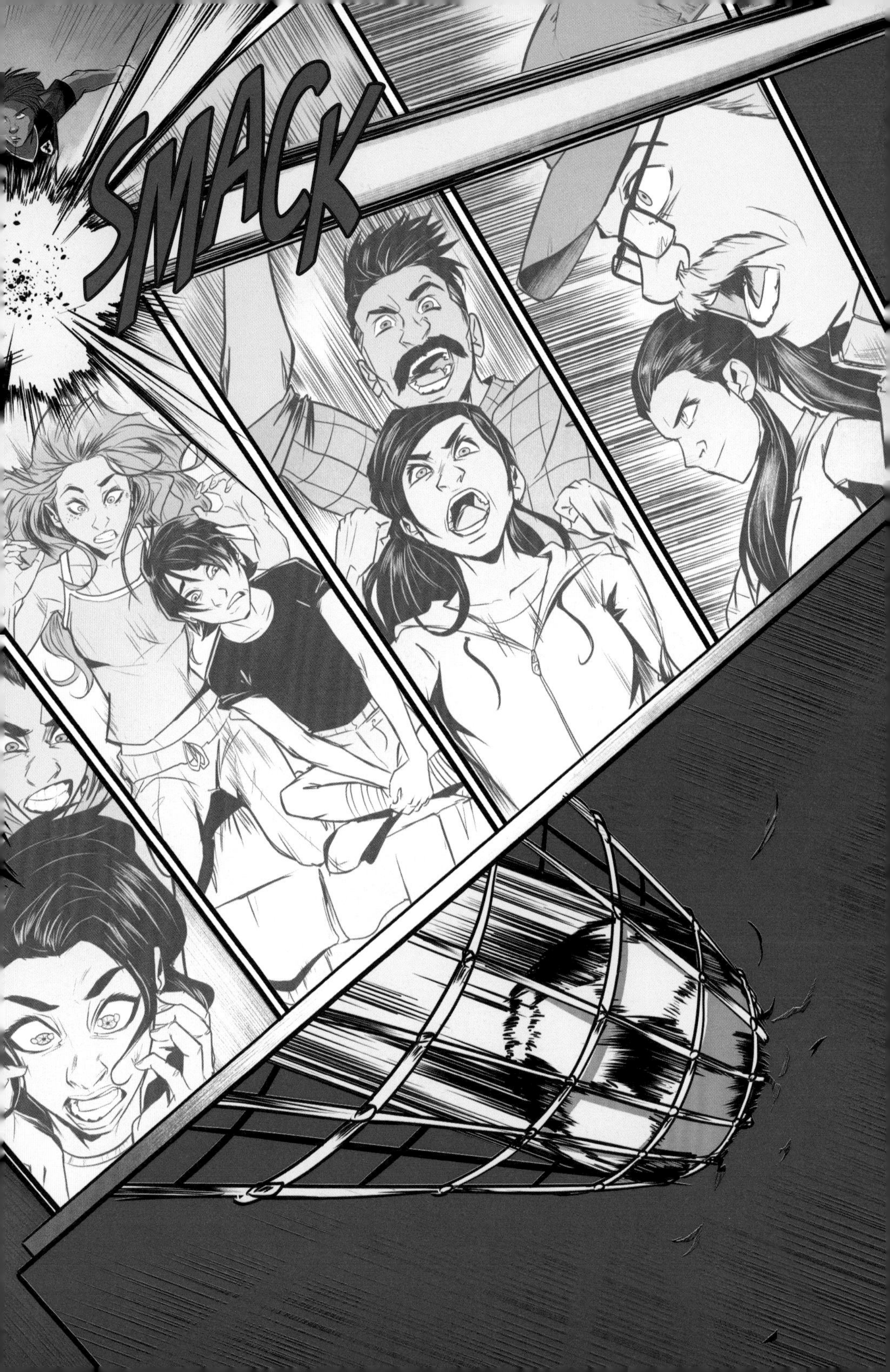
SMACK

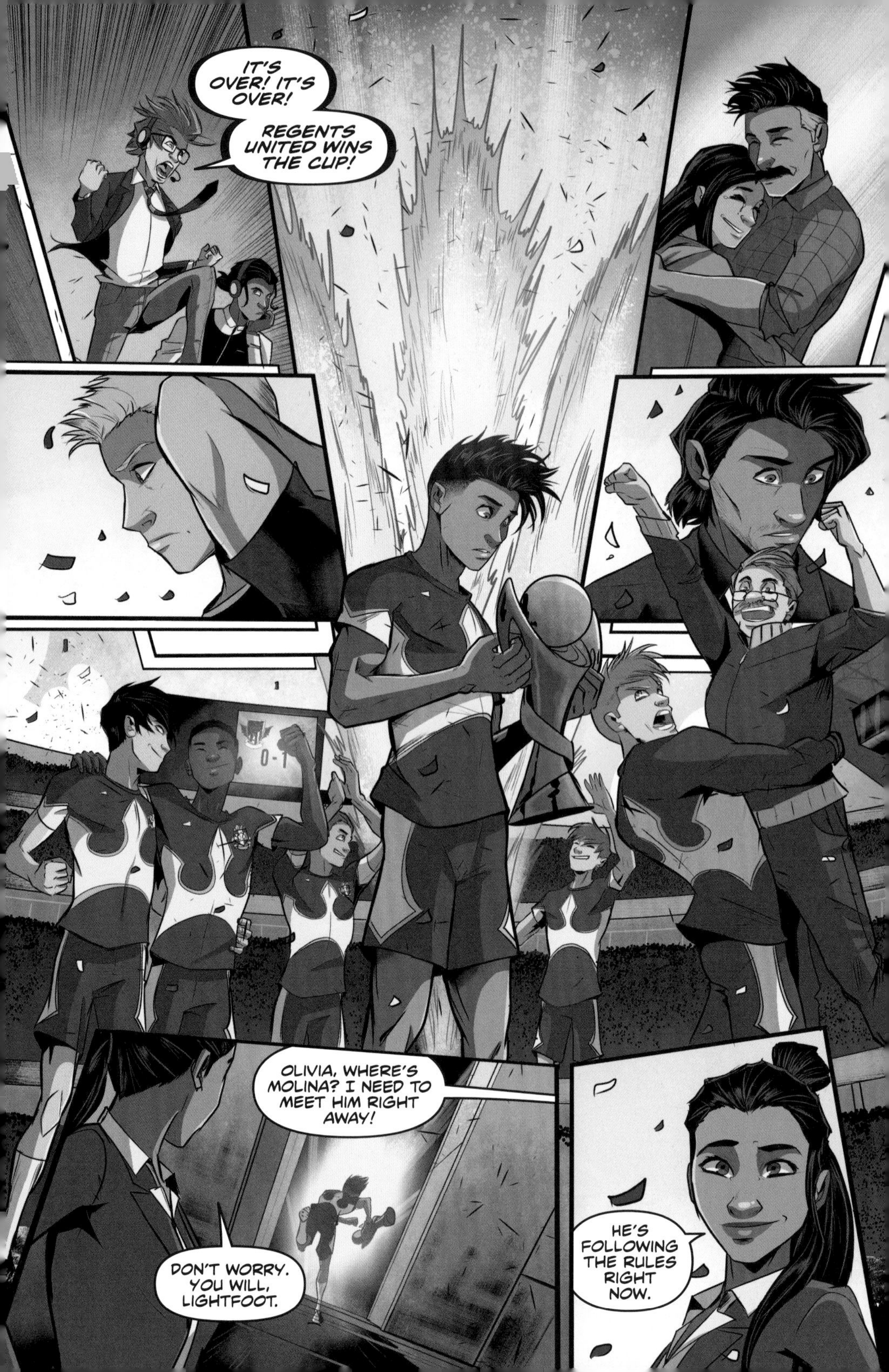
IT'S OVER! IT'S OVER!
REGENTS UNITED WINS THE CUP!
0-1
OLIVIA, WHERE'S MOLINA? I NEED TO MEET HIM RIGHT AWAY!
DON'T WORRY. YOU WILL, LIGHTFOOT.
HE'S FOLLOWING THE RULES RIGHT NOW.

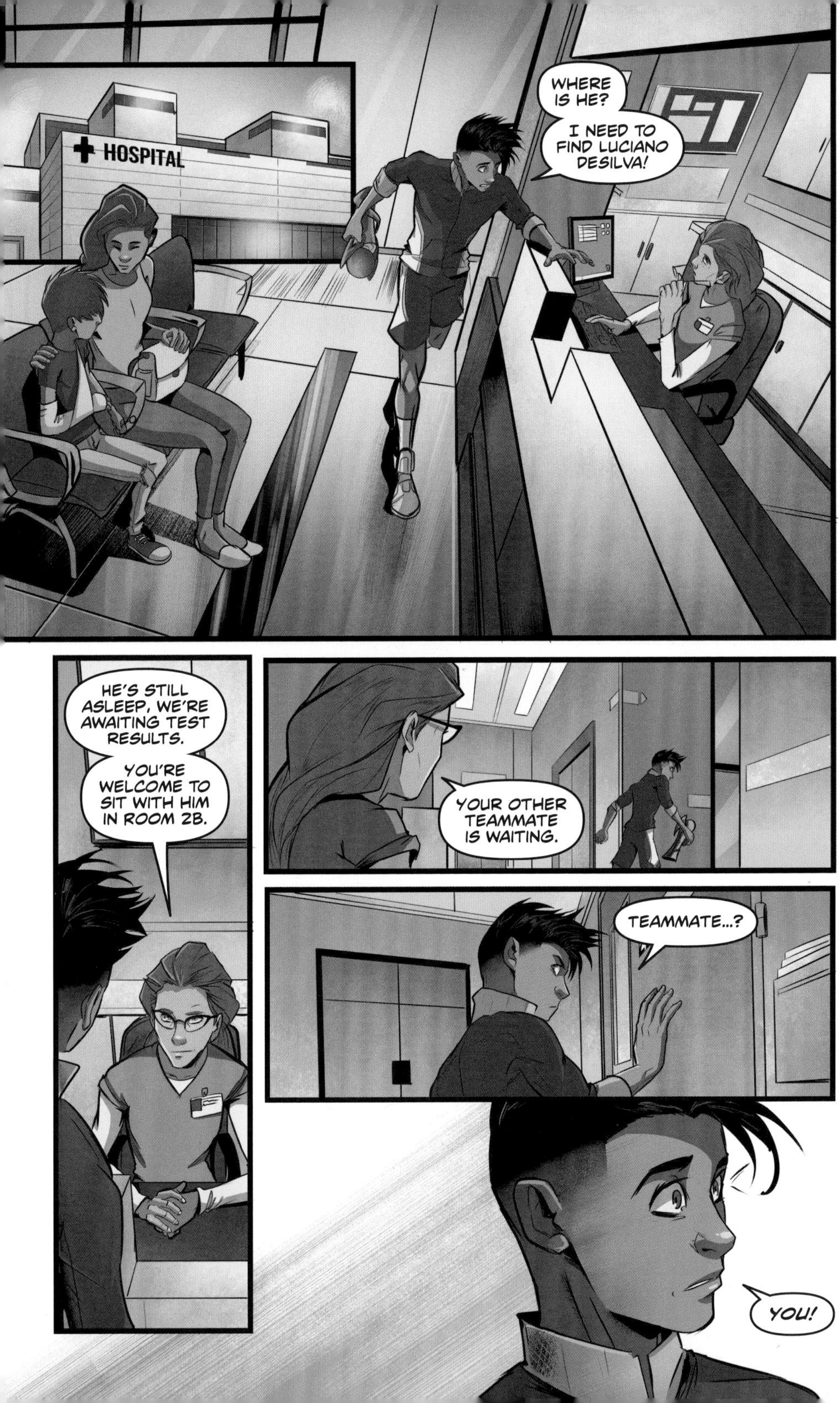
HOSPITAL
WHERE IS HE?
I NEED TO FIND LUCIANO DESILVA!
HE'S STILL ASLEEP, WE'RE AWAITING TEST RESULTS.
YOU'RE WELCOME TO SIT WITH HIM IN ROOM 2B.
YOUR OTHER TEAMMATE IS WAITING.
TEAMMATE...?
YOU!

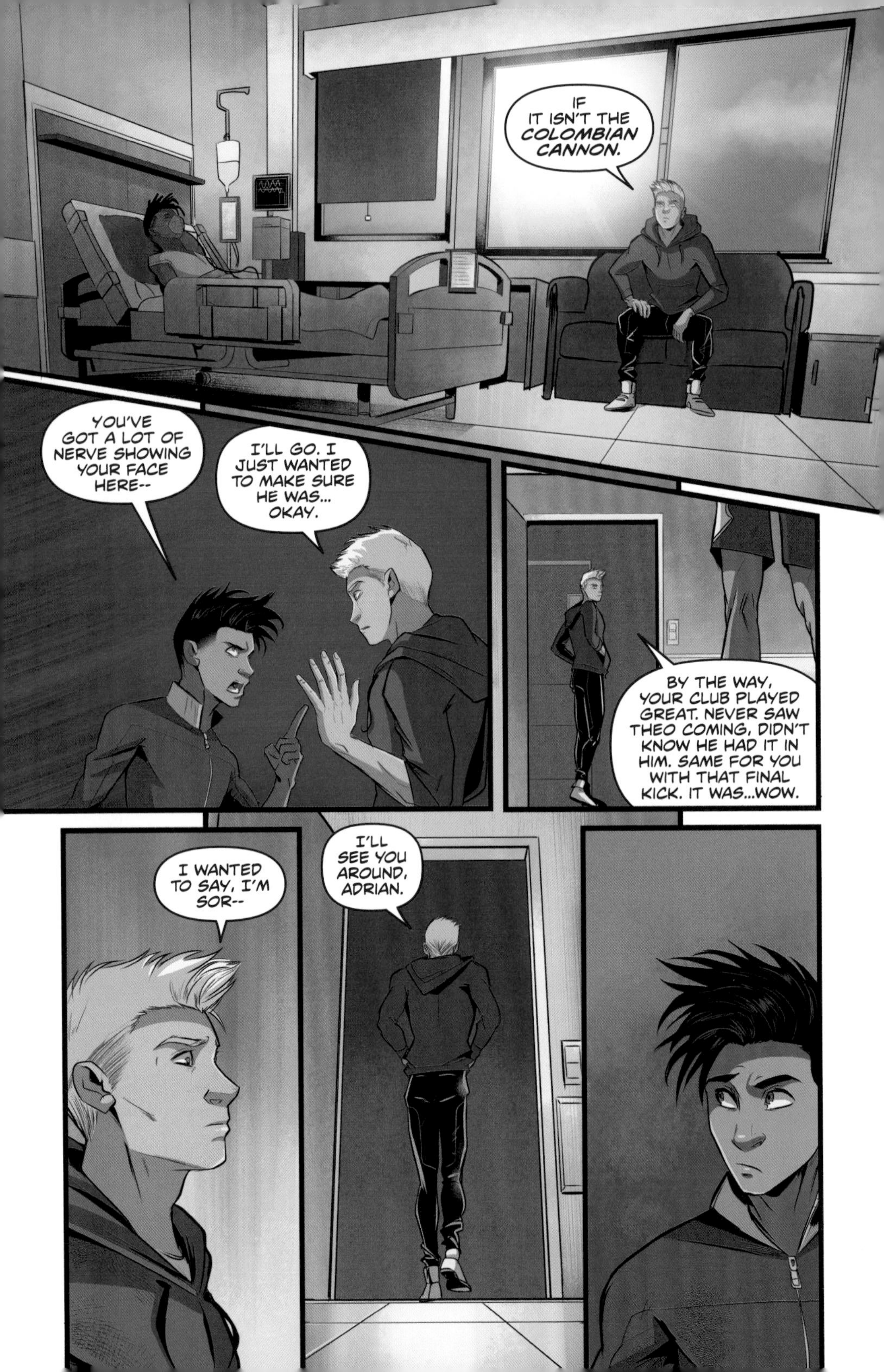
IF IT ISN'T THE COLOMBIAN CANNON.
YOU'VE GOT A LOT OF NERVE SHOWING YOUR FACE HERE--
I'LL GO. I JUST WANTED TO MAKE SURE HE WAS... OKAY.
BY THE WAY, YOUR CLUB PLAYED GREAT. NEVER SAW THEO COMING, DIDN'T KNOW HE HAD IT IN HIM. SAME FOR YOU WITH THAT FINAL KICK. IT WAS...WOW.
I WANTED TO SAY, I'M SOR--
I'LL SEE YOU AROUND, ADRIAN.

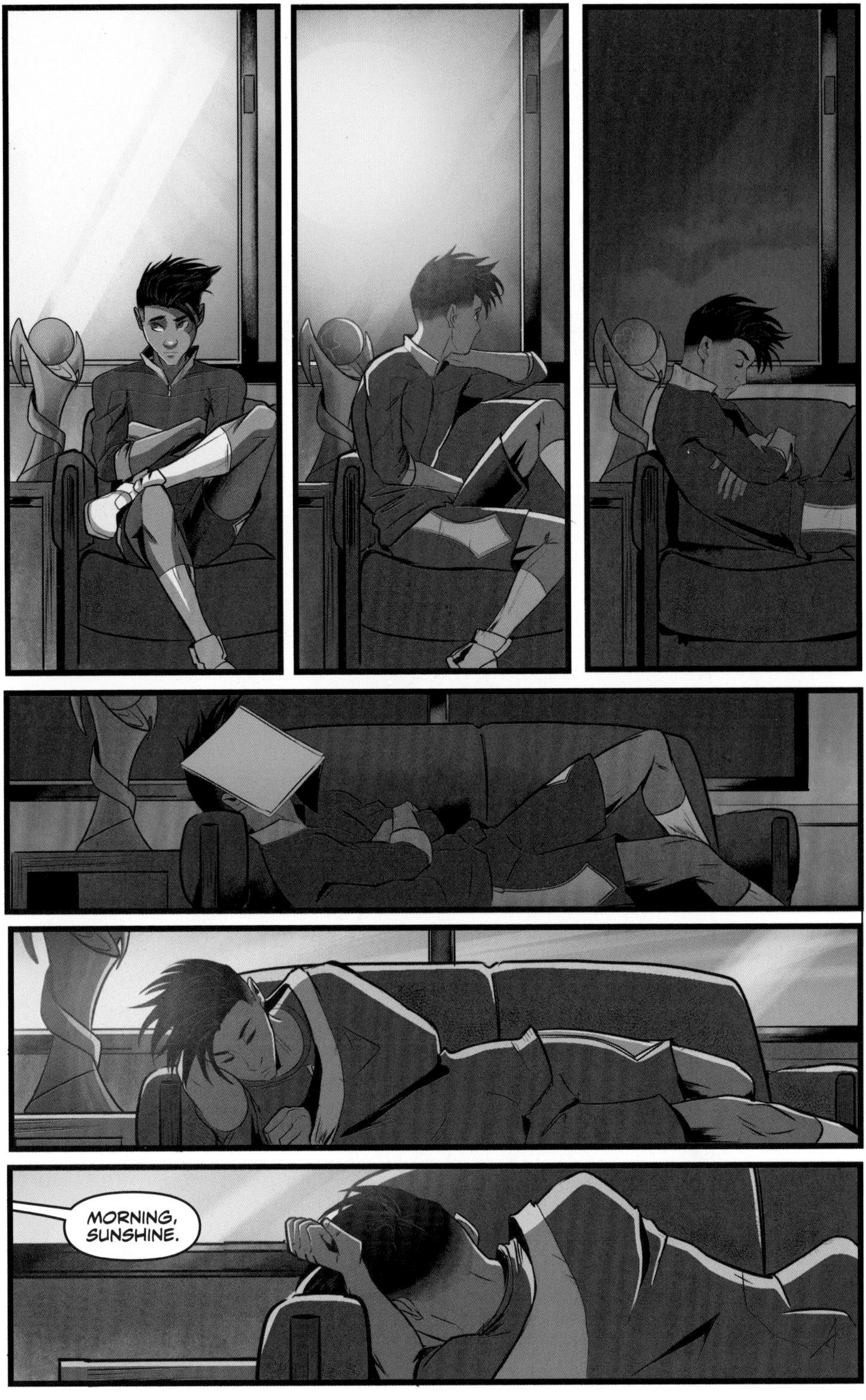
MORNING, SUNSHINE.

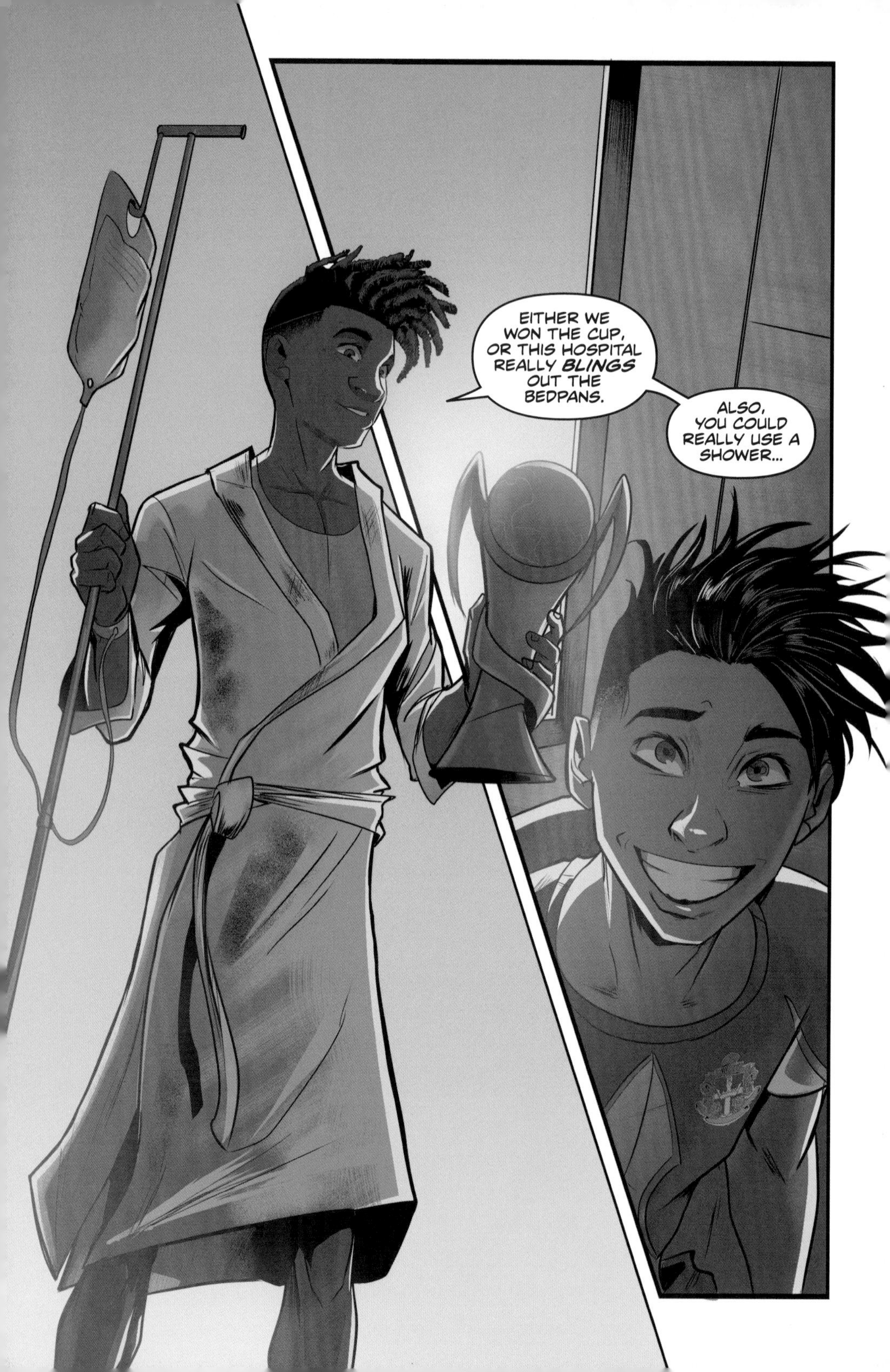
EITHER WE WON THE CUP, OR THIS HOSPITAL REALLY *BLINGS* OUT THE BEDPANS.
ALSO, YOU COULD REALLY USE A SHOWER...

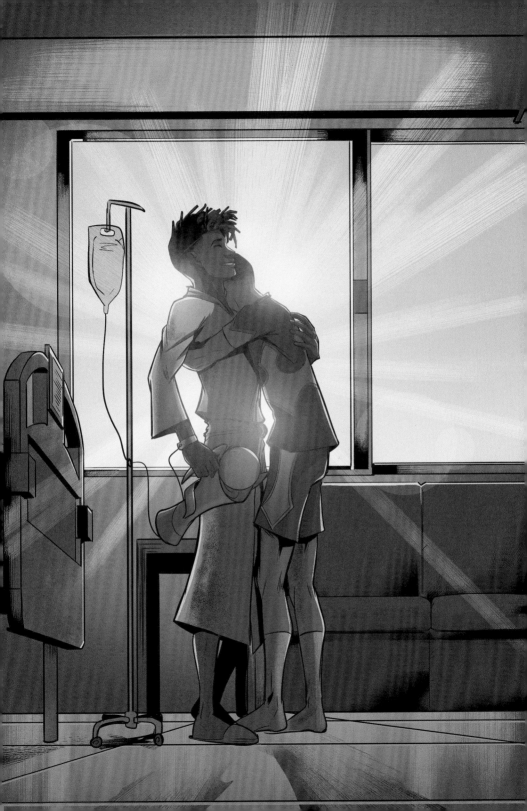

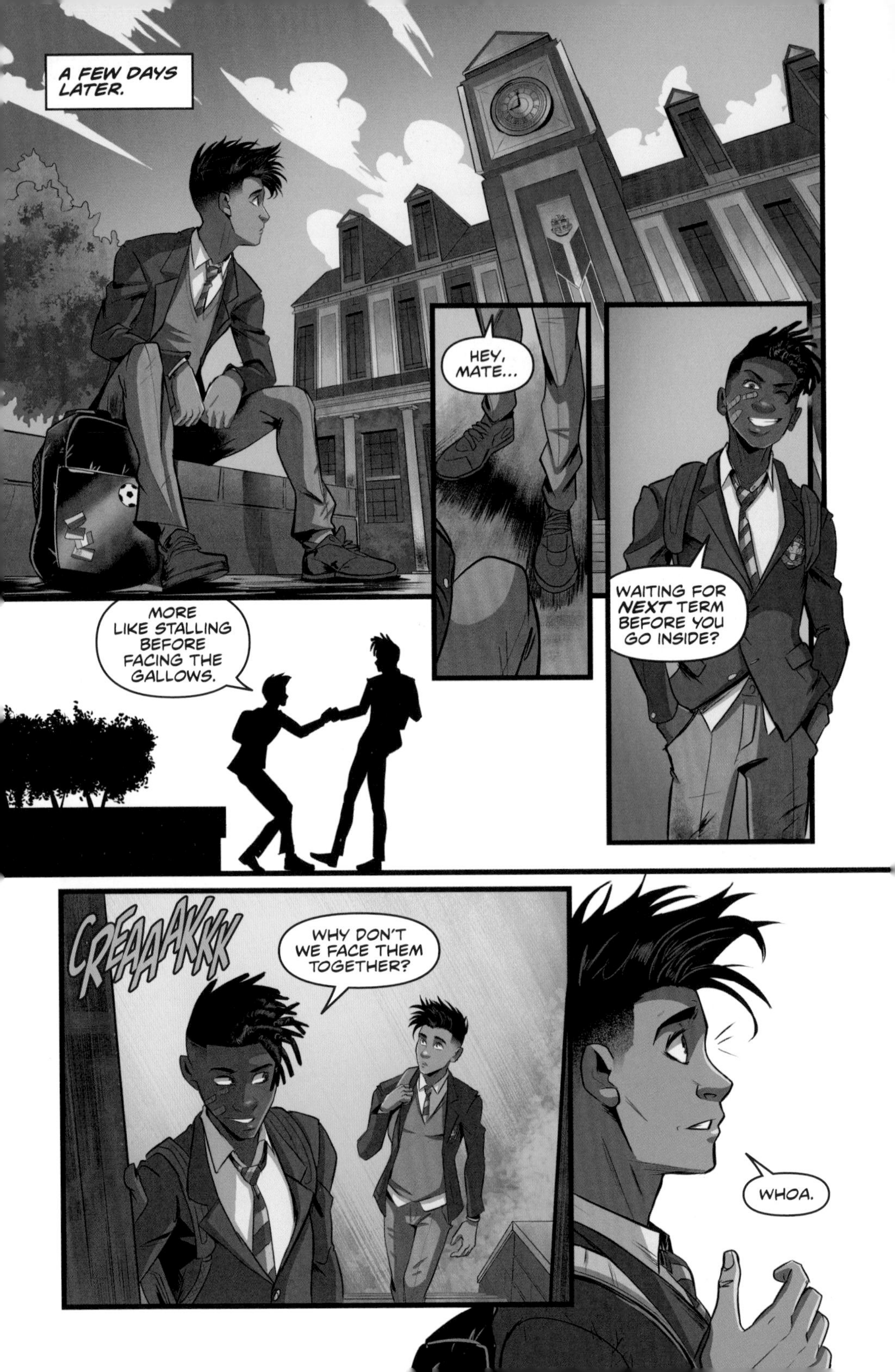
A FEW DAYS LATER.
HEY, MATE...
WAITING FOR NEXT TERM BEFORE YOU GO INSIDE?
MORE LIKE STALLING BEFORE FACING THE GALLOWS.
CREAAAKKK
WHY DON'T WE FACE THEM TOGETHER?
WHOA.

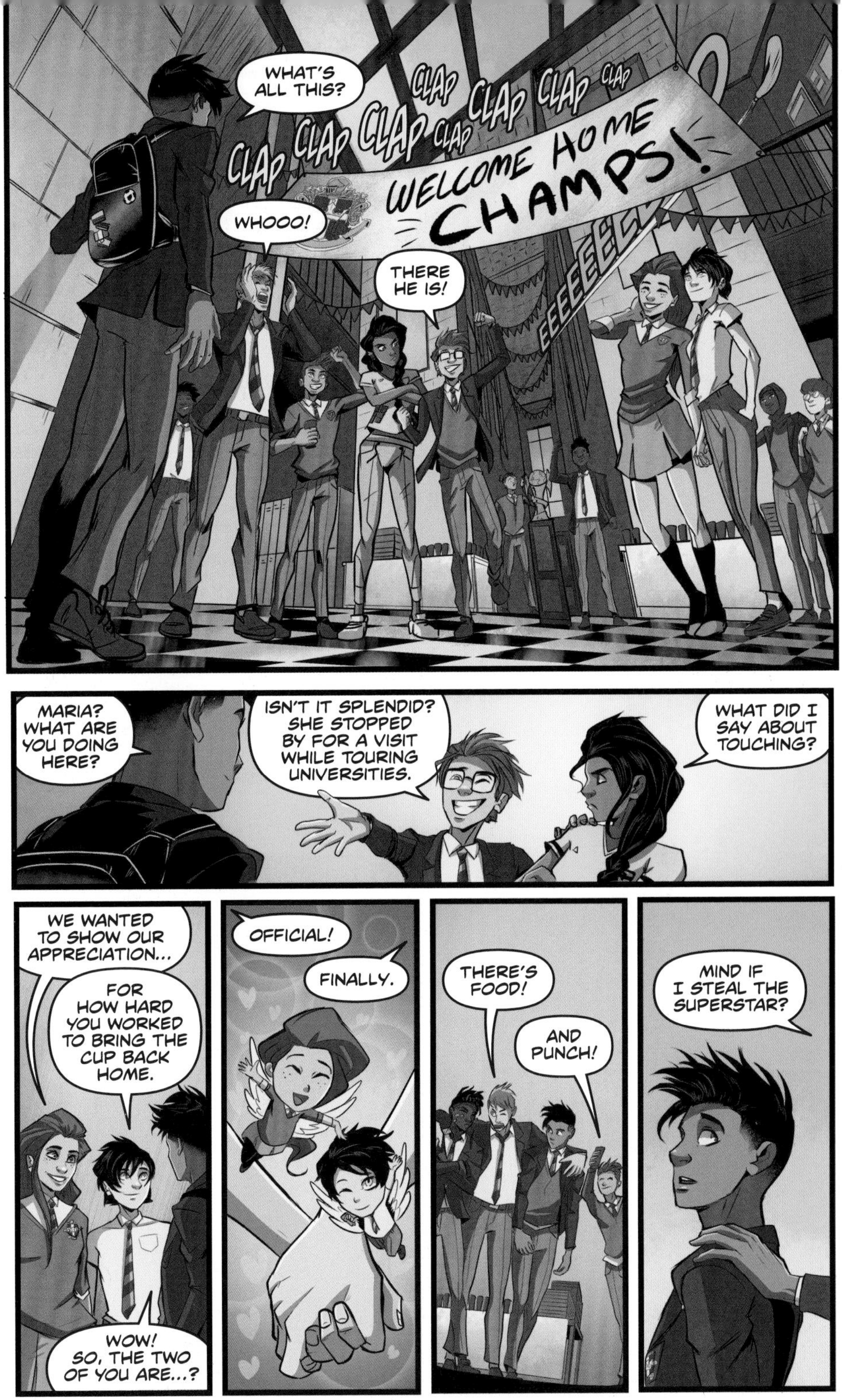
WHAT'S ALL THIS?
CLAP CLAP CLAP CLAP CLAP CLAP CLAP CLAP
WELCOME HOME CHAMPS!
WHOOO!
THERE HE IS!
EEEEEEL
MARIA? WHAT ARE YOU DOING HERE?
ISN'T IT SPLENDID? SHE STOPPED BY FOR A VISIT WHILE TOURING UNIVERSITIES.
WHAT DID I SAY ABOUT TOUCHING?
WE WANTED TO SHOW OUR APPRECIATION...
FOR HOW HARD YOU WORKED TO BRING THE CUP BACK HOME.
WOW! SO, THE TWO OF YOU ARE...?
OFFICIAL!
FINALLY.
THERE'S FOOD!
AND PUNCH!
MIND IF I STEAL THE SUPERSTAR?

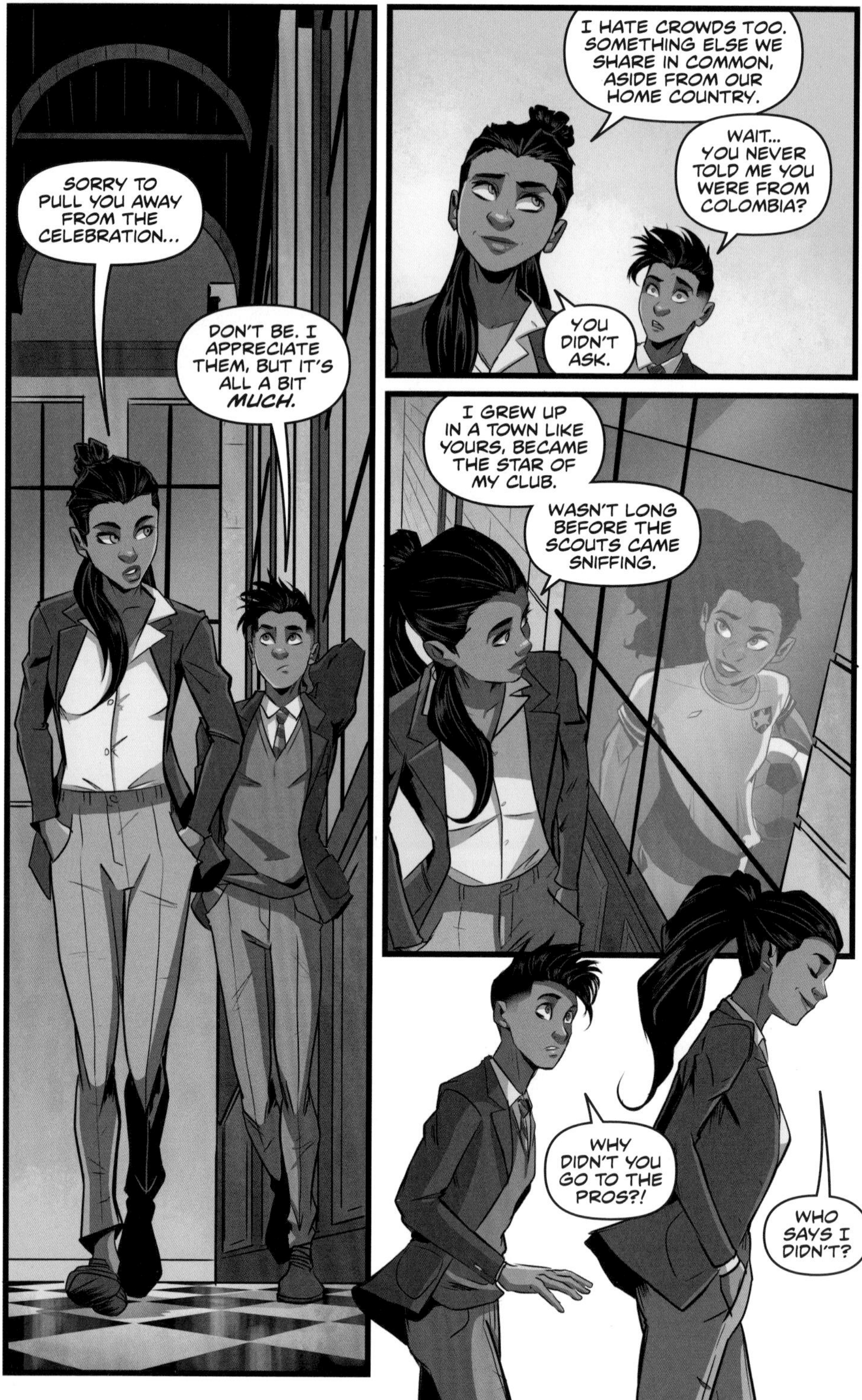
SORRY TO PULL YOU AWAY FROM THE CELEBRATION...
DON'T BE. I APPRECIATE THEM, BUT IT'S ALL A BIT *MUCH.*
I HATE CROWDS TOO. SOMETHING ELSE WE SHARE IN COMMON, ASIDE FROM OUR HOME COUNTRY.
WAIT... YOU NEVER TOLD ME YOU WERE FROM COLOMBIA?
YOU DIDN'T ASK.
I GREW UP IN A TOWN LIKE YOURS, BECAME THE STAR OF MY CLUB.
WASN'T LONG BEFORE THE SCOUTS CAME SNIFFING.
WHY DIDN'T YOU GO TO THE PROS?!
WHO SAYS I DIDN'T?

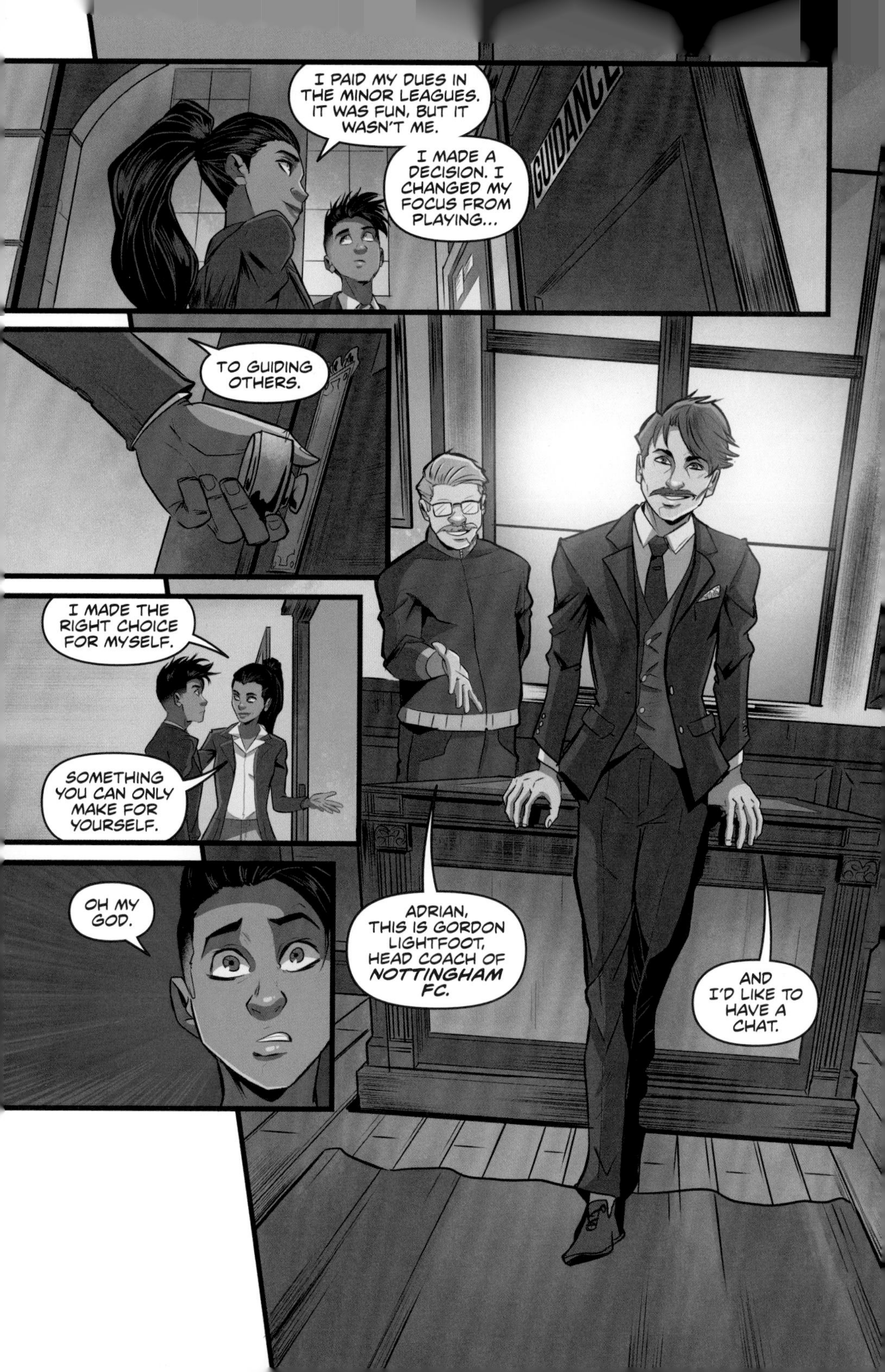
GUIDANCE
I PAID MY DUES IN THE MINOR LEAGUES. IT WAS FUN, BUT IT WASN'T ME.
I MADE A DECISION. I CHANGED MY FOCUS FROM PLAYING...
TO GUIDING OTHERS.
I MADE THE RIGHT CHOICE FOR MYSELF.
SOMETHING YOU CAN ONLY MAKE FOR YOURSELF.
OH MY GOD.
ADRIAN, THIS IS GORDON LIGHTFOOT, HEAD COACH OF *NOTTINGHAM FC.*
AND I'D LIKE TO HAVE A CHAT.

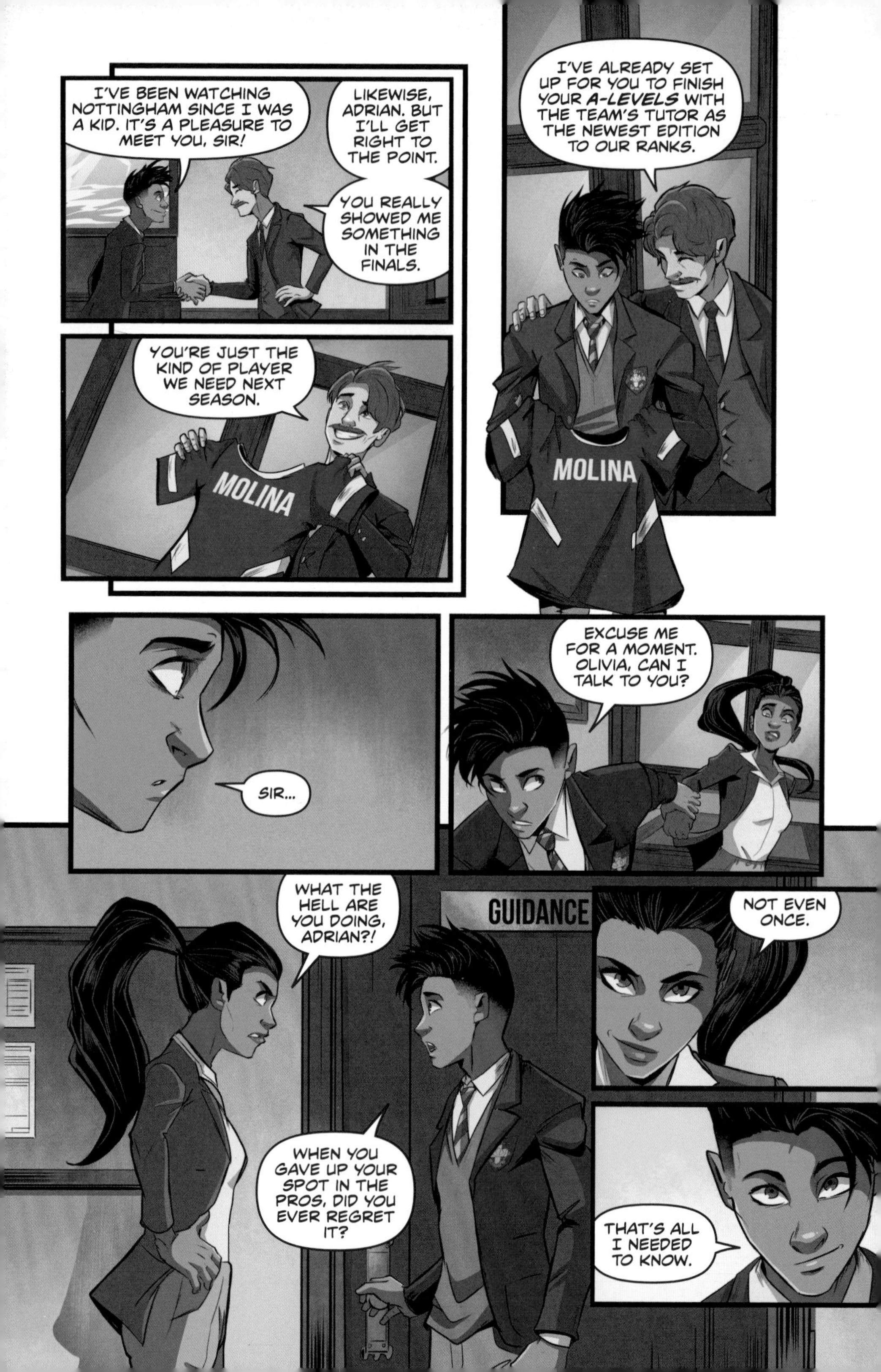
I'VE BEEN WATCHING NOTTINGHAM SINCE I WAS A KID. IT'S A PLEASURE TO MEET YOU, SIR!
LIKEWISE, ADRIAN. BUT I'LL GET RIGHT TO THE POINT.
YOU REALLY SHOWED ME SOMETHING IN THE FINALS.
YOU'RE JUST THE KIND OF PLAYER WE NEED NEXT SEASON.
MOLINA
I'VE ALREADY SET UP FOR YOU TO FINISH YOUR *A-LEVELS* WITH THE TEAM'S TUTOR AS THE NEWEST EDITION TO OUR RANKS.
MOLINA
SIR...
EXCUSE ME FOR A MOMENT. OLIVIA, CAN I TALK TO YOU?
WHAT THE HELL ARE YOU DOING, ADRIAN?!
GUIDANCE
WHEN YOU GAVE UP YOUR SPOT IN THE PROS, DID YOU EVER REGRET IT?
NOT EVEN ONCE.
THAT'S ALL I NEEDED TO KNOW.

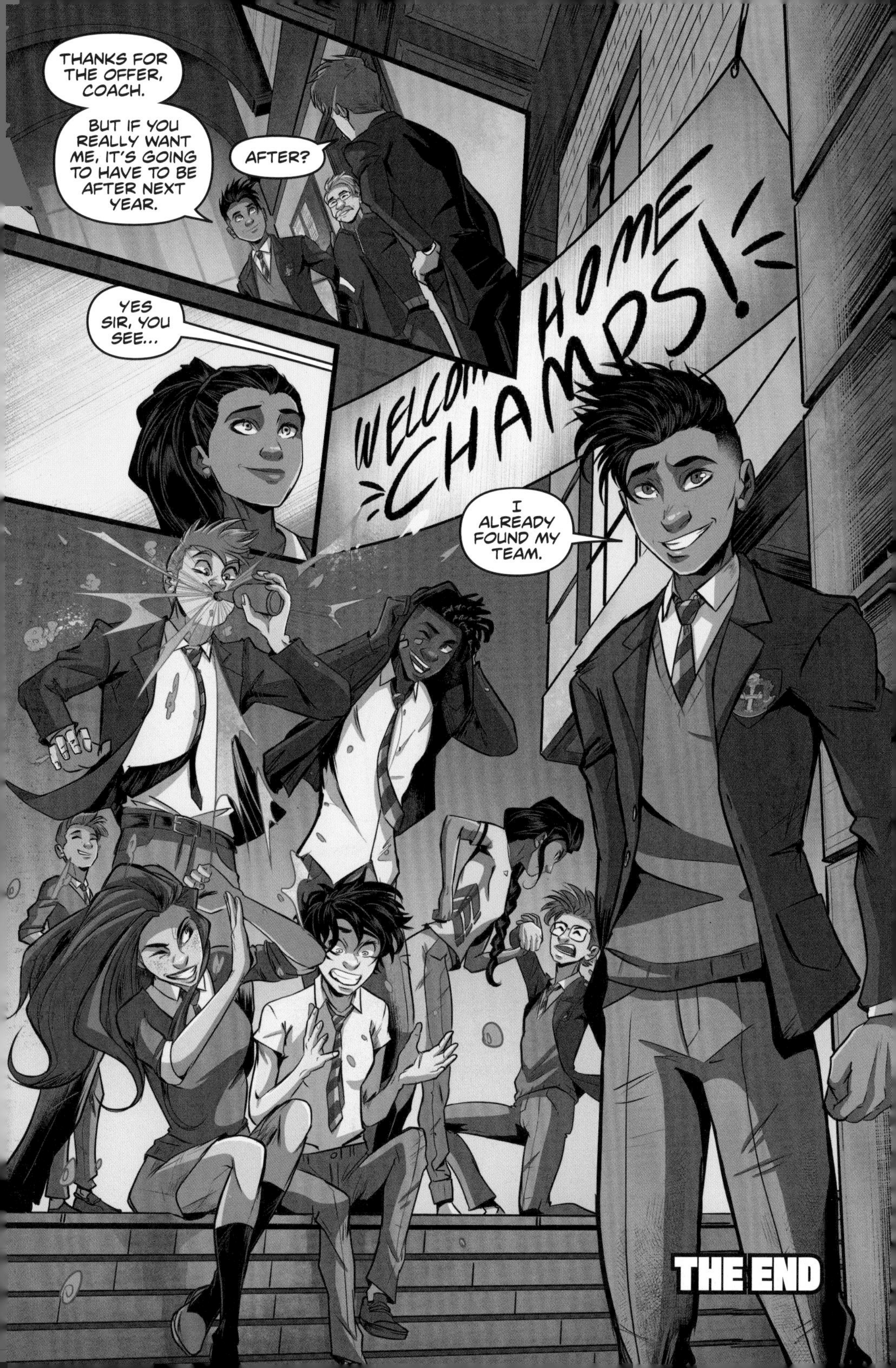
THANKS FOR THE OFFER, COACH.
BUT IF YOU REALLY WANT ME, IT'S GOING TO HAVE TO BE AFTER NEXT YEAR.
AFTER?
YES SIR, YOU SEE...
WELCOME HOME CHAMPS!
I ALREADY FOUND MY TEAM.
THE END

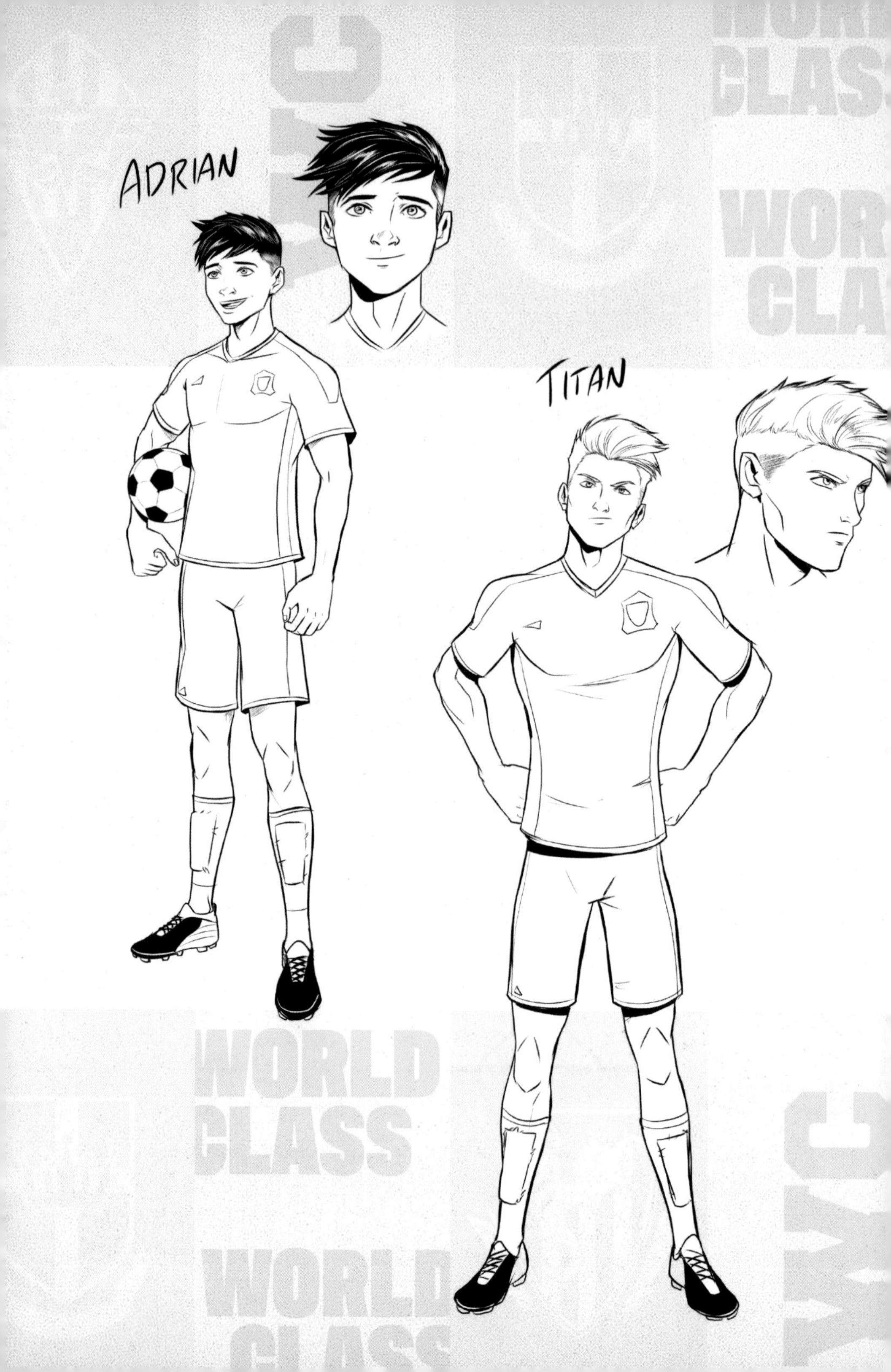
ADRIAN
TITAN

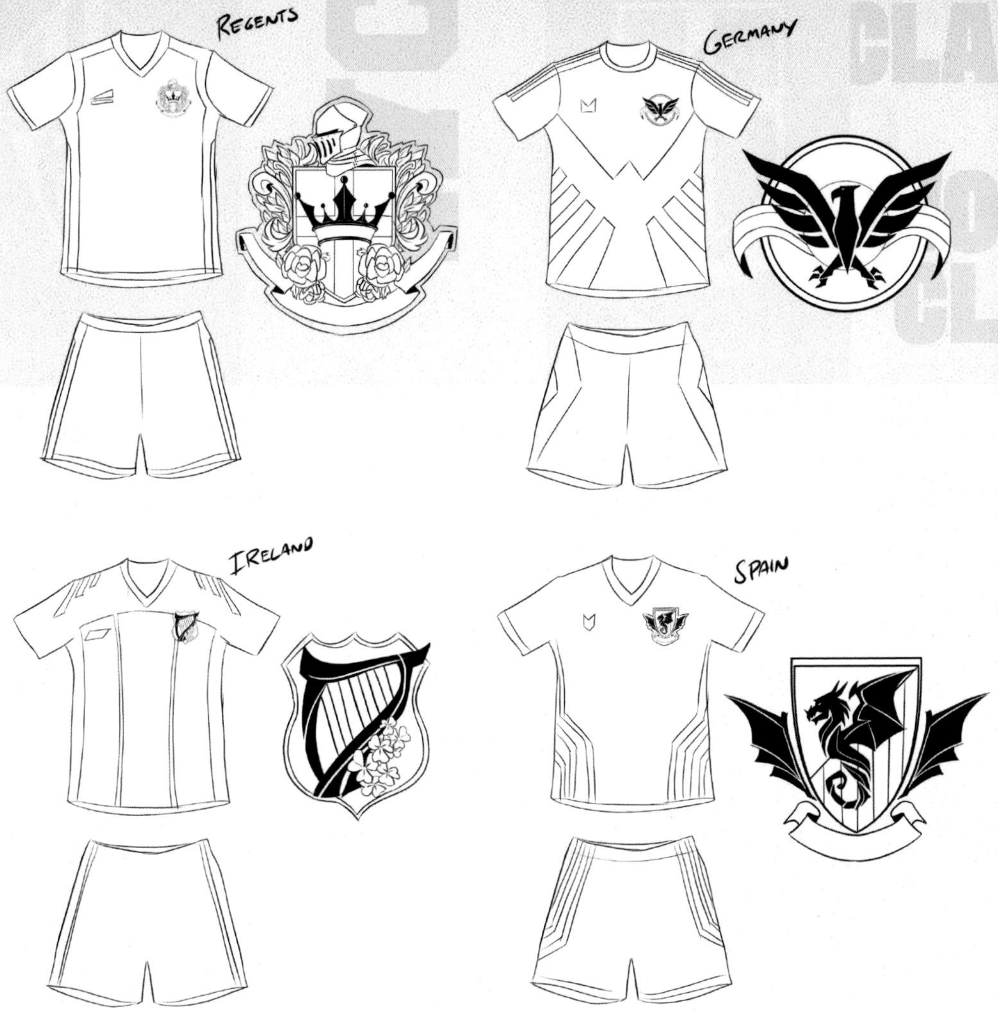

REGENTS
GERMANY
IRELAND
SPAIN

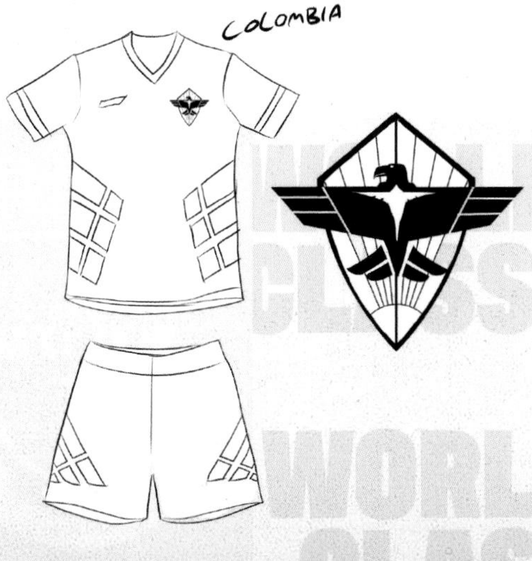

COLOMBIA

CHARACTER DESIGN

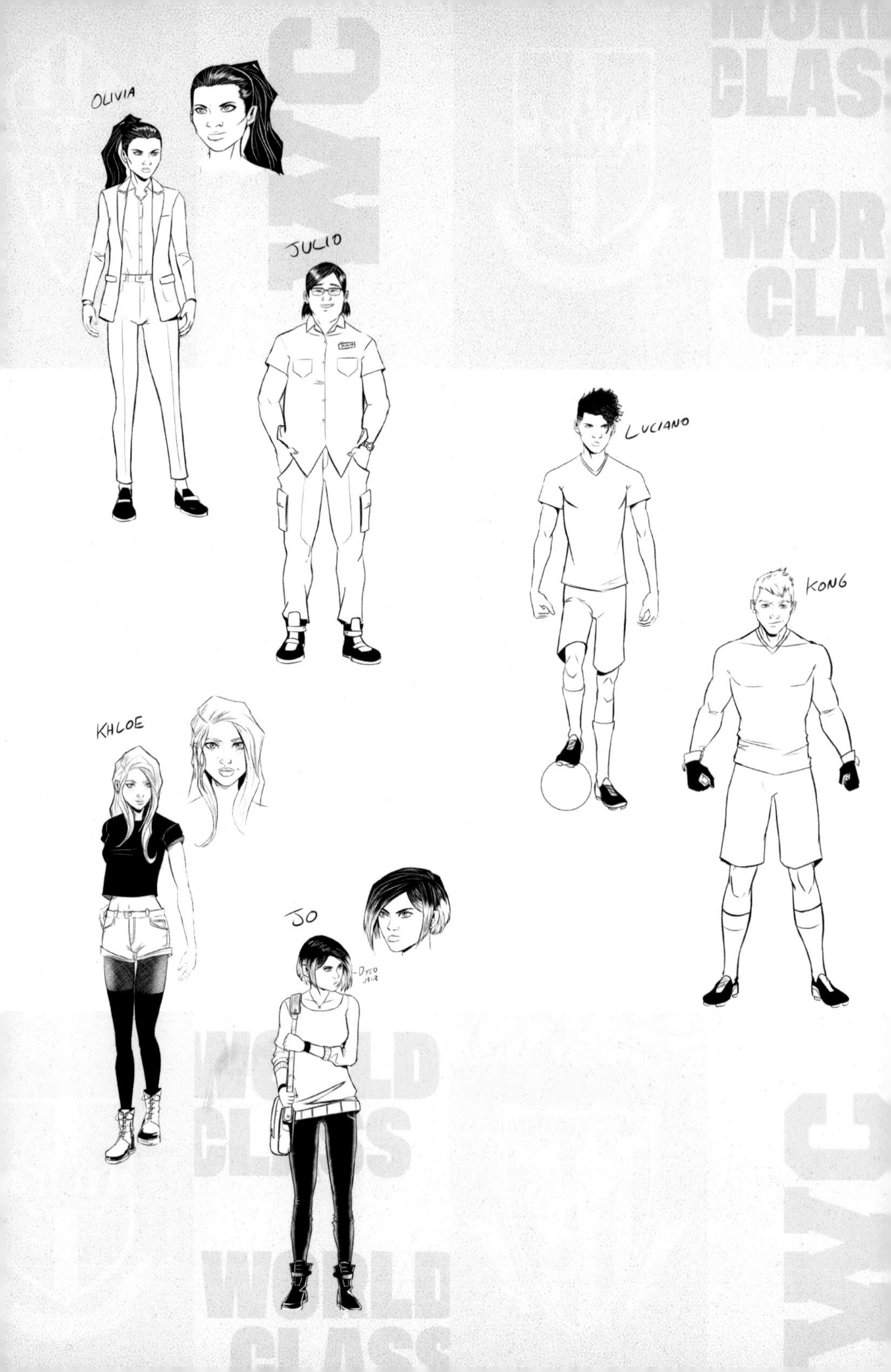
OLIVIA
JULIO
LUCIANO
KONG
KHLOE
JO
DYED HAIR

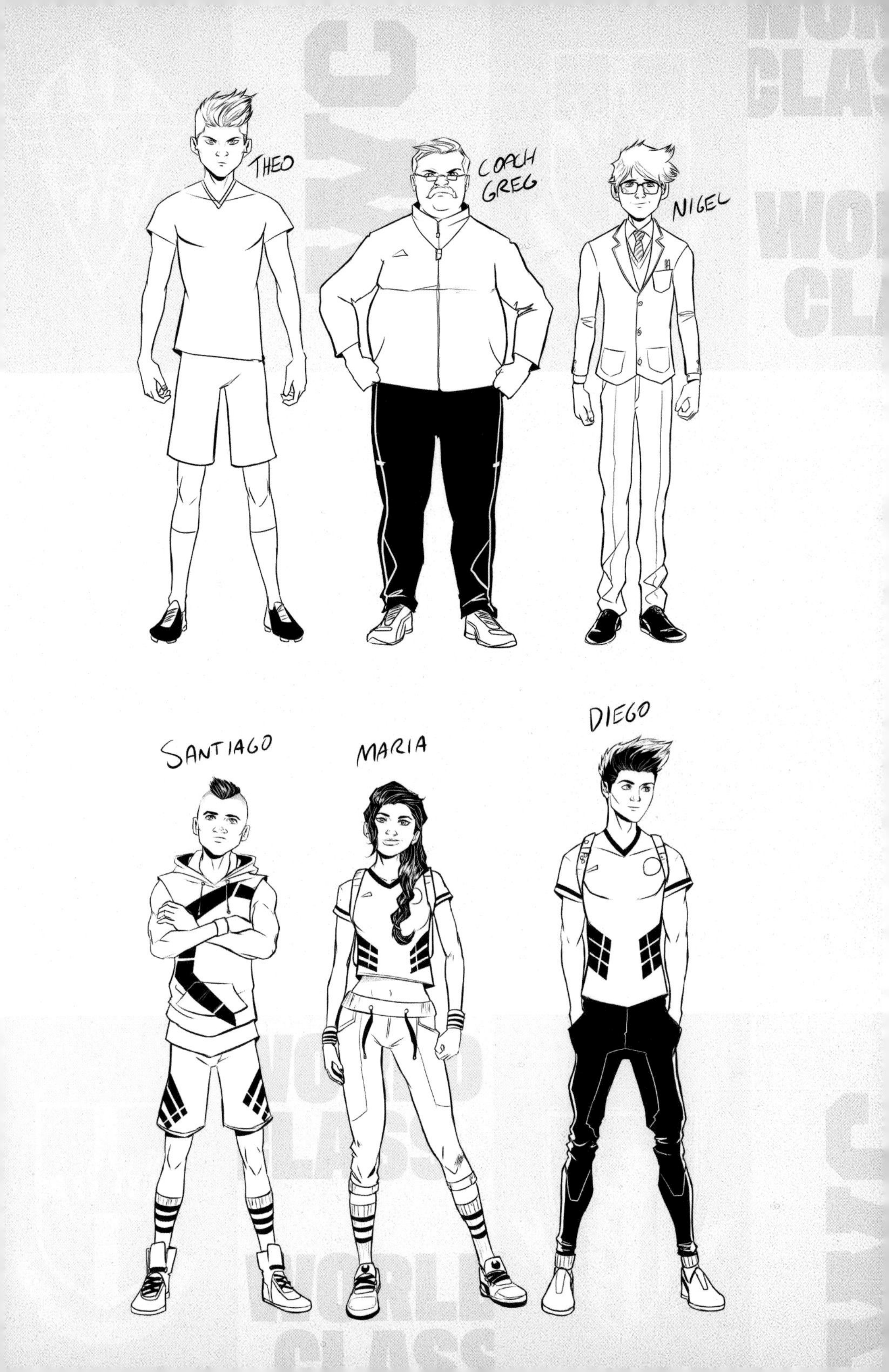
THEO
COACH GREG
NIGEL
SANTIAGO
MARIA
DIEGO

CREATOR SPOTLIGHT

Jay Sandlin

Jay Sandlin is a visionary writer and podcaster, as well as a history buff. Since self publishing his first anthology and picture book back in 2017, Jay has gone on to release Over The Ropes and Hellfighter Quin with Mad Cave Studios, as well as his first young adult graphic novel, World Class.

Patrick Mulholland

Patrick Mulholland is an artist from Belfast, Northern Ireland. He is most well known for his work on Power Rangers and the mini series Zero Jumper. Most days you can find him at his desk finding excuses to draw action scenes on every page.

Rebecca Nalty

Rebecca Nalty is a colourist currently living in Dublin, Ireland. Some of her previous projects include GLOW, Red Sonja, and Bog Bodies. When she's not working she enjoys spending time with her dogs and playing video games.

Justin Birch

Justin Birch is a Ringo Award nominated letterer born and raised in the hills of West Virginia. Lettering comics since 2015, he is a member of the lettering studio AndWorld Design and has worked with numerous indie publishers. Justin still lives in West Virginia, only now it's with his loving wife, daughters, and their dog, Kirby.